I Believe in Yesterday

Tim Moore's writing has appeared in the *Daily Telegraph*, the *Times*, the *Sunday Times* and the *Observer*, on whose behalf he was voted Travel Writer of the Year at the 2004 UK Press Awards. His books include *French Revolutions*, *Do Not Pass Go*, *Spanish Steps* and *Nul Points*. He lives in West London with his wife and three children.

I Believe in Yesterday

Tim Moore

JONATHAN CAPE
LONDON

Published by Jonathan Cape 2008

2 4 6 8 10 9 7 5 3 1

Copyright © Tim Moore 2008

Tim Moore has asserted his right under the Copyright, Designs
and Patents Act 1988 to be identified as the author of this work

First published in Great Britain in 2008 by
Jonathan Cape
Random House, 20 Vauxhall Bridge Road,
London SW1V 2SA

www.rbooks.co.uk

Addresses for companies within The Random House
Group Limited can be found at:
www.randomhouse.co.uk/offices.htm

The Random House Group Limited Reg. No. 954009

A CIP catalogue record for this book is available from the British Library

ISBN 9780224077811

The Random House Group Limited supports The Forest
Stewardship Council (FSC), the leading international forest
certification organisation. All our titles that are printed on
Greenpeace approved FSC certified paper carry the FSC logo. Our paper
procurement policy can be found at
www.rbooks.co.uk/environment

 **Mixed Sources**
Product group from well-managed
forests and other controlled sources
FSC   www.fsc.org Cert no. TT-COC-2139
© 1996 Forest Stewardship Council

Typeset by Palimpsest Book Production Limited
Grangemouth, Stirlingshire

Printed and bound in Great Britain by
Clays Ltd, St Ives plc

To my old self

MY TRAVELS in LIVING HISTORY

THE IRON AGE | THE ROMANS | THE VIKINGS | THE MIDDLE AGES | THE TUDORS | THE PIONEERS | THE U.S. CIVIL WAR

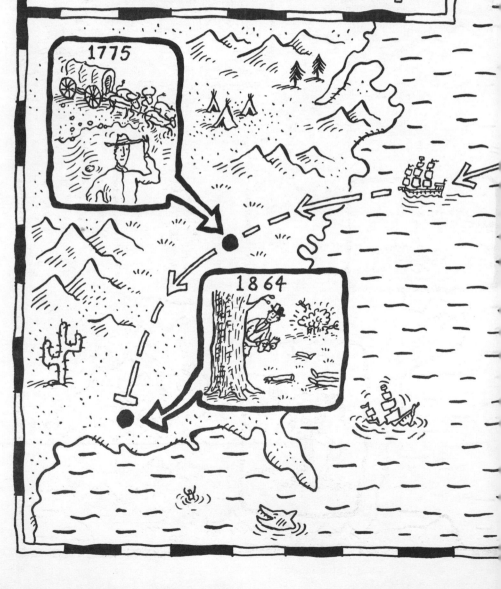

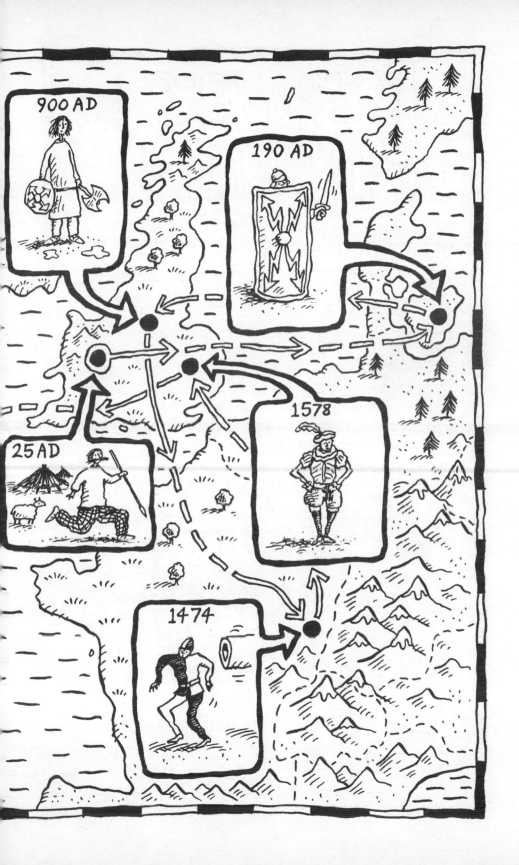

Acknowledgements

Thanks to Neil Burridge, Will Marshall-Hall, the fine men of the Legio VIII Augusta, Aurificina Treverica, Mick Baker and the warriors of Tÿrsliŏ, Christian Folini and the Company of Saynt George, Mistress Joan, Bella, Ed Boreham, Butch Hauri, the Douglas Texas Battery, Louisiana's war widows and refugees, and the incomparable Gerry Barker.

Oh – and Birna, for sending me off into the filth and fury with a kiss and a clean tunic, and not making me sleep in the shed when I came home.

Prologue

'Seven of us born up there.'

Sponge in hand, I looked around from the car's soapy roof and saw a venerable gentleman in a flat cap and scarf, trim and upright, nodding slowly, his gaze fixed on my bedroom window. 'Sorry,' he said, blinking himself back to focus and giving me a gentle smile. 'I'm a sparrow.'

My fingers tightened round the sponge, releasing a thick gobbet of dirty froth down the front of my trousers; then relaxed, releasing another: here was a Sparrow, scion of the fabled W.D. Sparrow. The W.D. Sparrow who had appeared on a 1923-postmarked envelope we found behind a doorframe after moving in sixty-five years later, and on the occasional utility bill that arrived in the months that followed. The man whose poignant legacy of this epic tenure, in a house stripped of all other domestic accessories, was an old red telephone and a BT directory, open at a page of Hounslow borough's residential care homes, with one such shakily circled in pencil.

In quiet suburban cockney, the son of Sparrow began to reminisce on his upbringing at number 29. The night he and a couple of brothers sneaked back in by shinning a drainpipe (one had slipped and broken a leg); the Luftwaffe bomb that had landed just behind the garden wall, entombing the Anderson shelter the family had vacated moments earlier;

1

the bus-stop chats with Dirk Bogarde, who had learned his craft at the end of our road, in a theatre that was now an office car park; and, yes, the seven new Sparrows hatched in the nest since soiled by three fledgling Moores.

I listened enthralled, oblivious to the sponge-chilled damp in my wrinkled fingers. If his tales came embued with a special resonance, it was because the home in which they were set was in every important detail the one we acquired. W.D. Sparrow was a careful owner, whose hardcore seven-decade redecoration habit revealed itself to our blowtorches like the layers of a house-shaped gobstopper. But that telephone and a gas stove aside, he was not a man who set much store in contemporary lifestyle comforts. It was quite a thing, in 1988, to walk into a home in an affluent area of West London and find its water supply restricted to a single cold tap in the kitchen, with fresh evidence of solid-fuel heating solutions smutting the hearths of every room. There was no bathroom, indeed no interior sanitation of any sort: the council's awe-struck building inspector had congratulated us on acquiring the very last residence in London W4 serviced solely by an outhouse.

'Would you like to, um, have a look around?'

Sparrow junior's nostalgia well had run dry, and it seemed an appropriate offer. For a moment those old eyes widened in anticipation; then he forced a wistful smile, declined politely, tightened his scarf and walked away. I watched him for a while, then turned back to the house. His reluctance wasn't hard to understand. The interior that in 1988 was almost exactly as he remembered it would now, fewer than twenty years later, be entirely unfamiliar. Almost everything behind his old front door, in fact even his old front door, had long since been rent asunder with crowbar and sledgehammer, and carried away in a skip. I couldn't say I still parked my behind on alfresco porcelain, or poured pans of stove-boiled water into a tin bath, or had a hundredweight of smokeless delivered every week. These were commonplace traditions that had defined the previous occupant's existence, and that of his predecessors, yet to have continued even one of them would have marked me out as an unwholesome eccentric. One short step away from encouraging pigeons to roost in the kitchen, or storing my excretions in labelled biscuit tins. How close I was to the life and times of W.D. Sparrow, yet how very, very far.

I returned to my distracted sponge-work, pondering how abruptly we had cast aside an age-old way of life, and the universal skills associated with it. In a single generation, life-changing luxuries had become necessities: with sporadic access to electricity and running hot water, my parents had endured well-to-do upbringings that would now be decreed almost inhumane. I pondered it all again one morning shortly afterwards, reading a newspaper report on a recidivist German youth offender sent by the exasperated authorities to 'fend for himself' in a remote Russian village. 'If he doesn't chop wood, his room is cold,' said his social worker, 'and if he doesn't fetch water, he can't wash. He must cope as we all did a few decades ago. It's the last resort to re-educate him.'

What had become of the Western world, that managing without sockets and taps was now the ultimate sanction against young rule-breakers? Were the everyday challenges faced by our forefathers from the dawn of civilisation until 'a few decades ago' already so remote and alien?

The TV schedules certainly suggested a nation mourning the loss of workaday, Sparrow-pattern life skills, and nurturing a perverse fascination with its own pampered uselessness: almost every month saw a new series in which hapless volunteers relived history by failing to fasten a stiff collar or pluck a chicken or bail out a trench. Watching as an aimless throng failed to recreate the erection of Stonehenge, a reworking of Jarvis Cocker's withering dismissal of rave culture ran through my head: is this the way they say the past is meant to feel, or just 20,000 people standing in a field?

Happily, encountering history face to face was a generally more rewarding balance of education and entertainment: at sites of historical significance one would routinely encounter elaborately costumed participants proficiently going about their period business. As my children failed to churn butter in the kitchens at Hampton Court one spring afternoon, their tutors – an engaging pair of leather-aproned Tudor cooks – brought me up to speed with Britain's thriving 'living history' scene.

Until a decade or so back, re-enactment had ticked along as a regional hobby for weekend warriors – the Cavalier and Roundhead Midlanders of the Sealed Knot, the hardy Roman legions clustered around Hadrian's Wall. It's no accident that the first official definition ('any presentation or other event held for the purpose of re-enacting an event from the past or of illustrating conduct from a particular time or period in the past') appeared in a clause that exempted historical re-enactment from the Violent Crime Reduction Bill, 2006.

Yet the cooks seemed refreshingly unimpressed with the pain-based end of the spectrum, and talked instead of a pastime that had developed into an erudite national sub-culture. Some of their associates were bona fide social historians, test-bedding theories on how people worked and played – it was all rather more academic these days. And significantly more diverse: 'I've heard you can go right back to the Stone Age if you want to.'

This was an extraordinary revelation. At a stroke, surviving in *The 1940s House*, even *The W.D. Sparrow House*, seemed feebly unambitious. Could I handle a spell in *The Prehistoric Hovel*? Were there really people who pressed the rewind button that long, who willingly embraced a grunting, filthy existence ruled by fear and hunger?

Intrigued, and just a little terrified, I spent the balance of that weekend delving into the history of re-enactment. It was a surprisingly long one, even if you didn't count the Roman battle victories refought in the Coliseum, which you probably ought to in honour of the many combatants slain therein on the altar of realism. Reliving famous triumphs for the purposes of prop-aganda or simple gloating proved enduringly popular – in 1895, the Gloucestershire Engineer Volunteers boldly recreated the defence of Rorke's Drift at Cheltenham's Winter Gardens (let us not dwell upon the seventy-five 'Zulu' participants).

The world had to wait until 1638, and an indoor confront-ation played out between 'Moors' and 'Christians' in the

Merchant Taylors' Hall, for the first recreation of something that hadn't just happened, and another 200 years for a re-enactment that wasn't a big fight. Though which was a succession of smaller fights.

The 1830s was, for Britain, a decade of disorientating change. The opening of the Liverpool and Manchester Railway; the Reform Act; the Poor Law – the old order was being swept away, and with it the old way of life. The rustic, semi-feudal, slow-paced existence that had been the centuries-old template for British society was being melted down, and no one quite knew what would replace it. One reaction, much as it would be 150 years later when the next technological revolution transformed daily life, was to seek nostalgic succour in the comforting past. Hail Archibald William Montgomerie, 13th Earl of Eglinton, and curse the 1982 A-level history syllabus, which in failing to mention him failed to leaven the dreary bilge regurgitated above.

Memorably encapsulated as 'one of the most glorious and infamous follies of the nineteenth century', the Grand Jousting Tournament of August 1839 was conceived as a spectacular celebration of medieval chivalry and pageant. When the young Earl called together 150 prospective participants from across Europe in a Bond Street armour-dealer's showroom, he pitched his dream as an antidote to the smutted drudgery of the new Industrial Age, and the insidious democracy following in its wake: one chronicler described it as 'symbolic of romantic defiance in the face of modern practicality'. The costumes, the catering, the tents, the jousts themselves – no expense would be spared in ensuring an authentic experience.

Learning that they were to fund this expense, and that here was a sport where defeat might leave a 10-foot pole lodged in your face, a large number promptly shuffled out. The room emptied further when Eglinton announced that his tournament was to be held at the family seat, a remote estate not especially near Ayr. In the end, just forty patrician diehards remained to be fitted up by the dealer – quite literally, it transpired, as a twentieth-century examination proved the 'original Medieval armour' he sold them to be entirely fake.

As the event approached, Eglinton began to suspect he had underestimated its Zeitgeist-tapping retro appeal. Beyond all the chivalric romance, the tournament winningly blended glamour with bloodlust: the flower of British aristocracy taking on *Hello!*-style Euro-royals, with excitingly lethal possibilities. Emperor-in-waiting Prince Louis Napoleon v the Marquess of Waterford, Count Lubeski of Poland v Viscount Glenlyon . . . The press build-up was feverish, and the Earl failed to dampen what soon became a national enthusiasm by promising free entrance to anyone who arrived in medieval dress. Having planned on a crowd of 1,500, he belatedly stuck up enough grandstands to seat three times as many.

Eglinton's excitement on learning that every inn and hotel in south-west Scotland was filled with codpieced, Rapunzel-hatted revellers from across the land soon evolved into a creeping sense of dread. Homeowners rented out rooms at exorbitant rates, and when there were none left, gentryfolk in fancy dress had to bed down in hedgerows. On the morning of the tournament, traffic on the thirty-mile highway from Ayr to Glasgow was muzzle-to-wheel; abandoned carriages blocked every road around Eglinton Castle. The most conservative final estimate of the colourful but careworn crowd that trudged through his gates was 100,000.

Eglinton was still wondering where to put them all, and what to feed them, when a crack of thunder split the lowland heavens. The epic cloudburst that followed leaked blood-red rain on those huddled under the scarlet grandstand canopies, and made a wet blur of the half-mile opening parade. Midway through the ill-tempered, malnourished hiatus that followed, the Earl sent a court jester out to appease the crowd: few could see him, fewer still could hear him, and those who did responded to his material with physical displeasure.

Three hours behind schedule, a squeaky fanfare heralded the inaugural joust: on cue, the rain became sleet. Unable to see the end of their own lances, the combatants tentatively converged across the quagmire, missing each other by some distance at low speed. The crowd had by now dispersed, yet soon returned: the rivers that ringed the estate were in full flood, stranding Eglinton with 100,000 unfed, blood-faced guests in tights. His ultimate reward for organising the world's first proper historical re-enactment was a bill for £40,000, lingering national ridicule and a very poor haul of Christmas cards.

Over-ambition, bad planning and worse weather, public humiliation, ruinous equipment of dubious provenance . . . in highlighting all these, Eglinton's Grand Jousting Tournament presciently introduced what I would discover to be many of living history's defining traits. If there is a more uncomfortable and expensive way of making a gigantic tit of yourself, only Richard Branson knows it.

Chapter One

If I was to start at the very beginning, then on the BC scale how low could one go? The online answer corroborated those Hampton Court cooks, and provided compelling evidence that re-enactment was a very broad church, with a far-flung congregation. A man in New South Wales was gamely trying to set up a neolithic group – 'Hi. Any takers for 4500–3300 BC?' – and some Californians had organised a re-enactment of the ancient agrarian rite known as Beltaine ('we recommend that children not be brought to this ritual'). Certainly, I hadn't expected to find an active Ancient Greek re-enactment scene in Watford. Yet a contest for the Apple of Hesperides held in a grammar-school hall wasn't quite what I had in mind – my intention was to experience, as intensively as feasible, the actual day-to-day life of our distant forefathers.

I scrabbled around in time and geography, and at length returned to my roots. The British populace at the embryonic stage of its historical development appeared depressingly resistant to progress – while great civilisations rose and fell in Egypt and Greece, we remained stubbornly mired in the rural, tribal Bronze Age for roughly 1,400 years. After the techniques for smelting iron were finally imported in the fifth century BC – some 800 years after their perfection in the Near East – our forebears happily played with their new metal for the next half a millennium, until the Romans pitched up. In those parts of our islands the invaders didn't reach, the Iron Age endured for a further 500 years. Over 2,000 years, and all we'd done was fit different tips to the spears stacked up outside our thatched-roof roundhouses.

Still, 2,000 years is a hefty chunk of recent history, and what with a reawakened national passion for Boudicca and the Celts, I imagined Bronze/Iron Age re-enactment to be a popular choice amongst living historians. It quickly became plain that this was not so, and for reasons that should have been obvious (though, as my forebears had found in the field of metallurgical innovation, only when a foreigner explained them). 'The problem with prehistoric re-enactment,' posted a Dutch living historian on one of the many relevant forums, 'is that because they didn't write anything, we don't have any information on how they interacted. From archaeology we know how they dressed, and how their tools and houses looked. But re-enactment is only a guess – all we can do is show how they might have cooked and worked and performed their ceremonies.'

Of my fellow Britons happy to declare a public interest in Bronze Age re-enactment, Neil Burridge was one of the very few who seemed to do more than 'outreach' – earning a few quid touring local schools daubed in woad. Neil's website focused on Bronze Age sword-making: a mere facet of his all-encompassing passion for weaponry, as became plain when I rang him. A deafening explosive blast assailed my ears as his wife carried the phone out to the garage; a trailing echo, a moment of shocked silence, and there I was, speaking to my first re-enactor. 'Sorry about that,' said Neil, brightly. 'Just trying out a – what do you call it? – a percussion-cap navy pistol.'

With a cheerful candour I frankly hadn't expected, Neil outlined the various rival factions in the small world that was the native Bronze Age scene. 'You've got the weekenders who just like to dress up – a bit iffy and amateur in my book, though I'll certainly put the gear on if you're paying – and the super-authentics, always fighting about who's doing it right.' I'd already encountered a couple of those, duking it out in a heated online debate on knotwork that was the essence of historical correctness gone mad: *You state that the design was brought to Britain in the sixth century by Saxon Christian monks – this simply isn't so.* 'And then there's your actual fighters. You know – the warrior syndrome, guys that just want to drag people out into a field and hurt them.'

This prospect became less unattractive as Neil described some of the other characters I might otherwise be spending the Bronze Age with. There was the droning know-all who never tired of boasting that no living man had spent more nights in a roundhouse; the lascivious eccentric who held pagan rites in his bedroom; the 'complete fruitcake' who had recently diversified into Nazi re-enactment.

For a week I worked through the more promising online resources Neil helpfully directed me towards. Some period enthusiasts were motivated by myth-busting evangelism ('The Bronze Age is stereotyped as ignorant and malnourished, but these were profoundly adept people who often grew to six-foot-six'), and some by the lifestyle trappings ('They had nice big houses, chariots, hair gel – lots of fun stuff!'). But no one seemed willing to translate thoughts into deeds by actually getting out there and reliving the Bronze Age. As a fully rounded prehistoric experience, one of Neil's sword-making weekends on Bodmin Moor wouldn't quite cut it, and nor would the residential workshop introduced by this memorable phrase: 'Why not treat someone you love to the ultimate gift – a voucher for our two-day flint-knapping course?'

Happily, the field opened when I put my clock forward a few centuries, and upgraded from bronze to iron. Very soon I had my first face-to-face encounter with a re-enactor, a man of modest stature and boyish voice, hauling a rucksack twice his size through a crowded pub opposite Victoria coach station.

A Welshman now resident in Canada, Will Marshall-Hall was in town to interest the British Museum in his plans to establish an Iron Age village in his adopted homeland. 'The lack of written records means the only way to research how people lived back then is to try and live that way now,' he said, thunking his rum and Coke down on the table. 'Prehistoric re-enactment comes with a built-in academic function.' How heady was the prospect of making a personal contribution to the social history of my homeland, until Will pointed out that as an average pre-Roman Briton, I'd have been dead for twenty-four years.

Keltica Iron Age Village, as I understood it, was to be a tourist attraction-cum-educational resource, as well as a labour of love for a living historian who had rewound from youthful dabblings with medieval re-enactment. An encounter with a battleaxe during this phase had endowed him the new-moon scar above his left eye: 'In Casualty they asked when I sustained the injury, and when I told them they said, "So was that 12.15 p.m., or a.m.?" and I said, "No, AD."'

What Will had to say regarding his passion for the Iron Age introduced themes I would find common to re-enactors from all periods. 'It's a back-to-basics thing, a rebellion against consumerism and commuting and all that crap,' he said, dismissing our fellow drinkers and their lifestyles with a flick of his hand.

It was Canada's primeval landscape that had lured him, along with a timelessly rural existence that until a couple of decades back had often been led without electricity or plumbing. 'It really doesn't take long to fall back into the natural rhythms of prehistoric life,' Will said. He raised a stubby finger and thumb. 'We're *that* close to our ancient selves.' Looking at his scarred, round face, now ruddy with rum and excitement, I suddenly found it very easy to imagine a horde of Wills scuttling down a hill towards a column of Romans, spears raised, tunic tails flying.

This was what kept the dedicated re-enactor going back for more: the quest for that elusive, almost mystical moment – Will called it a 'period rush' – when all those elapsed centuries slipped away, when then became now. 'It might only be ten minutes, it might be a whole week,' he said, with studied intensity. 'Last time it happened was at an Iron Age village in West Wales – I just suddenly knew that if I'd looked over at the fire and seen a couple of bona fide Iron Age guys sitting there, I wouldn't have been surprised. Just for that brief moment I completely understood their world, their outlook.' He gazed blankly through the fag smoke and jostle. 'Next morning it was gone. I'd blown it.'

Regrettably, the settlement in question was no more, but as we parted Will described a nearby surviving rival that he thought might offer what I wanted. Cinderbury Iron Age Village comprised a clutch of roundhouses built on a hill near the Forest of Dean's Welsh border. The area was apparently a focal point of Iron Age Britain – Will held forth at breathless length on the village's authenticity, both in terms of location and construction.

As a tourist attraction, however, and therefore a model for Will's own project, Cinderbury had yet to prove itself. The pair of Iron Age enthusiasts who'd built the place with borrowed money had over-estimated its appeal to drive-by holidaymakers, and after a period of bankrupt abandonment the site had recently been acquired by a local man who, as an accountant named Wayne, one might have thought an unlikely proprietor.

'Taste history, feel history, be history.' Laid bare on the website, Wayne's vision had a captivating and ambitious ring. Under his aegis, Cinderbury aimed to offer visitors a uniquely immersive experience of British daily life as it was led 2,000 years ago. Though a drop-in day visit remained an option, the stated hope was that most would book in for a week. Dressed in authentic costume, guests would sleep in a communal round-house, learn period skills from iron smelting to animal husbandry, eat authentic food and spend fireside evenings drinking 'historically accurate fruit juices' amid tales of heroes, demons, myth and legend. 'You may bring a toothbrush,' advised a footnote, 'which can be stored out of sight in your roundhouse. Make-up, jewellery and perfumes are however strongly discouraged and may be mocked.'

Wayne had seemed a little distracted when I phoned him to arrange a little time travel. Having been contracted to work in London three days a week, he wasn't presently able to attend Cinderbury as often as he had. As we falteringly cobbled together an itinerary – with a whole week currently unfeasible, he could only offer me four days in July – I struggled to imagine Wayne's curious double life, commuting between neck-tied financial consultancy and woad-daubed animal husbandry. Then he asked if £150 sounded all right, and I found it slightly easier.

I drove into the Forest of Dean halfway through the hottest July day in recorded British history. Serene and fecund, it wasn't hard to see what had made this area one of the great heartlands of Iron Age Britain. Or rather it was, because at 55mph you don't tend to get a good view of small-scale surface ore deposits.

Bronze, the copper/tin amalgam that lent its name to the previous 1,500 years of British life, had been a rare and shiny rich-man's alloy. Strong, crude and cheap, iron was a more democratic metal. Its raw material was a humble orange rock found in surface seams throughout the known world, and the end product's versatility was to revolutionise every aspect of prehistoric life. Before its arrival in around 500 BC, the vast majority of Britons still went out hunting with a bag of rocks, and struggled to master the rudiments of agriculture by scraping away at the soil with flint hand tools. Iron pulled us out of the Stone Age, and bequeathed the technology that would characterise daily life right up to the Industrial Revolution. Indeed, considering the metallurgical basis of the steel that underpins modern industrial society, the Iron Age lives on today.

The problem for our prehistoric forebears was that this miracle metal's grubby, utilitarian appearance belied a production process considerably more complex than anything they had previously mastered. The temperatures required to coax liquid metal from the rocky ore were stupendous, and procured only a hopeless, spongy material whose impurities had to be wearyingly hammered out. Even then you had a substance that remained a poor match for bronze until reheated, and in a precise manner that caused charcoal to combine with the iron to produce a bar of crude but highly resilient carburised steel. Take that, and after several further hours of highly skilled red-hot battering, you might finally have a knife.

Producing decent iron was a royal pain in the ancient behind, but less so than trying to skin a boar with a pebble. The wide-spread availability of decent hand tools, heatproof cookware and above all agricultural equipment – principally the iron-tipped ploughshare – had a profound impact on daily life. And in a strangely circular manner, so did the arduous complexity of the iron-making process itself. Once your tribe or extended family had pitched up near a supply of ore, and set up its forges and furnaces, you'd want to stay put. You'd clear woodland to make charcoal, and plant crops in the space left behind. The itinerant lifestyles still prominent in Bronze Age Britain became gradually redundant: after centuries of having to supplement their diets and lifestyles through trade or plunder, communities around Britain found they could co-exist in self-sufficient agricultural harmony.

Not that they always did, of course. Immigration was by no means a recent phenomenon – isotope analysis of teeth found near Stonehenge has shown that many of those buried there were born in what is now Switzerland – but during the early Iron Age, Britain's population was swollen by a steady influx of continental Celts: some of them economic migrants or refugees, others determined invaders with conquest in mind. (On behalf of all those irked by the global spread of the Irish pub, I'd like here to emphasise that the word 'Celt' was coined only in the eighteenth century, and the concept of a united Celtic culture contrived only in the nineteenth, partly to endow the very German Prince Albert with some sort of ancestral link to Britain. In fact, beyond vague similarities in language and religious ritual, there's little to connect what are commonly described as 'Celtic' peoples.)

This was the era of the great hill forts – I'd driven past one at Lydney Camp, just down the road from Cinderbury – though rather uselessly, no one is sure whether these were built by encroaching 'Celts' or retreating native Britons. It seems, though, that by about 300 BC the shakedown had endowed most of Britain with a largely integrated populace, albeit one generally under the aegis of regional warlords.

A modest, ring-fenced farmstead such as Cinderbury, generally home to a single extended family, was the default Iron

Age settlement. The small, ordered fields the inhabitants worked – such a distinctive feature of the English countryside even then that Caesar commented on them after his abortive invasions in 55 and 54 BC – would have produced enough oats and barley and hay to subsist on, with a modest surplus for trading. There would be pasture for sheep and cattle, and maybe a couple of pigs.

By 100 BC these first permanent farming communities were well established, and the template set for a rural way of life that would see us through the next millennium. The late Iron Age was an era of unparalleled peace and relative prosperity – historians have estimated that Britain's population at the time of Claudius's invasion in 43 AD was as high as 2.5 million, roughly what it would be 1,300 years later once the Black Death had done its worst.

An enhanced respect for the achievements of a neglected age – and the heady anticipation of recreating them in person – propelled me with windows-down, whistling enthusiasm through the Forest of Dean's shaded byways and surprisingly ugly market towns. The settlements thinned, the trees encroached, the traffic dwindled; by the time I swished past a mildewed billposter promoting The Wurzels, the whole isolated, overlooked, land-that-time-forgot vibe had long since silenced my cheery tootling. Just a few miles over the Welsh border, I recalled, a rambler had recently blundered across a ghost town in the woods: two dozen cottages, a bakery and even a public convenience, all laid out along a half-mile high street and entirely forgotten for 150 years.

And then there I was, pulling off the B4228 and crunching to a halt before a banner that relayed an evocative but strangely sinister message: 'The holiday of a lifetime – just not this lifetime!'

Flat on his back beneath this was the jauntily handpainted image of a Celtic warrior, his woad daubings and droopy moustache streaked and faded by the elements. 'Welcome to Cinderbury,' proclaimed the legend encircling his tangled blond hair. I got out, hauled the sign upright, then continued bumpily along a dusty path that passed a padlocked, plank-clad Portakabin starkly labelled 'SHOP' on its way up a low green hill. At the brow, beyond a rank of timbered public conveniences, the track ended before an Alamo-type palisade, behind which poked a trio of pointy, turf-capped roofs. My heart leapt. Then sank a little as I got out of the car and detected the unmistakable sound of a strimmer at work.

Its operator was a few-toothed young man who spotted me as I scaled the goods pallet that served as a gate. In between parched guzzles of Lucozade – the bottling plant was up the road, he revealed with a wink – he told me that Wayne, who lived nearby with his family, had asked him to spruce the place up for a film crew scheduled to arrive the following morning. Slightly unsettled, I asked where I might find Cinderbury's current residents. He responded with a look of sweaty bemusement. 'Here? Been no one here for a bit. Odd school party, couple of passers-by.' A glance around the fenced compound gave weight to his words. The unstrimmed areas lay knee-high in straggly weeds, and the magnificence of the two adobe-walled roundhouses that dominated the enclosure was compromised by the careworn third, whose sagging, desiccated turf roof had partly fallen away to reveal an inner sheathing of black polythene.

The groundsman inclined himself into the welcome shade of a thatched lean-to, home to a noticeboard detailing period pottery techniques, and the remnants of childish attempts to replicate them. 'Yes, always nice and quiet up here,' he said, shielding his red face from the sun. 'Fantastic reception, too,' he added, and tilted his chin at a mobile-phone mast that towered above the furthest roundhouse.

I left him to his work, and climbed back over the pallet gate in a state of confusion. Wandering the palisade's external perimeter I accepted that the bustling Iron Age community I'd pictured owed more to my hopes than Wayne's words. But was I really to do this utterly alone, and be filmed doing it? Maybe even followed around and prodded by daytrippers, for the ambience-soiling signs and weed-skirted information placards suggested a half-baked tourist attraction rather than a hardcore, bona fide living-history experience. Hard to imagine capturing that elusive 'period rush' wearing Gap shorts in the shadow of a telecommunications mast.

Round the back, amidst a nettle-crowned mess of builders' rubble, I refreshed myself from a standpipe; I relieved myself in the sawdust hell-pit of an earth-closet outhouse. Where were my Celtic clothes? What would I eat? This latter worry intensified as I passed a board that described the importance of fruit, nuts, herbs and vegetables in the Iron Age diet, and which presided over a patch of bald scrub whose solitary living resident was a thistle.

A path of recent construction led away from the settlement, heading down through the yews and hazels to a sun-dappled labyrinth of peculiar rocky hollows. These, as the relevant information board informed me, were an example of the local feature known as scowles, host to the region's iron-ore deposits, and an apparent inspiration to Tolkien, who came here to participate at an archaeological dig in the late twenties. This might have been *The Hobbit*'s birthplace, but it was also Cinderbury's death knell. In a poignantly literal manner, you could see where the village's founders had come to the end of the road: having impressively bridged a couple of deep holes, the path came to an abrupt, taped-off halt at the lip of a third.

The strimmer fell silent as I was halfway back, and when I returned Cinderbury was mine and mine alone. I'd earmarked the roundhouse nearest the gate; ducking in through the low entrance I found myself in a cool, earth-floored gloom redolent of woodsmoke, caves and pee. Once my eyes had adjusted I took stock of my new home. It was larger than it seemed from the outside, perhaps fifteen foot across, its circular wall flanked with sheepskin-topped haybales. At the hut's centre a cauldron hung from a tripod over a well-used open hearth, beside it a low, earthen half-dome that could have been a beehive but was more realistically some sort of oven. A pair of rectangular shields decorated with brass bosses and Celtic-type swirls stood propped against a wooden chest. Sitting down on a bale, I began to feel more positive about my forthcoming experience. In here, away from the clunking anachronisms that intruded into every external vista, I at last felt just a little bit ancient.

The roundhouse, as I knew even before yet another information board told me, was the hub of Iron Age life. When the villagers weren't out in the fields, they were in here – eating, talking, sleeping. Each of these impressively functional living units was an open-plan family home, focused around a fire that was kept going twenty-four hours a day, for cooking, warmth and light.

I recalled Will's account of the first archaeological attempts to recreate a roundhouse, extrapolated from foundations excavated across Europe. On commonsense grounds, the academics incorporated a chimney-hole in the straw roof; when the inaugural fire was lit in the open hearth beneath, the upward current drew embers into the thatch and in minutes the entire structure was ablaze. Only by trial and error did they realise a chimney was unnecessary: in a closed-roof house, the smoke rose to a layer conveniently just above head height, then filtered out gently through the thatch of its own accord. The archaeologists established that this process also kept the roof fumigated against insect damage, and created an airless upper atmosphere that extinguished any errant sparks and embers, as well as offering the perfect conditions for smoking meat and fish.

The whole experiment was billed as a triumph for the academic value of hands-on living history, but from where I was sitting the tributes were principally due to our Iron Age ancestors. Contemplating the lifestyle that Cinderbury was intended to recreate, I was awed by the multi-talented practicality it demanded. These people ground their own corn, and baked it into bread in an oven of their own construction. They raised their own crops and livestock, then cooked them in pots and pans they had crafted themselves. They sheared sheep, and spun the wool, and wove it into clothes. And at the end of the day, they sat down in the house that they'd built, and drank the beer that they'd brewed.

The most humbling consideration was the universality of

these diverse skills. You might be better at some than others, but you'd have to be capable of doing them all. Two thousand years ago, even I would have been pulling honeycombs out of trees and hollowing out antler drinking horns. Now all I could do was sit there and poke at the cold hearth, wondering if the nearest petrol station sold logs and matches. Where had it all gone wrong?

Over the following six hours, solitude and the mind-softening heat combined to reinforce this sense of inadequacy. Powerfully so once nightfall was added to the mix, and the occasional whoosh of traffic from the B4228 faded to leave me only a chorus of rural scuttles for sonic company. With no means of communication or illumination, I found that the authentic enhancements which had so recently made my situation seem better, now made it seem much, much worse. In through the dim roundhouse entrance crept loneliness and fear; out of it, in the last squinting snatch of half-light, swooped a bat.

What else lurked up there in the unseen eaves, or out there in the hobbity scowles? And why, now that my mind inevitably came to alight on it, did those eerily well-preserved Iron Age corpses that periodically bobbed up out of peat bogs invariably display evidence of ritual death preceded by torture? I hunched down against a haybale and drew one of the shields towards me, looking every inch the craven sacrificial offering.

Time passed, and I lacked the spiritual wherewithal to find out how much by making a dash for the car and its clock. I began to hum, reedily at first but soon with desperate, tuneless gusto. It was no relief to hear myself drowned out by the judder and rumble of neglected machinery bumping up the track, and creaking to a nearby halt.

A car door opened and clunked shut, and after a few scuffles and thunks, I detected the approaching sound of a big man dragging something heavy towards the roundhouse entrance. I stopped humming and pulled the shield up so that it hid everything but the top third of my head. The scraping ceased, and into the hut came footsteps and the sound of breathless huffing. Rustles and the snick of a lighter followed; with discovery imminent I whitened my knuckles on the shield's rim and hailed the interloper.

'Hello?' Half whimpered plea for mercy, half preparation for death – it wasn't a great Iron Age sound.

'Oh, right you are. Wayne told me someone might be here.' The lighter was held to a candle, and I saw myself looking up at a damp-faced, shirtless man of late middle years, an unlit cigarette in his mouth and a five-foot spear under one arm. 'I'm Dai the blacksmith,' he said, lighting his fag and letting the spear drop carelessly to the floor. 'What you doing behind that shield?'

The pitiful relief engendered by the comradely nature and forthright competence revealed as Dai strode about preparing the roundhouse was partly offset by the nature of these preparations. Lighting was a couple of dozen IKEA tealights placed atop the adobe oven and around the floor; bedding a pair of grubby sleeping bags sourced from the wooden chest – also home, I noted, to an empty half-bottle of Bacardi and two-thirds of a Kellogg's Variety breakfast assortment. I thought of all those deep-breath discoveries I'd made during my Iron Age acclimatisation research at home: 'Gruel was generally mixed with stock or fat, then left to set in a "porridge drawer", to be sliced and eaten cold over the coming weeks.' And here I sat, watching a man in trainers drop Silk Cut ash in our Frosties drawer.

As comforting as this was to the very large part of me that dearly wished to be back in my nineteenth-century house, in my twentieth-century bed, watching twenty-first-century telly, the whole point of being here was to peel away that part, bury it in the porridge drawer, then eat it sliced and cold. 'Taste history, feel history, be history' – it was clear now that the website's grand mission statement, along with its promise of historically accurate fruit juices, was not the work of Cinderbury's current owner.

My hope – or fear – that Dai might now settle into period character by refusing to discuss anything but matters ancient, possibly via a stream of primeval gibberish, was quickly laid to rest. In Welsh tones pruned of their singsong swoops and leaps by an adulthood spent largely on this side of the border, Dai explained that Wayne had hired him for the benefit of the film crew, who he believed were documentary makers. He also fleshed out Will's account of Cinderbury's troubled genesis: one of the original partners had 'pissed off abroad with half the money', leaving the other with no option but to sell up. 'Lost ten grand of his own,' sighed Dai, sparking up another fag. 'But he's been a lot happier since last autumn, when him and a friend made 180,000 gallons of cider.' By tealight, Dai laid out the principal tools of his trade: a pair of bellows, cleverly constructed from thick linen and a hollowed-out log, and the 'travel anvil' I'd heard him dragging over from his car. 'Bit of old railway track,' he said, tapping his nose. 'Right – let's eat.'

Anticipation, heat and terror had taken turns to sap my appetite, but I correctly surmised that Dai would not sap it further with a parade of challenging prehistoric comestibles. He strode out into the dark, quickly got a campfire going, and ten minutes later I was scraping two well-done Tesco mustard-and-onion beefburgers off an abused catering-sized saucepan.

Dai tossed me a can of Grolsch, and we sat down on logs to talk. Like Will, he'd started out in medieval combat, after meeting some enthusiasts in a pub; unlike Will, he struggled to explain what had then lured him further back through time. 'Just . . . all this,' he mumbled when I asked him straight, waving a helpless hand at the campfire, the roundhouses, our immediate environment in general.

As an enviably practical man, Dai was certainly well suited to the many-skilled demands of prehistory. 'We have it too easy now – we don't know how to fix things, let alone the joy of making things in the first place. Everything's disposable. When I come to places like this the big thrill isn't that I've come back to the Iron Age, more that I've left the Plastic Age.' Having been captivated by a demonstration of period black-smithery three years before, he'd gone off and taught himself the exacting ancient art of processing lumps of rusty rock into spear tips and knives. 'There's only a half-dozen or so of us in

Britain that can do it all, from start to finish.' (Another was his girlfriend, who he'd met at Cinderbury the year before.)

As Dai talked on, I sensed that here was a man whose historical hobby was an expression of his hankering for a simpler, smaller society with a more straightforward value system, focused on personal responsibility. And violent retribution: he spent an eager half-hour relating his father's no-nonsense approach to street justice – 'One time he just shoved a lit fag-end right up some lout's nose' – and proudly revealed that a black belt in karate allowed Dai to carry on the family tradition. 'The other week some little shits tried to mug me at a cashpoint,' he seethed, his genial, fleshy features alarmingly puckered with firelit malevolence. 'I grabbed one and said I'd throw him through a fucking shop window.' As a PE and maths supply teacher in the Midlands, he was unsurprisingly handed many of the more troublesome classes, and given a remarkable degree of freedom in how he chose to educate them. Here his belief in the value of practical skills came to the fore. 'I take them out in the woods and we build things – got a great log cabin on the go. It's amazing what you can get out of them once the ground rules are set.' There weren't many. 'I just tell 'em: mind yourself with the saws, and don't use the C word.'

Dai washed up the Iron Age way – turning the saucepan upside-down over the fire to burn the grease off – and at an unknown hour we headed back to the roundhouse. 'One thing you learn,' he said, dragging haybales clumsily around in the blackness, 'is to do whatever needs doing before it gets dark.' After a while he'd assembled the bales into two beds, and very shortly after, the nocturnal rustles outside were filtered out by Dai's profound, reassuring snores.

An inadequate number of hours later, a great metallic cacophony and the smell of bacon lured me blearily over to the sag-roofed roundhouse opposite. Within, the perennially shirtless Dai squatted before a filthy, sizzling trivet, a strip of bright blue M&S waistband asserting itself above his period drawstring trousers. 'We're going to work hard today,' he said, without looking up. 'You need fuel – fried meat and lots of it.'

23

Working the bellows for a day, he explained, equated to 2,000 one-armed press-ups. The physique endowed by this regime was more six-pint than six-pack, but it certainly did the job. When a fellow teacher recently choked in the dinner hall, Dai's slap on the back had knocked her unconscious.

Replete with Somerfield unsmoked streaky, we headed down towards the scowles in search of forge-fodder. Heating iron ore to well over 1,000ºC – and keeping it there for hours on end – is a fuel-intensive process: using Iron Age methods and raw materials, a team of Danish archaeologists recently found that over a ton of wood was required to source the charcoal needed to produce just 5kg of forged iron, the useable end material. By the time the Romans landed, it's estimated that over half of Britain's wild woodland had already gone up the chimney. It could have been worse: historians have suggested that the great Indus Valley civilisation, which abruptly disappeared around 1700 BC, destroyed itself through a frenzy of iron-related deforestation.

The year before, Dai had been down in Cinderbury's scowles to help build an authentic 'clamp' – a turf-covered bonfire employed to produce charcoal – and we now dug around in its remains for any usable surviving lumps. It wasn't the time to admit my blighting phobia of the small invertebrates that had made this place their home in the interim. For half an hour I delved whey-faced in the scuttling, many-legged awfulness; doing so without excreting tears or bacon was a small but significant step in the quest for my inner ancient.

We hauled a fertiliser sack full of our muddy harvest back up to the village and found the film crew milling listlessly about. Their welcoming address revealed an arresting truth – they were Australians, here to shoot a segment for a holiday programme. A quick word with the cameraman confirmed that they'd come all the way here to capture a genuine – if offbeat – vacation choice for Antipodean tourists, and were nonplussed to discover Cinderbury in a state of mothballed neglect. A woman called Diane introduced herself as the presenter, and with the refreshing candour that defines her nation enquired what the bloody hell was going on. I was formulating a diplomatic response when a convoy of vehicles pulled up in the now-crowded parking area, and disgorged half a dozen people of local appearance, led by an expressionless man in jeans and glasses. 'Sorry we're late,' he murmured. 'I'm Wayne, and these are your, um, extras.'

The tiny voice that had been bravely assuring me that Wayne's arrival would herald the sudden onset of hardcore prehistoric authenticity piped down to a whisper as he laid out our Iron Age lunch: petrol-station pasties and packets of crisps. It was silenced for ever when Cinderbury's owner led the way into a fly-floored, semi-derelict caravan hidden away in the woods, and thumbed at a soiled jumble of grubby fabric. 'Your outfits,' he mumbled, and slipped away. We didn't see him again until nightfall.

Our grasp of Iron Age fashion is based on patchy archaeological evidence, and the second-hand accounts of ancient scholars. Striped or plaid trousers, a tunic and cloak, unisex plaits and long moustaches – you could do a lot worse than picture Asterix and his fellow villagers. Greek and Roman contemporaries were most intrigued by the unusually colourful dyes used, and the facial hair: 'When they are eating the moustache becomes entangled in the food,' wrote Diodorus Siculus, 'and when they are drinking the drink passes, as it were, through a sort of strainer.'

A quick investigation of the caravan clothing heap suggested an unfamiliarity with the works of Diodorus Siculus, or indeed of fashion trends in fictional Gaul. The extras blithely pulled on pink acrylic smocks and orange trousers with the air of people who didn't often have much to do, and were about to be paid to sit around in the sun doing even less. I was left with a pair of golfing-uncle checked trousers and a clay-smeared white jerkin that was more of a cap-sleeve T-shirt. 'Don't we get any shoes?' asked Diane, tying a rope round her dress to offset its machine-stitched nylon-ness. Apparently not. My Clarks Wallabees were coming along for the time-ride.

It was a sweaty, peculiar day which I spent largely in Dai's company, envying him his strength, skill and authentic period sandals. As I sat in the precious shade of a willow fence, he swiftly dug up a barrowful of clay, and fashioned from it a crucible the size of a cereal bowl. Extracting iron from its ore was a process that – like filming a holiday-programme segment, as I was to discover – demanded long hours of repetitive tedium. Instead Dai had come prepared with a big sack of scrap-iron brackets and bars as his raw material, to be heated to glowing malleability by his calm, efficient work on the bellows, then belaboured with brutal finesse atop that railway-track anvil. With me as a gormless background apprentice the Australians filmed Dai hammering out spear tips and curly-handled knives from an exhaustive variety of angles, then noticed he'd had a fag in his free hand throughout, and had him do it all over again. Eventually they wandered off to record their introductory sequence, which required our inactive silence. 'This was life in the Iron Age,' Diane told the camera for the eleventh time, stooping out of a roundhouse with a spear in her hand. 'Everything you ate, wore and fought with, you'd have to . . . to . . . oh, bugger.'

When at length the Aussies ambled away to film extras trying not to giggle as they poked sticks at a half-built kiln, Dai let me have a go on the bellows. It was desperate, punishing work, and more than once my fatigue-addled technique allowed a nugget of glowing charcoal to be sucked back up the length of central-heating pipe that focused its output into the crucible. Reluctant to watch his most important tool destroyed in an idiot's conflagration, when it happened for the third time he gently asked if I'd like to try my hand at hammering. With these words all weariness vanished. Show me a man who'd spurn an invitation to batter seven bells out of a length of red-hot metal, and I'll show you a liar.

Sadly, the next stage – fashioning the abused ingot into something recognisably useful – involved the transition from labourer to craftsman, a transition for which we soon found I was not ready. I cannot therefore claim full responsibility for the splendid five-inch spear tip that now sits on my desk, though in fact I have, and often. Surveying it I note widespread evidence of corrosion, and am reminded once more just why we know so little about an era that endured longer than the Roman Empire.

Cinderbury emptied as the shadows lengthened. After polishing off the last of their hidden Lucozade stash – it's *Glucose Galore!* in this part of the Forest of Dean – the extras drove home into the sunset, followed by the hotel-bound Australians; the presenter's unfulfilled desire to churn butter on camera meant the latter group would be back in the morning. To my mild unease, the exodus was promptly swelled by the departure of Dai, who rumbled away in his Vauxhall-badged mobile foundry as soon as Wayne turned up and paid him. When Cinderbury's beleaguered owner trudged off to his own car I felt a more powerful twinge of insecurity, which persisted until he trudged back out of the twilight bearing a mighty flagon of local scrumpy.

The contempt I'd been nurturing for Wayne's shambolic stewardship melted into pity as we sat by the campfire and worked our way through this 7.5 per cent curse of the rustics, and a stash of combustible building materials I'd found round the back. It all came out. He'd acquired Cinderbury the summer before as an escape from that debilitating split existence, desperate for gainful employment that didn't demand his absence from the family home for half the year. But visitor numbers, already modest, had dwindled further when the nearby Clearwell Caves attraction launched their own 'spoiler' Iron Age settlement. 'It was made out of fibreglass,' said Wayne vacantly, 'but no one complained.'

The reason they hadn't, as he saw it, was that no one really cared about the Iron Age one way or the other. 'It's just not . . . sexy. No shiny uniforms, no big war machines, sod all in the way of art and culture.' At last his blank face furrowed. 'Eight hundred years of nothing.'

Beyond an astonishing level of disillusionment, the Cinderbury jinx had also caused Wayne untold sleepless nights, ratcheting debt and reacquaintance with a nicotine habit that had lain fallow for a decade. Yet he hadn't quite surrendered. There were plans to promote the village as a music venue, to hire it out to live-action role-players and new-age spiritualists. The school-party visits had gone fairly well – 'kids are great, really easy to please'. And then there were the half-dozen weekend guests who I learned were to arrive the following afternoon: the first such intake under his ownership.

It seemed no stone would be left unturned in Wayne's quest for profitability – quite literally so with regard to the Roman villa whose foundations lay just behind the mobile-phone mast. 'Archaeology students excavating their own Roman ruin, and staying in an Iron Age roundhouse while doing it . . .' He aimed a rare smile into the fire. 'Imagine what the American universities would pay for that.' With difficulty I forced out a small hum of encouragement, thereby inspiring Wayne to reveal the triumphant zenith of this extraordinary proposal: the roadside stall where everything that was dug up would be flogged off.

Certain it was only a matter of time and scrumpy before Wayne dragooned me into some 'What the Blacksmith Saw' period peep show, I greeted his departure with quiet relief. And the noisier sort, once noting that he'd thoughtfully left me the considerable balance of our gallon of peasant's ruin. Yes, I was going to make a one-man Iron-Age night out of it: just me, the starlit sky, the roaring fire. Oh, and this diseased sheep here.

The feral quartet of flyblown woollybacks I'd regularly encountered outside the Cinderbury walls were survivors of a flock of authentic ancient breeds brought in by the village's creators. The rest, I gathered, had long since been sacrificed to provide the original owners with something appropriate to eat, and their roundhouse guests with something appropriate to sleep on. Considering this as I chivvied my grubby, unkempt guest back out through the entrance and blocked it up with the pallet provided, I felt a pang of compassion. This swiftly evolved into an adrenaline surge of alarm when, not yet halfway back to the fire, I wheeled round to investigate the source of a sudden clackety stampede. In the fire-lit gloaming I found myself face to blank-eyed face with the same animal, as in the dim background his three associates trampled clumsily in over the upended makeshift gate.

Four sheep, I recognised immediately, were many more than four times as unsettling as one sheep. One was a sorry, stupid object of sympathy. Four was a gang. I knew it, they knew it, and most significantly they knew that I knew it. I took a pace towards them and they stood their ground; I essayed a threatening bark and they fanned out into a four-square, head-on attack formation. The effect was compounded by their neglected disfigurement. Strips of filthy, matted fleece sloughed off unshorn flanks imparted a look of haunted, mutant decay that connected powerfully with the childhood nightmares I'd suffered after reading an illustrated magazine account of wartime anthrax experiments.

What had possessed these creatures to act with a fearless, focused determination so far beyond the feeble capabilities of their species? The only herbivorous sustenance within these walls had been strimmed down to a parched stubble, and on such a balmy night they could not be wanting for warmth. Had these leprous, forsaken animals come in search of companionship? I had only to picture myself amongst them to know they had not. The proffered hand, the playful nuzzle, then a nudge, the nudge trumped with a butt, another, two more, then a stamp and a Buckaroo back-kick, and as I went down the first probing nips and gnashes . . . Backing slowly away from their ghastly yellow gaze I understood what had impelled them here. Before them stood a man who had taken his ease upon the flayed hides of their colleagues, and must now face vengeance.

What, I speculated frantically, would my Iron Age self have done? The question was no sooner asked than answered. Teenage memories of a Paleolithic-set film entitled *Quest for Fire* flooded my brain, and filtering through the depressing bulk that centred on muddy nudes being pleasured from behind, I recalled that the primeval obsession with flickering redness was less about warmth and cooking than warding off predators. With this in mind I retreated briskly to the fire, snatched

29

up a blazing length of four by two, and, before allowing myself to wonder how it had come to this, charged at the invaders, a ragged, warrior death-yell shredding the warm, black air.

Their unhurried withdrawal was half-hearted, even patronising. My cloven-hoofed tormentors ambled blandly out through the gate, passing en route the information board reminding visitors that the modest fortifications which encircled settlements such as Cinderbury were there not to deter human assault – generally benign co-existence was one facet of those '800 years of nothing' – but to keep destructive wildlife at bay. It wasn't a good time to remember a film extra's excitable account of the boar he'd spent many nights trying to hunt down through these very woods: 'Half the size of a donkey, nine-inch tusks – if he comes at you, it's all over.' Bar the awful, pleading screams.

Working fast, I resurrected the pallet-gate, bracing it with four spear-poles, jammed obliquely into the sun-hardened earth. Bed now seemed sensible, but pausing at the roundhouse's grim, black portal, I understood this was not an option. Instead, I walked very quickly back to the fire, pausing to sweep up a great armful of the only fuel to hand within my shrinking radius of fear: the stack of wooden tiles reserved to display visiting school parties' attempts at period pottery.

In the re-enactments that lay ahead I would become well acquainted with man's spiritual bond to fire, but never again would I feel it so intimately. Hunched up on a log, I didn't so much gaze at the flames as stare into them with a kind of desperate intensity. Be gone my scrumpy, my Clarks, my Fiat Punto – here, blazing savagely before me, was the competitive advantage that set my genus apart from and above the spiteful, dumb beasts outside those wicker walls. First created, then tamed, man's red fire had allowed my woady forebears to prosper where other mammals could barely survive. It had seen them through ice ages and raw leftovers, catalysed the very process that defined the era I was here to experience.

The fire was there to offer solace and displacement when the sheep rallied for a noisy and persistent assault on the rear wall, and when a moth the size of Dai's fist slammed blindly into my right temple. In more dwindled form, the hypnotic mind-balm applied by those flickering orange fingers helped me through the moment I grabbed hold of Wayne's flagon and felt a large slug being pulped in my grasp. I stayed until the scrumpy was drained, the last wooden tile no more than a fading ember. Then I tramped dolefully back to the round-house, pulled off my sweaty, smutted clothing, blundered on to the nearest haybale and lay there, feeling small things explore me and cursing myself for failing to anchor both arms around Wayne's departing ankles when I had the chance.

I was boiling my morning bathwater when the film crew turned up. 'You all right there, mate?' breezed the sound man, who could have seen from some distance that I was not. I looked up from a one-handled saucepan of oily, brown water and showed him a matching face, one deeply lined with physical and spiritual exhaustion. 'Bad night, yeah?'

It seemed best to respond with a shrug. Hard to imagine any Australian sympathising with my ovine ordeal. Particularly its most testing episode, wherein an apocalyptic overhead crash had propelled me from the hut at the break of dawn, nude and spear-wielding, to find that a sheep had somehow vaulted the stockade and was now grazing contentedly on my turfed roof. It had taken a direct hit with the scrumpy flagon to get him down, and in the chase that ensued to expel the repulsive beast out through the gate we'd disturbed a fox in the act of plundering Wayne's snack pantry.

I hauled my steaming saucepan round the back and sluiced off at least some of the sweaty filth that is the lot of the excitable blacksmith's assistant. This was my debut experience of period bathing, and it laid out what would prove an enduring circular truth: historic body-dirt could only be shifted with a lot of hot water, a valued commodity whose onerous creation accumulated much additional historic body-dirt. Ergo, it was best not to bother. If you can't take the grime, don't do the time.

When I returned, smeared and damp, Diane was standing

before the camera whisking a twig in an earthenware pot of double cream. 'Do you hanker after days gone by, when Lycra didn't exist and the butter' – pause for theatrical pot-sniff – 'was real?'

It was a matter of considerable relief when a hefty old Jeep clunked up and delivered a primitive technologist into my faltering prehistoric experience. Stubbled and down to earth in every sense, combat-trousered Karl Lee was an archaeologist who had made a name for himself as a hardcore practitioner of ancient survival skills.

Before the film crew stole him – to his great credit Karl refused their insistent demands that he don one of Wayne's Caveman-at-C&A jerkins – he accompanied me for a walk through the woods. 'You've got ground ivy, comfret, wild raspberries, colts-foot and beech nuts,' he said, scanning the vegetation. 'All perfectly edible. Acorns too, once you've boiled them to get rid of the tannin.' He stooped to snatch up a bramble leaf, then thrust it towards my mouth. In thrall to his manly certitude, I opened wide without protest: pleasantly nutty, if a little acid. Even better was the almost moreish wild garlic, and though Karl's subsequent harvest proved of diminishing appeal, I only spat out the beech leaves. 'Not that long ago, anyone could have walked through these trees and come out the other side with a meal,' sighed Karl as we marched onwards. 'We were all Ray Mears in the Iron Age.' Later he confessed that a medical condi-tion – unfortunate in most other lines of work – had deprived him of any sense of taste.

Wayne was waiting for us, or rather Karl, when we walked back in through the village gate. He explained he was off to get supplies for the 'Iron Age feast' that would welcome the soon-to-arrive weekend visitors, and wanted a primitive tech-nologist's input into the menu. This wasn't the first time Karl had been booked by Cinderbury's owner, and his deadpan reply was delivered with careworn brevity: 'A pig.'

Wayne pushed his specs up the bridge of his nose, squinted at us, and cleared his throat. 'Um, how about pork chops?'

Once he'd been filmed boiling nettles, Karl did his best to

make an Iron Age man of me. He dug out a bag of hefty chunks of flint, and in the shade of the boundary fence schooled me in the art of crafting stone hand tools. Because they were so quick and simple to make and use, Karl was certain these would have been common long after the introduction of iron smelting. 'The fields are full of them round here,' he said, alluding to the youthful finds that had first fired his enthusiasm. 'Go out after a night of heavy rain and you'll see flint tools and arrowheads all over the place.' In parts of the land, they're still in use: Karl had met Scottish deerstalkers who carried flint scrapers, attracted by the no-cost aspect and finding them 'more effective for some of the, ah, heavier work'.

Hoping I wouldn't be asked to disembowel Bambi with it, under Karl's watchful eye I fashioned some sort of flattish, pointy stone by hacking a large bit of flint obliquely against a smaller one. On occasion parts of my hand came between the two. Karl's subsequent demonstration of the flintknapper's art involved a flurry of clacking strikes that left a scattering of stone flakes on his lap and a straight-outta-Bedrock handaxe in his left fist. Then it was into the roundhouse for a practical seminar on the daddy of all survival skills: man make fire.

Squatting on the cool earth, in the hour ahead, Karl energetically ignited bits of singed linen, cedar bark and tinder fungus, which grows in black clumps on birch trees and was thus close to hand in ample supply. The necessary sparks were coaxed from the manual interaction of flint, metal and quartz, though he never quite managed it with his bow-drill, the string-powered wood-on-wood method that is the primitive-technological apotheosis of rubbing two sticks together.

Neither did I, of course, though you should have seen my face when I procured a couple of sparks from a flint shard and a flat piece of hardened iron: sweaty, it was, and flecked with spatters of blood from those ravaged fingertips. Yet how magical to watch the spark evolve into a red glow on the tinder fungus's corky surface, to spread and intensify as I cupped it in my hands and blew. A fistful of straw, a single well-aimed puff, and whoompf: fire, and the acrid whiff of singed eyebrows. It was the most impressively red-blooded achievement of a sheltered life, and I hailed it with an incoherent, primeval growl of triumph. When Karl stamped my fire out a moment later I could have clubbed him to death.

Leaving a trail of hot testosterone, I followed Karl down to the campfire, and his one-I-made-earlier cauldron of nettle tea. The common stinging nettle, he revealed, was of such versatile importance that Iron Agers would probably have cultivated it. I certainly wasn't aware that the leaves could be eaten raw (by Karl), if picked from the non-stinging underside and carefully folded. But the nettle's main use was to provide cordage, better known to you and me as string – an often overlooked survival essential. 'You can't use a bow or set a trap without it,' said Karl, grasping a bunch of benign, boiled stems from the tea cauldron. 'And they'd certainly have made a lot of their clothes out of nettles.'

Together we stripped off the fibres, then rolled them together atop our thighs, like Cuban virgins making cigars. 'There you go,' he said, as I held up my nine-inch mess of straggle. 'After flax, that was the strongest twine known to man.' Sceptical in the extreme, I tied it round my right wrist. Eight months – and 1,500 years – later, its last strand finally snapped as I helped manhandle a cannon through a French castle.

Karl drove off with Wayne's cheque in his pocket, leaving me with a handaxe and an improbable glow of authentic achievement. I'd be ready to face those woolly mutants tonight, nude or nay. Though ideally nay, as the arrival of a large van reminded me that this night, I would not be holding Cinderbury alone.

Dai was a stalwart chap and a supreme blacksmith, but he wore blue Y-fronts and flattened his spearheads on a railway line. Karl knew every skill necessary for recreating ancient life, but didn't go in for actually recreating it. A minute in the company of the van's occupants made it plain that Cinderbury's past was at last to become its present.

John ('call me Tinker') was the compact, lightly bearded half of the husband-and-wife team hired by Wayne to entertain his weekend guests. Despite their flippant name, my later research backed up John's businesslike assertion that the 'Time Tarts' ranked amongst the nation's most sought-after teams of professional re-enactors. 'There's maybe 45,000 serious re-enactors in this country,' he told me as I helped him and the cheery Karen unload their looms and drums and straw palliasses, 'and nearly all of them dream of making their hobby their job.' He showed me a gap-toothed grin. 'But not many have the discipline to make it work.'

A former deputy headmaster with a recreational background in medieval combat, John had arranged multi-period filming assignments around the world, from documentaries to adverts, as well as countless public displays. The easy part of the job was getting the props right; finding reliable re-enactors to wield them was a different story. 'It always comes down to ego and arrogance,' he said, passing me a basket full of prehistoric crockery through the van's side door. 'Most re-enactors hate admitting they're wrong, and being told what to do.' Confirming what I'd heard from Neil Burridge, John said the comparative dearth of evidence and an associated breadth of interpretation made earlier periods particularly vulnerable to this syndrome. During the recent filming of a documentary on Viking Britain, he'd endured a terrible time with the Dark Ages group his company had hired. One of the 'chieftains' had insisted that the film crew address him at all times as 'my lord', and another responded to the director's request to remove the white top he had on with a furious diatribe rounded off thus: 'Do you even care that I bleached this in my own piss?'

I was expecting John to greet Cinderbury's many compelling anachronisms with a gurn of outrage, but as a man who'd once been asked to erect a Roman camp for a Vodafone ad, he was clearly used to worse. When Wayne pitched up and breathlessly enquired what he might do in the half-hour before the first guests arrived, John calmly advised him to remove the school-canteen cookware, and the large plastic chemical drum that would otherwise welcome them as the village's gate-stop.

'And you might want to do something about those,' he added, indicating one of the many carrier bags snagged in the perimeter fence and roundhouse roofs.

I'd had no idea what sort of people might pay £200 for a weekend in the Iron Age, but as they began to arrive Wayne must have been delighted to note their principal shared attribute: a look of benign tolerance not associated with those accustomed to demanding their money back. The first was a very quiet middle-aged woman who worked for an examination board, followed shortly by a posh and hearty chap with a predictably underwhelmed young son in tow. Wayne – who'd taken the trouble to don a Guantanamo-orange jerkin, but not to remove his glasses – led them off to the caravan, and they returned a while later wearing brave faces and the standard Cinderbury uniform: knee-length cotton dress, shoes model's own.

By then Karen and John – barefoot in simple, heavy tunics hand-sewn from beige-dyed flax and linen – were well advanced with the dinner preparations, and the latter held forth as we sat down by the fire to help shell peas and skewer duck parts (Wayne's Safeway pork chops were quietly set aside). The frisson of disappointment that accompanied John's failure to address us in some kind of pre-Chaucerian rustic dialect was familiar to me from my first encounter with Dai, but as before, darkness brought the Iron Age to life. Particularly once Cinderbury's youngest resident had been packed off to the car with his GameBoy.

Nursing mugs of sickly warm mead, we allowed John's words and the flickering fire to draw us back through time. The Iron Age was by no means his speciality – a Time Tart has no fixed historical abode – yet he certainly knew enough, and delivered it with an involving sense of theatre. 'Our life here would be just working in the fields around,' he intoned, 'and we'd none of us ever leave this valley. If a chap who lived a day's walk away turned up, it would be like meeting a weird foreigner.' We all nodded into the fire. John explained that this humble, self-sufficient way of life persisted all but unchanged from 5000 BC to perhaps AD 1100, 'when feudalism came along, and

36

with it the concept of having a surplus, and widespread trading and all that. So when you talk about "the olden days", you really aren't making a lazy generalisation.'

Again I thought how strange and sad it was that our current lifestyle had rendered redundant the human skills honed over all those millennia. But how fortunate for me personally that it had: the lesson of the previous three days was that I'd have made a pitifully inadequate Iron Ager, capable of nothing more than poking the fire and a little light weeding. For 6,000 years, this hefty roster of physical, technical and spiritual failings would have rendered me utterly dispensable to mankind, a makeweight – or a millstone – in any community. As it was, in the modern era these sundry handicaps hadn't inconvenienced me since the days of being picked second last in playground football.

By the time the final guests arrived – a rather harassed mother and her eight-year-old daughter, who'd driven right across the country from Norfolk – I was flat on my back looking up at the Milky Way, as John and Karen serenaded Wayne and I with thumpy-flutey period music. The other residents could be heard dragging haybales about as my roundhouse was converted into a multiple-occupancy dwelling; the exhausted new arrivals clicked on torches and went to join them. This was John's signal to lay down his drum, and deliver to the blank-faced Wayne a friendly but forceful tutorial on where Cinderbury was going wrong.

'The hard work's been done here,' he began, 'but when you have twenty-first-century stuff around, even if it's shoved away round the back of the huts, it punctures the atmosphere.' The Bacardi-bottle stashes were right out, and those information boards should be hung from hooks, John sagely advised, so that they might be removed during living-history stayovers. 'And you know those goatskin bellows over by the kiln?' Wayne's impassive gaze said he might or might not. 'Well, I can see someone's taken a lot of time making those, but the frame's been put on back to front, so they don't work. And that, to me, is worse than not having them at all.' His searching look at Wayne went unreturned. 'It's just a matter of putting things together with a little care.'

For the first time Wayne turned his head from the fire. 'But I don't care,' he said. 'Not about the Iron Age, and not about re-enactment.' And for once there was a light in those lifeless eyes, a burning glower that said: the only good flint-knapper is a dead one.

This was my disheartening cue to turn in, and a moment later I was clumping through the unseen yielding forms that now lay between the roundhouse entrance and my haybale. A stumbling foot on a sleeper's arm, a blindly probing hand on a young face, much yelping and whispered apologies and there I was at last on my relocated bed of straw.

Prone in the snuffling, shuffling blackness, I could hear John still at it out by the fire; having failed to awaken Wayne's inner historian, he now appealed directly to his outer accountant. There were snatches of grim marketingspeak ('it's all about building a brand'), and a stark primer in how to milk the undiscerning cash cow that was the visiting school party: 'Each kid comes in with six or seven quid, right, and their parents don't expect to see any of that again. You can get some old coins knocked up for next to nothing – kids love those. Build up your school contacts and you can pull in three, three and a half grand a month, easy.'

My final day began by the campfire with a wooden bowl of porridge and the difficult aroma of onion skins, boiling in a cauldron to make dye. Karen played a prominent instructional role in what was to be a day of more delicate, perhaps more feminine, period skills. Yet more intensive, too: 'In the Iron Age, no one sat around doing nothing,' she reminded us, unaware that I had spent large chunks of the previous three days doing precisely that.

After an hour or two in the cauldron, yellowed skeins of spun wool were hauled out to dry in the hot sun, then painstakingly woven into wristbands on a fiddly handloom that the men weren't allowed near. Instead, we twisted and tapped lengths of brass wire into distant approximations of decorative cloak-brooches.

As we bent and banged and wove, Karen asked my fellow Iron Age newbies what had drawn them to Cinderbury; I could sense that she herself was curious to discover the appeal of this unfashionable and unglamorous period. Yet it had been plain even to me that their willingness to sit by this fire in Reeboks suggested none harboured a passion for authentic re-enactment, and many of their questions ('So was the Bronze Age before or after the Iron Age?') betrayed a cheery ignorance of ancient history in general. There were mutters about an interest in traditional crafts, and the posh dad spoke of a distant though still inspirational encounter with primitive societies in Burma. But the common theme that emerged was a refreshingly simple impulse to get away from it all, one so assertive it had overpowered the chortling contempt of friends and family. 'Everyone thinks I'm mad,' smiled the late arrival, draping smelly, wet yarn across a log, 'driving five hours to sleep on the floor with strangers in a place with no running water.' The examiner had faced workplace jeers ('Give my love to the Flintstones!'), and the absent wife/mother of the father-and-son team had responded to the news with a dumbstruck gawp.

It was almost as if they'd been drawn here against their will by some dormant part of their ancient consciousness, one that had briefly broken through what – on the timescale of human evolution and social conditioning – was after all just a recently applied veneer of urban sophistication. And that didn't just go for the adults: I'd thought our youngest villager seemed un-utterably bored until she looked up from her lapful of unspun wool and announced, 'I wish I could always be in the olden days.'

As the sun rose higher, it became ever more challenging to concentrate on the finickety tasks at hand. After a couple of hours, having fashioned a passable ringhead bodkin (oh, look it up), I moved on to a very brief career as a fletcher. I was endeavouring to split and trim my third and final goose feather into something that might conceivably improve the accuracy of an arrow, rather than just remodel it as an anorexic Gonk troll, when John issued a very strange hiss of warning.

'MOPs! MOPs!'

Not yet fluent in re-enactorese – here was an acronym denoting 'members of the public' – I was taken aback to look round and see a quartet of red-faced pensioners ambling towards us. 'Er, are you open?' called out one, and before any of us formulated a reply, in through the gate jogged Wayne, along with a young boy who he'd shortly introduce as his son.

'Yes!' he blurted, approaching them breathlessly. 'Yes, yes. That's, um, five pounds a head.' He stood there rubbing his hands as they scanned the village and exchanged questioning looks. He was still rubbing away when the small figure at his side broke the awkward silence. 'Dad,' he piped up, introducing what was to prove a trademark pronouncement, 'I'm gonna kill your bum.'

Wayne accepted the ensuing barrage of rearward slaps and punches with no more than a twitch of those stonelike features. 'Tell you what,' he offered, once the assault subsided, 'how about fifteen quid for the lot of you?' And we watched as the visitors tapped vaguely at their watches and wandered back towards the car park.

We toiled through our period tasks as the children ran sweatily amok under a limb-wilting sun. Some time in the afternoon, as the examiner and I were squishing heated goat's milk, sour cream and vinegar into an authentic cheese press, John subtly raised the stakes by inveigling the present tense into his conversation. 'See, we can trade this, maybe for salt,' he announced quietly, and, despite the heat, our labours thereafter were characterised by a gathering sense of purpose. Particular enthusiasm was devoted to our Diane-emulating efforts at twig-whisking cream into butter, though try as I furiously did it wouldn't work for me. Surveying the slurried whey that was the fruit of my twenty-minute manual frenzy, John solemnly announced that such a failure could be interpreted as evidence of witchcraft.

'Smirk if you must,' he whispered, holding out a finger, 'but first let me tell you a story.' And so, with the roundhouse shadows stretching out across Cinderbury's barren stubble, he told us the tale of a pagan acquaintance who, having been teased at work, cursed his tormentor so effectively that he was soon tearfully begged to lift the hex, and indeed handed a great deal of cash to do so.

'And the nature of this curse?' John's small, bright eyes darted from face to sunburnt face. Then, with a grim smile, he leaned towards me until that blistered nose was almost touching mine. 'See this face?' he hissed, jabbing a whey-flecked digit at his beard. 'Tonight, when you're shagging your wife, at the point of orgasm you'll see this face again, and you'll keep seeing it every time you shag her from now on.' All I can say is that this statement affected me a lot more than it would have done three days previously. A year on and I still have occasional cause to hate him for it.

Walking into our roundhouse in AD 25 – the year John had recently opted to place us in – and walking out of it two millennia later had a jarring, *Mr Benn* quality to it, though it might have felt more jarring had I not been wearing the same shoes in both shots, and been offered a shave and a shower in between.

En route to my fireside farewells I glanced through the door of the roundhouse commandeered by the Time Tarts, where Karen was collecting instruments for the after-dark festivities to come. A shield lay against a plank-framed bed draped with sheepskins, and on a low chest beside it sat a pair of wooden bowls and the cluster of Romanesque oil lamps that bathed the scene in soft, warm light. It was a most becoming still life; standing there in my tourist shorts and a Woodstock T-shirt, I at last felt a nape-tickling frisson of Will's 'period rush'.

Sensing this just as I was about to leave should have seemed a frustrating disappointment, but approaching the fire and its encirclement of tousled craftsmen, I accepted that the reality of my experience was this: you could have fed me from the porridge drawer and dyed my clothes in wee, you could have locked me up in Cinderbury for a year with only the Time Tarts and those sheep for company, you could have done all that and still I'd never have made it to the Iron Age. My clock just couldn't be turned back that far.

The night before John had railed at length against a distant

BBC historical-reality show in which a couple of dozen me-type urbanites were left to cope alone in an Iron Age village in Wales. Describing the consequent shambles, he'd rhetoric-ally wondered what the series was attempting to prove. 'You were just watching people without any period skills faffing about – any Iron Ager would have known that if you cook chicken in the dark, you'll end up with food poisoning. We didn't learn anything about their period at all.'

Perhaps not, but we learned a little about ours. Mainly that most of us in the developed world have mislaid all the funda-mental talents that were once hardwired human nature, but which in the space of a breathless couple of centuries have been rendered utterly irrelevant. Appraising my least ridiculous cloak-brooch, John diplomatically commented how difficult it was to master tools and crafts that had played no part in one's formative years. And there we were: I was simply too modern, too pampered and closeted, all that ancient know-how jettisoned in favour of more contemporary life-skills, like digital copyright theft and sarcasm.

Yet there was hope, and it lay just beyond those wooden walls. Buried out there were the remains of a structure that would have astounded Cinderbury Man perhaps more than the phone mast erected beside it 2,000 years later. The invaders that built it brought with them the sophisticated technology and culture that would at last haul our filthy forebears towards civilisation as I recognised it. They were, in short, the kind of people I might more convincingly pretend to be.

Chapter Two

They pioneered our urban way of life, and left behind vast lumps of epic civil engineering. They conquered a huge swathe of the known world with their winning blend of ruthless tactical efficiency, big catapults and splendid helmets. They lived it large, and wrote about it. Everything that Wayne felt the Iron Age lacked, the Romans had in shiny spades. No surprise that, in contrast to the dearth of prehistoric re-enactors, the problem now was an overwhelming surfeit.

Britain alone hosts more than a dozen very active Roman groups, most with a military bias, some boasting over 100 members and a history stretching back to the sixties. Germany is another stronghold. Switzerland, Spain, Norway, Holland, Russia, Australia, Venezuela . . . no matter how far I cast my Google net, it came back with a haul of sandalled legionaries. Shamed by their subsequent decline, or just bored with an era whose relics cluttered their city centres, Italy could muster only one mothballed group; indeed it seemed that the Romans were most popular in those countries they had either failed to annex in totality or never even knew existed. Perhaps inspired by Hollywood's enduring fascination with the era, no fewer than twenty-one practising legions patrolled the United States. The Legio XIV had declared Buffalo, New York, a 'formally recognised province of Rome'; I watched in silent awe a

YouTube video depicting period military drill solemnly performed in a Las Vegas parking lot.

Aware that soldierly lifestyles were likely to dominate many of my forthcoming re-enactments, I spent some time tracking down civilian-oriented Roman groups, pretending I was doing so in search of a more rounded experience, rather than just to avoid pain and humiliation. Fruitlessly so. Hope was raised by a post in livinghistory.co.uk's Roman section headed 'For those inclined to gentler pursuits', then dashed by the message beneath: 'We always need body draggers, arena guards and someone to portray Pluto ushering the fallen into the after-life.' Of all the historical enthusiasts I would contact, only the Vikings proved more singularly bent on violence.

My misgivings were eloquently encapsulated in the pages of www.gladiator.hu, a Hungarian organisation whose annual 'Traditional Fighting Club' attracted period hardmen from across the world. 'Our training camp reflects the mentality of Roman gladiator schools, and besides developing your endurance and fighting skills, you will also find people with similar interests and a strong sense of fellowship. The quality of training is guaranteed by magister gladiators.' It seemed impossible to imagine a less appealing event, though researching the Dark Ages I found one: 'Although such encounters are well documented in European history, Beth believes this was the first nude battle re-enactment. By all accounts, it was a great success, and there is already talk about next year's event. Hopefully the weather will be more cooperative.'

In the end, I applied to join the half-dozen pan-Continental groups whose website photo archives featured members at least occasionally doing something other than hurting or being hurt. The first to come back with a positive reply was the Legio VIII Augusta, a French group based predominantly in the Toulouse area. It was a happy result: their commanding officer expressed his genial enthusiasm in mercifully fluent English.

'We are invited this summer to spend some days in Denmark in an archaeological park, living in historical conditions. You will be our first British. It's great because in the Roman days in the period we depict it was the same, a mixture from different origins. Jean-Luc Féraud SIG LEG VIII AVG.'

A week with French Romans in Denmark sounded irresistibly cosmopolitan, and the legion's website uniquely depicted the presence of a great number of young and attractive female camp followers. I signed up without hesitation, and three months later wandered through the gates of the Lejre Experimental Centre.

'Oh, it's very late for a visit,' said the woman manning the trim and very contemporary reception area. 'This is a big place and I'm really sure you won't have time.' In doing so she presented me with my first opportunity to grab bragging rights over a MOP. 'But I'm not here to visit,' I announced, airily. 'I've come to join my legion.'

I might have announced an intention to hold my breath for an hour.

'You're a *soldier* – a *Roman* soldier?'

If my pride was hurt by the tone of her response, it slunk off in a corner to die during the sceptical, lingering appraisal that followed. In the end I scrabbled through the large bag at my feet and retrieved my helmet. I held it up for her inspection, and we both watched as a crumpled crisp packet snagged in one of the cheek-piece hinges freed itself and fluttered down on to her souvenir pens. 'Please,' she said, almost sadly, 'you will find your colleagues behind the hill.'

It was a hot day, and my journey had been a stickily protracted trudge up and down the public-transport hierarchy: train then coach to Stansted, plane to Copenhagen, inter-city to Roskilde, once-an-hour local service down a branch-line shin-deep in weeds, then an otherwise empty bus through the wheatfields and windfarms of the gently undulating, well-ordered Danish countryside. Throughout this odyssey I endeavoured to comply with Jean-Luc's final communiqué, a request to attain familiarity with the legion's orders – in Latin.

Culled exclusively from Roman sources – principally Caesar's own account of his nine-year campaign in France – these offered at once a thrilling insight into the truly immersive, fully codified realm of ancient military history I was about to enter, and a sobering foretaste of what I might have to endure when I got there. Wedged on benches between solemn, Scholl-sandalled Scandinavians, I'd worked diligently through the relevant website printouts, doubly hampered by the complete absence of English therein. I'd hopefully do the right thing if a snarling centurion barked out *'Pergere!'* (*'Marche!'*), followed by *'Ostiose!'* (*'A votre aise!'*), or if an unlikely cry of *'Ad impedimenta!'* (*'Chargez les bagages lourds sur les chariots!'*) rang around the camp. But there wasn't much to be made of *'Gladium condere!'* or its runic translation *'Rengainez!'*, and it was hard to imagine a happy outcome to any interpretation of *'Ad aggerem!'* (*'Elevez une butte!'*).

No such confusion – once I'd foolishly researched its true meaning – muddied the fearful last command of the hundred or so listed in the legion's compendium. The Roman Army's base unit, the *contubernium*, was an almost claustrophobically close-knit squad of eight legionaries who shared a tent, ate together and fought side by side. If one of the group showed cowardice in the face of the enemy, their centurion would declare *decimatio*, the cue for the most inhuman practice ever conjured up by a civilisation synonymous with merciless brutality. The squad, coward and hero alike, would draw straws, with the unlucky loser sentenced to death. Not at the point of an executioner's sword, but with stones and clubs forced into the hands of his own squad, his closest colleagues, in strong statistical probability including the coward himself. As a back-up to this apparently inadequate deterrent – you don't really want to know where the moral compass was pointing back then – the survivors were for some time thereafter obliged to survive on barley rather than wheat.

The prospect of living for a week on either of these period victuals encouraged me to lay down an impressively thick base-layer of twenty-first-century calories throughout my journey. Doritos, hot dogs, a big tub of curried potato salad – in it all went, repulsing even the most stoic Dane into affording me a little extra bench space. It also fuelled my laboured manhandling of a vast holdall containing the most curious selection of personal effects I had ever carried out of my front door.

After the poly-cotton shambles that was my Cinderbury wardrobe, I'd been boyishly enthralled by the prospect of striding about as a fully tooled-up legionary. Particularly once it became apparent that the ratcheting demand for re-enactment kit had attracted a number of Indian craftsmen into the market, meaning period equipment could be snapped up on eBay for significantly less than I'd imagined.

Having sourced a gleamingly splendid, brass-trimmed helmet for under £50 I proudly emailed Jean-Luc the relevant image. In doing so I inspired him to a tone of icy disdain at odds with our previously cordial communications: 'This helmet is completely wrong,' began his reply. 'Not one thing is good on it. Do not buy this helmet.' Chastened, I checked the picture against those worn by the Legio VIII Augusta's jovial membership in their website photo archives. Only very gradually did a tiny, single difference – two decorative brass roundels on the hinged cheek-pieces where there should have been three – assert itself to my untrained eye. Yet as I trained that eye, through a long after-noon of online research, I could feel myself being drawn into a comfortingly male realm of obsessive authenticity and slavish attention to the finest details of make and model.

I learned that the Legio VIII Augusta's chosen period – the late first century AD – would have seen them equipped with the helmet subsequently codified by archaeologists as the Imperial Gallic G, examples of which have been retrieved from the Rhine near Mainz, and – in battered fragments – from the rubbish pits where they were hurled during the Boudican Revolt of AD 61. Inspired by a Gaulish design, the Gallic G incorpor-ated protective plates intended to reduce the evident regularity with which legionaries found themselves being decapitated from behind or deprived of their ears. It was the dominant helmet of the Roman Empire's most dominant age.

I came to appreciate the nuances of form and function, the vocabulary of steel gauges and rivet work, the thrill of owning a precise copy of an actual helmet worn in battle by a legionary stationed in Colchester, then kicked off his severed head into a compost heap. Extracting the fruit of this research from a big square box some days later, I found I didn't care that the attached invoice featured a total precisely double that of my eBay find. No time for such concerns when there was a house to march around, and fragments of schoolboy Latin to bark out whilst doing so: 'One, two, one, two, Caecilius is a banker, three, four, three, four, Grumio is in the garden.' I was still at it when my youngest daughter returned from school, with a friend who hasn't come round since.

The helmet was the heaviest bit of kit, followed by the hobnailed sandals, or *caligae*. Despite sharing the same sub-continental origins, these proved less satisfactory reproductions. The glossy, unyielding straps were machine-stitched to soles decorated with smooth, dome-topped studs, which succeeded only in severely compromising traction. Every night for a week I skated around the patio in an attempt to weather them down to some semblance of authenticity. The look I achieved was that of a pair of cheap ankle boots that had been bunged into an office shredder full of drawing pins. A few smears of curried potato salad, applied in some waiting room or other, had proved oddly successful, but still I dreaded unveiling them.

My progress through its verdant, rolling grounds confirmed that Lejre was a rather larger operation than Cinderbury, and a vastly more successful one. Hot and happy families thronged the path as it skirted a pair of mighty Viking-model longhouses and a lake upon whose bulrushed foreshore lay a hollowed-out log canoe; others availed themselves of the wood-burning barbecue pits laid out in accordance with Lejre's oft-encountered motto – 'Let's Picnic in the Past'. The predominant flow of visitors, however, was towards the brow of a hill and through a gate in the fence that topped it. I shouldered my burdensome kitbag, laboured upwards and found myself before a multilingual notice of events. '11 a.m. and 3 p.m.,' read the English part. 'Romans fighting against Celts.' The massed, bellowing yell that now ripped up from the valley below made a glance at my watch unnecessary.

Over the transfixing half-hour that followed, I saw what I had let myself in for. Squatting on my holdall high up a hot hillside dotted with spectators and the odd ram-goat, I watched a dozen-strong phalanx of Romans file out through the gates of a stonewalled Celtic village – a clanking, shuffling, red-and-gold column of chainmail and hobnails, helmets gleaming, each member bearing a stubby wooden sword in one hand and a tall curved shield in the other. At its head, a glowering commander whose golden helmet was memorably topped with a desiccated fox skin; at its rear, half dragged, half frogmarched by a trio of grim-faced legionaries, a bound and bare-chested villager whose arrest had presumably aroused all those furious decibels.

Their goal, a couple of hundred yards beyond the straw roofs that poked above the village walls, was a small encampment confined within a pointy-sticked defensive palisade: four tents, some kind of wheeled crossbow-cum-catapult – a ballista? – and a smouldering fire. SPQR central. My home. The stubbled and muscular prisoner struggled impressively en route, at one point spitting on a proximate shield in an act of defiance that earned him a volley of ungentlemanly kicks. A few good-natured boos rang out from the crowd, but as his captors manhandled him brutally towards their camp entrance I felt my innards aglow with anticipation. I thought: I can do this. I can don the gleaming colours of a glorious empire, bringing the light of civilisation into a pagan darkness. I can take my place in this merciless snatch squad, extracting contemptible, topless Luddites out of their filthy huts for an awed glimpse at our brave new future, then torturing them to a complex death.

This reverie was interrupted when a duo of long-haired Celtic archers popped up from behind a rock on the opposite side of the valley, launching a quickfire succession of rubber-tipped arrows which, with commendable accuracy but no more, thwacked into a close formation Roman shield barrier erected with efficient haste. Nice try, I thought, just as a swelling roar from the hillside behind alerted both audience and Romans to a rampaging mob of furious Bravehearts, staves and mighty iron swords held aloft. The spectators around me visibly recoiled as the ambushers steamed headlong into the heavily outnumbered Roman ranks; together we watched in harrowed silence as the Legio VIII Augusta was frenziedly battered, clattered, stabbed and clubbed to swift and total destruction.

At the end of a mad half-minute, the valley floor lay scattered with prone, motionless legionaries, their corpses already being looted by giggling Celtic children who had formed a redundant second line of attack. The victors untied their liberated comrade, then turned to the crowd as one, weapons and plundered helmets held high. '*Toutatis!*' they yelled in unison, and as the spectators emerged from their shock to hail the triumphant rebels, I understood what was going down here. This was to be a re-enactment of Roman history as written not by Tacitus and Livy, but by Goscinny and Uderzo.

The imperial fallen were brought to life with a dramatic cry of '*Que les morts se relèvent!*', but five minutes later they were once more face down in the Denmark daisies, annihilated in a revenge attack on the village that backfired horribly. After a second resurrection the Romans regrouped, and armed with tennis-ball-tipped javelins marched away for a set-piece coming together, and a further brutal pasting, on the far side of the valley. And that was it. The dead and living took a bow; the audience applauded and filed away. They had come not to praise Caesar, but to bury him.

For some time I sat alone on the hill, brooding on the deluded, wrongheaded injustice of what I had just witnessed, and the pain and humiliation its repetition would shortly accord me, twice a day at 11 a.m. and 3 p.m. prompt. The land we now called Denmark lay some way north of both the limits of Roman imperial expansion and whatever might be defined as the Celtic region of influence, yet considered as a geographically transplanted re-enactment of Caesar's Gallic campaign, what had taken place here was a ludicrous travesty. A moustachioed comic-strip dwarf gulping magic potion to despatch hapless Romans by the oafish dozen helmet-first into a gorse bush was not history. History was the Battle of Bibracte, where in 58 BC Caesar and 30,000 troops had routed ten times as many Gauls. History was the

decisive Battle of Alesia, six years later, where 'as in other examples of ancient warfare, the disarrayed retreating Gauls were
easy prey for the disciplined Roman pursuit'. History was Gaul
being entirely absorbed within the Roman Empire by 50 BC, and
remaining so – without a single notable act of nationalist rebellion or resistance – for over 500 years.

Yet no such indignant concerns seemed to plague my future
colleagues, whom I now watched strip down to their authentic
loin-swaddlings and jump gleefully into a small, murky lake
near the Gaulish village walls. Once I was sure they weren't
talking in Latin I sidled up to one, a considerable young man
with a reckless twinkle in his rather rheumy blue eyes, as he
climbed back to shore through the reeds. He cut short my
introductory mumbles with a jovial, rasping call to attention.
'*Eh! Eh! L'anglais est arrivé!*'

An hour later, squatting on the straw-strewn floor of the
tent I'd be sharing with five fellow legionaries, I unpacked in
a mood – new to me as a living historian – of exultant anticipation. Everything was going splendidly; already, the daft false
start of Cinderbury seemed a distant memory. I'd been cheerily
invited to join the Legio VIII bathers, and accepted with an
apparently convincing display of enthusiasm: no casual observer
would have guessed that the man in the non-period pants had
never before voluntarily entered a body of water he couldn't
see the bottom of.

They did not speak Latin, and though none but the grizzled,
Gainsbourg-eyed Jean-Luc spoke much English, the hostly willingness with which most gave it a shot was touching and
entirely unexpected. ('I pree-fair le rugby,' replied Vincent, the
chap I'd first approached, when I mumbled some football-
related ice-breaker in my hopeless French. 'No acting, more . . .
men.' Though I'd rather he hadn't emphasised this last word
by punching himself very hard in the chest.)

Laying out my wardrobe for their inspection as we dried
ourselves afterwards, I'd faced no worse than modest ribbing
for my Startrite *caligae*, and only a dash more for the billowing
mainsail of a tunic my wife had hand-stitched using Jean-Luc's

measurements and a hemp/linen bedsheet purchased from French eBay – pre-1920, as advised, and thus woven on hand-looms, which imparted the requisite rough-hewn, unbleached look. ('Be aware it was surprisingly large,' he'd advised me, though judging by the conspicuously less generous cut of his and everyone else's more dapper tunics, I alone had faithfully adhered to the authentic dimensions.)

To marshal the torso-swallowing capaciousness of this sleeve-less, knee-length workwear staple, Jean-Luc had lent me a belt. 'This is really something special, the best in the legion,' he'd told me, handing it over with grave ceremony in a small tented pavilion just outside the camp walls. This accommodated both his private quarters and a craftwork stall selling ancient knick-knacks, most conspicuously a fertility symbol in the form of a winged erection. The proprietor was an auburn-haired German woman, Ira, whose workshop, Aurificina Treverica, had produced the belt in question: lavishly decorated with hand-worked tinned-brass rivets and plates, and finished off with a sort of clanking sporran – a curtain of five medallion-studded leather strips that hung down before the groin.

This splendid accessory elevated my appearance above that of a failed trick-or-treat ghost, and when teamed with a borrowed pair of well-seasoned, properly hobnailed old *caligae* – three sizes too large, and thus worn with a great fat pair of Hadrian's Wall-issue socks – imparted a look my new comrades seemed to find very nearly convincing. No less importantly, walking about in all this stuff felt much less blaringly daft than expected, particularly once they'd shown me how to make sense of the leather spaghetti that was my *caligae* lacing.

At this fledgling stage of my re-enactment career, I could not have wished for a more welcoming group of time trav-ellers, nor a happier compromise between hardcore historical accuracy and contemporary reassurance. A barefoot legionary had pressed upon me a honey-smeared slab of some sort of bread-pancake hybrid he'd prepared by baking dough on a flat rock extracted from the fire, then handed over a bottle of Heineken to wash it down. Linen drawn over a convoluted framework of wooden poles, the tent was self-evidently of period design, though jumbled in the straw amongst the armour and swords and leather-sheathed drinking vessels lay the odd Nike trainer and custom-car magazine.

Squeezed together on benches in the fly-happy heat of what I'd come to know as the mess tent, we effected more detailed introductions over an incomprehensible Roman dice game. Vincent was by some distance the most flamboyant of our number, an archaeology student with an unshakeable passion for roll-ups and the bellowed lyrics of Led Zeppelin. Ex-commando Renaud, an ever-smiling prop forward with calves the size of my waist, and a waist the size of a water-butt; goateed wisecracker Jean-Charles, a younger military veteran whose evidently uncanny impersonations of absent legionaries provided much of the after-dark entertainment; gimlet-eyed Paul, a modest, thoughtful man most often to be found reading in our tent; Germain, the quiet one; Francky, a six-foot-two, seventeen-stone teenage colosseum from the badlands of Marseilles; Laurent, a teacher at a technical college who'd sneakily persuaded his students to build the legion's ballista; and two beaky, companionable brothers, Jean-Michel and Thibault, respectively a plumber and a tax inspector.

Aside from Ira and Jean-Luc's teenage niece – both quartered in the flying-penis pavilion – the female contingent I'd beheld on the legion's website were conspicuous by their absence. No place for them on this big boys' scout camp, this swig-from-the-same-jug, five-to-a-tent, superglue-grade male-bonding belch-fest.

The park closed at five, and with the sun still high and hot it was just us, the unseen Gauls, and a creeping plethora of ram-goats gathered in vast-bollocked, blank-eyed malevolence outside our palisade. (Rare breeds, of course, which after my Cinderbury alarums I dearly wished to make rarer still.) Jean-Michel sat flaking wood into a barrel for fire-lighting purposes, Thibault was off jogging in his Reeboks, Renaud emerged from the leather-covered provisions tent with a bottle of Pernod. For an idle, comradely hour we slumped on the rope-handled chests that served as mess-tent benches, sipping pastis and lethargically slapping flies off our bare legs.

53

Ferried from wooden bowls to sweat-rimmed mouths with wooden spoons and iron-bladed daggers, dinner was bread dipped in olive oil, sausage, walnuts and figs, copiously accompanied with red wine decanted into earthenware jugs from the plastic jerry-can stashed behind a chest in the corner. An endless flow of chatter that included the words *romanisation*, Charlemagne and Peugeot evolved into a series of emotional monologues on the ideal of a simple life, the tyranny of the alarm clock and the dehumanising nature of office work; my understanding of all this was heavily dependent on the legion's very French habit of illustrating almost everything they said with a flamboyantly expressive mime.

The sun sank lower and we wandered out of the tent. Shield bosses, the business ends of the rack-stacked javelins and ballista bolts, Renaud's zebra-plumed helmet slung jauntily atop a spear wedged in the dusty earth – the legion's many metallic possessions gleamed softly in the golden sidelight. Off past the lake, a coil of wood-smoke rose into a cloudless sky above the thatched roofs of the oak-girdled Gaulish village, along with muted strains of a jolly, pagan singsong. It was all terribly becoming.

'We fight two hour only in one day, but it's hard,' yawned Vincent, heralding a tent-bound exodus. 'You will find so tomorrow.' Before I could nod, a rock exploded in the fire, flinging shrapnel and English yelps right across the hillside.

Nine hours later, ladling porridge out of a smutted copper pot hung from a tripod over the fire, I felt I'd coped as well as could be expected with the sardined intimacy that was an almost universal human experience until perhaps a century back, and still defines military life today. In the tent it was elbow to elbow, knee to buttock, nose to ear; those who didn't snore, farted. To my right: the immovable boy-mountain Francky, his bum-fluffed, Easter Island-sized face never more than a snuffling twitch away from mine. If Francky had snored they'd have known about it in Copenhagen, but instead he talked, an urgent mutter that invariably included '*Maman*' and many instances of the word '*non*'. Here was the teenage conscript who didn't hate Gauls and just wanted to go home.

Germain, to my left, never once made a sound or even moved a muscle, yet unsettled me more than all the restless, guttural snorters combined. The legion were restricted to wooden mock-weapons in combat, but every soldier had brought along a honed and gleaming *gladius* – a stocky, fat-bladed short sword lethal in close-quarter, over-the-shield stab-work. Most came out only for the after-hours photographic posing that was to become a nightly ritual, but for Germain that wasn't quite enough. As we pulled off sandals and tunics and laid out our bedding on that first night, I watched him tenderly inveigle his *gladius* into the sleeping bag he was about to rustle into. How I wished he had not done so. At least half a dozen times, woken by some thunderous guff or Francky's plaintive mumblings, I lay for long minutes studying the somnolent Germain's blank, freckled features for any flicker of emotion that might betray an imminent rampage, any sign that he might be set to go Brutus on my ass. Every night it would be the same.

Thibault and his barefoot brother, my most forgiving soldierly mentors in those early days, came up as I was decanting espresso dregs into a wooden beaker. ('*Eh, c'est italien comme les Romains,*' apologised Renaud with a blithe shrug.) 'Alors, Teem,' breezed Thibault, clapping his tunic-clad thighs. 'It's now your special moment!'

Concern that this might be the prelude to some outlandish initiation, apt to involve oiled nudity, had receded by the time I took my place in the Legio VIII's ranks. My sense of sore-thumb unreadiness had not.

Paul had insisted I don his *lorica segmentata* – a kind of half-suit of armour, with overlapping steel strips that sheathed the torso and shoulders. A magnificent piece of kit whose burnished, martial splendour had dominated the foot-end of our tent, when teamed with my voluminous shin-length tunic and the spindly limbs protruding therefrom, the effect suggested Wee Willie Winkie off to play Rollerball. Thibault, who with his brother had assumed a genuine and most touching concern for my welfare, did what he could by tightening everything – armour bindings, helmet chinstrap, belt – but his girding thumbs-up after a final appraisal failed to convince.

The park gates had opened as Germain and I washed up the porridge pot at a standpipe near the Viking longhouse, and a small crowd of camera-toting families stood in wait when we filed out of the camp entrance. *'Legio expedita!'* barked Renaud, calling us to attention in his capacity as *optio*, our sergeant-major. *'Venire . . . pergere!'* Delighted to have recognised the command to march, I raised my shield and turned smartly towards the Gaulish village. Francky's colossal chest blocked the way. *'Avant la bataille,'* he whispered, *'un petit promenade.'* A clumsy, clanking about-turn later and I was rattling off in pursuit of my legion.

'Sin, sin, sin-dex-sin! Sin, sin, sin-dex-sin!' With Renaud doing his NCO bit at the rear and Jean-Luc in that road-kill helmet raising our battle mascot – a cat-sized brass bull on a pole – at the fore, the Legio VIII paraded briskly through the park's already busy central attractions, a promotional tour that took in the barbecue lake, the Viking village and a number of forges and workshops whose presence had previously eluded me. I can't pretend not to have enjoyed the very considerable attention our progress invited, even when expressed in the form of laughter and pantomime-villain boos, issued by those who had learned their Roman history from *Asterix* and *Monty Python*.

The acclaim initially anaesthetised the physical demands of our undertaking, but by the time we tramped back to the camp entrance Renaud's *sin-dex-sins* were passing unheard beneath the laboured exhalations rasping around my helmet's interior. The shield, the armour, the helmet itself – all the state-of-the-ancient-art imperial kit that had seemed so pleasingly uncumbersome as I stood in line outside the camp now weighed me down to a bowed shuffle. My weary, hobnailed feet scrabbled noisily for purchase on the stone-paved sections, and my shield-bearing left arm was expressing its distress through a sort of spasmodic shiver over which I had no control. When the command came to stand to with shields rested on the ground, I all but threw

mine down in exhausted distress. Perhaps fifteen seconds afterwards Jean-Luc raised his bull once more, and off to the
village we headed, marching as to war.

Thibault had already explained that our engagements with
the Gauls would always follow the four-stage routine I'd
witnessed the day before, and thus forewarned I determined
to savour the snatch-squad raid that would be act one. But it
wasn't easy, and not just because my belt fell off as we charged
through the village gates.

The first small, windowless house I ran inside to search was
empty, but dashing into the second, sword drawn, imperial
sneer in place, I found myself confronted by a cowering Gaulish
mother, a dirty-faced infant half-hidden in the russet folds of
her tunic dress. She could have been my Cinderbury wife, with
our Cinderbury son. It recalled that scene near the end of *The
Sound of Music* when the male half of the 'I am Sixteen Going
on Seventeen' duet comes at the von Trapps with his SS-issue
Luger. As I stood there in breathless confusion, a pair of fellow
legionaries ducked in through the low door, paused briefly to
kick over a basket of carrots, then rushed back out, trailing a
yelled order – in French – to follow them at the double.

Trotting outside I spotted our quarry being dragged screaming
across the threshold of the village's most prominent structure,
a thatched longhouse with spears and gaily coloured oval shields
propped against its outer walls. The prisoner was the same
man apprehended the day before, and he resisted Paul's and
Germain's attempts to bind his wrists with familiar desper-
ation. But no more success: as they yanked him upright, I noted
the many fresh and half-healed gashes and abrasions gouged
into that impressive torso. By the end of the week it was as
if he'd been thrown from an express train.

What had looked so grimly satisfying from the hillside was
uncomfortably harrowing up close, and the keening wails of
the prisoner's bereft family hardly helped. As I brought up the
rear guard back through the gates, I couldn't help being aware
that not one twenty-first-century spectator, not a single MOP,
had been inside the village walls to witness what we'd just

done. The faithful brutality was purely for our own benefit, and that of our oppressed underlings. *Pour encourager les autres*.

The crowd jeered as we hauled our spitting, flailing freedom fighter back down the path. 'This is typical for us,' Laurent told me later, explaining how an enduring national guilt complex caused many of his countrymen to regard Roman re-enactment as a treacherous collaboration with an occupying enemy.

A little light dawdling allowed the archers to take their positions, and then, with a cry of *'La tortue!'* (in the heat of battle, Latin always went out the window) the legion jostled itself into the crowd-pleasing 'tortoise shell' defence against incoming missiles: the first rank of four holding their shields before them in tight formation, the second raising theirs above their heads, and the optional third (*moronicus brittanicus*) jogging around trying to find a gap to wedge his shield in that doesn't – sorry! – include his colleagues' fingers.

The mighty thunk of arrow on shield did enough to suggest that even a rubber-tipped strike would down a better man than I, but from what I'd seen the day before it was plain that worse was soon to come. What I didn't anticipate was how soon, and how much worse. One moment I was almost enjoying the close, heavy-breathed fraternity of under-tortoise life, and the next a rearward wave of roaring pagans had crashed upon us, staves and swords swinging wildly.

I retain only snapshots of the calamitous seconds that followed. There were beards and bad teeth; there was wood and metal and noise. The battle cries and the clatter of sword and shield, alarming even from the range I'd heard them as a spectator, were at close quarters amplified to an overwhelming, murderous cacophony. Spittled rage and full-blooded blows assailed me from all sides, blasting away Renaud's desperate rallying cries to hold my position: 'Tim! *La ligne! Gardez la ligne!*' Then, without even knowing how or at whose hand, I was down, winded and bewildered, hot, shallow breaths filling my helmet, blinkless gaze fixed at the blue heavens. When a grinning youth in a grubby jerkin scuttled up and wrenched the sword from my hand, I realised I hadn't even attempted to wield it.

'Que les morts se relèvent!'

I hauled myself groggily upright to see the Gauls acknow-
ledging the crowd's cheers, holding aloft their pillaged booty;
a stocktake of the rising dead revealed we'd taken only three
of them down with us. Would my legion never be allowed to
make a closer fight of it? More than an affront to history, this
seemed an unnecessary humiliation to those charged with
recreating it.

I tried to ask Paul as he diplomatically relieved me of his
precious *lorica segmentata,* and watched that small, round,
stubbled face pucker in confusion. The truth, falteringly
explained as we made our way back to the village for round
three, struck me almost as hard as the Gaul or Gauls unknown
who had laid me out a minute earlier. For there was no preor-
dained outcome to any of these skirmishes, no script to follow;
of the four battles fought in the morning before my arrival,
the Legio VIII had actually won three. Far from going through
the motions, we were here to fight competitive duels with
honour and glory at stake.

And how on earth were such battles won and lost? Miming
energetically, Paul and Thibault laid out the rules of engagement. Any sword strike to the face, neck or unarmoured torso
meant death, with limb blows obliging the sufferer to hand-
icap himself in homage to *Monty Python*'s Black Knight: take
a hit to the arm and you folded it behind your back, cop one
in the leg and you hopped. If I had yet to behold this memorable phenomenon, they said, it was because anyone thus
disabled was almost instantly put out of their idiotic misery.

So I was here not to make up the numbers, not to lie down
and die on request, but to kill or be killed, to be judged on my
skill and courage as a warrior, to uphold the legion's repute
and fight for the glory of Rome. This new information seemed
too large for my brain, and was soon sloshing around in my
queasy innards. I wondered if the enhanced responsibility might
prove overwhelming, and during our subsequent attempt to
storm the village gates, found that it did. Once again a rearward attack did for us: as I stuck an arm over the fence, wafting

blindly away with my sword, some unseen enemy shield-charged me from behind with the force of a runaway skip lorry. Shock, a badly dented back and whiplash were the immediate legacies of this encounter, but these were swiftly driven away by a jostling stampede of shriller discomforts: I had been propelled, face first and half naked, into a dense and extensive patch of nettles.

We lost that bout 11–1, and went only a couple better at the morning's final coming together, round the other side of the lake near the village's rear entrance. Additionally equipped this time with our Slazenger-tipped safety javelins, we stood in two lines as the enemy steamed raggedly towards us; only when Renaud saw the yellows of their eyes did he yell the command – '*Pila jacere!*' – that allowed us to release these ludicrous sticks skywards. Mine, which stalled and nosedived after a flight of perhaps seven feet, was by no means the least threatening deployment.

The Gauls paused briefly, tracking each javelin's stunted trajectory in the manner of Road Runner observing some farcical, Acme-sponsored attempt on his life. '*La ligne!*' yelled Renaud, and this time I dutifully held the authentic formation, one which allowed a large section of the enemy to outflank us at a gentle trot before slaughtering the might of Rome in the now traditional hindward manner. In a pitiable inversion of Nietzsche's adage, that which killed us did not make us stronger.

My fourth death of the day was the least painful but the most infuriating: felled by a light strike between the shoulder blades, while obediently sinking to the earth I saw the fat-faced young Gaul responsible actually skipping along behind our back line, despatching each of its members with a dainty flick of his sword and an update of his running tally of kills for the day: '. . . *douze, treize, quatorze!*'

We were again resurrected, and lined up to return the distant crowd's applause by banging swords against our shields. It was a hateful duty in the circumstances, like taking a loser's medal after an embarrassingly one-sided cup final. I came, I saw, I was conquered. Only as I dejectedly wedged my sword back in my belt did I spot the delta of blood rivulets coursing down my left hand and forearm, their source a trio of deep abrasions on the central knuckles. '*Oh, c'est normal,*' breezed Thibault, when he saw me surveying these wounds with an expression of aggrieved disbelief. He held up his own left hand and indicated the livid scar tissue sheathing the relevant area – shield-bearer's knuckle, I came to note, was a universal legionary's complaint.

Other complaints asserted themselves during the trudge back to camp as the adrenalined anaesthesia of combat wore off. Most severe was that pulsing crater near the base of my spine; most mysterious an angry red weal that almost encircled my upper right arm. Running like a constant prickling fizz beneath them all were the numberless nettle stings that riddled my limbs like some medieval pox-rash. With four sound thrashings still to come in the afternoon, and then another eight a day thereafter, what in the name of Caesar would I look like at the end of the week?

Lunch was restorative, and not just because of Renaud's generous decantings from our secret plonk cache. Between battles the legion's camp was open to visitors, and in Jean-Luc's absence I found myself asked to field queries in the Scandinavian lingua franca that English has long been. This was my first taste of the strange quasi-celebrity bestowed upon the public re-enactor, and how sweetly moreish it proved.

Wide-eyed youngsters gazed up at me in slack-jawed awe as I sated their parents' curiosity, my gigantic ignorance apparently camouflaged by the reassuring authenticity of my outfit. It soon became clear that to a certain junior visitor I could say no wrong, like a fireman on a school visit telling wonderstruck children that his smoke hood was a kind of space bucket, and that the helmets were that colour because arsonists were allergic to yellow. 'That? Well, it's a . . . measuring pole. Used by sanitary engineers. Precisely the length of Julius Caesar's forearm.' 'I see you're rather taken with our ballista. Bit of a mean machine, isn't she? At the Battle of Cinderbury, three of these babies accounted for 4,000 charging Waynesmen.'

It was no particular surprise to find that a very vocal minority of fathers had come not to ask questions, but to give answers. The way to silence these dangerous saboteurs, I found, was to whip my helmet off and offer it to one of their children. 'But from my detailed study of such shields . . .' they'd begin, and I'd abruptly plonk that Imperial Gallic G down on another small blond head. It never failed. 'Always room for a new recruit,' was my standard accompanying drawl, delivered to the disarmed father with an infuriating wink. 'You have a name please, soldier?' croaked one enchanted mother as her little girl tottered happily about beneath two kilos of 16-gauge Indian steel. 'Caecilius,' I replied without hesitation. 'Private Caecilius Grumio of the Eighth Augustan at your service, ma'am.' The Roman salute that now shot involuntarily from my right arm would have earned me rather more than a gawp of surprise had I tried it out a couple of hours south in Hamburg.

I'd noted Laurent hanging about with an expression of concern as I spouted disinformation all over his beloved ballista – more accurately a 'scorpion', he informed me – but I only got told off once, after Vincent overheard me being sidetracked by a garrulous Swedish visitor into a critique of Tony Blair's foreign policy. 'When you wear zis,' he said, grabbing my belt in both hands, 'you are Roman legionary, in Roman epoque, and nussing more.' Everything Vincent said and did was said and done with manic intensity. Five minutes later I saw him furiously masturbating a javelin.

The afternoon battles followed the established pattern, though before being slaughtered in fight three, by the village gate, I did at least manage to kill someone – a tubby, walrus-tached Obelix who stumbled in mid stave-lunge and landed navel-first on my diffidently proffered sword.

Perhaps to atone for the monstrous unrealism of the combat – as Jean-Luc truculently pointed out, our *'gardez-la-ligne'* tactics made no military sense on the tiny scale we were re-enacting them – when the crowds left, the legion threw itself into authentic military maintenance. Exhausted by eight deaths and a bullying sun, I slumped vacantly in the mess tent as all around armour was buffed, belts restitched, *caligae* re-hobnailed.

Thibault had begun fashioning himself a chainmail vest, a nimble-fingered labour of unfathomable dedication requiring several thousand tiny steel hoops, three pairs of specialist pliers and the sort of personality never tempted to hurl all of these down on to a hard surface and batter them with the back of a shovel, again and again and again.

It was always a pleasure to watch my legionaries engaged in precision period toil. Particularly as the ribald, barrack-room banter that typically accompanied it – tightly focused on bodily functions and the intimate congress of Gaul and goat – could without warning evolve into an arcane discussion of fletching techniques or Mark Antony's tactical failings. Jean-Luc held forth with some passion on the genuine academic merits of what he called experimental archaeology – only by actually making and using armour, uniforms and instruments of war could you hope to understand how the Roman Army fought, and with a success that saw it dominate the known world. 'We discover that a legionary must have many skills,' he told me. 'He is engineer, baker, metalworker, shoemaker, chef . . .' With the multi-talented evidence of this all around us, I could only think how wonderful it would be if even some of it – along with the ability to injure large men – rubbed off on me.

It was dark and raining when half a dozen tartan-trousered Gauls pitched up, droopy moustaches limp with drizzle. Their spokesman, the one I'd accidentally killed a few hours back, trooped into the mess tent to announce that the womenfolk had thrown them out of the village, furious that their *après-guerre* revelries had woken the junior Gauls. Vincent welcomed them into our already well-populated quarters, and as they squeezed up on the box-benches each took time to gawp in wonder at the trappings of a superior civilisation.

Aside from our extraordinary range of foodstuffs and alcohol – one that their efforts in the hours ahead would render much less extraordinary – what seemed to astonish our visitors most was the period technology on display, and how we had mastered it. One, a goateed skinhead whose leather wristbands I'd had a very close look at while their owner pillaged my corpse, simply could not believe that the Pompeii-issue lamps illuminating the table were authentically fuelled with olive oil. I gathered that having failed to coax a reliable flame from their own close equivalents, they'd resorted to paraffin. Except that didn't work either, and each Gaulish homestead had now been forced to choose between Maglites and blackness. You could not wish for a more effectively literal demonstration of how the Dark Ages happened.

'*Attention, attention! Il arrive!*'

I never had much luck decoding the Gauls' harsh and throaty French, but there was no mistaking those words, stage whispered as I climbed back over the camp palisade after a goat-anointing comfort break. The odd half-glimpsed nudge and suspect snigger had already caused my highly tuned paranoia sensors to twitch, and now they shrieked like klaxons. I shuffled back into the suddenly silent mess tent, cheeks aglow, and wedged myself in the tiny gap between Francky and a grubby, grizzled pirate of a Gaul with a smile like a pub ceiling. He showed me this at uncomfortably close quarters, then in tones cultivated on the wrong side of Hadrian's Wall, croaked, 'All right, pal?'

The detected presence of a fellow Briton far from home is in most situations a happy one. But not this kind of Briton, in this kind of situation. It was instantly impossible not to picture the man they called Ross rubbing his grimy hands at the unanticipated bonus of some simpering Sassenach stave-fodder. His greeting was delivered like a gauntlet slap, and of the four further words of English that were all I would hear from this expatriate Scotsman over the days ahead, two were 'off'.

If there was an awkward silence to puncture, Vincent always had the pin. In a moment he'd whipped out his knackered acoustic guitar and was bellowing out a lewd folk song which brought the mess tent to its unsteady feet, thus granting me a low-profile exit. It wasn't just the Ross factor, or the winks and giggles. I simply couldn't bring myself to fraternise any further with men who'd spent all day hurting me to death.

Alone in our tent I savoured the soldierly satisfaction of

unbuckling my belt at the end of a hard day's fight, its many rivets and medallions warm to the touch, hearing the darkness jingle as I tossed it into the corner and hit armour. I lay there in that darkness amid the muted wassailing, feeling myself settle into the one authentic period duty I could ever hope to master: really hating those fucking Gauls.

And so I began to adapt to the routines of military life. Those frenzied blurts of pain and fear were interspersed with long, idle hours in the mess tent, playing dice, buffing armour, eating vast slabs of very red meat and aimlessly shooting the *merde*. There were occasional unbilled excitements. A murderous cacophony from Jean-Luc's pavilion one afternoon had us all dashing out of the mess tent, unhealthily exhilarated that the curious (but very Roman) *ménage à trois* resident therein had come to a messy (but very Roman) end. In fact, they'd all gone out for the day. A ram-goat had somehow slipped through a gap in the canvas and laid expensive waste to Ira's jewellery cases.

One hot *après-midi* was devoted to Renaud's paratrooping tales from Africa and Croatia; another to Vincent's hoarse and lusty singalongs ('Tim, you help wiz ze lyric to "Johnny B. Goode"? No, no – "Go" we know already.') And then there were the moments of quiet self-doubt, when a legionary would sidle up and discreetly enquire how I really felt about what was going on here. Except their unease was focused not on the moral validity of war, but the lingering fear – common, I would find, to even the most hard-bitten re-enactor – that everyone watching them recreate it thought they were total idiots.

The worst part of every day was the village raid: with homes to defend and no MOP witnesses about to curb their enthusiasm, the enemy would set about us with furious abandon. As I crouched into the longhouse on the second morning, shaking sword at the ready, a junior Gaul dropped down on my back from the gloomy rafters. I tottered blindly around for a while as he clung on and pummelled me with feet, fists, knees and elbows, then bit cinders and goat crap when some heftier tribesman whipped my ankles away with a stave. An attempt to surprise them that afternoon with an attack through their rear gate introduced a new nemesis: a wiry old berserker with flowing white hair and a Bismarck 'tache, who looked like Getafix but fought like a thousand cornered polecats. He approached me at a bellowing gallop, kicked my shield aside without breaking stride and unleashed a frenzied volley of sword blows, the majority of them post-mortem, accompanying each with a horrid Jimmy Connors grunt.

If that appointment with Great Uncle Punishment was my daily low, the highlight was scorpion drill. The public demonstrations Laurent organised every afternoon were safety-first affairs, with the machine we called Charybdis aimed at a patch of bare hillside and fired well below full velocity. How much more exhilarating were the freelance trials we held before the park opened, winding the tensioning gear as far as it would go and strafing the distant countryside with fat-shafted, iron-tipped bolts. One thunked so deeply into a tree trunk half a kilometre away that Germain and I had to use axes to hack it free. 'With Charybdis,' smiled Laurent when we returned, patting one of her solid wooden wheels, 'an accident is a death.'

A couple of days later, Laurent went off in the legion's minibus to visit a nearby Viking museum (along with Vincent, who had insisted on doing so in full Roman kit), leaving me alone to present Charybdis – and more challengingly the mysterious tangle of plumb-lines that was the legion's surveying equipment – to the gathered visitors. They were a predominantly teenage intake; all morning their unusually partisan jeering had irked me, and now, in camp, they swiftly took unkind advantage of my flustered naivety.

'Hey, dude, why don't you just use a laser?'

'Wit dis measure stick – how many metres from my ass to your face?'

Worse was to come when I raised my shield and thoughtlessly trotted out the standard lecture-ending challenge: 'So, if anyone wants to try their luck against the Roman defences . . .' That this would be the prelude to something other than the usual drumming of infant fists was apparent when the first kick landed. I hunkered down behind my shield as the Nike-powered impacts intensified into a fearsome tattoo, and the warm Nordic air was soon alive with my curse-studded cries for a ceasefire.

A pair of the most vicious assailants – one I recognised as having thrown an apple at us during the pre-battle walkabout – ambled up as I laid my shield to rest against our weapon rack, shaken and breathing heavily. 'You are many times defeated today,' began the smiling elder, tracing a finger along the point of an authentic display *pila*. 'It's maybe because of a tactic problem?'

His accomplice weighed in before I could reply. 'Or because you are wearing a dress?'

'Careful with that javelin, sonny,' I hissed. 'That's how I got *these*.' And I pressed my weeping, purulent knuckles right up to his freckled nose. Later we learned that Lejre had been host that day to a visiting party from a residential school specialising in the treatment of serious emotional disorders.

Debilitating as the many physical strains of pretending to be a Roman soldier surely were, I came to realise that my almost constant state of exhaustion was due in no small part to the brain-hungry efforts involved in making sense of what Frenchmen were saying to me. One night, having been introduced to a pastis and mint-syrup combination and made very good friends with it, I stumbled through some portal of alcoholic omniscience and heard myself debating speed-camera technology with Laurent. The linguistic fallout was dreadful. Thereafter, whenever I tried to convey a lack of comprehension – typically through the catch-all shrug/wrinkled nose/headshake combo – Laurent would be on hand with a dismissive gesture and some wink-accompanied comment about continuous-wave radar.

Yet all the while, I was slowly progressing. By day three I'd discovered an unexpected aptitude for certain period talents, prominently splitting logs and not washing. Dropping an axe on my foot while engaged in the former, I heard myself swear in French. I began to develop a genuine appreciation for the prêt-a-porter, pee-on-the-go convenience of the Roman tunic. And I had not died – twelve times – in vain. Blow by blow, parry by parry, I was getting up to fighting speed, able to at least see who was killing me and how they were doing it.

It was during the third round of the second day's ruck, my already prominent hackles raised after Ross spat on my shield as I lay dead, that I noticed thoughts more focused than the white noise of panic and terror running through my head in battle. 'I'll fucking have you, you fuck-faced fuck-sucker,' was one such example. The discovery in that same encounter of a Gaulish reluctance to go down when killed translated these thoughts into loud words.

We still lost, of course, but fuelled by fury I rose from the dead in a state of let-me-at-'em euphoria. I slapped backs. I clenched my fists and yelled incoherent, steroid-faced encouragements, so pumped up that my tunic seemed a snug fit. I found my sympathy for the villagers replaced by a powerful desire to burn their filthy houses to the ground, to heave a dead goat down their well, to hurl their mewling, smut-faced young into the nettles.

If the Gaul's superior aggression in combat was authentic – when push came to shove, and then to stab and slash, you would after all expect a freedom-fighting warrior to out-brawl some tired mercenary a million cubits from home – then so too was my ugly lust for extracurricular vengeance. The morning after I made sure to get a couple of kicks in at our prisoner. And that sunset, assessing the benign arcadia beyond the lake, with its gentle smoke plumes, its comely thatched structures, its ambling, shirtless men ferrying water about in twin-bucket shoulder-yokes, I gazed at the shields stacked up against the longhouse and thought: One night, maybe not tonight, but one night, I'm going to get in there and piss all over those.

Dressing up in full regalia was a regularly indulged after-hours pastime, and, from that evening on, one chronicled with almost pornographic relish. Set-piece tableaux were painstakingly set up and photographed: Germain about to be ambushed by a pair of piratical pagans; a line of Gaulish warriors spread out across a hilltop, silhouetted dramatically in the gloaming;

Vincent in Caesar-era kit staring flintily into a setting sun. As the primary instigators of these nightly posc-fests, the Gauls became an after-dark fixture in our camp. This proved useful in terms of keeping my hatred levels topped up. When the conversation strayed beyond social and military history in the first millennium, our guests seemed incapable of offering anything beyond belches and boorish unpleasantry; in war as in peace, the Gauls were always too near the knuckle. Ribald and cutting as my legionaries could certainly be, their banter was always underscored with a basic human decency, and offset by moments of pensive philosophy. It was the Roman way.

By the same token, when it was done belittling Hollywood depictions of ancient combat, and had run out of insulting adjectives to describe the plastic-helmeted centurions who badgered tourists outside the Colosseum, the legion would revitalise itself with a little experimental archaeology. One afternoon we cleared our tent of all rucksacks, sleeping bags and mobile phones – *'les affaires civiles'*, as they were tactfully dubbed – and set about establishing whether such a structure could indeed accommodate the ten men that comprised each *contubernium*: eight legionaries, plus the two support servants who carried water and looked after the mules. We just about managed it with Francky decimated from the equation, and the servants doubling up as footrests, but the principal lesson for me was just how far the European definition of miserable discomfort has evolved over the last 2,000 years. In the ancient world, a good night's sleep meant one uninterrupted by violent assault: being babysat by nine strong men was one reason why the average Roman legionary looked forward to a life 15 per cent longer than his civilian counterpart's.

Regular meals contributed to this statistic. It was Napoleon who said that an army marched on its stomach, a logistical maxim that his countrymen in the Legio VIII had taken very closely to heart. My first encounter with the catering corps – Jean-Michel squatting barefoot by the fire, mopping up cauldron dregs of lentil stew with a crumbling fistful of leftover dough – was to prove misleading in the extreme. The dark and ever-sweltering interior of the legion's well-stocked leather provisions tent was alive with the muscular aromas of ripe cheese and conserved meats; from tinned peaches to pastis, their definition of admissible foodstuffs seemed to encompass anything whose ingredients had been cultivated within the Empire's generous confines at any point in history. However awkwardly this sat with Jean-Luc's revelation that a legionary was in effect paid largely in wheat and for long periods ate little else, it was somehow wonderfully faithful to the epicurean spirit of both ancient Rome and modern France. It was just not possible to imagine sweaty, ostentatiously flatulent men of any other nationality rounding off every meal as the Legio VIII did, with a heartfelt round of toasts to the *cuisinier*.

Raising a wooden beaker to Renaud as he doled out seconds of chicken cassoulet, I looked around the table, from face to grazed and stubbled face, and wondered if wine and Stockholm syndrome alone could account for the warm fellowship I now felt for these men. We were a band of brothers, who ate as one, slept as one, fought as one. When, playing dice on an idle mess-tent afternoon, Vincent soporifically wondered aloud if soldiers eventually thought as one, we all smiled and nodded. Even the one who'd spent much of the day thinking about the three earwigs he'd found in his sleeping bag that morning.

So intimate was our bond that I soon found it disturbingly hard to sense where the nothing-to-hide, close-knit comradeship ended, and the Romoerotic coquetry might begin. Mini-length tunics and the almost universal eschewal of underwear meant that a flash of *saucisson de Toulouse* was never more than a crossed leg away: Laurent's after-lunch routine included a splayed catnap on the camp's straw-heap that sent many younger visitors reeling away in distress.

If this was a hint that the decadence which destroyed Rome might be corroding the legion's self-control, many others revealed themselves in the ignominious events of day four. 'Discipline is our god,' went a favoured Jean-Michel catchphrase. How shameful to find myself – first through incompetence, then blind hate and rage – desecrating the relevant altar.

That morning, addled with the toxic aftermath of their mint and pastis abomination, I shuffled out of a village house and pronounced it clear with a bleary call of '*Vide!*' The great many insurgents who followed me out a moment later made short and brutal work of our entire search party; as we lay dead together, sharing another moment of esprit de corpse, Thibault berated me in an unusually tetchy whisper.

Desperate to atone for what was the most humiliating defeat yet, Jean-Charles and Vincent enlivened the ensuing battle with a commando flank attack, stripping down to their loin-cloths, slapping on mud camouflage and wading out through the lakeside reeds in the hope of reaching the village walls by stealth. With gesticulations and warning cries, the crowd betrayed them to the defenders; vengeance was swift and terrible.

Before he was even out of the water, Jean-Charles copped an awful blow which seemed to burst his face, spraying that muddy torso crimson and – in conjunction with a simultan-eously cracked rib – putting this sizeable ex-paratrooper *hors de combat* for the rest of the week. As we watched him struggle back to camp, black of eye and flat of nose, I was consumed with powerful emotions: a piquant dash of vengeful fury in the nauseous gloop of there-but-for-the-grace-of-Jove-go-I terror.

In the same engagement we came under aerial log bombard-ment; in the close-quarters thick of the one after, I hazarded a tentative peek above my shield and had its top edge driven straight back into my lower face. That meant a lip split three ways, and a spectacular recurrence of shield-bearer's knuckle. Thereafter the wounds were reopened eight times a day; the scabs didn't have a chance to form until I got home.

Unhinged by these relentless calamities to a state of shell-shock, in the morning's final engagement I took leave of my senses. When a volley of Gaulish spears fell some way short, I dropped my shield, dashed unthinkingly from our line, snatched one up in either hand and, with a lunatic, throat-stripping roar, hurled both back at the enemy.

'In battle, anger is as good as courage.' So goes the old Welsh proverb I've grown so grimly familiar with as it scrolls across the intro screen in Medieval II: Total War, never imagining that I would one day assess this aphorism at first hand, and discover it to be bollocks.

The javelins plopped harmlessly to earth at the feet of a quizzical enemy; my bestial howl faded into a sudden and profound silence. The audience laughter that presently filled it suggested parallels with a notorious incident in the 1974 World Cup, when a Zaire player ran out of his defensive wall as Brazil lined up a free kick, and joyfully hoofed the ball into the crowd.

The immediate consequence of this moment of madness was another as-we-lay-dying admonishment from Thibault; in the longer term I earned myself a permanent demotion to the '*légères*' – the unarmoured, ultra-expendable first line of attack. When that evening Jean-Michel led me up the hill for the first of many patient tutorials in *pila* hurling and the shoulder-bruising art of shield defence, I had to conclude he was following orders from the top.

By then, however, the Legio VIII already found itself under new management. Infuriated – or, who knows, inspired – by my deranged indiscipline, Jean-Luc had apparently conducted himself with excess vigour in its aftermath. The precise details of his rush of blood were regrettably never discussed, but Gallic petulance would seem to have taken hold of the internal inquiry that ensued; our commander surveyed all future battles from the comfort of his pavilion.

If the red headbands wrapped around our skulls to limit helmet-chafe aptly imparted a kamikaze bearing, the dispirited lethargy with which we donned them after lunch did not. Our morale was shot. When Laurent asked me to shoo a goat off the scorpio firing range, I complied with a furious gusto unknown to the quivering mute hunched pitifully behind his shield in human combat. It was my only honest victory of the week.

Embittered by invalidity, Jean-Charles wearied of imper-sonating the legionaries who weren't there, and over lunch started on those who were; focusing on Francky's occasional stutter was a mock too far. Most particularly as throughout that inglorious afternoon our young giant alone stood firm in battle. Francky's extreme youth had been underlined when I came out of the shower – hidden away in some distant admin block it had taken me three days to locate – to find him doodling tanks and fighter jets on the whiteboard outside. In combat, though, he was more of a man than the rest of us combined, and nearly always the final Roman down. The consolation of premature death was a worm's eye view of Francky's last stand, watching through the dandelions as his ponderous but titanic blows hewed gaps in the closing circle of opponents, until at last they overwhelmed him.

So closely did we adhere to the unflattering *Asterix* stereotype that afternoon – the crowd-pleasing low point was a demonstration of artillery-camouflaging techniques which ended with the vegetation we'd draped across Charybdis being eaten by goats – that even the enemy felt sorry for us. Ludo, their lead archer and good-natured chieftain, and one of the very few Gauls I didn't mind being killed by, came over that evening to organise a keep-fit session; he tried very hard to hide his incredulity at the number of Romans who couldn't touch their sandals. Watching us pant and redden and sweat, he quietly asked if we'd prefer to make it four fights a day instead of eight. Everyone but me seemed to think he was joking.

It had become plain that we were all entitled to a day off, what in military circles is known as a little R & R, and the following morning I came back from the showers to find Thibault, Jean-Michel and Germain scuffling about through our tent-straw in casual sportswear. 'Vite, Tim – *nous allons en ville!*'

Ville was Køge, a trim medieval port twenty minutes drive away. The way things had gone the day before I should have been glad of a break, but I clunked the car door shut without enthusiasm. A short while earlier, striding towards the ablution facility in my tunic and hobnailed sandals, I'd felt the heady stirrings of that period rush alluded to by Celtic Will. Emerging from our tent thus clad on previous mornings was an act accompanied by a twinge of looming ignominy, as if that linen flap was a stage curtain, with an audience of my unkinder friends and associates waiting in malicious expectation. But this time there was nothing but a bland and soothing, what's-for-breakfast sense of routine: just the start of another day in the Eighth Augustus. Despite the best Gaulish efforts to batter him back inside, the Roman within me had begun to emerge. And now here he was in a Citroën Berlingo, wearing Gap shorts and a Duke Nukem T-shirt. Back to square 2005.

In blustery sun the four of us trailed dutifully through Køge's squares and churchyards, nibbling very expensive seafood sandwiches and photographing statues. After the intensities of combat, it seemed to me so inane, so pointless. Sneering at Denmark's third-oldest house I began to wonder if I could ever again function as a normal tourist. In their trainers and polo shirts, my comrades were diminished in my eyes. By the same token, the colossal hatred I'd built up for the Silver Psycho was inevitably eroded when we encountered him wandering about in civvies with a wife and two kids, his deranged hair tamed into a wanky ad-man's pony-tail. How oddly glad I was when we met him again back at the Lejre car park, and he returned our nods and waves with a snarl that was the final whistle for our ceasefire kickabout in no man's land: '*Et maintenant, la guerre.*'

The day after was 14 July, Bastille Day, and despite the inevitable banter about foreign royalists I kept my head, rather than having it wind up in a basket. Someone had taken the trouble to bring along an enormous French flag, and when the public had departed we all – Gaul and Roman alike – piled into the large chalet that served as Lejre's function hall, and serenaded it with an iron-throated rendition of 'The Marseillaise'. After a traditional Gallic feast of plonk and spag bol, Ludo stood to deliver an announcement that my recent experiences had rendered almost humdrum: in half an hour, for those who were interested, a dead chieftain would be cremated on a funeral pyre by the tumulus.

As someone who likes a good fire, and loves a bad one, I counted myself very highly placed amongst the interested. Jean-Luc, quite vocally, did not. The tumulus was a slab-sided mound on the hillside just behind our camp, and as the rest of us rushed about with the pyromaniac enthusiasm of the fairly drunk he stood at a haughty distance, red cloak draped impressively about his shoulders, condemning the staged stupidity of what we were up to in a multi-lingual mutter.

A substantial pity, as constructing the funeral pyre represented the Eighth Augustus' finest hour. Working with a controlled and wordless intensity that was exhilarating to spectator and participant alike, half the legion dragged Gaulish cartloads of wood up from both camps to the hilltop, whilst the rest surgically removed a precise eight-foot-square patch of grass and topsoil, neatly stacking the green turfs for later replacement in accordance with Lejre's environmental code of conduct – twenty-four hours later, you would have spent a long day searching for any evidence of pagan conflagration. When the camp wood stores were exhausted, three of us marched off to an adjacent forest and stumbled back ten minutes later, each shouldering a gigantic dead bough in convincing homage to the Romans' most famous victim. In half a breathless hour we assembled a mighty and geometrically faultless pyre, fit for a dead king. Even the Gauls, surveying our imperial hyperactivity in a state of gormless inaction, had to concede that co-ordinating such a multi-tasked synthesis of labour and materials would have been beyond them. It was only right that when the last log was laid, and we stood back to appraise our work, spent but content, their appointed spokesman should come over to shoo us all brusquely away.

The entire edifice, as became clear from our permitted viewpoint outside the exclusion zone, had been erected for the benefit of a slapheaded little Gaul, here on a two-tiered mission to assemble a photographic impression of life in pre-Roman France, whilst hurting me. We watched as he dressed his set, laying sheepskins and shields atop the wood, all the while fussing about with a light meter. These were but the early stages of an excruciatingly pseudo-portentous pose-athon, one that filled the twilit horizon with shaggy silhouettes and the muted glint of ancient weaponry. If they'd let us light the fire I'd have at least considered surveying the scene with the flinty stare of appreciation befitting a fallen warrior. As it was, watching Ludo clamber on to his combustible deathbed, then half-tumble off it with a cry of *'Putain de merde!'*, I could think only of a Spinal Tap cover shoot. It would take them at least a dozen attempts to get the thing ablaze, and when they did the 'ghost of Ludo', asked by the photographer to hover mysteriously in the smoke, scorched himself on a sword left too close to the fire. As his shrieks rang out we were already down by our own campfire, toasting their uselessness. And in that moment, the Legio VIII was reborn as a fighting force.

Our failure to win a single battle since I'd joined the legion's ranks had become a source of profound embarrassment, and when the duck was broken on my penultimate day, I cared not that it was more down to enemy ennui than to all those sinew-yanking training sessions with Jean-Michel. A certain flexibility with the rules of engagement also played a part: taking my lead from the many Gauls I'd seen fighting on in defiance of a mortal blow, when a sword tapped me lethargically from behind during the morning war, I wheeled about and knocked its adolescent wielder to the floor with a vicious shield-shove. All around, listless Gauls were being hacked down, and suddenly Francky, Thibault and I found ourselves standing alone in the valley of death. For a moment the three of us stared at each other in bemusement, then we turned as one to the Saturday-swollen crowd, raised our swords and let forth the cry I had been waiting to deliver in earnest all week: *'Victrix!'*

Legio expedita . . . sin, dex, sin . . . legio consistere . . . legio in aciem . . . The sunbaked earthen paths of Lejre were by now liberally stippled with our hobnailed imprints. I'm not sure when I decided that the afternoon battles would be my last. It might have been the moment a ten-year-old son of Gaul stood over my body, squeaking at his dad to come and look at the Roman he'd just killed. It might have been five hours later, when Vincent cut short his fireside folk bellowing to scold himself for excluding the legion's guest, and then for my benefit struck up 'O-Bla-Di, O-Bla-Da', causing me to regret more deeply than ever my intrusion into a Roman holiday – half lads' outing, half family reunion – that was for most their only annual break. Or it might have been the hour after that, when half a dozen Gauls stumbled into our camp in a state of moonshine-powered disarray, and began chuntering on about '*les blacks*'.

My withdrawal from combat, announced over porridge on what I had just realised was my final morning, meant the legion would be fighting its last battles in a much depleted state. A twisted knee and a brick-sized bruise on the thigh had accounted for Jean-Michel and Laurent, with Jean-Charles and Jean-Luc still in their tents nursing face and pride respectively. So feeble was the rollcall turnout that Ludo and the scarred hulk of our oft-abused prisoner came over to offer their fighting services as '*Romains auxiliaires*'. That evened things up until Vincent saw what was going on and promptly defected: all week he'd nurtured a typically masochistic desire to play the prisoner, and this was his chance.

Taking my place amongst the hillside spectators was an unsettling experience, and not just because I had done so still wearing my *caligae* and that Demis Roussos kaftan of a tunic. Watching Paul and Germain mete out the beating Vincent so dearly craved, it seemed absurd to think that only seven days had passed since I'd witnessed this scene first played out. A week might be a long time in politics, but how much longer it was in war. Especially one you've travelled 800 miles and 2,000 years to fight in.

I learned over lunch that the afternoon battles, Lejre's last, were giving way to a farewell skirmish at a pagan ceremonial site somewhere behind the village. This was an area I hadn't previously explored, and when at last I found it, sliding through the nettles down a forest-girdled hollow, how glad of that I was. The 'sacrificial bog', as an information board undersold it, was a nightmare made flesh – rotting flesh, indeed, for before me lay a stagnant, stinking lake of black water girdled with flyblown animal parts. Most compelling were the two wizened horse corpses slung over makeshift gibbets above the waters' edge; most malodorous the oozing pig's head that looked up at them through carrion-clustered eyes of grey jelly. It was Picasso's *Guernica* reimagined first by Salvador Dali, then Damien Hirst. Why had I come here early? It was certainly the most appalling place I had ever willingly visited, and I had it all to my quivering self. When pus-hungry greenbottles began to take an interest in my seeping knuckles, I was enduring an ordeal that would have scared the prehistoric piss out of better men than I. And it would be fifteen long minutes before two armed columns of those marched down into the swamp of death from either side.

A generous crowd followed them in, but dwindled rapidly once the stench and the first wave of mosquitoes hit them. By the finish, as for one last time Francky fell loudly to earth to join his long-dead comrades, there were no more than two dozen witnesses to hear that stirring, godlike cry ring out through this most grimly appropriate arena: '*Que les morts se relèvent!*'

I was packing in the tent when the legion marched back into camp. With the passing of days, our belongings had over-lapped into a communal straw-bedded heap of sandals, helmets, washbags and paperbacks. In the most profound expression of our comradeship, I noted how we'd even begun sleeping closer together: all through that final night, with my arms flat by my sides, one elbow lay in permanent contact with Germain's *gladius*, and the other with two or more of Francky's consider-able limbs. I barely seemed to notice the snoring any more, though when I crept out for a nocturnal pee it was stridently audible from a great distance. The hills were alive with the sound of mucus.

They wouldn't let me leave without a final dressing-up parade. It was all terribly affecting. Renaud held out his zebra-plumed *optio*'s helmet, and Thibault his chainmail vest; thus clad I was handed Germain's hallowed *gladius*. How good it felt, striding about camp dressed like a million denarii, at least until the hottest day of my visit began to interact with 15 kilos of chainmail (as I'd discover, precisely double the weight I'd shed over the week). We stood in line for a final photograph, then one by one they came across to brush their stubble against mine in the Gallic manner. Paul was last. 'Teem,' he announced, placing a hand on my hot and sagging shoulder, '*tu es un bon legionnaire.*' Despite the welter of evidence that this was not the case, it would do for me. A moment later I was walking out through Lejre's giftshop in tourist civvies, abruptly demobbed from both the army and the ancient world.

The park was closing, and as I picked through my week-old travel rations at the bus stop, two stick-wielding boys ran out through the park gates in noisy but jocular pursuit of a third. It wasn't difficult to deduce what had inspired them. Almost all the re-enactors I had thus far encountered were in revolt against today's not-my-fault, who-can-I-sue compensation-culture, passionately convinced that a society that failed to teach its citizens to take responsibility for their own actions could not survive for long. Watching Vincent relocate logs from wood pile to crowded fireside by hurling them over his shoulder, I'd been reminded of blacksmith Dai's cheery eschewal of goggles and gauntlets: 'I'm made of asbestos, me,' he'd chuckle, brushing another super-heated ember from a lavishly scarred forearm. 'Bottom line: it's my lookout.' At moments like those, I was invariably possessed of an evangelical enthusiasm for living history. If we could all go back to our roots for even one week a year, I'd find myself thinking, how much more competent, more grown-up our society might be. Look at me, one of the modern world's feeblest whiners, sitting here now on the bare gravel with great big wounds all over one hand and a mouthful of rancid banana.

Yet as the two boys caught their quarry on the far side of the car park, and the noises evolved to a rather less jocular blend of clatters and yelps of distress, I began to wonder if the skills we'd been displaying for their benefit were not just irrelevant to the modern European lifestyle, but dangerously malignant. Could I really be proud that the helmet glinting from my unzipped holdall was no longer a shiny dressing-up accessory, but a functional counter-measure against fellow humans bent on cleaving apart my skull? Was it a shame that most of us no longer knew how to fend for ourselves, or a cause for gigantic celebration that most of us no longer had to?

'Goodbye, soldier!'

It was the woman from the welcome desk, walking out to her car. Returning her smile I belatedly appreciated that the previous seven days were the closest I had ever been, and ideally ever would be, to experiencing war. In depressing reality, this was a product of my life in cloistered, first-world suburbia, rather than evidence of any grand historical march towards global harmony. Since 3600 BC the world has known fewer than 300 years of peace; the 14,000-odd wars packed into the rest have accounted for more than three billion human lives. In any given century, more people died in wars than in the one before, and the sombre truth was that twenty centuries back I'd have been one of them. Though my age put me right at the end of a legionary's twenty-five-year career-span, I'd fought like a quaking new recruit. There would have been no second chances, no learning curve; I'd died a swift and panicked boy-soldier's death, over and over again.

Something that was impressed upon me as I flicked through a discarded local newspaper at Copenhagen airport some hours later, and found myself confronted with a half-page photograph of a legionary in a familiarly oversized tunic, cowering, head down, almost apologetically accepting a heavy sword-strike to the back of the neck.

Chapter Three

As the husband of an Icelander who can trace her lineage back to the last great Viking kings, it is my well-worn spousal duty to correct erroneous and hurtful historical stereotypes wherever I encounter them, or pay for it with a drunken scalping.

At any rate, it was certainly a surprise to attend the Reykjavik Viking Festival some years back, and find that those attracted to the Dark Age lifestyle were fired not by a determination to overturn lazy clichés about meaded-up berserkers, but a desperate eagerness to reinforce them. For every quietly toiling craftsman seated at his stall rubbing beeswax onto a drinking horn or carving runic symbols into a sheep's knuckle, there were three dozen woolly coated, hugely bearded madmen waywardly clattering each other with stubby axes. The overbearingly dominant emphasis, at least to a man who'd rather foolishly come along with two very small children in tow, was on full-blooded violence and bellowed obscenity.

It was a matter of some relief to find my initial research suggesting that active interpretation of this era and its people had matured considerably over the intervening decade. A helpful representative of Britain's largest period group, which with a prosaic restraint rare in the re-enacting world styled itself The Vikings, replied to my enquiries with a businesslike rundown of its activities, one that found space for the phrase 'fitting a show around the client's needs'. That its 1,000 members were a breed apart from the sweary barbarians I'd encountered in Iceland was made plain by his assertion that 'in having local groups who are themselves members of the national society, we can be likened to the scouts'.

With the wardrobe shame of Cinderbury still fresh in my mind, proper kit was a prerequisite. 'Re-enactors should be happy to lend you authentic clothing,' advised my friendly pagan scoutmaster, 'but footwear is expensive and made to fit.' So it was that a few evenings later I found myself drawing around the soles of my feet, and posting the result – along with sufficient arcane measurements required to map my ankles, heels and arches to NASA-satisfying detail, and a bankers' draft for €250 – to a specialist German cobbler called Stefan. It was an improbable introduction to the age of craftsmen, one that endured for thousands of years and died only recently. I was the wrong side of forty and had never before had anything made to fit me, nor spent as much on an item you couldn't inhabit, drive or plug in. When the neatly wrapped parcel arrived I tore it open with Viking impetuousness.

The browned foot-wrappings thus liberated, stinking of gamey death, seemed an unlikely introduction to the world of bespoke couture. By appearance and odour, they might have been pulled off the feet of one of those eerily preserved peat-bog bodies. The untanned leather was stoutly unyielding; when I tried them on they fitted like a glove, a glove made out of bark. What an effective indicator of the befuddling shifts in relative economics over the last thousand years that reproducing such harshly spartan footwear, hardly recognisable as shoes, should now cost more than nine water-resistant, softly cushioned pairs of Primark's finest. Or, I don't know, half a new flat-screen telly or loads and loads of DVDs and crisps and stuff.

Hobbling, blistery discomfort aside, the principal issue revealed while wearing them in around the house was one of traction. Picking myself off our parquet for the third time, I began to credit Jean-Luc's explanation for the difficulties even he experienced staying upright in *caligae*: humans, he believed, actually walked differently back then, placing the whole foot flat on the ground with each stride, in the manner of rural Africans. What chance of talking the old-time talk, if I couldn't even walk the old-time walk? I could already foresee my end, slipping skull-first onto the stone threshold as I ran from some longhouse in a period rush.

It was becoming clear from their online event calendars that even the most resilient living historians were reluctant to re-enact winter, and with the nights drawing in I seized upon an invitation to attend a three-day, participants-only 'living-history camp' in Leicestershire. Hrothgar, *né* Mick Baker, was leader (sorry, *jarl*) of a group that convolutedly styled itself *Tÿrsliŏ – Vikings! (of Middle England)*. Unfailingly genial as he had shown himself during our multi-media communications – after a couple of emails he referred to his members as 'Vikes' – as a grammatical statement of intent, that exclamation mark was a cause for some concern. Particularly once I'd scoured the group's website, and found my gaze snagging on words like 'shock', 'scare', 'unsanitised' and 'visceral'. And that was just on the homepage introduction.

A jocular multiple-choice quiz in their forum, intended to assess a Tÿrsliŏ (pronounced tear-sleath) warrior's spiritual authenticity, included these 'correct' answers: 'Chainmail is for poofs', 'Smack him so hard he cries and looks like a twat' and 'Meths, mixed with mead or paraffin'. Scrolling down the index I came across a less flippant, and hence more worrisome discussion on the mechanics of combat: 'May I remind you all that we fight in accordance with the principles of Western Martial Arts . . . The whole body is a target. I do not want to have to slap anyone who says "it wasn't a kill because it hit my forearm".' Here, plainly, was a group hewn from the same bloodstained rock as those I'd seen in Reykjavik all those years before, belting seven shades of sheep-shit out of each other in a playing field. How glad I was, at least now that the scars had formed and half-healed, of the inoculatory beatings endured in Denmark.

It was a matter of some relief to find this pagan brutality tempered with more academic period-based concerns. 'Sorry to sound picky,' began a thread headed 'Taking the camp to the next level', 'but has anyone noticed that the picture on the food-stall living-history page shows a loaf of white bread and very modern orange cheese?' There followed a lively debate on historical interpretation. 'Too many of you turn up in Vike bling,' sneered one poster. 'I've been a member since 2000, and this is my first full season with shoes.' For another, the devil was in the detail. 'We should all STOP buying bowls in non-European woods. It should not be a question of "can the public tell the difference" but "I want it to be correct".' 'You try buying proper stuff with one wage and three kids to feed,' came one riposte to this; another muttered darkly about 'a disturbing trend towards fundamentalist sharia authenticity in the group'.

A 'green jade phallus' topped the lost and found section, and there was a goat for sale in the classifieds. Regardless of which faction now held the upper hand, I was evidently in for a hard-core time of it.

A week later I wandered down the aisles of the Co-Op in the Leicestershire market town of Anstey with Hrothgar's brief shopping list and a furrowed brow. In my basket lay a turnip, two leeks and half a dozen eggs; I picked up a couple of apples, making a note to peel off those sticky labels before laying them out on the Dark Age smorgasbord, and tossed them in. How grateful I was for my nutritional trump cards: two packets of Icelandic wind-dried haddock, one of which I'd torn open in a moment of calorific weakness on the North Circular Road, thereby obliging me to drive 100 miles up the M1 with all the windows open.

What else might qualify as Viking sustenance? Carlsberg? Danepak? Online research had certainly reshaped my concept of timelessly basic foodstuffs. Amongst the principal catalysts that drove the Vikings to foreign plunder, I'd learned, were the meagre nutritional possibilities of Scandinavian soil – onions, cabbage, barley and oats if you were lucky, barley and oats if you weren't. Broccoli, cauliflower, celery, lemons – none would grace a northern European market stall until well into the Middle Ages. It was still difficult to imagine life without the potato, but I'd also be deprived of spinach, sprouts and swede – a root vegetable which almost literally had Viking written all over it, yet wasn't mentioned in England until 1781. Carrots weren't encountered in the former Viking lands until the early medieval period, and even then were available only in purple or white – the carrot we know today was not developed until the late sixteenth century, rather splendidly by Dutch agricul-turalists eager to show their allegiance to the House of Orange.

Half an hour on I was I bumping off a muddy forest track and into a muddier car park, past a sign that welcomed me to Markfield Scout Training Ground. A troop of army cadets jogged into the woods with a stretcher, followed by half a dozen weary boy scouts. Then, through a thicket of sycamores, I spotted a huge swathe of orange and green striped canvas being raised aloft in a clearing, by a number of loud men with very long hair. Some of these, and the many wives and children helping to pitch camp, were clad in dour smocks, others in vibrant tracksuit tops. As I walked through the trees, the glint of weaponry asserted itself; so too did that of prescription eyewear. There was wood smoke and fag smoke, sheepskins and sleeping bags. Amid the striped pavilions so winsomely evocative of longboat sails stood an olive-green army-surplus tent. The battle for authenticity was evidently far from won. I didn't know whether to be disappointed or relieved.

I announced myself to a very tall man with flowing auburn locks and a Hawaiian shirt. 'Oh, there you are,' he said, in amiable Midland tones. 'I'm Orc.' He talked me through some basics as I helped erect the vast tent that would house his family. 'I'm on the Council of Elders,' he said, 'so I could have insisted on a pitch near the bogs.' He thumbed at a brick struc-ture in the clearing opposite. 'But come on: what are the woods for?' All the while, Vikings of both sexes and most ages, perhaps twenty in all, walked in from the car park bearing ominously battered shields, archery targets, charcoal briquettes and crates of lager. The pervasive sense of the new age meeting the old was neatly embodied by the half-dozen children scurrying around, with hair and clothes that could have slotted in at Glastonbury or Cinderbury, and names to match.

'We don't throw axes, Indigo!'

'Emrys! No bare feet near the fire!'

An elderly dog shambled up and stared at me sullenly, followed by a mead-toothed man in baggy Gaulish trousers and a well-worn jerkin, bespectacled and all but bald. He introduced himself as Bede, and told me he'd be in charge until Hrothgar arrived.

Tÿrsliŏ took its hierarchy seriously – full membership was granted only after twelve months of dogsbody servitude as a *thrall*, and warrior status came to those who had proven themselves in combat over at least two years. 'Don't worry,' said Bede, gruffly, 'you don't have to grovel until I put my collar on.' From within his clothing he extracted a torc, the open-ended ring of braided metal that designated status and leadership from the Iron Age to the Vikings. 'But for now, I'm ordering you to help put the chapel up.'

Only when I'd helped erect the relevant small tent did I ask myself, and then a portly and pallid young Vike called Flosi, what place a Christian edifice had in Thor's own campsite. 'We're Saxon crossover,' he said, in a rather piping voice. 'There were actually a lot of Christian Vikings, though strictly speaking—'

'Off he goes,' interrupted the weatherbeaten Kevin Costner who was tautening a rope-sprung double mattress in the tent beside us. 'You won't get away for an hour.' It didn't take long to deduce that Flosi was the most vocal of the pernickety pedants on the group's forum, and the only one present here; winding him up – and catching him out – was a favourite pastime amongst the others. A raucous jeer accompanied Flosi's mumbled admission that he'd repaired some utensil with superglue, and when he disappeared to the toilet block I was sniggeringly urged to peek beneath the sheepskins that carpeted his strenuously accurate tent: the garish blue vinyl of an air bed revealed itself.

A rheumy-eyed, straggle-haired young man and his female companion appeared through the trees, the former covering the ground with a conspicuously lopsided gait. 'Ah!' barked Bede, happily. 'It's the fucking one-legged Cornishman.' It would be a couple of hours before I had the most conspicuous of these adjectives confirmed, via a glimpse of flesh-toned prosthetic, and an account of the motorcycle accident that bequeathed it.

'You forgot epileptic,' came the wearily laconic reply.

'I won't next time,' said Bede, with a wink.

The afternoon evolved into a pleasant if rather nippy early evening, rays of smoke-filtered autumn sun angling in through the trees. A mobile rang; an infant bawled; someone lit up. ('About a third of us smoke,' estimated Orc, who was amongst the most enthusiastic.) A raven-haired valkyrie they called V approached with a sack of spare clothes, and upended it before me and my fellow novices, a stocky young couple who'd come to sample *thrall* life (only now do I realise that the phrase 'in thrall' is thus derived). I ended up with a pair of baggy brown trousers held aloft with a tramp-style rope belt, and a long, rust-coloured linen tunic that our wardrobe assistant said had once been hers. Three re-enactments in, and already I couldn't care less. I went back to the car to change, underlaying that rough and thermally inadequate dress with a couple of T-shirts, and finishing my outfit off with those million-dollar peasant boots. With no footwear available in the dressing-up bag, the novice *thralls* were obliged to spend the entire weekend barefoot.

By now everyone in camp was fully Viked up, the kids in tunics, the men in thick felt cloaks, the women largely headscarfed. But the specs and fags were still out in force, and Kevin Costner was slumped outside his family's pavilion in a Millet's camping chair. Flosi swiftly spotted my shoes and offered his appraisal. 'Not bad,' he murmured, 'though it looks like you've got a pair of M&S socks on under them.'

'Two pairs.'

'And obviously the laces let them down. Vikings had toggles

like these.' He showed me those that fastened his own shoes. 'These were actually knee-length sea-boots until last year. Cost me a fortune, looked great, but then I did a bit of research and found they weren't quite the ticket.' I could just picture that round, boyish face contorted in flagellatory penance as he hacked them down into the spartan, ankle-high foot coverings I saw before me.

As he talked I recalled some photos I'd seen of the 1967 Peel Viking Festival, a pioneering event that had seen the Isle of Man sands thronged with warriors, valkyries and beached longships. What struck me about the monochrome festivities wasn't so much the preponderance of beehives and Dr Scholl's sandals – or indeed a captioned revelation that their vessels were customised lifeboats salvaged from the *Titanic*'s sister ship – as the fact that to a hairy-coated man, every Viking on show sported a horned helmet. I'd like to think that even those of you who aren't shacked up with a direct descendant of Harald Hardrada would be aware that no Viking ever wore a horned helmet. Yet those trailblazing re-enactors weren't naive or ill-informed – they just didn't know any better. No one did: it's extraordinary how far our knowledge of ancient lifestyles has developed since the *Sergeant Pepper* era.

'The trouble with this lot,' Flosi continued, lowering his voice, 'is that they tend to dress how they want, not how Vikings actually did.' He tilted his head at a pair of Vikes sporting fur-trimmed hats of Cossack appearance. 'Those are Rus hats, worn by ninth-century Russians. They'll tell you that the word Rus means "Viking invader", but that's just conjecture.' He explained in detail how the Vikings' eastward forays might well have brought them into contact with the wearers of such hats, but emphasised the dearth of evidence that they ever brought the fashion home. 'There's far too much kit being justified on the grounds that it *could theoretically* have been worn or used.' He shook his head sadly, and took a sip of ale from a soapstone cup he'd found in Tesco, being sold as a toothmug.

Every so often a patrol of scouts or cadets trotted past,

angling looks of curiosity and amusement in our direction. One group of the former tentatively approached the camp with cameras at the ready, and one of my Vikings urged them hither with a practised chorus: 'Photo opp-or-tun-ity, photo opp-or-tun-ity!' As the scouts snapped away the Vikings merrily yelled and charged and brandished; no pose was too cheesy. 'We're all shameless tarts here,' whispered an English teacher named Hoketil, raising a shield and sword high above his head. A couple of months before I wouldn't have joined him; a couple of hours before I might not have done so with a scout-blanching roar.

It is the Vikings' unfortunate historical lot to find themselves synonymous with violent sexual assault, yet my in-laws see off all related jibes with the arresting insistence that their Dark Age antecedents ran an equal-opportunity society. With their husbands invariably abroad trading, they tell me, Viking women would have taken charge of both farmstead and family. Obviously I've never had the heart to debate with them the nature of Viking commerce ('Here's my final offer: two kicks and a stab for that sack of grain, oh, and I'll throw in your dad's ear for those bracelets'), nor suggest how they'd react if I went off to try my hand at it, and sent them a postcard explaining I'd done so with the sole and noble intent of expanding their daughter's domestic and administrative capabilities.

Evidence of Tÿrslio's even-handed approach to maniacs of both sexes emerged when a bit of playful slappery between the Cornishman and his girlfriend flared up into a full-on grunting scuffle, and then a knife-versus-stave stand-off.

'Don't panic,' whispered Hoketil, sensing that I wasn't enjoying this spectacle as much as everyone else seemed to be. 'It's not sharp.'

The splinters of wood that flew up from the subsequent coming together suggested otherwise, but before these had settled on the ground the fight was over: the Cornishman stuck his good leg forward, hauled his girl across it and despatched her to the earth with an extremely hard punch in the chest.

A mass cheer rang out, and barely faltered when the felled warrioress shot to her feet and stormed off into the forest.

As darkness came, the community lapsed into a more traditional division of gender roles. The women busied themselves with childcare and catering, some herding reluctant mini-marauders to bed, others filling pots with hunks of meat and turnips, and tending these as they bubbled atop the kitchen-tent fire; the rest of us got stuck into beers and blokey pyromania, chopping wood with big axes, and heaving the resultant logs into the bisected oil drum that was our brazier. Perhaps to atone for this glaring aberration, the lushly goateed Rodstaff, a British Museum numismatist, told me he'd be lighting our showpiece fire with tinder fungus. I cleared my throat as a prelude to recounting my related triumph at Cinderbury – in shaming reality still the only moment that suggested I had a future in the past – when he remembered he'd left it at home. Bede then extracted a flint striker to bring light to the Dark Ages, and when that didn't work Kevin Costner bent down with a Zippo. Our de facto commander snatched it from his hands. 'Remember what I told you five minutes ago about being a leader? Well, that's being a fucking knob.' It seemed a little inconsistent coming from a man with a roll-up in his lips.

Bede's reign as *jarl* ended soon after, when a small Rover bounced up the path and disgorged a twinkly eyed, grey-bearded fellow of modest stature. With a chirpy and very un-Viking giggle he donned a fur-banded hat of precisely the type condemned by Flosi, and introduced himself as Hrothgar. 'For heaven's sake, let's get that going,' he said, surveying the moribund brazier. 'Anyone got a lighter?'

Night had long since settled on the camp when the stew and dumplings were ladled out into well-used wooden bowls. The most prominent non-martial accessory was the sea chest, in essence a wooden toolbox that was the repository of a Vike's period effects, and a good place to hide his phone and car keys. Half a dozen of these were dragged up to the now roaring brazier, and on them we sat, steaming bowls in our laps, wooden spoons in our hands.

Having enjoyed so little success asking previous re-enactors what had attracted them to their chosen period, I didn't really feel like despoiling the companionable fireside ambience with the same stilted enquiry. Oddly, as soon as the womenfolk went off to wash up, the men of Tÿrsliŏ asked it of themselves. Perhaps my presence inspired these neo-Norsemen to see themselves through outside eyes, to wonder for the first time how on earth they came to be sitting round a fire in hooded cloaks, prodding embers with a pike staff, when all their friends were watching *Taggart* in bed. Or perhaps they were just more expansively drunk than I realised.

'Quick straw poll, chaps,' chirped Hrothgar. 'Why do we do Vikes?' The first answers were shrug-and-a-swig-of-lager jobs, tales of simple happenchance. Kevin Costner had run into Tÿrsliŏ at some sort of pagan Halloween event, and joined up on a whim when he found out they were based just up the road from him. 'To be honest,' he confided later, 'I'd rather be doing Robin Hood stuff.' The Cornishman had experienced a similarly indirect introduction, getting into medieval combat while working in an Oxford pub frequented by a fourteenth-century group, and transferring to Vikes by default when he relocated. Hrothgar's own re-enactment career had begun in the Napoleonic army – he remained a member of a period group called L'Artillerie Légère – but he didn't seem quite sure how this had led him to the Viking life. Perhaps he'd got a taste for unhinged mayhem at the Waterloo-era event that had degenerated into cannon crews firing diseased rabbits at each other.

For a few, as I'd guessed from certain references on their forum, this was the end of a natural progression from symbolic dressing up and combat to the real thing, one that had begun with school holidays spent rolling many-sided dice across an orc-strewn Dungeons and Dragons board. There followed studenty weekends devoted to LARP, live-action role-playing fantasies acted out by dozens, sometimes hundreds of costumed obsessives in fields or warehouses, and then a more focused interest in reliving real history with real weapons. To offensively patronise this section of the latter-day Viking community, it seemed to me that a dominant attraction of the Dark Age way of life was how closely it permitted them to dress and behave as if the world had been created by J.R.R. Tolkien. Referring to children as 'hobbits' didn't help their case.

'It's just a good look for me, I suppose,' said Dagmar, who didn't seem to mind when informed that he'd given himself a popular Icelandic girl's name. It was a good look for almost all of them. Dagmar was unusually tall, and his nose more obliquely broken than most, but otherwise he displayed the characteristics that made the Tÿrsliŏ male the convincing embodiment of well-fed wealth and hirsute virility in an age where these were prized, and which had failed to invent the toothbrush.

For a while we all gazed into the fire. Then Orc seemed to lose patience with himself and his fellow Vikes. 'Cut the crap, guys,' he blurted. 'It's the fighting.' He placed a large, firm palm on the meaty hand axe tucked in his belt (crafted, like his antler-handled sword, by the group's own blacksmith), and stared at me through those gingery curtains of hair. 'What I've learned with this lot has given me an awful lot of confidence in real-world situations.' He took a deep draught of Fosters, then smiled distantly. 'Funny to think I used to run away from trouble.' I was hoping for a chorus of fatuous laughter to swell up out of the fireside shadows; instead, many heads nodded in thoughtful assent.

It was a new experience to hear a violence buff calmly rationalise his passion. Orc offered an analogy with American football, another of his brawn-centric pastimes. 'I guess it's just that buzz when you leather a guy – I mean, *really* leather him.' He scratched his patchy beard. 'Anyway, you'll see what I mean tomorrow.'

The cat was out of the bag, and my Vikings now took turns to boot it around the fire.

Tentatively at first, but then with competitive, beery abandon, they assailed me with tales of physical ruthlessness. I learned of the twenty-three admissions to Accident and

Emergency spawned during Tÿrsliô's weekly training sessions in the previous year alone; I was shown how repeated metallic blows to unprotected fingers had endowed many of those around the fire with hands set in a clawed curl, one that made grasping small objects a challenge. I heard of the growing number of once-bitten Dark Age groups unwilling to accept a rematch with their warriors: 'Oh, bollocks,' said Orc, recounting the tremulous mutter he'd once overheard from the opposition lines as Tÿrsliô took to the battlefield, 'it's that full-contact lot.'

Their proud refusal to fight to a script had meant history being rewritten before the public's flinching gaze. Supposedly victorious Saxon and Norman armies had been regularly battered to defeat, and recreations of inter-Viking conflict settled in the actual loser's favour. Had Tÿrsliô been asked to perform a Canute re-enactment, it might have ended with the North Sea in full retreat.

Visceral combat realism was Tÿrsliô's mission, and any tale that embodied it was worth a boast. Rodstaff told me of the occasion he'd taken his sister and her son to their first Viking battle event, engineering his own violent death right before them. 'Oh, great,' he overheard the boy mutter as he lay there motionless, fake blood pulsing from his abdomen, 'so who's going to drive us home now?'

Dagmar described a battle so gruelling to participant and observer alike that a horse and an elderly female spectator had both suffered cardiac arrest; Hrothgar dug about in his sea chest for their promotional brochure, whose cover featured a pinioned pagan having his prosthetic stomach luridly sliced open below the headline 'We Maim To Please'.

The images revealed within detailed Hrothgar's own obsession: honing the group's special effects to forensic levels of gory detail. I saw Tÿrsliô warriors being disembowelled, strung up, set ablaze, even beheaded. For years, Hrothgar had toiled with an alchemist's passion to perfect the recipe for blood, a blend of golden syrup, food colouring and washing-up liquid whose proportions he would not reveal. The apogee of his dark art was showcased in the newspaper cutting he now presented. Dominated by a picture of a smiling Hrothgar arm in arm with a wizened corpse, this was a souvenir of the occasion a large number of policemen had descended on his house after a horrified neighbour spotted him lugging the pictured dummy, a favoured Tÿrslið prop (nicknamed Kenny in honour of the oft-slain *South Park* character), into the garage. 'One of life's great pleasures,' Hrothgar sighed as he closed the book and settled back on his sea chest, 'is driving to a Vike meet with Kenny in the passenger seat.'

I gasped, I drank, I gawped, I clapped my dress-clad thigh and drank some more. Because when all was said and done, this was the sort of stuff I wanted Vikings to say and do, and how I wanted them to say and do it. What of it if they sliced orange cheese on a board of non-European wood, if every so often an electronic warble asserted itself from the sea-chests beneath us?

In one of the very rare quiet moments, Hrothgar stated how re-enactment groups could be sorted into five levels of authenticity. First up were the bibulous casuals who wore eBay fancy dress and taped hessian over their trainers; grade two re-enactors generally rented outfits from theatrical costumiers and 'looked OK from a distance'; he placed Tÿrslið in grade three, on the grounds that 'we do machine-stitch our clothes, but only on the inside where it doesn't show'. I never quite pinned him down on what defined grades four and five, but his respect for those groups who reached this level was tempered with scorn for the joyless sobriety that apparently characterised them.

'You get these obsessives who rope their camps off at events: they won't even talk to the public, and never want to party after hours.' Hrothgar shook his head, bemused by those whose re-enactment agenda found no place for alcoholic silliness. The odd muttered hint suggested Tÿrslið was something of a Viking Foreign Legion, an ask-no-questions refuge for those expelled from more sombre re-enactment groups for crimes against authenticity and decorum. But how glad I then was to be here sharing dirty jokes and supermarket lager round an oil-drum brazier, not squatting amongst moody Dark Age zealots, dyeing clothes in piss and silence. To be with people who were Vikings because Vikings got drunk and fought, not because they rotated crops and invented the stirrup.

With every passing hour and emptied crate, the group's already relaxed stance on historical accuracy relaxed further: cans were no longer decanted into wooden beakers, and someone popped open a tube of Pringles. Every so often an elder bawled, '*Thrall*! Wood!', and Leicestershire's newest Viking would totter obediently off into the forest with an axe, barefoot. In three days we must have got through at least a couple of trees' worth: it isn't hard to see how the great forests that covered most of Iceland when the Vikings arrived are now barren arctic deserts.

We burned and drank; they held forth and I listened. Somewhere along the increasingly fuzzy line I learned that women were permitted to fight for the Tÿrslið cause ('in drag'), but that Bede no longer was. 'Ex-paratrooper, trained to kill at no regard to his own personal safety,' said someone. 'A psycho, basically.' Hearing himself thus described, the object responded with a yellow-eyed wink. He winked a lot more throughout Orc's account of how he'd been ambushed by Bede, Kato-style, at some recent event: 'Broke an ankle and snapped my Achilles, but I still fought on until the end of the day.'

The brutal camaraderie recalled my time with the Legio VIII. At one point Bede threatened to burn the Cornishman's false leg in the fire, only to be told that carbon fibre wasn't combustible. Any Vike who fell asleep in the minibus on the way home from an event could expect to awake in a state of imaginative comic humiliation: banana-horns would be lashed to his helmet, or his groin, or he'd find himself mummified in gaffer tape and somehow tied to the inside of the roof. Happy times, smiled their indulgent *jarl*, explaining with a sigh that things had calmed down now that so many Vikes brought their kids along. 'Gone are the days when we stayed out until 3 a.m., breaking things.'

Gone, perhaps, but not forgotten. There was the time they'd all been out on a beach after an event near Portsmouth, throwing pebbles at what they thought in the twilight was a marker buoy; moments later, a helicopter caught them in its searchlight and informed them through a loudhailer that they'd been stoning a nuclear submarine. Oh, and that Tÿrslið camp that was stormed by riot police, tipped off by locals convinced that a horde of crusty travellers had moved in. The bulk of Bede's army stories ended up with a grenade going off in someone's face, and when the men of Tÿrslið weren't hanging each other off cliffs by their fingertips, they were confronting intruders with shotguns, setting light to restraining orders or reversing fork-lift trucks into their former places of employment. Their many tales of derring do – both as Vikings and as civilians – would later oblige me to take a long hard look at my suburban lifestyle and see it for what it really was: happy, secure and generally rather wonderful.

Quite the most repellently evocative tale was Hrothgar's account of the 1,000-a-side siege re-enactment he'd attended some years previously at a castle in Sweden. One afternoon, as he drank with his fellow defenders at a makeshift bar they'd set up along the battlements, the enemy had opened up with a volley of cabbages fired at great velocity from their hefty trebuchet; the soldier beside Hrothgar was left holding only the neck of the vodka bottle he'd been about to refresh himself from. The besieged army had two days to hone their revenge: when the invaders duly massed outside the castle gates for the final showdown, the gigantic butt of 'boiling oil' emptied upon their heads was a-brim not with water, as they'd been led to expect, but the manifold excretions of 1,000 unwashed inebriates, collected over forty-eight hours. The gathered audience watched the outraged event organiser stamp furiously up to the gates, cursing furiously; then saw him again, a short while later, being dangled by his ankles from the highest tower, trouserless and bleating. Well, whatever floats your boat. Then burns it.

The conversation turned briefly to Spangles, the Ford Capri

and other areas of consumer nostalgia, interspersed with
chorused one-liners from *Monty Python and The Holy Grail*,
a cultural phenomenon I suspected was a dominant inspiration
for Dark Age combatants. For a while the woods around us
were alive with the mutters and rustles of some bumbling
teenage patrol on a night mission; like Bede, Orc had served
time in the army, and for a vivid minute or two he described
how easy – and entertaining – it would be to stalk and snatch
a cadet, and bring him back to camp.

As these rustlings receded and the last distant scouting
singalong faded, my Vikings once more filled the night with
hairy-chested, hairy-coated reminiscences, euphemistic 'inci-
dents' involving landladies, firemen, coastguards and – always
– hog-whimpering insobriety.

'You sometimes have these "Superviking" moments,' smiled
Orc, who dutifully recounted a great many. The common theme
was retribution wreaked upon disrespectful civilians: the
drunken MOP who smashed Hrothgar's windscreen and was
chased at axe-point into Leicester town centre, where he hid
under a car and refused to emerge until the police arrived; the
taunting youths dispersed from outside a North London chip
shop by a judicious display of weaponry; a group of the same
punished in an undisclosed manner for spitting upon slain
warriors at a battle re-enactment in Oxford.

It was no surprise when raucous words evolved to bellowed
selections from Tÿrsliŏ's extensive repertoire of ribald, self-
penned drinking songs. Halfway through the first, Bede hauled
himself groggily aloft and weaved off into the night, murmuring
about 'a bad bottle'; we didn't see him again until morning.
Flosi, who'd hitherto nobly restricted himself to wooden mugs
of the 12 per cent cough syrup that is mead, now succumbed
to the lure of bottled cider, and then – disastrously – Pernod
blended with dandelion and burdock. It wasn't long before I
found myself addressed with thick-tongued urgency.

'See, I'm just trying to set a standard, to stamp out all the
really rubbish kit,' he shouted above a chorus of 'The Well-
Hung Ploughboy', waving a chubby finger about. Forgotten now

was a recent episode in which he'd fanned our waning fire with a battery-powered pump, brought along to inflate his air bed. 'But I mean, we're good at fighting – *the best*. Don't you forget that.' I told him I wouldn't. 'Those Romans you were with . . . I did some of that crap once, just poking each other with sticks . . . We don't have a routine or shit like that, we just . . . *go right at it*. Yeah? You'll see.' I told him I would, but wasn't at all sure I now wanted to.

They were roaring about badgers when I turned in, and were still at it long after I'd rolled out my sleeping bag in a corner of the coach-sized, orange-and-green striped, open-fronted tent I was to share with Hoketil and many tottering stacks of shields, table trestles and wooden chests. Here in the dark, away from the comfort of the fireside, that pagan wassailing had a distinctly less homely ring to it. Aglow with flames and ale, the distant faces I could see through the tent's open awning seemed increasingly sinister. '*You'll see*.' Setting Orc's earlier words against Flosi's recent unsteady pronouncements, I wondered how I'd taken them as a warm invitation, rather than the cold threat they so starkly were.

How would it feel to be leathered, *really* leathered? I spent some time trying to rationalise the experience in terms of Newton's laws: it was all about momentum, probably, and the disastrous effects of resisting it. As a featherweight leatheree struck by fifteen stone of charging berserker, would I simply bounce lightly off into a distant part of the forest, like a plastic skittle struck by a wreckers' ball? Or would it be more of a hammer-on-peach job? The important thing, I decided, was to ensure that when someone hit me, I was already travelling in the same direction: this meant rolling with the punches, and counteracting an imminent shoulder charge, or similar, by running at least slightly away.

None of that, though, would be much use when the hardware came out. '*It's that full-contact lot*.' The Cornishman's palsied grasp explained just what that meant: heavy lengths of metal aimed at human flesh and swung without restraint. I flexed both hands in my sleeping bag, as if for the last time.

My exhalations steamed out into the cold air ever more rapidly. One ballad ended, and before the next began I caught the click-hiss of liberated lager, and snatches of Vike-talk: 'The thing about Bear is, when he hits someone they know about it . . .', 'So this guy whacks me in the guts, but he doesn't know I've got a blood-bag under my tunic – poor bloke almost fainted . . .', 'Ah, belt up, Flosi, you ponce.'

I awoke to the thwack of willow on skull. Two of Orc's boys were clattering each other with staffs by the kitchen tent, and with an intestinal lurch of foreboding I once again questioned the violent infliction of pain as a useful twenty-first-century life-skill. No more soothing was the stentorian reveille with which Hrothgar mustered the slumberers – a quavering blast on a cattle horn, precisely as delivered throughout *The Vikings*, an account of Kirk Douglas and Tony Curtis's epic struggle for the throne of Northumbria. 'That's not nearly as funny as you think it is,' croaked Hoketil after Hrothgar discharged right into his blanket-shrouded head.

We breakfasted on wooden bowls of porridge, and then, after Flosi went back to 'authenticate his tent' prior to inspection, on Nescafé, bananas and many packets of supermarket bacon. None of it went down well with the butterflies that had made my innards their home.

The ensuing inventory of correctitude, ordained by Hrothgar at Flosi's nagging insistence, was a two-tier event. Flosi stood haughtily before period accessories hewn from European wood, while everyone else idly punted anachronisms out of sight or stuffed them into linen bags, shouting 'Au-then-ti-cate!' in Dalek voices. To the men and women of Tÿrsliö, anything was historically admissible as long as it could be concealed at short notice. Hrothgar did his best to affect an air of stern disapproval, no easy task for such a reluctant disciplinarian, nor a Viking with a digital camera round his neck. 'Right, I'm going to walk round and take a few pictures, and I don't want to see anything out of period when we look back through them.'

Shortly after, we huddled around the little LCD screen at our leader's beckoning. 'Well, straight off in this first one, we've got two . . . three people smoking, and it looks as if Otto there is sending a text.' Kevin Costner's teenage son aimed a truculent shrug at the fire. *Booze gr8*, I thought. *2nite we mutil8 newbies*. Hrothgar clicked on through the photos, tutting at a cotton headscarf here, a sleeping bag (mine) there. 'Now *that's* better,' he said, arriving at a shot depicting the interior of Orc's tent. 'Nice arrangement of weapons and shields . . . proper crockery . . . and I like how you've hung the cloaks up over the bearskin standard.' ('Great eBay find, that,' someone whispered.) Flosi leaned forward and squinted at the image. 'Er, what's that, by the sea chest?' Hrothgar zoomed in, and we found ourselves looking at a huge packet of Pampers. He tried to frown, then let out one of those soprano chuckles: his Vikes were just too unruly, too flippant for all this, and ultimately so was he. 'Who am I to talk anyway?' he sighed, helplessly. 'Look at my sea chest – it's supposed to have rope handles, and they're metal. And that lock is fourteenth century at best, for God's sake.'

There was a loud tut from the rear of the group. 'Look, have we come here to fuss about bloody stitching, or fight?'

'Fussing sounds good,' I mumbled, amidst the roar of bloodlust thus unleashed.

And so, a moment later, two five-strong lines of heavily armed warriors stood facing each other across an adjacent forest clearing. Through a necessarily prolonged visit to the latrine block, I had missed being conscripted into this first round of battles, and watched proceedings from a hunched position on one of the tree-stumps that formed what Bede, newly returned to camp and a rather more reluctant spectator, had already dubbed death row.

The *thrall* couple, drawn on opposite sides, clutched their swords and circular shields in whitened fists; if maintaining balance in the dewy grass had already proved beyond my slick-soled peasant boots, then how would they cope in bare feet? 'Right!' bellowed Orc. 'Five on five, no running through the camp, Martini rules!'

Any vestigial misgivings at having not yet been conscripted to the Tÿrsliŏ ranks evaporated when Bede revealed what this meant. 'Any time, any place, anywhere,' he mumbled, as the first grunt-accompanied clang rang out. 'You know – anything goes, no holds barred.'

I spent the following quarter-hour in a blinking, cringing flinch. Pikes, hand axes and mighty swords were wielded at full strength, meeting shields with a thudding crack and each other with a painful, grating slash. Worst of all was the softer, yielding thump that accompanied a body blow. After a while I became aware that the defensive twitches with which I reflexively showed empathy with those being hit were being precisely mirrored by Bede's jabs and swipes, enacted on behalf of the hitters. 'Bugger,' winced Dagmar in response to a lusty axe strike to the forearm, without interrupting his combat manoeuvrings. Even without a sharpened edge, the heavy-gauge steel their in-house armourer used was capable – as I now beheld – of cleaving a fat pike shaft in two.

A cloak was slashed from nape to hem, a shield splintered to inutility. Everything I knew of Flosi suggested I'd be watching him hacked to the ground, repeatedly, mercilessly and with only bleating resistance, but far from it – he showed himself amongst the more fearlessly accomplished warriors of the many on display. When the Cornishman and V came to join the fray, it was swiftly apparent that no quarter was given nor expected on grounds of sex or mobility. In her third battle, V copped a mighty blow to the hip that would still affect her gait when we packed the tents up two days later, but which she didn't deem sufficient to stop her fighting on. This, I thought, was how it must have been at a Gaulish training session in Lejre: an attritional loon-on-loon onslaught, sharing little with the stunted blitzkriegs that had brushed us legionaries aside.

What rules there were seemed to correspond to those I'd largely failed to learn in Denmark: a blow to the hand meant you fought on with it behind your back. As was the case there, though, these proved difficult to enforce. Once the barefoot *thrall* and his girl had been brusquely put to the sword, the battles were protracted, vicious and rounded off with bitter recriminations.

101

'But you only had one arm!'

'Yeah? Well, you had no fucking legs!'

'He never takes his fucking hits!'

'Piss off – I got you on the follow-through!'

Orc, who I now learned was the recently appointed head of combat training, had a terrible job adjudicating these disputes, and offering tips to the embittered slain. 'I understand that it's a natural reaction, but if you raise your shoulder like that you're going to get hit in the neck, and . . . Fine, off you go, spit your dummy out and we'll see you later.'

Hrothgar and a few others had by now gathered expectantly around me on the sidelines, and when the battle in progress drew to another violent and ill-tempered conclusion, Orc came across to conscript the bystanders. As I prepared myself to die, Bede felt compelled to run through the more memorable battle-field injuries he'd suffered, inflicted or witnessed. How glad I was, as with wet-lipped glee he told me of a spleen burst by the thrust of an armoured knee, that I would at least not be facing him across this God-forsaken clearing.

Orc strode towards us, cloak flowing, a Valhalla-despatched angel of death. 'Right, you and you are fighting on Dagmar's side, and . . . let's see . . .' His long, outstretched finger moved towards me; I felt my entire frame stiffen. 'Er . . . Hrothgar with Rodstaff . . . and . . . ah . . .' In the end I could stand it no more. Abruptly determined to jump before I was pushed, I breathed hard and shot up a hand. So be it; the runes were cast; it was my fate to be put to the sword, here in this boy-scout training ground, wearing a dress.

Orc wrinkled his long, freckly nose. 'You? Er, sorry, mate – that's a non-starter.' I felt my pale cheeks redden. And this only days after my youngest daughter withdrew a bottle of chilli sauce from our supermarket trolley, with a look of genuine concern and the words, 'But, Daddy – on the label it says "Not for wimps".'

The shame of rejection eased slightly when Orc hastily explained that a minimum of two training sessions were a pre-requisite for 'Martini' combat – the *thralls*, he said, had earlier that week undertaken their third. Insane these Vikings might be, but they were never irresponsible. No matter that their expressions of shellshocked exhaustion – and indeed my own subsequent conversations with them – suggested the newcomers wouldn't be back for a fourth. 'Most of our new recruits last a month,' said Hrothgar later, which was some comfort to those of us who wouldn't have lasted an hour.

For the balance of the morning I squatted on my mossy tree-stump, watching my Vikings, as Flosi had promised, go right at it. Clack, yell, thunk, crunk-thunk, squelch, howl, swish-smash, clack, shriek . . . As the clearing rang with angry blows and cries of rage and pain, my humiliation receded ever further.

Scrish, whomp, thwack . . . I thought of Hrothgar's revelation that Tÿrslið had been blacklisted by English Heritage, organisers of the multi-period Festival of History at Kentmarsh Hall, the country's largest re-enactment event: highlights of the sniffy letter he'd been sent included the phrases 'excessively wild and reckless' and 'insufficient emphasis on reality'. But the Nescafé and fags didn't really seem to matter any more: here before me, now that I could appreciate the scene through the curious eyes of a bystander rather than the tear-filled equivalents of a prospective participant, was the very essence of that brutal, fearless determination which had defined the Vikings, no matter what my in-laws and the po-faced revisionists had to say about advanced naval construction techniques or the runic alphabet.

At length the warriors were all fought out, and I followed as they shuffled wearily back to camp, grumbling over hits and kills and wiping sweat from their hairy red faces. A swishing thwick-thunk lured me round the back of the kitchen tent: there the non-combatant women were launching metal-tipped, feather-flighted arrows at an archery target, and most particularly at the apple wedged on a stick in front of the bull's-eye. Other than being made of wood the bows they were using hardly looked overwhelmingly authentic, but if I'd imagined this might make for a more forgiving introduction to the sport of pointy-stick stretch-twangery, I was soon to be proven wrong. From a range of perhaps twenty feet, in a dozen attempts I grazed the target's outer ring only once, and – despite accepting the optional gauntlet – really, really hurt my hand. In fairness, it was almost dark when a yelp from behind the kitchens informed us that someone had finally enjoyed a William Tell moment.

By then the *thralls*, Hoketil and a few others had packed up and gone; our after-stew campfire congregation proved rather less uproarious, in volume if not content. I now learned of the secret scoring system that kept Tÿrsliŏ on its toes at events: a point for every member of the audience you made cry, faint or vomit, with double marks for having the St John Ambulance called on to the battlefield. A failsafe way to rack up a big score, I gathered, was covertly tying a blood bag round a willing Vike child's neck, then extravagantly biting its throat out before the crowd. Hrothgar hoped this might be trumped by a scenario the Cornishman had recently suggested – after succumbing to a 'leg wound' on the battlefield, he'd be visited by a Viking 'surgeon', who'd surreptitiously replace his carbon-fibre attachment with a joint of pork and a blood bag, then treat the crowd to a graphic amputation. 'Imagine the smell when we cauterise it,' our leader murmured, smiling dreamily.

This imaginatively ruthless determination to distress the spectating public was, I concluded, at least partly incited by the witless enquiries the warriors of Tÿrsliŏ had to endure between battles. A MOP would ask if that fire was real, or this baby, or those horses, then seek confirmation of the supplied answer by jabbing the relevant entities with a stick or finger; an apology for the pain or alarm this caused them was invariably demanded. We chortled at the gormless confusion with which spectators learned that a wooden bowl of stew was indeed to be eaten or a sheepskin to be slept upon. But even as I chortled, I accepted that this ignorance underpinned the whole re-enactment movement: a stew-pot bubbling over a fire was now an exotic spectacle, one worth giving up your money to behold, or giving up your weekends to recreate.

When raindrops began to hiss on the brazier, Orc and Flosi dragged the whole thing under the awning of my open-fronted tent. How particularly grateful I now found myself that, perhaps out of chivalrous respect to the women, the men of Tÿrsliծ had deemed flatulence less integral to the historical experience than the Legio VIII. As we pulled a trio of sea chests up to the relocated fire, someone even excused themselves after belching.

The restrained ambience lent itself to more considered conversation. I found time to question Flosi on something that had bothered me since he'd flaunted his toggles: how, over many centuries, had the Vikings failed to envision the modest refinement that would have produced the inestimably more practical button – apparently not in common use until the fifteenth century? An awfully big stumble along the march of progress: like inventing the jug, and taking 500 years to realise you could cut the top half off and have yourself a cup. And while I was about it, what about pockets? Flosi laboured to defend his heroes, demonstrating the superior carrying potential of a belt slung with leather pouches in a manner that caused the most heavily laden of these to swing back forcefully into his groin. 'Well, I don't know,' he winced, pallidly. 'They'd just grown up managing without them.' Had our forebears consistently adhered to this argument, I might have said if I'd been more drunk or he'd been in less pain, we'd all have been sitting there naked, grunting and fireless.

The introspection deepened in the hours ahead. Some campfires make you want to drink and shout and sing, others seem to encourage sombre rumination. And so, as the embers subsided, I came to hear of the tragedies that had befallen this outwardly boisterous tribe, the breakdowns, the illnesses, the bereavements. I learned that V's husband Hereward, like her a Tÿrsliծ member of long-standing, had been killed the year before in a motorcycle crash. V had been riding pillion: the legacy was a 'leg full of metal', which explained why she was still limping from the blow received in combat, but not how on earth she'd been able to fight in the first place. From Rodstaff I heard of the car accident that had very nearly claimed his life the year before that, when he'd hit a tree on the way home from an event. 'Thor saved me,' he said simply: he'd watched a lightning bolt strike the road ahead a few seconds before his crash, and was therefore driving very much more slowly when it occurred. Many weeks in intensive care and many months of facial reconstruction had followed; I understood now that the many scars etched into his cheeks and forehead were not legacies of combat. When at last Rodstaff felt able to attend a Tÿrsliŏ training session, he was greeted with the words: 'Look – it's Quasimodo!'

It was already plain that this camp, though ostensibly a 'living-history workshop' to showcase newly acquired kit and debate the promotion of historical accuracy, was at heart a weekend away with likeminded friends. Now I came to understand that what bound these people together was more than a shared love of beery sadism – theirs was a deep fraternity that went beyond companionship. Indeed, the word 'family' now emerged with touching regularity: as in Viking days, as in modern Iceland, they were a close-knit tribe, who lived in near proximity and looked after their own. This bond asserted itself through visits to each other's grandmothers, to the bedside vigils for Rodstaff, and the dreadful aftermath of V's tragic accident. Inevitably, it found its most eloquent expression in Viking vigilante missions: 'Rodstaff called me up and said he was having a bit of trouble with some yobs outside his house – we were all there in five minutes.' That was Orc again, of course. His own part of Leicester was notorious as a joyrider's playground, yet the odd judicious display of Dark Age weaponry had proved so effective a deterrent that he could now safely leave his keys in the ignition.

The rain intensified dramatically after the Vikes shuffled off to their sheepskin-covered beds; by daybreak, those in the leakier tents had already driven home in a sodden huff. Mrs Orc followed them soon after, taking that high-spirited brood with her; one of my default images of the camp was the final sighting of young Emrys as he dragged his tunic tails through the car-park mud, pike staff in one hand and an upturned mead empty in the other.

Having shared my tent with a fire it was very difficult to stop thinking about hot running water; pulling on that wood-smoked, mead-stickied tunic was an act accompanied with a loudly guttural shudder of self-loathing. I had fresh pants and a toothbrush in the boot, but being caught with either would raise those mumbles about southern pansies to an unacceptable volume. Why hadn't I snatched the opportunity during my covert mid-campfire mission to catch the ten o'clock headlines on the car radio? Why instead had I snatched three packets of salt and vinegar from the glovebox, and mindlessly shovelled them into my mud-stubbled maw as I hunched down in the footwell? What a horrible price I'd paid for that – my very eye-sockets now seemed rimed with soured trans-fats, an oily penance for this nutritional transgression. The dried Icelandic haddock I proudly laid on the breakfast table might have redressed the historical balance, but after devouring two butter-smeared lengths of it without recourse to cutlery I hardly felt less like a shower.

It was treacherous underfoot; after my second mouthful of campsite I understood why Nikes now poked out beneath many cloak hems. We gathered under the food tent, stirring wooden mugs of tea with huge and filthy daggers, and dispensing muted ribaldries. Asked to help wash up – frankly no onerous task, given the unchallenging quality control – young Otto embarked on an epic teenage sulk, flailing with such impressive abandon that he knocked his own tent down from the inside.

We pottered about, packing up; I helped take down the chapel tent, decommissioned without once seeing active service. The rain briefly evolved into canvas-clattering hail: 'Hail, Thor!' went up a lone, almost apologetic cry. 'Repeat after me,' mumbled V to no one in particular, '"I like doing this."' I sensed that if a few of them hadn't, it was because there'd been no public to dress up for, show off to, petrify, repulse.

The unquestioned highlight of these downbeat final hours was having Hrothgar inflict a deep wound to my left cheek. A livid, two-inch gash, dribbling patent-recipe crimson from a brownish central scab – it was the work of a mere moment for his practised hands. The mysterious clear fluid he first applied somehow caused my skin to contract, giving the impression of a deep, stab-like fissure; there were no mirrors around, but the effect was evidently convincing. As I walked around what was left of the camp, offering thanks and farewells to the few Vikes who remained, Bede – a trained army medic – strode up with a merry glint in his eye, tapping his left cheek referentially. 'Ooh, tasty! Argument with a pike, eh?'

A couple of hours later, cruising down the M1 with my longbow-blistered fingers curled gingerly around the wheel, I wondered what I'd brought away from a long weekend in the Dark Ages. On a micro level, the lovingly collated *Big Book of Fire-Stuff* in my head now included indexed entries for rosemary (a sprig thrown in a smoky blaze considerably reduces eye-sting) and wool (a superlative flame-retardant, as the Cornishman had demonstrated while idly extinguishing a skillet inferno with a corner of his cloak). I had become a little more accustomed to the unchecked accumulation of smoke-scented bodily filth, to everything that passed my lips being powerfully tainted with damp wood and onions, to the challenging discomforts and intimacies of communal outdoor life.

And there was certainly evidence of a more bluffly practical approach to personal mishap, as I discovered just before Newport Pagnell, when a disheartening flappity-slap from my off-side rear obliged me to pull over into the hard shoulder. My routine in changing a wheel is not to even look for the jack until I've spent at least fifteen minutes howling at the accursed injustice of my predicament. But there I was, bounding out on to the hard shoulder without hesitation, and effecting the necessary pit stop with swear-free focus and almost alarming vigour.

It was difficult to pat myself too hard on the back, though, and not just because I'd just burst all those blisters on the jack handle. Because the overbearing legacy of my stay with the Vikings, as it had been with the Romans, was that violent conflict, such a dominant feature of modern history's first millennium, really wasn't my thing. Try as I might to pretend otherwise, I was still very much a man of my time. The first thing I did when I got home was to alarm the children with my scar, but the second – after being frogmarched at arm's length into the shower by a wordlessly disgusted spouse – was to update my sat-nav's speed-camera database. It was the most twenty-first-century thing I could think of.

Chapter Four

How many of us are familiar with the Battle of Towton, fought just south of York in 1461? I certainly wasn't, until the morning I accompanied my children's leftover Shreddies with an article that described how this single clash in the drawn-out Wars of the Roses accounted for more than one in a hundred of all Englishmen – at least 20,000 were killed, more than on the first day of the Somme, indeed more than have ever died in a single day in our nation's history. And as the writer went on to remind his readers, this was not 'industrial killing from a distance': 'Every Englishman who died at Towton was pierced by arrows, stabbed, bludgeoned or crushed by another Englishman.'

With dukedoms and principalities battling for supremacy, mid fifteenth-century Europe resembled some attritional game of Risk, with borders constantly redrawn, and war an ever-present threat. In almost every village in Europe, men of fighting age were expected to exist in a state of permanent military readiness, maintaining weapons and armour in combat-ready condition, and participating in regular training.

No one played this game with more ruthless panache than Philip III, Duke of Burgundy. His fluid empire, an extensive agglomeration of prosperous fiefdoms laid out along both sides of the largely notional border between the French kingdom and 'Germany', brought in such vast wealth that his court outshone any in Europe. When he went on tour – which was almost constantly, given that his ever-expanding realm lacked a fixed capital – he took with him a tent that was 'more a town than a pavilion', with wooden towers, crenellated walls and sufficient space in its many subsidiary canvas enclosures to sleep 3,000 courtiers and servants. And he partied hard: at one Burgundian bacchanal held on a boat on the Rhine, the guests danced with such reckless abandon that the deck gave way; 140 partygoers drowned in the subsequent capsize.

Much of Philip's success was down to skilful diplomacy – alliances, political marriages and so on – and some was down to simple wealth: in 1443, he bought Luxembourg. But the elephant at the bargaining table was his army, influenced in tactics and organisation by that of imperial Rome, and widely acknowledged as the most efficient fighting force of its time.

In 1467 Philip went off to that 3,000-man tent in the sky, and, as was often the way back then, with the main man gone everything swiftly went breastplates-up. His distinctly less canny son and heir, Charles, made so many enemies that he had to employ six people to taste his food, as well as having everything that passed his lips checked for poison by 'assay with a piece of unicorn horn'.

Impetuously eager to outdo Daddy, and perhaps figuring he'd better live up to the new tag he'd given himself, in 1476 Charles the Bold invaded the Swiss Confederation. After laying successful siege to the castle of Grandson, and dutifully stringing up every member of the surrendering garrison, he turned his 20,000 troops to face the Swiss reinforcements that now belatedly pitched up.

What followed ensured the battle's place in history: Grandson, grandmother of all cock-ups. Ordered to about-face and retire a certain distance to allow the Burgundian artillery a clear view of the enemy, Charles's front ranks somehow became so confused that when a scattering of Swiss troops appeared through a nearby forest they panicked, sparking off a disorientated, full-scale retreat. Having barely fired a shot or swung a pike, the astonished Swiss soon found themselves wandering through the abandoned Burgundian camp – the traditional mobile city with a perimeter of around 5km, now populated only by an estimated 2,000 'camp girls'. The Burgundians regrouped, but never won another battle. Less than a year after the Grandson debacle, Charles met his end at the battle of Nancy; the mighty empire built up by his father died with him.

A cautionary tale of arrogance, ineptitude and bloody comeuppance, and one that after my previous two historical adventures I had no desire to experience outside the pages of *The Golden Age of Burgundy*. Yet somehow here I was, setting off to enlist with the Company of Saynt George, a military unit in Burgundian service, *circa* 1474. If I'd hoped that the Battle of Scoutcamp Wood was my war to end all wars, I'd hoped in vain.

The past is a foreign country, said L.P. Hartley. And this time he was right: fifteenth-century France, via Switzerland. I flew into Bern with Darwin Air, which prompted inner speculation on the 533 years of urban evolution I was soon to undo. Banking over the ominously snow-slathered peaks that girdled the Swiss capital, these wonderings intensified: even here, in the prosperous, technocratic heart of the planet's most modern and densely populous continent, the clustered hill villages and pine-dense valleys exuded an air of unhurried timelessness. Pick a square foot of Europe at random and the chances are man won't have done much to it in the last half millennium. Yet if I'd been plonked down in that square foot in 1474, dressed and equipped as I currently was, even the least significant of my possessions – forget the quartz watch and mobile phone, I'm talking about a single machine-stitched sock or even a sheet of lined notebook paper – would have dumbfounded the locals, then compelled them to burn me as a witch. For all I knew, so might the men I was on my way to meet.

As secretary of what I'd soon start calling the Company, Christian Folini was effective leader of a group whose reputation for hardcore medieval authenticity was familiar to re-enactors around the world. Even a cursory glance at the online details of the event he had kindly invited me to attend made it abundantly plain that I was about to enter the upper echelons of Hrothgar's Scale of Historical Accuracy.

Most prominently, I would be accommodated not in a campsite or some ersatz period reconstruction, but garrisoned in a starkly bona fide castle – Haut-Koenigsbourg, a many-towered medieval fortress stuck atop a ridge near Colmar in the Alsace. On the bus from Bern airport I'd re-acquainted myself with my downloaded précis of the castle's history: its twelfth-century origins, its strategic importance on the Burgundians' eastern periphery, and the subsequent centuries of crumbling abandonment ended by Kaiser Wilhelm, who celebrated Alsace's annexation into his empire by having Haut-Koenigsbourg lavishly restored to its medieval – and, um, 'German' – pomp.

Of more immediate concern was Christian's emailed introduction to the life I would shortly be leading within its brick-red sandstone walls. The 150-odd participants would sleep 'under the roof', which sounded cosy but probably wasn't: 'It can get quite cold,' he'd written, 'and we permit only a straw-bag and woollen blanket.'

One re-enactment season had ended; another had just begun. But only barely: Christian's final weather report – 'The snow inside the castle has almost gone' – despatched me off down Chiswick High Road in search of thermal protection. That I would be donning this furtively had been made plain by an illustrated article in the Company's newsletter, *Dragon*, detailing approved designs of hand-stitched linen underwear. 'Fig i: a common style of fifteenth-century underpants, based on several contemporary illustrations (Flemish Decameron *c.*1430–40, Ducal Palace, Dijon, etc.) . . . fig m: underpants with ties appear in some Swiss sources.' The best I could manage was fig z: shorts of boxer, inside out, labelling excised (Company of St Michael). These boys weren't so much the period fashion police as the inquisition.

I came home with long johns, two woollen vests and a pair of ankle-high cycling socks that I had proved to myself – and a curious bike-shop assistant – could be covertly worn under my Viking peasant shoes. I could only hope all this would do. Whatever a straw-bag was, I figured Darwin Air wouldn't welcome one into their hold, and the only un-patterned, natural-fabric blanket I'd been able to find was luridly Jackson Pollocked through many years service as a hapless decorator's dust-sheet.

With its wobbling pushbikes and trundling trams, Bern's pace of life could not be described as breathless. I sat on a bench outside the station for a last run-through of the 'useful phrases' printed out from an edition of *Dragon*, and felt uncomfortable squaring the uncouth contents with the well-presented lunchtime shoppers ambling benignly by. Was that headscarfed old dear really the direct descendant of a folysh bitchfox and a dyrty shitten knave? Could I picture some forebear of those satchel-backed, bespectacled schoolboys hoofing a doltish horson in the jewylls?

Pressing a buzzer marked C. FOLINI an hour later, I found such imaginings rather easier to entertain. I had by then experienced central Bern's overwhelmingly medieval ambience, the walk-through astronomical clocks, the codpiece-flaunting statues, the Gothic cathedral in whose cobbled shadow I now stood. A brief tour of the city museum had taught me that Bern meant 'bears', and that its unlikely status as Switzerland's capital dated back to the late Middle Ages, when Bern dominated a large swathe of the region as the largest city-state north of the Alps.

I also now knew that Bern's armies had been on the winning side at Grandson: the 500 years of peace that Harry Lime derided so flippantly in *The Third Man* dated only from the end of the wars that did for the Burgundian empire. For many decades before that time, and many more after, Swiss mercenaries were so highly esteemed that almost every court in Europe employed them as guards. The Pope, famously, still does. In re-enacting the fifteenth century, a resident of Bern was re-enacting not only his city's glorious zenith, but a time when the menfolk of Switzerland, however starkly implausible it seemed, were feared across the continent as Europe's hardest bastards.

Trim, slight and possessed of a blindingly toothy smile, the pony-tailed young man who welcomed me through the door was not an obvious incarnation of this past. Christian's apartment was the first re-enactor's home I had entered, and it did not disappoint. Up in the eaves of a venerable townhouse, it looked out across a dishevelled sea of gabled roofs from one side, and the cathedral's gargoyles from the other. Within its austere, almost monastic interior there was no sign of a television, and peeping through into the bedroom I noted that Christian and his quietly charming girlfriend Saara – a theology student who hoped to apply for the ministry – slept in single beds. The frisson of pious disapproval I detected while placing a bottle of red wine on the tiny dining table made me very glad I'd left my intended token of gratitude – a litre of single malt – back in my hotel up the road.

Over a simple repast of pasta, Christian cheerfully recalled his teenage LARPing ('A feudal-era shogun, surveying his desert kingdom from a youth-hostel window'), and how it had led him by stages towards the Company of St George.

I never quite grasped precisely how or why the group acquired its name, though it appeared connected to the Swiss-resident British expats who founded the Company back in the eighties (one, I later learned, was a fantasy artist who had helped design orcs for the *Lord of the Rings* films). Famously, though, George – very probably a third-century martyr, tortured and beheaded in Palestine – never set foot in England, and it's not at all clear how or why he bagged the national-saint job.

The re-enactment group that bore his name described itself as 'a small late-medieval fifteenth-century military company of castle garrison with its attendant craftsmen and their families'. Christian was at pains to emphasise the banality of this unit: 'We are in Burgundian service,' he told me, in flawless, lightly accented English, 'but under a very minor lord who pays us only moderately well.' He also eagerly cited the historical evidence that authenticated his group's very mixed nationalities – it's apparently common to find multilingual graffiti, including English, in places right across Europe where such companies were billeted.

More glumly, Christian related the political ructions that had riven the group in recent months. I'd read on the Company's website that his ascent through the ranks had begun with an 'extraordinary' article he'd composed for *Dragon* on 'luggage and transport'; it seemed that some of the original founders, now in their sixties, resented both Christian's sudden rise to prominence and what they saw as his overbearing authoritarianism. He sighed, then gave me another of those full-beam grins. 'So, anyway – let me see your equipment!'

My unshared titter of ribaldry died away, and I faced up to the moment I had been dreading since my first encounter with *Dragon*'s online back issues, with their great treatises upon correct handsaw designs, and statements redolent of tireless, devotional toil: 'I have yet to find drawers in a table as early as the 1470s'; 'There is a tendency to leap to conclusions – an observation that applies especially to trestles'. The Viking shoes aside, all I'd dared bring along was a drawstring suede purse stolen from my daughters' handbag collection. The afternoon before leaving, I'd endeavoured to age this accessory by pulling it over my right foot and performing a sort of one-legged *Riverdance* on the patio. Witnessing this scene over his fence, then hearing my mumbled explanations, my neighbour Stephan, an experienced set designer, advised rubbing powder paint and cooking oil into the suede.

Christian gingerly examined the greasy aftermath of this procedure and smiled less brilliantly than was his wont. Then he went off to his equipment cupboard, and returned with a great many items: a pewter cup, a wooden bowl and spoon and a great long woollen cloak he'd fashioned from an East German army blanket. 'And here, to tie your clothes together.' He tossed me a ragged square of pigskin, then laid down a pair of scissors and an open tub of lard. Who knows in what idiotic fashion I'd have combined all these if he hadn't then shown me. When the last lace-length strip had been manually impregnated with congealed fat, I wiped my fingers on my stupid purse and shook Christian's hand. 'See you tomorrow morning, six forty-five,' he said.

'Sorry,' murmured Saara with a little smile. 'I know how difficult it is for you English to get up early.'

After a few fitful hours of sleep and an epic shower apparently intended to wash away many days of medieval filth in advance, I was sharing the back seat of Christian's small hired Peugeot with two baskets of beeswax candles, a bundle of grey blankets and some sort of entrenching tool. It was raining; I dozed. We stopped to pick up a jolly maiden named Kaja, and then at a stonemason's, from whose workshop Christian emerged with two buckets filled with cannonballs.

The purpose of these became apparent in a very quiet village soon after, when Christian creakily raised an up-and-over garage door to reveal two artillery barrels marooned in a jumble of trestles, stools, cauldrons, earthenware, ironware, wickerware, saws, axes and a great many savagely spike-topped halberds and pikes. It was a dumbfounding moment, the closest I've ever come to knowing how Lord Carnarvon and Howard Carter felt that day down in the Valley of the Kings.

A professional haulier rumbled up in a big lorry, which over two very wet hours we almost entirely filled with the contents of the garage. When it was done we stood back, rested our rusty, damp hands on our hips and looked up at the extraordinary load. 'So,' said the driver, in the perfect English I was already taking for granted, 'where is your theatre?'

There was still a lot of driving to do, and while other people did it I hunkered down with my candles and mattocks for a last run through the incredibly detailed background scenario Christian had laid out for our event. The days before the Company arrived at Haut-Koenigsbourg had not been uneventful: a Burgundian messenger had been ambushed and his nose cut off; a group of burglars had attempted to scale the castle walls; a noblewoman had slipped on a wet step in the inner castle, 'but luckily, her leg did not break'.

Then it was into the routine we would adapt to once garrisoned at the castle, one largely dictated by the rule that 'the Company does not function as a democracy'. Participants would be split into ten-man *dizaines* under the command of a *dizainier*, himself responsible by turn to the quartermaster, the provost, the petty captain and the captain. With a curious blend of dread and excitement I re-familiarised myself with the daily drill: 'The wake-up call will be around 0700. We will have morning prayers before breakfast. The provost has an eye to check they are being attended. Each *dizaine* will by rota help in the kitchen, clean the cauldrons, provide the artisan stations with food, chop firewood and support the quarter-master with whatever work there may be. Two of the *dizaines* will be on guard during the night.' The reward if I could stick all this until Friday: 'the arrest and trial of a Polish agitator for causing unrest'.

The expectation of utter authenticity went without saying, alluded to only in a footnote: 'As usual, no smoking visible to non-smokers. Likewise, no use of cameras in costume. If you want to take pictures, please put on modern clothing.' I wiped a porthole in the condensation, gazed at the grey-misted hills and thought again of the troubling paragraph I'd found in the 1990 issue of *Dragon*. 'This year at le Puy, a very small group of the Company indulged in an extremely personal "hobby" that finally tested the good humour and tolerance of their comrades, and brought semi-official complaints on the flight back.'

I'd wondered if there would ever be a good time to find out more about this 'hobby', and if it was still practised. At any rate, this was not that time: with our destination now apparent as a tall red smear on a distant hilltop, Christian's right foot eased towards the floor and the gleam in his eye evolved from cheery to manic. His mobile rang, and in distracted impatience and three languages he brusquely despatched an enquiry related to his work as a web-server engineer. '*Ja, ja, ja . . . eh bien*, reboot *le* router!'

The road shrank and rose and twisted; a vast battlement the colour of dried blood reared out of the mist; Christian wrenched up the handbrake, leapt out, and scuttled in through an arched doorway the height and breadth of a double-decker. I followed him and stumbled straight into a Bruegel.

The slushy, snow-bordered courtyard within was alive with medieval scurrying: a clay-slathered potter in pointy boots and a pointy felt hat, shouldering his wheel; dangly capped minstrels lugging lutes and flutes; florid, linen-coiffed wenches with spinning wheels and baskets of apples; frowning gentry in fur-trimmed cloaks; shrieking urchins in bring-out-your-dead cowls. Liveried soldiers were stacking breastplates, standards, shields and helmets beside a barn, home to a small mountain of hay, half a dozen comatose figures in tights, felt caps pulled over their faces, three pitchforks and perhaps 200 crates of bottled alcohol.

For a while I gawped from the foot of the mighty witch-hatted tower that bore down on us, overwhelmed by the scene's scale and faultless plausibility. Then a lofty, green-cloaked man with a fat armful of fabric and a huge smile breaking through his riotous facial hair strode up, and addressed me in high-pitched Germanic English. 'Tim, yes?'

This was it: I blinked hard and launched recklessly into my rehearsed opening gambit. 'Hail-fellow-tis-pity-indeed-God-hath-not-sent-us-a-faire-day-how-goes-it-with-thee.'

The big man's smile faltered; in horror I realised I had shown insufficient respect. 'Sire!' I blurted. 'Lord . . . master . . . my liege?'

He wrinkled his sizeable nose, then let forth a shrill guffaw. 'Welcome to 1474, dude!' And he handed me a big pile of multi-coloured clothing.

Feeling my whole head burning, I grasped this bundle and a linen sack, which, on his instructions, I stuffed haphazardly with barn hay. Tottering beneath this load, now supplemented with my holdall of personal belongings, I followed him up a wooden staircase, along a rickety covered walkway, through a series of dim chambers strewn with barrels and baskets and finally – stumble, curse, juggle, drop – up a narrow stepladder. 'Your bedroom!' he beamed, then scuttled back down through the trapdoor before I'd had a chance to thank him.

Before me, sparsely illuminated by candle lanterns hung from a cat's cradle of eaves and crossbeams, yawned the largest attic

I had ever encountered. Whispery shufflings encroached from unseen corners; as my eyes attuned I could make out caped and cowled figures laying out bedding and possessions. Hourglasses, daggers and iron-hooped buckets lay strewn around; in vain I scanned the glazed earthenware, wood, leather and linen for any trace of modern life. As one of the many Scandinavian participants would later tell me, with a mixture of pride and shame, 'When it comes to re-enactment, we are the real super-nerds.'

This previously unencountered level of dedication was embodied by the Jewish merchant I'd seen carrying his seven-branched candlesticks across the courtyard. That evening I learned he had not only personally tailored his entire outfit, from those Star-of-David belt studs to that bobble-topped yellow skullcap, but hand-fashioned an oil lamp and other accessories from period designs on display only in Jerusalem museums, learned how to bake the requisite type of unleavened bread, and – despite not actually being Jewish – mastered the Hebrew text and speech necessary for performing religious ceremonies. And he had done all this in six months.

I made my home at the attic's far edge, just by a sizeable gap where roof failed to meet floor. Trying to ignore the graveyard mist curling up through this opening, I stripped off my twenty-first-century wardrobe, bundled it away with my nylon holdall and paint blanket under the straw sack, and set about making sense of the outfit I'd been given. It was a task that would prove distantly beyond me in the four days ahead.

Night had fallen when at last I creaked back down the stepladder. First into shot came my death-scented peasant shoes, followed by two tightly woollen-clad legs: one Lincoln green, one off-white. Somewhere around mid-thigh lay the bottom hem of an extremely capacious scarlet wool tunic, bunched in at the waist with a thin leather belt from which dangled that shrieking sore thumb of a patchwork bag and a linen knapsack heavy with thigh-battering utensils. Next up a red sleeve the girth of a Brotherhood of Man trouser leg, then another, a quick flash of moss-coloured linen jerkin and the

119

greasy pig-strips that half-fastened it at the neck, a crumpled
sliver of the raw linen shift beneath this and just the hint of
the thermal vest beneath that, and then the crowning glory –
a skull-clinging, eyebrow-grazing dome of a cap, one half red,
the other black. Manchester United's court jester.

I slipped and scuffled along the dark walkway, stopping many
times to yank up my green and white hose, unsatisfactorily
attached to my jerkin using the eyelets and a dozen-odd metal-
tipped laces (sorry, 'points'). Very cold moisture was already
blotting through those thin leather soles and the covert cycling
socks, and my long johns didn't seem nearly long enough. But
if I was shivering, it was largely down to a sense of appre-
hension more powerful than I had experienced at any previous
re-enactment. Because already, this didn't feel like one.

I tagged on to a column of hooded, lantern-carrying
mutterers, and followed them through an archway, up a
perilously slick-stoned path against the outer wall and into an
open area flanked by soaring walls and towers. In one corner
a fire was bringing a cauldron of root vegetables to the boil,
and amongst its circle of Smurf-hatted huddlers I found many
forms of comfort. Most principally, there was confirmation all
around that the Company's lingua franca was not fye-on-thee,
but MTV. One of the half-dozen Brits warming their hands
amongst the Swiss, Germans, Frenchmen, Poles and Czechs
explained why: 'If it can be done properly, like the kit and food
and that, then we do it properly. If it can't, like getting everyone
to talk medieval, then we don't. No point. Same goes with
daft period names. I'm Baz.'

Baz was a crop-headed ox of a man who I'd earlier seen
shouldering three of the Company's hefty standing shields at
once; no one else had managed two. He filled my tiny pewter
cup from a vast flagon of ale and aimed his thousand-furlong
stare up at the battlements. 'No matter how many times I do
these things,' he said, in pancake-flat Yorkshire tones, 'that
thrill never goes away. Fuck: I'm living in a castle.' Baz went
on to tell me of his day-job as a fencer, his past as a roadie,
bouncer and hardcore punk, his dalliance with Second World

War re-enactment as a Russian infantryman, his £1,500 peasant outfit.

His oft-heard pronouncement as the kitchen area was prepared became a catchphrase: 'Show me where you want the hole and I'll dig it.' As the physical embodiment of a stout yeoman, Baz was plainly back where he belonged. If it was true of the Vikings, it was even truer of this lot – I couldn't avoid concluding that many Company members had gone medieval largely because their face fitted. Put-upon slap-headed fatso in the twenty-first century; respected friar in the fifteenth.

We filed past the cauldrons for a ladle of soupy stew, and after a mumbled, desultory grace, washed it down with a monstrous surfeit of ale. In the days ahead I would learn that in glorious contradiction of Christian's domestic precedent, getting medievally tanked up was one of the duties of castle life: you don't have to be drunk to work here, but it helps. Only when ordered to do a run to the booze barn, there to decant ale from deposit bottle to glazed earthenware, did I discover our brew of choice to be the monk-strength ruin of many a Belgian. And by then, it was already much too late.

At some indeterminate point in the night I found myself ricocheting along the covered walkway, my muddied hose bearing testament to a fitful mastery of the medieval walk that was apparently obligatory: a sort of cocksure, rolling gait, half cowboy, half costermonger.

This method of progress proved very poorly adapted to the terrain encountered once I'd ascended the trap-door stepladder at the third attempt. After two swaggering strides into the attic blackness, it was made vocally apparent that many more people had made their beds here during my absence, and that most of these were now in them. For a minute I stood there, swaying gently as I waited for my eyes to adjust. When I accepted they wouldn't, I inched unsteadily across the dusty boards, outstretched arms probing the dark.

Twice my forehead impacted forcefully with some ancient beam; twice I recoiled and felt my wet heels make human contact. Chivvied off course by tuts and hissed Teutonic curses,

I was soon utterly, utterly lost. At one point I tripped over something, or someone, and, finding myself prostrate on a stretch of unoccupied floor, very nearly didn't get up again. Only after an almost tearful eternity of hunched fumbling – and one very unfortunate false alarm – did I locate my straw-bag. Effortfully I removed one sodden shoe, and after yanking in vain at the other flopped backwards, half covering myself with the paint blanket and Christian's cloak. Shortly after I pulled both of these off, and stuffed them into the numbing blast that rushed in through the gap by my head.

It was a predictably trying morning. Terrified by the prospect of a day in the stocks – the default punishment, I imagined, for any idle heathen who forswore morning prayers – I'd blundered about the castle's many courtyards in search of the chapel, at length finding a plain and very damp chamber where a stubbled and bleary Englishman in a crumpled white habit was lighting candles with a shaky hand. For half an hour he mumbled schoolboy Latin at his filthy, frozen and very modest congregation; evidently, threats of a headcount were included only to add a little colour to the scenario.

My drunken failure to wash up the night before meant a breakfast of turnip-tainted porridge, and as the assembled Company stood in silence for our debut morning muster, the toothbrush I'd secreted down the front of my tunic dropped to the flagstones with a tell-tale plasticky tinkle. The harlequin throng around me wheeled about as one; I laughed foolishly as I stooped to pick it up, but I laughed alone.

Standing on a low wall before us, Christian – resplendent in the red and white Company livery – ordered us into *dizaines* by name. I wound up in a largely Scandinavian unit, headed by a man called Johann who was by some distance the most conspicuous human presence at Haut-Koenigsbourg. At six foot four he was the tallest Company member; with an exuberant Prussian-general moustache he was also the most facially flamboyant. Most compellingly, in that keenly fought contest for the castle's daftest wardrobe, no one ever came close. That morning he teamed his fur-trimmed scarlet coat and red and cream hose with a towering bell of a hat, silly of itself, but also quite plainly intended to suggest the business end of a great big cock. Yet somehow – perhaps because of the defiant, preening self-confidence with which he carried himself – he got away with it. Somehow, in fact, he looked like the coolest man in all Christendom.

Our *dizaine*'s first duty was guarding the main gate, which meant kitting up in armour and helping ourselves from the jumble of weaponry piled at the foot of the tower beside it. I picked up an eight-foot halbard with a metal end as viciously complicated as a giant Swiss Army knife with all the blades open. Everyone else had brought their own protection; a very cheerful Dane sourced a breastplate, helmet and gauntlets, and helped me on with them. Cursed as I am with the hands of Miss Muffet and the head of Mr Happy, this was not a straight-forward process. The gauntlets' giant articulated fingers were a knuckle's length out of sync with my own, making the simple act of grasping the halbard a feat of pain-defying endurance. The helmet was a kind of cross between a Nazi stormtrooper's and one of those boat-brimmed conquistador jobs; with it perched atop my bulbous skull like a party hat, I could be fairly certain the effect was not sinister. Moreover, with the chin strap fastened, I could barely open my mouth. 'Is that OK for you?' asked my kindly Dane, stepping back and trying to mould his latent guffaw into a smile of encouragement. 'Go, got geally,' I rasped through clenched jaws. 'It gurts like guck and I geel lige a gogal gickhead.'

This latter sensation intensified impressively when I learned that the castle was soon to throw open its gates to several hundred French schoolchildren, and that the Dane and I were to stand outside these gates, halbards at our side, as the Company of St George's welcoming committee. We could hear the massed squeaks of Gallic impertinence even before the castle staff arrived to unlock the mighty wooden wall that lay between us. 'Those about to die,' said the Dane with a wink as it creaked ajar. 'Oh, shuh uh,' I replied.

Being eight years old, the first few dozen visitors didn't give us much trouble. A few even called me '*monsieur*'. The Dane and I worked up an effective good-guard, bad-guard routine – he strode around, brusquely corralling the children into a double column, while I did my best to contort my jaw into a smile whilst conveying a welcome in ventriloquist French. 'Gonjour, et giengenue au chateau de Haut . . . Gerggisgerg.'

We waved in each group then waited for the next to shuffle up the steep and twisting woodland path that led from car park to castle. It was a happy time. 'Take away that postbox,' sighed the Dane, 'and you've got a perfect view.' I surveyed the misty plain beneath us and saw just what he meant: a scattering of rural settlements whose only eminent structures were church spires, and not a car to be seen on the byways that connected them.

The trouble began with the first group old enough not to be scared of the Dane, tall enough to see how stupid my helmet looked, and bold enough to tell me. Our routine quickly fell apart. The Dane aimed his glower at them and they sneered; I attempted a throttled greeting and they jeered. When we noticed their accompanying teachers nudging each other and giggling, we gave up.

For the next half an hour I stood in the cold, white sun, gazing in resignation through the leafless trees as sniggering young Frenchmen flicked my breastplate, rapped my helmet and employed me as a prop in an endless series of demeaning photographs. It was an ignominy I'd so often seen busby-clad guardsman enduring at the hands of junior tourists on the Mall, and one I endured with appropriate stoicism. At least until a youth in a turquoise tracksuit snatched my halbard away, and I trotted off in clanky pursuit screeching gritted, incomprehensible abuse.

I'd only just retrieved it when Johann, somehow resplendent in a sort of metal skullcap accessorised with crimson ostrich feathers and what looked like giant steel earmuffs, led the balance of his *dizaine* out through the gates. Relief that my shift was over lasted as long as Johann's announcement that we were, at this very minute and in this very place, to put on a display of halbard drill.

'Raise halbards . . . carry halbards . . . turn . . . prepare to . . . ah, Mr Englishman?' Hiding in the middle row had been a mistake – four orders in and my unschooled recklessness with this enormous weapon had cleaved a huge hole in the ranks ahead and behind. The Dane's reward for whispering quickfire tips over his shoulder was an errant spike snagged in the nape of his cowl; while detaching this I endeavoured to whack a passing teacher with my weapon's stump end. In my subsequent research I found the halbard thus described: 'In the hands of an agile trained man a formidable weapon, but otherwise more dangerous to the wielders' companions.' They might as well have given Buster Keaton a ladder, nailed a big saw to one end and sent him off down a crowded high street.

After a quiet word it was agreed that I should stay guarding the gate while the drill continued; I watched as my *dizaine* clumped off into the woods for a formation march around the walls. It was much quieter now, with most of the school parties already inside the castle, but reflective appreciation of the timelessly bucolic plain laid out distantly beneath was no match for the ratcheting discomfort of my vice-like finger and headwear. By the time Johann led his boys back up the forest to meet me the pain was so great I could barely focus. My pulsing brain seemed set to escape through whatever head-hole it could find; it was as if a door had been gently closed on my halbard-holding right hand, and not opened.

Johann brought the halbardiers to attention, then sauntered across and gave me a quick up and down. 'Listen, ah . . .'

'His name's Tim,' supplied the Dane, noting my wan distraction.

'Listen, Jim, there's this thing about armour.' My commander lightly clanked his own breastplate with both gauntlets. 'Because I'm tall and slender, armourers love me. I look *really great* in this stuff.' He allowed himself a smile of deep content, then sighed. 'But I have to say you just look really stupid.'

This seemed more than a little rich from a man with a huge bouquet of feathers on his head, but I gazed up at him without reproach: it was a statement of inarguable fact, delivered with commendable simplicity.

'I'm thinking perhaps you could . . .' He broke off, idly fingering his moustache with a steel-plated digit and looking vaguely about. 'Go somewhere else and never return,' was doubtless his preferred conclusion to this sentence, but after a while he concocted something more diplomatic. 'Perhaps you could go to the top of this tower, and help with the handgun.' I followed his gaze up and spotted a thick, hexagonal barrel poking out of a space in the red stone. A moment later, gleefully relieved of my armour, I bounded up three rickety flights of wooden stairs and found my medieval career relaunched with a glorious, shattering bang.

Being a four-foot tube of heavy black iron with a bore the size of a golf ball, the handgun proved inaptly named. More accurately it was a sawn-off, wheelless cannon, or perhaps a fifteenth-century bazooka. The Swedish crew preparing this crudely magnificent firearm for action included the self-taught blacksmith responsible for its manufacture: the day after he offered to make me one for €900, and the day after that I very nearly placed an order. All my best memories of 1474 involved the handgun, but none are more treasured than those of the two afternoon hours I spent up in that smoke-filled, plank-floored turret.

Working as a crew of three, we rotated jobs. I spent my first shift carefully decanting crumbly gunpowder from a stoppered cow's horn into torn squares of paper, sealing each with a twist and passing it to the second in line (a lofty Dane whose physique, stubbled good looks and unusually stainless smile made him the undisputed goodwife's choice), who dropped it down the gun's gaping muzzle, followed by a wad of straw and a good damping down with the ramrod, then handed the loaded weapon to the gunner. He heaved the mighty beast through the small window, then waited as I tipped a little gunpowder over the touch hole to prime the charge, before number two ignited this with our linstock, a slow-burning length of rope wound round a pole. After a quarter-second of heavily pregnant silence, the known world was filled with an apocalyptic blast that shook the stone walls around us, caused some internal organs to change places and left our turret filled with sulphurous smoke and boyish peals of hysterical laughter. I might never make the mental leap back to 1474, but there I was in 1980, watching red-hot pieces of Dinky shrapnel scythe across our back garden.

It was an especially happy moment when my first turn at firing the gun coincided with the egress of the older school parties. We waited until the outside courtyard directly beneath us was thronged with truculent adolescents, then filled our cast-iron avenger with a double charge of powder . . . If I listen closely, I can still hear that chorus of harrowed, whimpering moans.

The three of us stumbled blinking out of the tower in a state of dazed, sooty-faced elation, looking like Guy Fawkes and his boys might have done if things had gone to plan. Aimless wandering was not tolerated for long amongst the lower orders, and a passing officer swiftly seconded me to wheelbarrow duty – ferrying wood from a necessarily huge pile to the kitchen fire, and returning with a load of festering scraps to tip in the neighbouring spoil pit.

The Dane was helping me shovel in turnip tops and fish heads when the next *dizaine* marched up to take their turn on guard shift. 'If you thought you had a bad time, watch this,' he said, as the crop-headed German *dizainier* barked out the first drill command. His furious displeasure at one soldier's response swiftly reduced the culprit to wobbly-lipped distress.

'Had enough? Want to go home to mamma? Huh? HUH?' A tear rolled down a bearded cheek, and a traumatised school party scuttled by.

At this point a liveried gentleman I hadn't seen before strode up, looking as stern as a man with an Emo Philips' bowl cut is ever likely to. He presented me with the breastplate I'd worn that morning, silently indicated its many rust patches, and before departing issued a single-word instruction: 'Remove.'

I spent the remaining hours of daylight, and a couple beyond, unsuccessfully engaged in a task that would deprive me of the Trial of the Polish Agitator. It seemed a ridiculous undertaking when everyone else had surely employed proprietary chemicals to bring their armour to a showroom shine. Seeing me work away at an orange scab with my thumbnail, a passing member of the kitchen shift suggested using 'abrasive material': after fruitless experimentation with charcoal and salt, I wound up furiously scouring the hateful object with handfuls of ground-up castle. The alarmingly counter-productive results of this meant that a short while later I found myself secreting the breast-plate behind a bale of hay at the back of the booze barn.

Friday night meant a fish supper, which would add pollocky undertones to the complex flavours impregnating my bowl. In the cauldron queue I eavesdropped on the loudest conversation: a debate introduced by its Austrian originator as 'why we do this shit'. A predictable majority, including nearly all the Scandinavians, were searching for life after LARP; a couple of Brits had more obscurely graduated to hardcore re-enactment from 'hippie fairs'; a German newbie said she'd found herself inspired during a tour of Scottish castles. Most intriguing were the three Dover customs officers whose curiosity was first piqued by repeated contact with tooled-up re-enactors in the red channel.

For a great many Company members, four days of unwashed medieval knees-ups applied a little historical balance to working lives spent, like Christian's, at the soulless, lonely frontier of twenty-first-century information technology. For a very few, like Jim the Potter, this was a full-time way of life: throughout the re-enacting season he travelled the continent, hawking his wares at events and fairs. Having made a career from his historical hobby, Jim was the envy of all Company members, or at least all who hadn't taken the time to imagine living for half the year in the back of a Transit van.

With the last cauldron drained, one of the Poles walked about with a wheelbarrow of straw hats he was trying to sell, while everyone leant against castle walls striking the standard medieval quaffing pose. Why not give it a go? Curl an imaginary drinking vessel to your puffed out chest, plant the other fist on your hip, splay your legs slightly and stick out a lower lip. A slight glower helps. Imagine Henry VIII down his local, warming his arse by the fire. I was getting quite good at it when two Company officers rushed up from the gate babbling theatrically about a hostile party in the woods.

'Here we go,' sighed Baz, reeling his lower lip back in as liveried guards scuttled along the dim battlements above. 'Some sort of daft "repel the invaders" thing's about to happen.' Over supper he'd delivered a rundown of his greatest battlefield hits: the Tewkesbury re-enactment where his one-man charge had broken right through the enemy lines, a street-based event in Spain which had evolved into a kind of human Pamplona, the Running of the Baz. The veteran of these and many other brutal victories shook his head and drained an impressively capacious tankard. 'It's dark, so you can't use sharps . . . and if we're not hitting each other, I mean *properly*, what's the bloody point?'

Reassured that I probably wouldn't be hurt, I left him there and jogged across to our handgun tower. There was a lookout already in place at the top; I recognised him as the dishevelled priest. 'Hello there,' he drawled, still peering out of the window. 'I'm Brother Balthasar, Andy, whatever. Oh – here they come.' I squeezed my head alongside his and squinted into the night. A glint of armour, a flash of red feather – it was the Swedes, of course, manhandling their handgun through the moonlit forest.

A rather desultory exchange ensued; the Swedes later complained, with much justification, at the lack of defensive activity. They let off a couple of blasts in our direction, then made a charge at the front gate; we shrugged a bit until someone tottered up the tower stairs with a bucket of water, and emptied it on the invaders through the 'boiling-oil' hole.

'All a bit too *Python*, this,' said Brother Balthasar, during the aimless stand-off that ensued. He snapped soon after, sticking his head right out the window to roar great chunks of John Cleese's silly-English-niggits speech at the puny enemy force gathered distantly beneath. All I really brought away from this experience was an enhanced appreciation of how much better it must have felt to be this side of the huge stone wall. To be – oh, *really*, Brother Balthasar – inside the castle pissing out.

It rained again, and sliding off to bed I wondered how anyone completed even a stunted medieval lifespan without shattering at least one limb, and thus ending their one-score-years-and-ten as a hobbled invalid. That dark and lonely walk back to the attic dormitory always seemed to shrink what you might call the time difference; the harsher realities of fifteenth-century life never seemed more tangible. Trailing my cloak through the mud and pools of whiffy froth, and flinching at every woodland scuttle, I was struck by the self-evident but otherwise elusive truth that this was indeed how all Moores had once lived. On the first night, this thought had been accompanied with pity for my forebears; just a day later, I found it giving way to towering respect. Perhaps, with two more days to come, I could still make that final leap to envy.

Being less drunk, I negotiated the trans-attic assault course in under ten minutes, and once at my palliasse successfully removed the lashed-together doublet and hose, using the 'babygro' method advised by Baz: untying the front two 'points', then pulling my arms and legs out in turn. It was the first time I had managed to remove any part of my medieval outfit.

Assured by the sound of a thousand snoring medievalists, I set off for an early-hours comfort break by the light of my mobile phone, and was navigating the trap-door steps when the frail illumination picked out an ascending hand. It belonged to a middle-aged German, one of the many Company members hairily decorated with a 'tache-less, Henry VIII face-girdler. 'Maybe we all have *this*,' he hissed, flicking a ghostly finger at the phone as I passed him, 'but only you have *these*.' And in the quarter-watt half-light I saw the beardless parts of his face pucker in elaborate contempt, his gaze fixed hatefully upon my thermal undergarments. Out of sight, in this realm, was never out of mind. Every night after that I peed through the hole in the roof. Or at least tried to.

First to arrive for prayers, I found Brother Balthasar arranging candles on the altar, mumbling Doris Day songs customised with yawned profanities. When the room was half full he uncrumpled his liturgical crib sheet, coughed horribly, and embarked on those sanctus-spiritus mutterings. Ten minutes in he briefly lost his place; believing the service at an end, his flock filed as one towards the door. Brother Balthasar stopped us in our tracks with a hoarse and loutish bellow. 'Oi! Not so fast. Plenty more where that came from.' And on he murmured, and on, and on.

Christian kicked off the post-breakfast muster with a rundown of found property; the presence of 'a pair of women's hiking boots' amidst the tankards and daggers sparked off loud jeers. He finished with a reprimand to the many artisans who'd been deserting their stations, and whose presence I had completely forgotten about. Later that afternoon I passed amongst the knife-makers, pewter-casters and blacksmiths who plied their fiery trades along the far side of the outer bailey – how fulfilling to engage this latter artisan in informed debate, and not just because there were those who called him Dwayne.

It would be two days, though, before I was given leave for a whistle-stop tour of the parallel kingdom that was the castle's only properly habitable tower, home to manuscript illumina-tors, fancy needleworkers, Jim the Potter and a shuffling surfeit of warmth-seeking visitors. I concluded that it was probably authentic to the spirit of a fifteenth-century castle that high-status craftspeople (if not potters) should exist in a rarefied world-within-a-world from which the low-born likes of me were excluded. And that as things in there seemed dreadfully insipid when set against the explosive excitements of outdoor life, this was a social apartheid I was happy to endure.

I'd first met Barbara when helping dismember her in a lock-up garage, and in the hours ahead I would acquire a very intimate knowledge of her every nook and cranny. Named after a saint – as was her sister artillery piece, Catherine – Barbara was the Company's apparently faithful reproduction of a fifteenth-century iron-barrelled, breech-loading cannon. Our *dizaine*'s morning duty was to lug her extremely weighty component parts, and the many iron pins and hoops that held them all together, from the stable block to the elected artillery courtyard, over at the far side of the castle. This was an uphill journey on rain-slick flagstones, one which demanded a degree of team co-ordination as yet beyond us. At one point a wheel got away from one of the Swedes and me; I watched it roll waywardly off down the inner bailey, imagining the deadly game of human skittles that would have enlivened the scene a few minutes later, when the castle opened its doors to visitors.

Our gun captain was a black-clad Englishman whose toneless, iron-throated sarcasm called to mind an officer addressing hopeless new recruits in the National Service years. A bevy of serving wenches arrived with a basket of bread and a jug of ale, which we worked through while half-listening to the instructional lecture and watching the small grandstand to our right fill with visiting families.

The drill he outlined required us to dismantle Barbara, reassemble her, then fire a round – blank, sadly, as the cannonballs Christian had picked up en route were merely for display. For perhaps fifteen minutes we dithered inefficiently, putting the wheels on the wrong way round, forgetting the axle bolts, mislaying the wedge that held the loaded chamber firm against the breech, and enduring the weary rhetoric with which our gun captain pointed out these failings and many more. At length, Barbara stood ready, a Swede applied his linstock to the sprinkling of primer powder, and a soul-shredding boom thundered about the ancient walls that towered around us.

Our reward from the audience was harrowed silence, then fitful applause and nervous laughter; but just as it had been up in the handgun tower, those responsible for this explosive cataclysm punched the air, whooped mindlessly and trotted about exhibiting most other male-pattern celebrations. It was as if we'd scored a thrilling goal at the end of a ponderous but ultimately brilliant team move. When the smoke had settled, I rolled up my idiotically billowing sleeves and rubbed my gunpowdered hands together: we were going to do this properly, and often. If it had all been a little *Jeux Sans Frontières* until this point, thenceforth things got very Royal Tournament.

It took time for our *dizaine* to find its best formation. Throughout the early afternoon I sat in the loading area with

Werner, a jovial, pug-nosed Belgian who had driven all the way from Brussels with 10kg of gunpowder in his boot. Our station was necessarily distant from the cannon itself: Werner merrily recounted the story of an English Civil War re-enactment that had ended in tears after windborne artillery sparks ignited dry grass in the spectators' car park, torching several vehicles and their unfortunate canine occupants.

My job here was to take the spent chamber from the runner who ferried it back from Barbara's breech, still smoking, clear away any debris and lingering embers by blowing through the torch-hole in this cast-iron facsimile of a beer tankard, pass it to Werner for a measure of powder, then grab a wodge of straw and stuff this on top, hammering it all down with a wooden rod and a mallet. 'The harder you hit it in, the bigger the bang,' said Werner with a wink. Quite soon he was doubling the powder dose, and I was clouting the straw wad so hard that the end of the rod began to split. The louder the boom thus procured, the more eagerly we worked.

Most involving was my subsequent stint as one of the heavy mob who took Barbara to bits and rebuilt her; most successful was the role I would assume in the final line-up: grabbing the loaded chamber from Werner, dashing over to the cannon and slotting it into the breech, clouting in the wedge and running away as a waiting Swede sprinkled the priming charge on.

We all had a go at applying that godlike *coup de grâce* with the linstock, but I would never enjoy a shift as our rammer/swabber. This crew member's twin tasks were to stick a big rod down the barrel in simulation of loading a cannon-ball, and then, post-bang, to douse any surviving cinders with a long-handled damp mop. My perception of what seemed at worst a tedious station was dramatically reshaped during our lunchtime discussions.

Even without a ball shoved down its gob, I learned, a primed cannon was capable of wreaking deadly havoc; if the swabbing failed to do its job, premature detonation would expel at great velocity anything that happened to be in the barrel at the time. Inevitably, this would be the ramrod; and when it was, the force of ejection meant that at least some part of the rammer's person went with it. Our gun captain had been part of a neighbouring crew when this occurred at a Battle of Crécy re-enactment in 1996; the unfortunate rammer, a noted military illustrator, had half of his right arm despatched to the horizon. (His brother, also an artist, visited him in hospital the next day with a paint brush and paper; in months he had trained his left hand to do what his right once had.)

'This is why you always stand at one side when you use the ramrod,' said one of the Swedes, before telling us of the Russian artilleryman who had failed to do so at a Napoleonic re-enactment. This unfortunate man's colleagues dragged his impaled corpse thirty metres back to their cannon, propped it up against a wheel, and continued with their work. I didn't quite know whether to believe this tale, but every time the ramming job came up for grabs thereafter I seemed to find myself paying very close attention to some part of my outfit, signalling at imaginary associates in the grandstand, or, as on one especially shameful occasion, actually hiding behind the powder box.

In fact, with artillery design still very much at the trial-and-error stage, in the mid-fifteenth century there was no such thing as a safe artillery job. In the early years, cannons accounted for as many attackers as defenders; King James II of Scotland added his name to the friendly-fire rollcall when a cannon barrel exploded during a siege in 1460.

A couple of times the primer failed to set Barbara's main charge off, meaning a call of 'Misfire!', a long wait, then a gingerly, rather whey-faced return to a lit cannon. I was never required to remove the still-live chamber, but if it had gone off halfway through this procedure there would have been more than enough shrapnel to go round. How wonderful it had felt to find at last my medieval *métier*; how distressing to learn that it was one that guaranteed being poured into a very early grave.

After lunch our gun captain was called away to drone disdainfully elsewhere, and with the matily gung-ho Werner promoted to the role, we found ourselves reinvigorated. Someone sneaked a digital watch out of their belt purse, and began timing our drill. Dismantle, reassemble, boom, dismantle, reassemble, boom . . . Once we employed Baz as a kind of *Big Bad John* human hoist, holding aloft Barbara's massive wooden chassis as Swedes darted about attaching things to it, the times began to tumble. Someone had told us the Company record for the procedure was forty point something seconds, and when – at perhaps our twentieth attempt – Werner stopped the watch at thirty-nine dead, Johann celebrated so exuberantly that he split his two-toned hose right up the arse.

Word of our achievement got around – no surprise given the stentorian length with which Johann announced it to all Haut-Koenigsbourg's distant corners – and as the light dimmed the Company's official photographer arrived to record a few re-runs. It was an honour indeed, though looking at the relevant images on their website now, I'm struck by the disappointing amount of gormless standing about I appear to be engaged in. Also by how, in a world of extremely foolish hats, few proclaimed their foolishness more stridently than mine.

There was to be fencing and dance after dinner, but as the Company lined up at the cauldrons for sausage casserole, the first of many rolls of thunder made it apparent that these would have to wait. Instead my fellow 39ers and I gathered in the shelter of the handgun tower and toasted our achievement, many times, and at length I swayed off dorm-wards through the rain, passionately determined henceforth to apply this new appetite for physical endeavour and logistical efficiency to every area of my life, instead of none.

How strange, I pondered some hours later during Brother Balthasar's unkempt grumblings, to find myself submitting so gratefully to a command-based routine. A couple of my Romans had spoken of the solace of subservience, and as a feckless, rudderless freelancer, I immediately sympathised: despite all the blathering about nanny states, these days fewer of us are told what to do than ever before. I had suggested as much during some aled-up fireside debate on the first night, though only now recalled my subsequent loud analysis of which particular nationalities were most likely to pine for the comfort of taking orders.

At muster something wonderful happened: Johann bent forward, parted the split in his hose and with a cry of purgative ecstasy laid a magnificent golden egg into my waiting hands. Or that was almost how it felt when our *dizainier* presented me, and each of my artillery companions, with a medallion ordered from the Polish pewter-caster. This depicted St Barbara, patron saint of cannoniers, and in honour of our achievement was etched with the numerals XXXIX. By sundown we'd all stitched them to our hats – at a stroke my berk-beacon head-wear became a badge of honour to be worn with pride, pride I still feel as I hold the medallion now. A pride whose glorious zenith came at muster's end, when Christian led the entire Company in a chorus of adulatory huzzahs, one whose soul-kissing echo faded only when Johann sidled up to inform us that we each owed the Polish guy six euros.

Now familiar with my squawking enthusiasm for loud ballistics, a select group of Swedes invited me to spend the day with them and Baz on a handgunning party. Johann – his split hose now concealed beneath a majestic fur-collared crimson cloak – had spotted a semi-derelict tower near the artillery court-yard, one that overlooked the main gate from the other side. Though this ramshackle structure lacked any means of ascent, we endeavoured to get ourselves and two handguns (Fat Butt and the smaller bored Long Butt) up to its rotten-floored turret by judicious use of ropes and a tottering human pyramid.

One of the most striking facets of Company life was the bond of mutual respect and practical competence – of course you won't drop this brimming cauldron if I pass it to you; of course that enormous iron tripod won't collapse into the fire the minute you tell me you've put it up; of course you won't yelp like a stepped-on puppy when I hand you these coils of rope and you find they're all covered in cobwebs. Having failed all these tests of time and many more, I had at last earned my stripes – and the *dizaine*'s respect – as a giggling, swivel-eyed explodophile.

Once we were all set up – barrels poking out of the window-slits and trained on the arriving tourists, gunpowder and smouldering linstock placed as distantly apart as our modest confines permitted – Johann dutifully endeavoured to kick-start an authentic scenario. 'The captain has told us to look out for enemy scouts, so we should—' Our opening volley drowned him out, and in the roof-raising high-fives that ensued, he somehow forgot to carry on.

We settled into a routine. Boom, giggling whoops, idle banter, boom. Extrapolating from my solitary relevant experience – a paintball session spent hiding atop an obscure gantry in some abandoned warehouse, firing hopeful pot-shots into the mêlée beneath – it was a wartime posting well suited to my temperament. Rightly confident that no one was watching, they whipped out tins of chewing tobacco, and insisted I take a muslin-wrapped portion – to look at and to taste, like a fag-end wrapped in a tea bag. Spitting it out through the gaping hole in the floor, I imagined this was how life would have been for gun crews through the ages: with his helmet-strap dangling loose across his stubble, the heart-throb Dane was more Iwo Jima than Bosworth Field.

Between salvos, as golden sunlight filtered in through the hazy, pestilential vapours released by our explosive butts, we talked. Sometimes the focus of debate was the relationship between fear, death and religious faith; at others – can't pretend this wasn't a surprise – it was Captain Pugwash. A brief foray into Middle Eastern politics ended after Johann named Benjamin Netanyahu as the Israeli Prime Minister, adding 'or at least he was when I stopped paying attention to the modern world'.

There was the now traditional exchange of hideous injuries sustained or witnessed – the fencing demonstration that had ended with an eight-year-old girl in the audience being carried off on a stretcher with a quivering épée lodged in her skull; the wayward shield parry that embedded a photographer's camera in his face; the re-enactor who somehow stabbed himself in the leg with his own broken sword, and bled to death in five minutes. After a fencing career that had left every one of his front teeth chipped, Johann celebrated his recent

137

retirement by having them filed down. 'So far this year I've broken a nose and two fingers,' said another of the Swedes. 'But luckily they weren't mine.'

In an unexpectedly introspective soliloquy, Johann traced his vainglorious, Muhammad Ali-like superiority complex to a distant LARP event, where for a week he had reigned as king of over 1,000 participants. Ten years on, he still found himself forgetting that it took more than a meaningful glance at his empty coffee cup for it to be refilled. 'And ever since I have always loved criticising, but hated being criticised.' Just as he risked a Fat Butt fragging, our leader disarmed us all with an account of the sweetly vulnerable dream he'd had the night before, in which the Company's provost had quietly asked Johann to resign, on the simple grounds that nobody really liked him.

Bang, spit, guff, bang. Baz outlined his theory on re-enactment's seven-year itch, referring not to the inevitable side-effects of the period lifestyle, but the breaking point of spousal tolerance for this all-consuming hobby. His inability to give up living in the past had already cost Baz more than one long-term partner. 'And let's be honest, it's basically a man thing, this.' Considering my historical experiences it was hard to disagree. The train-spotting dedication to mindless detail, the fighting, the casually exuberant, hose-rippling flatulence – most of re-enactment's dominant traits were predominantly male.

The latter was a grimly prominent feature of our day in that tower, and the former asserted itself when Baz, gallantly offering to retie my oily pig-string neck fastenings in the correct period manner, detected something untoward beneath my linen shift. 'Is that a *thermal vest* you've got on?' he asked, wrinkling that huge forehead and fingering the relevant hem in the manner of an underworld heavy exposing a hidden voice recorder.

Two days before I'd have shrugged fatuously, but now I was a team player, a member of an elite unit, and I didn't want to let my buddies down. 'It's wool,' I said in a very small voice, already lowering myself through the hole in the floor.

It was pleasingly restful up in the misty gloaming that passed for daylight in the attic. Over at the distant far side someone else was getting changed, a symphony of soft linen swishes and the creak of thick leather. When they had left me alone, I embarked on the harsh synthetic rustling required to extract my holdall from its under-mattress hiding place, and to stuff the shameful thermals inside. This was the first time I had bared any significant flesh, and I succumbed to the now familiar guilty thrill of sniffing my unwashed torso: those usual muscular aromas of hard labour and woodsmoke were now counterpointed with cannon grease and the acrid, eggy tang of saltpetre.

The extent of my explosive contamination was revealed on my way back to the tower, when I stopped off for a pee. The public loo was a vitreous enamel, stainless-steel microcosm of the life we'd left behind, and as such most Company males preferred to avoid it, instead taking great pleasure in loudly and very publicly anointing any vacant stretch of courtyard wall. Quite often they would manually vacate their nostrils while doing so: for well-bred, antiseptic Scandinavians and Teutons, Company life offered an outlet for activities that would in their home towns merit lifelong civic opprobrium, and several thousand hours of community service.

My own fear of the castle's smallest room was what I saw in its mirror. On this occasion, I learned that I had just put most of my clothes back on inside out, and that I had been walking about with a big black ring all round my mouth. For a day and a half: a little probing with my tongue detected the sulphurous legacy of blowing out all those cannon chambers.

I rejoined my crew just as they discovered that the bread we'd brought up for sustenance made a more than effective substitute for our straw gun-wadding. Serendipity was doubled after the bread ran out: a Swede returned with a big bowl of dough left over from its preparation, a material that proved itself the most deafeningly percussive wadding imaginable. We were thereafter able to reduce all arriving visitors to yelping, scuttling panic, despite the great distance that separated us from the public entrance. Later we found blackened dough splattered all over the facing walls; one of the guards on gate duty told us he'd managed to flick a smouldering lump from a push-chair cover just before the cowering parents noticed.

The most thunderous salvo of all was saved for a hapless young couple who arrived mid-morning in fancy-dress medieval kit: Rapunzel for her, Errol Flynn for him, cowboy boots for both. From their sober expressions – and game attempts to master the cocksure period swagger – I could sense the pair were in earnest; I am ashamed to confess this did not prevent me from gleefully agreeing to a double-charge from our Butts. As they ambled out through the gate, we let them have both barrels; the huge cloud of smoke released spared us their reaction.

Only later did I suspect that my fellow gunners were blasting away at the bumbling, ill-clad newbies they had all once been. I'd already noted the seasoned re-enactor's reluctance to reminisce upon their early days – there was no fond nostalgia for that first-time experience, just silence borne of cringing shame. The wooden spoon Christian had lent me belonged to a small fellow they called Seagrass, a voluble Company veteran who seemed to have a different outfit for every day. When at the end of our stay I handed this crude pine utensil back to him, he plunged it into his bag with evident embarrassment, before treating me to an extended eulogy to his current spoon, a forty-euro rosewood job 'copied directly from an archaeology find'.

A thoughtful young Englishman I'd talked with the night before believed that even as a re-enactor strove towards utterly authentic perfection, he secretly dreaded the sense of hollow redundancy that came with actually achieving it. The example he gave was of a medieval associate who finessed his character to the extent of calculating, through studious socio-historical research, the likely size and composition of his amassed family fortune; having reproduced this to the last groat with minted facsimiles of period coinage, he realised he had nowhere else to go, flogged the lot and started all over again, in 1942.

The light faded and we returned to the kitchen courtyard. I sat at a table with some of the Poles and joined them in a variant of nine men's morris, pushing ducats around a hand-painted board. After all that high-octane ordnance it was hard to sustain enthusiasm for such gentle entertainment, especially once the novelty of the nude-gargoyle dice had worn off: for the very first time in my life I understood what drove people to voluntarily enlist for active service.

Around us the preparations for the postponed feast were proceeding in earnest. A cauldron brimful with a broth of bratwurst and broad beans was coming to the boil, and great earthenware jars of rollmop herrings were being decanted into glazed bowls. Out in force were the mustards and many types of pickle, whose glorious presence made a piquant delight of even the most unpalatable leftovers. Notably excepting the grey, egg-based matter that had lingered undiminished on a side-table for days, the one substance to fully merit the repulsed disbelief that accompanied every visitor's inspection of our culinary receptacles.

With its bubbling cauldrons, bustling goodwives and burlap sacks of Harvest Festival produce, the alfresco kitchen was an exciting place to be. For days I had waited in vain for the kitchen rota promised to all *dizaines*; now, enticed again by the dull gleam of those culinary cleavers, I sat unbidden at a trestle table and laid into a pile of leeks with a small axe. In moments I was chivvied away by a pair of coiffed females, determined to protect their apparent monopoly on food preparation. 'This work is not for you! Go and play with your cannon!'

This was regrettably not an option; instead I joined a team carrying tables and benches up to the appointed party courtyard. On the third trip the Dane came up to reveal that neither he nor I would be going to the ball: Johann had put us down for gate duty. So it was that three hours later, as the huzzahs and hurdy-gurdies echoed down from the upper courtyard, we were stamping away the cold on the flagstones by the handgun tower. Through steaming breath we watched as the final grains slipped into the night-watch hour-glass, then for the third and final time I inverted it.

Wearied by what he saw as counterfeit revelry, Baz had some time previously wandered down to join us. He talked me

141

through his latest kitchen-fitting business venture, then moved seamlessly into an explanation of why theft – all theft – should be summarily punishable by death. Nostalgia for a more forthright stance on crime and comeuppance was emerging as an important appeal of The Olden Days: Dai the blacksmith and most of my Vikings had expressed similar views on a citizen's right to protect his property by any means necessary.

At any rate, it was something of a relief when the next shift arrived to take over. Particularly as this included the Company's silliest man – a tiny fellow whose huge tapering gnome-hat was mirrored by an identical beard, the two divided by an enormous pair of bottle-bottom, bone-framed pince-nez (the widespread use of period spectacles at the castle was ambitiously justified by their presence in a single early fifteenth-century portrait). 'You see?' shouted Johann, strutting down from the now silent feasting courtyard as I shuffled frigidly off to bed. 'Now you can say you were not the stupidest-looking guard!'

Our final morning began with a compulsory dawn procession around the castle's perimeter, a 'blessing of the walls' against enemy attack. Drawn along by the dependably seedy Brother Balthasar's droned incantations, the Company trailed about beneath battle standards, and a lovingly constructed icon of George slaying the dragon. It all seemed much less foolish than it might have done four days previously, but after half an hour the temptation to disrupt proceedings with an abrupt flurry of cruel anachronisms was almost unbearable. Oh, to pull on a pair of giant foam-rubber hands and run up and down the ranks of murmuring, bowed heads, bellowing 'Shaddap You Face'.

Indeed, this was precisely the sort of LARP-ish theatricality that Baz loudly derided as 'pantomime shit'; a rolling Yorkshire groan filled the courtyard when at the post-porridge muster Christian held aloft a reliquary containing 'a part of the dragon's hide', inviting all new inductees forward to press their lips upon this eBay-sourced sliver of stingray skin.

The hour-glass was emptying fast. A few Company members had left the night before, and the rest were now starting to pack up. Jim the Potter – red-cheeked, bandy-legged, pointyhatted and looking more than ever like a dishevelled Rice Krispies sprite – struggled past with a shoulder yoke hung with buckets of half-finished crockery; on his next pass I asked him for a go, and was swiftly grateful that he had loaded up with unbreakables.

Because this had been by a distance my most immersively authentic re-enactment to date, the bedrizzled end-game proved more than usually deflating. I was replacing turf over the kitchen hearth – a blackened mess topped with fragments of broken utensil – when a voice called out 'Cheerio!'; I turned round and there stood Mrs Dwayne, the blacksmith's wife, wearing a cagoule and jeans and holding a can of Fanta in her non-waving hand. I blinked: for a heady moment, she looked like the one in stupid clothes.

My task assumed a poignant significance. Lying there in the muddy charcoal, those earthenware shards and slivers of wooden cutlery were powerfully suggestive of an historical 'find', and here I was, reburying the past. Men now remarkable only for their occasionally ridiculous beards filed by with torches and fags and bottles of Heineken. With a lick of make-up and their hair released from linen confinement, many women were literally unrecognisable.

It seemed so jarring, so sudden, like the house lights coming on in the middle of a deeply engrossing film. I felt almost betrayed. When the Dane strode past in a fleece and hiking boots, rucksack on back and digital camera poised, it was like Dorothy coming face to face with the real Wizard of Oz.

I was dreading my last sight of Johann – catching him in a tracksuit would have paralleled the moment in *Quadrophenia* when Jimmy spots über-mod Ace Face trotting out of a hotel in his bell-boy outfit. When the towering Swede strode into the courtyard in plus fours and a tweed cap I could have kissed him. As I watched, a number of giggling young females from the castle staff rushed over to do just that: Johann's last act, before driving off in a Swedish minibus full of weaponry and *dizainiers*, was to pose for a series of photographs with a lovestruck girl on each knee.

There was an almost indecent haste in the departures, and not just because of the gastric complaint that several whey-faced Company members were taking home as a period souvenir. 'Oh, I'm not so fine,' groaned one sufferer when I saw him hunched over in the booze barn. 'And see what somebody have done to my breastplate!'

It was as if everyone wanted away before the spell was completely lifted, before that final strike of twelve turned our fairy-tale castle back into a twenty-first-century tourist attraction.

With the medieval make-believe suspended, the closeness and camaraderie of our co-dependent proximity seemed abruptly awkward. As we climbed out of our damp and filthy outfits up in the attic, there was none of the fuzz-buttocked flaunting that had been such a prominent feature of attic life. The chest-out, hail-fellow swaggers were gone, replaced by the diffident, eyes-down shuffle of modern urban life. Filth was suddenly undesirable and inappropriate: 'Bad combo, black denim and distemper,' called out a departing Dwayne the Blacksmith, seeing me lean against a tower wall. Yet the cataclysmically soiled clothing I'd returned to its owner a moment previously would have made a great medieval doorstep challenge: 'Gunpowder? Pottage? Cannon grease? Let's see you shift that lot without a boil wash, Gwenevere!'

The Company's head cook, Josianne, very kindly offered to drive me to Bern. Our opening conversation revealed that neither of us understood a single word the other said, but this didn't stop her delivering three straight hours of amiable-sounding chatter. Somehow it wasn't awkward: she talked and talked and talked, and I gazed out of the window, watching in mild awe as Haut-Koenigsbourg briefly emerged high above the gloomy, flooded fields in a Holy Grail halo of sunlight, then blurred back into the smudged grey.

A jack-knifed lorry, contraflows, rush hour – the twenty-first century wasn't trying very hard to win me back. As we crept through Bern's outskirts I compiled my usual post-historical inventory. The physical fallout was as disparate

as ever – if previously I'd paid a painful price for hands un-
accustomed to wielding shields or longbows, this time the
payback was for forty-two years of muscular unfamiliarity
with cannon barrels and shoulder yokes. More positively, my
first rain-dominated re-enactment had taught me the importance of not getting things wet, because if you failed, the only
guaranteed way to dry these things was to spend a whole
night with them shoved down the front of your tights. I had
almost mastered the art of laying items out in the frail
daylight of morning that you might need in the pitch dark
of night, and between these extremes could now with reason-
able accuracy estimate the hour by consulting the sun.
Having for once survived on strictly period rations, I'd come
to appreciate age-old epicurean pleasures: a long draught of
cool water, a nice crunchy apple, a finger dipped in the honey
pot. And under Johann's charismatic command, I had at last
emerged from the long period of history when leadership was
generally determined by brute physical strength, and the
eager willingness to assert this in mortal combat.

My first hours of freedom after previous re-enactments had
hitherto been occupied with an unsightly overdose of Homer
Simpson-type modern comforts. But after Josianne dropped me
off at Bern station, while waiting for the airport minibus I
succumbed to what felt a lot like contempt for certain aspects
of modern life. Yes, I went into a newsagent's and thumbed
through a three-day-old *Financial Times* in a vain quest for
football results, but did that warrant those tuts of theatrical
disgust from the hausfraus around me? Yes, I ordered two
kebabs, but when I smiled at the man who handed them over
the kiosk counter, did he have to recoil so visibly? Only when
I paid 45p to do something that for four days I'd been doing
up against a castle wall for free, and afterwards glanced in the
mirror, did I see that he did.

Chapter Five

If a common theme connected all the previous periods I'd stuck a grubby toe into, it was the daily struggle for survival. The Iron Agers had led a hand-to-mouth existence; with the others it was more fist-to-face. Only now, emerging from the Middle Ages, was I entering an era when a West European might reasonably expect to enjoy a life untroubled by the fear of war or famine, albeit one cut rudely short by disease.

In Britain, certainly, we had by the mid sixteenth century established a generally prosperous and stable society, where most people had a roof over their head and enough to eat, and therefore no longer routinely felt quite as eager to kill each other. The delightful consequence, as described in *Dancing in the Streets: A History of Collective Joy*, was a celebration of human happiness more universal than any previously known. Or, indeed, since.

'Beginning in England in the seventeenth century,' states the author of the aforementioned work, 'the European world was stricken by what looks, in today's terms, like an epidemic of depression.' Having at last resolved his basic human needs, European man looked around at the jolly, prosperous realm he had created and sighed, 'So, is this *it*?' The instant mankind was no longer preoccupied with the lower end of his hierarchy of needs, existential world-weariness kicked in. One minute our sample Englishman was gaily skipping around a maypole, the next he was bitterly pissing on the ribbons, despising himself for the empty-headed pointlessness of it all. In other words, I had better make the most of 1578. It was going to be all downhill from here.

Inaugurated in 1979, Kentwell Hall's three-week Great Annual Recreation is generally acknowledged as Britain's most venerable large-scale, long-term historical re-enactment. Hosted at a period manor house in Suffolk, Kentwell was familiar to me from a tiny box advert that ran for many years in the *Guardian*'s classified section, headed 'Live as a Tudor!' It had been yet more familiar to my wife, frustrated sixteenth-century aristocrat and card-carrying period obsessive (the card in question: her Hampton Court season ticket). This was the one event she envied me: when the application forms and brochures dropped on to the doormat she eagerly tore them open.

It was rather sad to see the vicarious excitement drain from her features as it became apparent that first-timers were not considered gentry material – by hallowed Kentwellian tradition, a place at the high table came as grace-and-favour reward for years of lowly servitude. No madrigal-backed feasting and erudite Shakespearian repartee; no velvet and lace. 'You should expect to perform dull but necessary jobs quietly and without complaining,' she read, with growing disgust. 'Menial . . . privations . . . exhausting hard work . . .' She tossed the welcome pack on the table. 'You're going to be some shitty peasant.'

Such was Kentwell's repute that a two-stage selection process was required to sort the Tudor wheat from the chaff. So it happened that a full four months before Kentwell would open its magnificent gates to the first jeering school party, I found myself approaching them up a muddy carriage drive flanked with blasted oaks. This was certainly the most peculiar job interview I was ever likely to attend, but also the one I most dearly wished to go well; only after much wardrobe-wringing had I decided against the paisley trousers that would have declared an eager willingness to make a vast and very public tit of myself.

The 'new participant's form' I now retrieved from the

passenger footwell read like a village idiot's CV. Having awarded myself a bottom-grade D for each of the thirty-four listed 'Tudor skills' requiring self-assessment, I'd thought better and Tippexed in a few face-saving Cs: Animal Care, Herbs, Part Singing and – as the closest approximations to Shitty Peasantry – Scything and Coppice Crafts. 'If you feel you have no talent,' one of the accompanying letters had stated hopefully, 'we may discover otherwise.' You may, I thought, aware that the absence of period ordnance at Kentwell made this very unlikely.

There were a good couple of hundred wet people queuing outside an octagonal gatehouse to register, perhaps a third of them fully Blackaddered up in doublet and hose or coif and kirtle; most wore weather-resistant expressions of bright-eyed, wide-eyed, almost evangelical glee. Beyond the queue lay a 100-yard stretch of immaculate greensward, and beyond that, girdled with a broad moat, the turreted majesty of Kentwell Hall.

I joined the queue behind a young girl in a parka with a big mod target on the back. The two basket-bearing, cloak-wearing veterans in front kept her fitfully supplied with banter as we shuffled towards the gatehouse. 'Thing is, you're always out under the trees, so it carries on raining for about four hours after it's stopped . . . I can recommend the Kentwell Diet – you eat loads, but shiver it all off . . . It's kind of like Glastonbury, in tights, with work.'

Our meeting point was the overcroft, an unheated barn attic filled with many rows of plastic chairs. We trooped in, sat down and watched through clouds of our own misty exhalations as an imposing rural statesman of late middle years, in tweeds, brogues and an age-worn Barbour, rose to address us. In sonorous, barn-filling tones this rather superb figure introduced himself as Patrick Phillips, resident owner of Kentwell Hall for the previous thirty-six years, and, for the previous twenty-seven, co-ordinator of what he billed as Britain's oldest and largest period recreation. 'Just to get things straight,' he boomed, fixing all newcomers with a challenging glare, 'this is my house and my show, so what I say, to a very large extent, goes. Feel free to tell me what job you'd like to do, but remember the final decision is mine.'

My relief as Patrick brusquely dismissed the trend for re-enactments dominated by 'all that fighting malarkey' was soon swept away by a wave of new misgivings. 'Can I just say how glad I am that it's cold and wet?' he announced, with a grim smile. 'We don't want any fair-weather fainthearts here.' He theatrically cleared his throat, looking about the overcroft as if expecting those who recognised themselves in this description to make an exit. When they didn't, he treated himself to a sceptical harrumph and continued. 'You are to be part of a genuine sixteenth-century entity,' we were weightily informed. 'Nothing should detract from that – no glasses, no false teeth. People tell me they're stone deaf without their hearing aid, and I say, "*How fantastically Tudor!*" It's a terrible crime in our world, a horror story, if you forget to take off your watch. These aren't minor things – these are our *core values!*'

No other event, Patrick declared, demonstrated so eloquently 'how we are all products of our past'. With his rich voice cracked and quavering, he reminded us that as Tudors we would know everyone we saw, and greet them accordingly; what a tragedy that the decline of integrated communities had now sapped Britain of its sense of mutual trust and fraternity. As he detailed how we were to resurrect the age of collective joy, his language, and increasingly strident delivery, seemed more consistent with a cult leader. 'You must unlearn almost everything you know – purge from your minds all knowledge of the last five centuries. The house is not some ancient monument, it's only forty years old!'

'Two score,' piped up a voice from the rear, inciting a round of sniggers which Patrick silenced with an imperious glower. He strafed this slowly across the audience, face by cold-cheeked face.

'What you are about to do is going to change your lives *for ever.*'

With these portentous words still hanging in the cold air, Patrick let it be known that without the funds the Great Annual Recreation brought in, Kentwell would not survive, 'at least not without a tainted government grant of some sort, which I certainly shan't be begging for'. This was his cue for a protracted, sweeping tirade against 'the astounding incompetence of today's politicians'. After a detailed indictment of Suffolk County Council's recycling policy, a weary sigh signalled that his ire was now spent. 'You may wish to put me down as a complete nutter,' he said, trailing off into a mumble, 'as others have.' With that, our lord and master turned away from the lectern and departed through a rear entrance, leaving the overcroft in a silence punctuated by the distant lowing of unhappy cattle.

Each Great Annual Recreation was set in a different Tudor year, and this time Patrick had stuck his pin in 1578. 'I'll need to get this outfit seen to,' said the cheery fellow deputed to show newbies around the grounds, glancing down at his red and black puffball hose through a pair of Reactolite prescription shades. 'Not baggy enough for 1578, even allowing for Suffolk being a little behind London fashions.'

We were led past the ice house and along a stretch of manicured yew. 'The thing to remember is that everyone services the manor,' he said, pointing out the Hall-adjoining moat house that would be home to the bakery, dairy and sundry herbalists and seamstresses. I gazed up at the mighty flank of red brick and soaring mullion windows: it wasn't hard to empathise with awed Tudor ruralites experiencing this unimaginably rarefied other world for the first time.

For an hour we trooped around the extensive grounds, inspecting each of the many far-flung outbuildings that would house all the 'stations' manned by craftworkers and tradespeople. The muddy tracks that linked these were topped with a frigid crust; a vicious wind, tainted with the pervasive stench of free-range, rare-breed agriculture, carried away our guide's words. The rain evolved into sleet, and then an ear-stinging hail. Someone shouted out a query about bathing facilities, and was told that the showers – both of them – were in a block about 400 yards from the campsite where all 200 of us would sleep under twenty-first-century nylon. Never before had the great unwashed been so aptly named. The bulk of my fellow first-timers were students or recent graduates in search of a budget summer break with a twist; but to paraphrase the Sex Pistols, this was a cheap holiday in your own misery. I looked at the many disconsolate faces around me and accurately predicted I wouldn't see half of them back at the second open day.

'What job are you going for?' asked one of the young women shuddering along beside me at the column's rear. In the previous hour my occupational ambitions had become very tightly focused. 'Anything fire-based,' I said.

We returned to the overcroft, now home to a period careers fair. Old hands with name tags identifying their 'station' rushed up, trying to secure our services; I looked vainly around for a badge reading 'bakery' or 'smithy'. (Later I learned that these stations, and a few others, operated long-established closed shops.) A kitchen job was out – in a humbling interview with the genteel head cook it emerged that even an entry-level culinary assistant would already have mastered several pastry-making skills I had never heard of. At her recommendation, I went off to meet the sutlers: outdoor-based camp cooks, serving up pottage for the masses. During a swift chat these hearty dinner ladies made it plain they would welcome anyone who could cut a turnip in half, and swear a lot while doing so. I gave them my provisional pledge, and joined a long queue leading to the storeroom where Patrick was passing final – and very feudal – occupational judgement.

'A *sutler?*' he repeated scornfully, when, over two hours later, I at last filed in to meet him. 'Oh, no, no, no, no.' He ran his patrician gaze over my application form, then over me, then over the hand-scrawled register laid on the crowded desk before him. 'I've been making these decisions for twenty-six years,' he murmured, 'and you can count my mistakes in single digits.' As he drummed his large fingers together ruminatively, I tried to imagine how these mistakes manifested themselves: some Lord Percy caught jet-skiing round the moat, perhaps, or the Baldrick who bellowed Kwik-Fit jingles from the dovecote roof, hose round his ankles.

At length Patrick clapped his hands, sighed magnificently, and delivered his verdict.

'Chamberlain,' he boomed.

I felt my brow furrow. 'Actually, it's Moore. Timoth—'

'Chamberlain!' he cut in, sharply. 'Head of the household. Second week. Next!'

How head-swelling, how chest-puffing Patrick's adjudication had sounded, even before I learned what a chamberlain was: I'd walked in to meet him as a shitty-peasant-to-be, and walked out as the grandly costumed master of Kentwell Hall's entire domestic staff. And how little these bodily engorgements subsided, even after I'd deduced that my appointment was entirely attributable to my advanced years, and a desperate shortage of age-appropriate male applicants for the role.

The first misgivings had taken hold at the follow-up open day two months later, in May, as we filed up to present our outfits for approval. I smiled encouragingly at all those queuing up with armfuls of unfinished linen and wool, many of them still stitching frantically away at ruffs and coifs – with the Great Annual Recreation now just over a month off, all costumes were expected to be very nearly Kentwell-ready. How fortunate I was to have stepped out of Patrick's interview and immediately been offered a complete outfit by a Kentwell regular who had served many years as a steward, a sort of assistant chamberlain.

'Who's doing the alterations?' enquired the wardrobe mistress when I blithely told my tale. I remembered the steward as a vertically conspicuous figure, but now learned – from an eavesdropper who revealed herself as his fiancée – that only a supreme feat of needlecraft could adapt for my use an outfit tailor-made for a man of six foot five with a twenty-six-inch waist. My wheedling attempts to procure this feat were shortlived: as an end-of-week-two steward, her fiancée would be needing the outfit himself. 'I expect he was just trying to be helpful,' she concluded, with a tight smile. Only through a great effort of willpower did I resist the graceless impulse to wish her a long and happy married life as Mrs Lanky-Arsed Twatbollocks of Cockshire.

An undertone of reedy panic accompanied me through the How To Be Tudor workshops that occupied the rest of the day. Like spies about to go out into the field, we were briefed on how to blend in to 1578 – what to wear, what to know, what to say and how to say it. There were lectures on everything the visiting public might ask us about, from current affairs to fashion. 'A few bullet points for you all,' called out one old hand. 'Mary Queen of Scots is still in prison, fears of Spanish invasion are very real, ruffs are big and getting bigger. Oh, and summer months always brought a terror of plague, so that's something to talk about.'

As a prominent go-between 'twixt gentry and serving folk, I would need to be familiar with all national news, as well as the minutiae of local gossip; another steward-to-be handed over a great sheaf of sixteenth-century family trees and advised me, with a look that implied he'd long since etched every name and date deep into his cortex, 'to have a little glance through'.

While compiling our own character's back story, we were urged to ensure it tallied with others. 'If you go around telling visitors that the cook's your mother, make sure she knows.' Because there was nothing the public liked better, it seemed, than catching a Kentwellian out. School parties – the only midweek visitors – were inevitably the worst. When an aeroplane passed overhead, they would mischievously point it out to the nearest man in tights; we were instructed to cup a hand to an ear and complain of 'loud hornets about the manor', or stonewall with a blank-faced 'I know naught of what you speak'. They would sidle up with cameras, hoping to elicit a telltale grin into the lens; the recommended response to all requests for a photograph was a quizzical shrug and the non-committal declaration, 'You may do what you will.' They would plunge their hands into your linen haversack in search of compromising possessions: the advice was to secrete asthma inhalers and the like in a smaller linen bag kept within this, and to ward away any concerted probings with a cry of, 'Away from my privy business!' (If asked to smuggle some larger item of modern contraband into the manor, the procedure was to wrap it in linen swaddling, move fast and repel curious enquiries with a disarming over-the-shoulder call of, 'A dead baby, master!' 'It's become a verb,' said Bella, Kentwell's resident administrator and a jovially reassuring presence. '*Could you dead-baby this first-aid kit to the limners?*')

It was Bella who chaired the masterclass on the event's curious lingua franca: some called it Kentwellese, others Desperanto. 'It's probably best not to speak for the first two days,' she began, 'but I promise you that after you get home you're going to find it hard not to greet people as "good master" and "mistress".'

As I knew only too well from my awful – but mercifully irrelevant – preparatory flounderings at Haut-Koenigsbourg, period speech was the most appalling historical challenge I had yet faced, and I scribbled desperate notes throughout Bella's lecture. Aye for yes, nay for no. 'The dreaded OK' – substitute with 'good enough'. Other dos and don'ts: don't say don't, or isn't, or any other similar contractions. Do say 'I spin', not 'I do be spinning'. No *Archers* accents or cockney, please.

Cruelly, I was to be denied the very tempting 'thee' and 'thou', which I'd hoped to sprinkle liberally into any flawed conversation as a kind of instant Tudor seasoning. Both were apparently appropriate only within one's own family, or when addressing servants or children: 'The next low player who addresses the high table as "thee",' said a stern voice from behind, 'is in with a good chance of a starring role in the stocks.' How grateful I was when Bella handed us a get-out-of-jail-free card, to be played when a visitor backed you into a corner, linguistic or historical. If no old hands were around to help you out, and pretending to be mad hadn't worked, one need simply run off, with a shout of, 'Prithee, master, I must away!' 'Though obviously,' she went on, 'you can't use that one too often.' Let me be the judge of that, good mistress, I thought.

I drove home with the notebook open in my lap, its arcane hints and tips consulted at every set of traffic lights. 'No scented toiletries (lavender ~~OK~~ good enough). Stop wearing watch now: risk of telltale tan-lines. Underwear? Half don't wear any. No slacking on Tudor etiquette – acknowledge betters with bob of head. Wear Tudor gear to supermarket – learn to think of it as clothes, not an outfit.'

This last one elicited a bark of mirthless laughter. I now at least had a hat, a musty, fifth-hand black velvet number of a design associated with obscure academic ceremonies, acquired along with a handmade wooden spoon and a thin black belt from a stall set up outside the overcroft. But given the complete and utter absence of other period apparel, that Sainsbury's run would probably have to wait.

Six weeks later, with a kiss, a snigger and a sigh of envy, my wife bid me farewell and drove away down Kentwell's tree-lined approach. We'd set off at dawn, and I hadn't slept well. Ill had I slept. I do be sleeping ill, master, bob my head, good morrow. The Great Annual Recreation had already been running for a week, and a scaffold-framed, self-proclaimed 'time tunnel' shielded the hall from view. I stepped through the plywood portcullis, from the now to the then, and beheld a front sward dotted with knights-of-old type stripy-canvas pavilions. A bead of sweat rolled down my back as I surveyed these and the imposing Tudor edifice beyond, and not just because since my first visit here we'd moved near a score degrees up the centigrade scale.

I dumped my camping gear at the gatehouse and set off towards the overcroft with a huge holdall, filled to jangling, knee-thunking bursting point in a fortnight of internet-centred panic buying. First to thud on my doormat had been a turned wooden bowl and beaker, followed by accessories to dangle from my belt: a handmade eating knife, a sheath to accommodate it, and a small black leather purse, now home to a pair of wooden dice, a goose-feather quill and reproductions of period coinage, tarnished – like the rather splendid set of hefty keys that would clank alongside – by four days' refrigeration in a sandwich bag full of boiled egg yolks.

With eight days to go I took delivery of a pair of black woollen tights and a pair of crimson-lined, black leather 'latchet' shoes, modelled by a Kentwell-approved cobbler on originals retrieved from the wreck of the *Mary Rose*. A day later my wife finished stitching Roman-tunic offcuts into the last of the many linen napkins and aprons appropriate to my office, to dimensions outlined on page four of Kentwell's *Guide for Liveried Staff*. And finally, less than a week before my reign as chamberlain was due to commence, I jogged across a field near Bedford, outflanking a skirmish between Royalists and Parliamentarians, to receive my robes of office from their diffident creator's pavilion.

'Er, there you go,' mumbled Ed Boreham, fingering his House of Stuart goatee with one hand and waving the other at a folded stack of black wool. 'Oh, don't forget these.' He handed me a bag: in it was a linen shift, its sleeves and neck fastened with pearl-tipped silk ties, and three bijou wonders of the period tailor's craft – concertina-folded ruffs, one for each cuff and one for my collar. It was only two weeks since Bella had put me in touch with Ed, and only days since I'd emailed him the dimensions of the widest part of my thigh when crouching, the distance from my waist to the lowest part of my crotch, and many other spouse-troubling measurements.

'I'm not fighting again for a bit,' he said, folding up my cheque for £250, 'so you might as well try it on.' Ed was coercing my bare limbs through four very tight woollen orifices when a woman he would identify as his wife ducked in through the tent flap. I'd met enough re-enactors by now not to expect her to duck back out; without a word she took my knee in an armlock and yanked a hose-leg over it. Ed tied the many sets of points that fastened skin-tight black doublet to baggy-arsed black hose, his wife attached the ruffs, and there I stood, gazing down at the thumb-sized codpiece that nosed apologetically forth from my groin.

'I haven't got a mirror,' said Ed, 'but honestly, you look . . . fine.'

'Absolutely,' nodded his wife. I walked back across the battle-field wondering how Adam Ant had got that correlation between ridicule and fear so very badly wrong.

Kentwell's lower classes were obliged to get changed in their own tents or caravans; as honorary members of the gentry, liveried household staff were accorded the honour of getting dressed in front of each other in the overcroft. I walked in and found myself surrounded by half-naked page boys and minstrels.

'You are lately come upon the manor?'

It was a man I recognised as having sold me my spoon, now topless, and with a lute in his hose-covered lap.

'Yeah . . . yes . . . aye.'

He cordially introduced himself as Master Symon, and gave me a prompting look; I pulled down my jeans, swallowed hard and heard myself say, 'God give you good day. I am Master Wat.'

'And I'm Dr Who!' called out an unseen youth, accurately reflecting the now-regretted flippancy with which I'd filled in the 'Kentwell name' box on the final registration form. How glad I was to see Master Symon's avuncular smile falter only slightly.

As I grappled with my outfit he introduced me to the many maids, mistresses and masters milling about us in various states of undress; one of the fully clothed former very kindly came over to help with the thirty-odd fastenings – points, hooks-and-eyes, ruff strings – that preserved a chamberlain's modesty. The final touches: a Walter Raleigh-style pearl earring, and a Johann-sized white ostrich feather clipped to my hat brim. A moment later, studiously averting my gaze from the overwhelming magnificence of its façade, I jangled across the Tudor-rose maze bricked into Kentwell Hall's courtyard, ducked through a dark doorway in its west wing, and found myself in the small and gloomy stewards' room, home to half a dozen of my liveried young charges, and the beeps of their incoming text messages.

'Good morrow, pages,' I announced, delivering my debut contribution to *Tudors Say the Funniest Things* at the only youth curious enough to look up from his phone. 'I'm an under-steward,' he answered, wearily, 'and the rest here are grooms.' With that he returned his attention to the small screen in his hand. It was the first of a long day's countless humiliations.

'Yet I know not of these *Gresham* Pastons, Master Wat,' responded the gimlet-eyed noblewoman who enquired of my origins as I squeezed past her corridor-filling farthingale. In the previous half-hour of frenetic but unfocused activity I had snagged my hose on a door handle, thereby detaching one of its strip-like woollen 'panes', dropped a wheelchair ramp on a house-maid's toe, and was now becoming messily entangled in my own back story. 'Perchance you are addled at this early hour?'

A big mistake to pick such a historically eminent East Anglian surname – the Paston family's medieval correspondence is a renowned period resource – and a bigger one to twin this randomly with the Norfolk village where I'd spent a family half-term week the previous year. There was nothing for it. 'Prithee, my lady, I must away!' And off I scuttled, hand on insecure hat, keys a-clanking.

I was alone on the moat bridge when the first school party emerged through our side of the time tunnel. For a grim eternity I tracked the jeering crocodile's progress across the sward, feeling a small thrill every time it entered a pavilion, side-tracked by a demonstration of some period art or craft, and dying a small death when it emerged. The entire weight of Kentwell's three-winged, mullioned bulk seemed to press down on me, and with it the burden of my looming responsibility.

What an awful, codpiece-shrivelling moment it was when the woman known simply as Wilmott – a white-faced, black-hatted veteran who had recently appeared on television as Queen Elizabeth's corpse – informed me that the chamberlain's principal morning duty was to greet Kentwell's young visitors with a welcoming lecture, then usher them through to the kitchen, first stop on the prescribed tour route. A welcoming *what*? 'Just, um, go on about the carp in the moat. "Know thee upon which day we do dine upon these fish?" That sort of thing.' She briefly surveyed the silent, carp-like motions of my mouth, then said, 'I'll send out Edmund to show you the ropes.'

Edmund, a sartorial mini-me but for his light grey doublet, swaggered up to my side as the children massed purposefully on the bridge. At twelve he was perhaps a year older than they were, but being of very modest stature he looked up at the majority. Though when he turned to me and delivered a big, freckled wink, I began to hope that things were going to be good enough after all.

'From whence come you this day, young maids and masters?' His strident, Artful Dodger tones rang out around the courtyard, silencing the juvenile jabber. 'And how many summers have you, childer of Romford, in the county of Essex?' For fifteen minutes I listened in awe as Edmund delivered his routine, a cocky, compelling amalgam of teacher-pleasing sociohistorical fact and pupil-teasing audience participation, honed over six previous days as an under-steward. Throughout this humbling masterclass, and the three that followed, my responsibilities were restricted to pacing about the courtyard having my codpiece sniggered at. Then Wilmott's Pilgrim Father hat shot out of the kitchen door, the mouth beneath it summoned Edmund away, and I was alone.

I can't remember too much about the first few parties, except that I didn't detain any for long. Having mumbled out what little I remembered of Edmund's spiel, I'd find myself reduced to wordlessly flourishing a hand at the courtyard, or a swan, or my own outfit, like a mute hostess displaying the prizes on *Sale of the Century*. Then someone would ask a question, and with an abrupt and deranged grin, I'd semi-frogmarch the whole group off towards the kitchen, like Basil Fawlty co-ordinating a fire drill. The suspicion that my performance was being monitored was confirmed when Mistress Joan, a history teacher who as head housekeeper was my female counterpart, gently called me in and sent out a couple of grooms to take over.

I spent the rest of the morning skulking in the dark and claustrophobic stewards' room. Every so often a jostle of schoolchildren trooped in from the kitchen, received a swift lecture on the room's modest contents by a pair of well-drilled grooms, and trooped out into the housemaids' chamber, next stop on their tour. In between, I learned a great deal about my fabled predecessor, Master Joshua, and the impressive extent to which I was failing to live up to him.

'He was brilliant at putting on a show,' said George, another of the more sympathetic under-stewards. 'Kept us on our toes, entertained the public.' A show? My ruff suddenly felt much too tight. 'Ticking us off, shouting orders. "Clean those knives, idle page," all that stuff.'

'Oh, and he let us work up this nice routine with the garderobe,' piped Edmund, nodding his velvet-capped head at a curtained enclosure on the far side of the stewards' room. They gave me a demonstration when the next group filed through: Edmund rushed towards the garderobe, clearing a path with a desperate cry of 'Prithee passage!', and once behind the curtain issued a long, straining grunt which culminated in a repulsively evocative spattering splash, procured by slowly releasing a handful of pebbles into the moat below. For the junior visitors, this was unalloyed comedy gold.

Twenty-four hours later, after enduring one eulogy too many in honour of Master Joshua, I attempted to conflate his collected dramatics into a single performance. Because this ended with me screaming 'Toilet!' as I forced a confused and alarmed page backwards into the garderobe at the point of my eating knife, nobody laughed. But on the plus side, nobody ever mentioned Joshua in my presence again.

Gentry dinner (it would be 200 years before anyone had 'lunch') was the big set-piece ceremony of the day, one in which I suspected the chamberlain would play an extremely prominent role. Not yet ready to face this, or the Paston-of-Gresham-type conversational awkwardness that was sure to accompany it, as soon as the under-stewards began lining up outside the kitchen, I turned on my flat leather heels and walked smartly off, right across the courtyard, over the bridge, and out on to the now very lively front sward. I had run away, and how glorious it felt.

For long minutes I waited for this sensation to diminish, either abruptly with a bejewelled hand clamped to my shoulder, or through creeping insinuations of guilt and inadequacy. Instead, the following half-hour of freedom was characterised only by a deep and burgeoning sense of gleeful wonderment. Striding around the grounds, past grubby limners boiling up their dyes amidst the venerable oaks, past a straw-hatted milk-maid skipping winsomely after a bleating goat, past whistlingly industrious potters and gardeners and laughing barefoot urchins, I found myself cast back into the poor-but-happy age of collective joy. Just like old times.

So this was the Kentwell Effect – the defining sensation, so often mentioned at the open days, of finding yourself in a living snapshot of Tudor England. The period rush of being there as a nation went about its daily business 500 years ago. I remembered Bella stressing the importance of 'having someone check your rear view before walking through the time tunnel', and now I understood why: it wasn't the postcard pomp of the great-hall gentry that made this whole thing come to life, but that half-glimpsed snatch of a woodsman striding into the trees with an axe over his sweaty shift, or two basket-bearing good-wives waddling distantly through the frame.

Yet there was something else, something more personally gratifying, and it was this: almost everyone who saw me was instantly reduced to a state of fawning, unworthy terror. If they were doing something, they dropped it to bow and scrape; if they weren't, their idle hands grabbed desperately for tools or baskets. As I ambled through the walled garden, hands behind my back, an elderly goodwife leapt off her stool and bid me please to take my ease. To those who recognised my livery I was the big boss foreman, the *capo di tutti capi*, and to these I was master. To the many who did not, I was a feather-hatted, quill-bearing emissary from the semi-mythical realm of impossible privilege that was The Big House, and to these I was my lord, my liege and even – to one gardener's boy rushing towards the kitchens with a trug of herbs – your majesty.

Our open-day guide had stressed that we were all in the service of the manor, and to these toiling unwashed masses, that meant me. *Le manoir c'est moi.* Inclining my head graciously at the genuflecting peasantry, I began to feel rather more than comfortable in my skin. My robes of office, a source of craven embarrassment as I shuffled about the courtyard that morning, seemed now a richly magnificent expression of my importance. I strutted back across the moat bridge, jutting my codpiece proudly forth like a Holbein made flesh. In thirty momentous minutes I had grown to love old Wat Paston of Gresham, king of the collective age of joy.

'Whence come you, Master Wat?'

It was Wilmott, standing in the kitchen doorway with her thin eyebrows arched and her black arms folded. I never quite established our relative positions in the domestic hierarchy, but this was no time for deference. Nor, I found, explanation or apology. 'God give you good day, Mistress Wilmott,' I breezed, and marched into the stewards' room to bawl out some school-children. This was *my* time.

'I like *Scooby Doo*, so I got *Scooby Doo* pants on.'

There was always an unsettling adjustment from our daytime realm of linen and oak to the brashly synthetic campsite 300 yards distant where we took our nocturnal ease – 'decompression', the regulars called it – and the first night proved the most jarring. With my glad rags on a hanger in the overcroft, I was just some bloke in shorts putting his tent up wrong. I went off with my toothbrush for a quick flail at the daddy-long-legs colony in the toilet block, then returned to my rude bedchamber, one ear assailed by the campsite chorus of swishing zips and the other – well, what the hell – plugged into commentary of Ukraine's World Cup encounter with Switzerland. It was a funny sort of relief to be awakened at dawn by a shrieking commotion, and find myself squinting through the zip-flap at two peacocks duking it out on a caravan roof.

Breakfast was Marmite on toast, despatched in full regalia in the overcroft courtyard. Just time for a quick linguistic warm-up – 'A most wondrous volley did Zidane strike upon the yester, Master Wat!' 'Er, aye' – before I repaired to the court-yard to do battle with the first school party.

'Gather forth, childer!'

After the fumbling idiocies of a score and four hours gone by, I found I was very nearly enjoying myself. Though I would never master the lingo – any attempt to veer away from Edmund's script saw me mired in 'proceeding in a northerly direction' model policeman-speak – I felt genuine pride watching those smirks and scowls dissolve into gawps of wonderment. Because of me they would go home to tell their families of their journey to a time when children their age had been in back-breaking physical employment for many years, when crows were lunch, when men wore trousers with dinkles sticking out the front. From my lips they learned that 'a square meal' derived from the wooden trencher boards that were the era's most common eating surface, and that 'upper crust' referred to the top half of a loaf that had not been in contact with the sooty, grubby oven floor, and was thus reserved for the master of the house. And if sometimes the response to all this was a prolonged expression of dismissive scorn, then perhaps those high-pitched jeers and hoots were an act of denial, one born of a reluctance to accept that they had all once lived such grim and filthy lives. Or perhaps it was because they still did, and in Essex.

'Marster Wart?'

I didn't need to turn around to know who was pacing across the courtyard: our transatlantic nobleman, a round-faced fellow in period specs, whose speech content was always flawlessly authentic, but whose chosen accent suggested Loyd Grossman impersonating Mel Gibson in *Braveheart*. In consequence, it took three repeats of his subsequent address before I understood what he was saying. If not what he meant: where in the name of Good Queen Bess were these coppicers, what was the 'wand for the clouts' I had been ordered to demand from them, and who were 'those that would dine without', the group which apparently required this worrisome instrument? Dine without what? Clothes, by the sound of it. But lacking the linguistic tools to formulate even a basic request for explanation, and unable in the midst of so many young visitors to drop out of verbal character, I thought it best to nod purposefully, then stride off over the bridge in a state of total ignorance.

William, the most senior under-steward, found me aimlessly humbling peasants in the paddock grove. He placed a hand on my shoulder, and as he led me back to the house explained the request he had now himself fulfilled: our noble lord had been asking for willow wands to smooth out tablecloths, as laid for the benefit of those gentry who had opted to eat outside. 'It's tough to get the hang of the language,' he said, when at length we reached the courtyard. 'But I just want you to know I think you're doing . . . *really well*.' If William had been older than thirteen, I would have felt less like burying my knee in his jewylls.

With those who would dine within waiting expectant in the great hall, we joined the grooms and stewards lined up by the kitchen. William had advised me I was to lead the procession of dishes and announce each to the seated gentry, but while assimilating this looming duty I found myself distracted by my first experience of the cook and her staff in action. It seemed more like a boiler room in there, a blur of smoke, fire and broth-spoiling industry. The utensils were crude and smutted, the raw ingredients of base and wholly unexotic appearance, and the ovens might more convincingly have been employed to power some pioneering pit pump.

How extraordinary, then, to see floury hands emerge from this filthy maelstrom bearing dishes of such aromatic and opulently decorative splendour, each passed into a waiting page's hands with the cook's flustered pronouncement: 'Marchepane tart of peaches . . . salat of portingales . . . snow in summer . . .' Pie of this, farce of that, brisket of the other – I didn't at this stage have any useful idea what most of these things were (marchepane is marzipan, in case I forget, and portingales – then shipped in from Portugal – were oranges), but that hardly seemed to matter. Each dish was at once a fabulous creation, and a sombre reminder of the dumbfounding gulf that divided the impossibly pampered few from the barley-boiling many. A gulf neatly embodied in the little ramekin of pease pottage that was last out of the kitchen: an ironic bit of rough, like those miniature cones of fish and chips they serve at up-market functions.

A maid rushed in from the dairy with a tray of butter pats fashioned into Tudor roses, followed by another bearing golfball-sized soft cheeses garnished with delicate blooms from the walled garden. I took them both, then turned to find the procession had left without me.

'. . . and marchepane tart of peaches!'

William's assured tones rang out around the great hall, giving way to a smattering of genteel applause from the high table, a dozen noblefolk seated Last-Supper-style behind the neatly marshalled pewterware. He turned as I walked in, shot me an infuriating wink, then nodded up at the minstrels' gallery, high above us near the distant hammer-beam ceiling.

On cue, Master Symon and his fellow musicians launched into some plucking, parping hey-nonny-nonnyism.

'Yeah, sorry, mate – we had to get cracking,' murmured my youthful usurper as I joined him and the other maids and pages by the serving table. Watching a moment later as he dispensed plcasantrics and portingales to his enchanted high-table fan club, I realised I was beginning to despise this child of thirteen. And pathetically, I despised him because I was jealous: jealous of his accomplished self-confidence, jealous of how he had won the hearts of every Kentwell notable with his cheeky (but authentic) banter and mischievous (but authentic) roister-doistering high-jinks. Jealous, most overwhelmingly, of the countless acts of reckless rebellion that always went undiscovered: refreshing himself from the wine jug, despite the ample crimson evidence that besmirched his ruff; hoisting surreptitious V-signs behind many a gentry back; idly flicking large amounts of food – soft cheeses, fruit, chunks of pastry – straight out of the window behind the serving table.

Contingent as they were upon my own poor showing, these resentments hardened impressively when I was taken to task by the high table's most terrifying resident, a forthright and aggressively flirtatious noblewoman. In a severe whisper, delivered as I proffered her a pie, she warned me that I was failing to display the authority befitting my role. 'Just *assert* yourself, man,' she hissed, her shrewish stare intensified by the wives-of-Henry headdress that crowned it, 'and for heaven's sake, work up a bit of chat, the odd witty rejoinder, *anything*.'

Half a dozen schoolboys now approached, gurning in automatic revulsion at the fare on display; presented with an audience, milady addressed me in ringing tones.

'Why, 'tis an ill place for a feather, Master Wat!'

A sudden silence entombed the hall; I tracked her prompting gaze to my quill, which through an accident of gravity now gave the impression of sprouting forth from my codpiece. A tinkling of noble laughter swelled then died away; many pairs of eyes, young and old, settled expectantly upon me. What

Would Joshua Do? A hundred klaxons went off in my head, with the unfortunate effect of evacuating it.

'Stuck right down my bell-end, innit?' I blared, or later wished I had. Instead, I looked back down at the feather, ears aflame, and directed at it an almost inaudible grunt of assent. My noble tormentor issued a strangled exasperation, and as the minstrels struck up afresh, leaned back and muttered, 'Well, maybe it'll come.'

After the nobility had had their fill and departed, the staff, as would henceforth be the case, dined in the next room along, on any leftovers not defenestrated by bored servants. The first school party filed in to find me mashing together pie crust, pottage and honey dressing in my bowl, and were filing out when, with an echoing report, my ale-filled wooden beaker split from lip to base.

I was dealing with the hose-soiling, William-cheering after-math when in walked the chap who had shown me round the manor all those months before. By dress and back story, the man I would know as Master George should have taken his rightful place on the high table; I was never quite sure why he had instead been obscurely seconded to ours. But how glad I would be of his and Mistress Joan's unfailingly cheerful guidance in the days ahead, and how glad I was that very moment when he spared me the ordeal of leading grace. In the bowl-clattering chatter that followed his amen, he sourced a spare cup from about his person and handed it to me with a smile. 'Master Wat, I bid you take this to the chamber yonder, and there refresh yourself from my vessel of squared form.' He flicked his head at a door marked 'Go Ye Notte This Way'; I slipped through into the off-limits realm beyond and there, on a side-table dense with silver-framed photographs of Patrick's forebears standing to monochrome attention, stood a three-litre wine box.

And so life about the manor settled into its peculiar two-speed, two-age routine. The days began with increasingly sweaty tent-reveilles, and long, hot mornings spent educating childer in the shadeless courtyard, clad from head to toe in thick black wool. 'A most fiery day about the manor,' said Master Symon each morning, trotting past with his lute towards the cool darkness of the house. My first duty was now to fill a huge zinc water-butt from a standpipe hidden under a sheet of hessian by the stewards' room door, for the purposes of rehydrating staff and visitors. Or, in reality, just the staff: the schoolchildren were invariably unwilling to spare themselves from parched death if doing so meant ingesting fluid which had 'got all bits in'.

Most of the days were now what they called 'free-flow', with the staggered school groups supplanted by a juvenile free-for-all: instead of seeing off regular waves of attackers, we now had to cope with an eight-hour blitzkrieg. The heat made the children more stupid and us staff more intolerant. It was very hard to give a straight answer when asked if those candles on the window sill were real, or that feather in my purse. Or the dead hare a teacher spotted rotating gently in the moat one morning, which a page and I fished out with a basket on a pole, and presented to the kitchen staff. Four hours later I ladled out jugged lumps of it on the high table.

Worst were those small groups with a very high staff-to-childer ratio, evidence of severe behavioural issues at best, impressive criminal records at worst. 'Is that a real knife? Can I have it? Are you a pirate? Are you a wanker?' Wilmott confided that though most Kentwellians came to escape the realities of modern life, she was here to get back in touch with them. I could see what she meant, but after such a gritty encounter it was very hard not to take it out on the next party of open-faced youngsters, beckoning them forth onto the courtyard, waiting until their rapt faces were angled up at mine, then shattering the expectant silence with a larynx-stripping bellow: 'I am Chamberlain, HEAR ME ROAR!'

On the most stifling morrow, a new batch of pages joined our ranks: I commandeered the smallest and most cherubic as my winsome courtyard assistant. After an hour young Nicholas, hitherto a silent and biddable prop, interrupted one of my interactive bow-and-curtsey workshops with a sort of extended wolf-like yodel. When I wheeled round to reprimand him, he looked straight through me, said, 'That's about right, David,' and embarked on a deeply unsettling drunken giggle. Then his eyes rolled up into his head; I caught him before he bit maze.

Mistress Joan took charge of the patient, and after we'd half-walked, half-carried Nicholas into the shade her suspicion of heatstroke was confirmed: we unbuttoned his doublet to find a thickly padded military jacket beneath. It later transpired that the poor mite had been turned away from the archery butts on age grounds, but had kept the uniform on out of stubborn pride. I wondered if he'd be carted off through the time tunnel in an ambulance, but the temptation of a bona fide invalid to work on proved too great for the herbalists. Nicholas was propped up in bed with an aromatic cold compress on his pale forehead, an object of curiosity for the endless stream of visitors jostling through the relevant bedchamber. He didn't so much convalesce as lie in state.

In the sparse moments of down time, Mistress Joan and I would find a patch of shade and stand there sharing murmurs of illicit vocabulary, the odd 'weirdo' or 'sod it', like two schoolkids splitting a crafty fag at the back of the hockey pitch. If she wasn't around I'd have to make do with a game of liar dice round the stewards' room table, plonking my plumply padded hose on a stool ('like having a built-in cushion, innit?', as Edmund pointed out). When defeat palled, I entertained myself by striking enigmatic *Man With a Pearl Earring* poses against the sunlit panelling, a period still life of fruit and pewter on the sideboard, frame-right.

It was an expression of how completely I had failed to subjugate them that the grooms and under-stewards all called me 'mate', if they called me anything at all. In the stewards' room I was accorded the stilted, rather reluctant companionship of some vaguely embarrassing cousin, or a French exchange student. And as Mr Barraclough to Joshua's Mr Mackay, how I dreaded ordering, asking, beseeching this room full of Fletchers to do my will.

All this was compounded by the fresh hell of Suffolk's Cockiest Page, a lumbering youth called Riece who one morning strode into the stewards' room to announce that we were all his bitches now. Riece called me 'chief', stole alcohol far more successfully than William and kept an out-of-tune bass guitar in the overcroft, meaning I had to take my tights off to the faltering strains of 'Smoke on the Water'. Somehow, though, he failed to get my goat, and not just because William had already ridden this metaphorical beast off over the horizon. There was no snide artifice in his exploits, just a barefaced and therefore oddly endearing cheek. Plus, as the son of a part-time poacher, he was a mine of era-appropriate trivia: if ever I need to skin a pheasant in a hurry, I now know to grab its tail, stand on both wings and pull.

Comfortably the most dreadful part of every day was gentry dinner, a parade of consistent ignominies that would begin with me announcing the dishes before I had transcribed each to memory. 'Salat of citrus and dates! Pease pottage! Pie of . . . bird!' Then it was into a wearisome hour of scuttling back and forth between high table and serving area.

'Salt, Master Wat, salt! There, doltish fellow, upon yonder mantel!'

'Whither go you, Master Wat? Wouldst thou show me thine arse?'

'Nay, nay, Master Wat, the *Rhenish* wine!'

Yet such theatrical chastisements were all part of what Mistress Joan called 'the game', and could – by a bigger man – be tolerated. What could not were the non-period grumblings of malicious discontent.

The most persistent dispenser of these was a moonfaced woman in a ludicrous dome of a hat that recalled *dizainier* Johann's 'knobhead' titfer. 'Do you think he even *knows* he's supposed to start serving from the middle of the table?' she muttered to her neighbour one day.

It was a fair point – I didn't – but one delivered with such odious spite that I could not hold my tongue. 'I pray most humble forgiveness, my lady,' I proclaimed, in a ghastly, obsequious sneer, 'for this foul and monstrous . . . monstrous . . .'

Oversight? Error? Nothing sounded nearly Tudor enough, and my indignant sarcasm fizzled out into red-eared silence. How maddening, how hateful that this day of all days William had been invited to dine with the gentry. As I retreated back to the serving table, he waved his pewter goblet and smiled broadly. 'Master Wat? I am run dry.'

I was now flat-lining through staff dinners in a state of humiliated exhaustion, wordlessly ingesting leftovers of heart pie, moat-drowned hare and – on Friday – the ample remnants of a bony and disappointingly bland carp. Inexplicably forgiving as they were of all my other failings, Mistress Joan and Master George both suggested that I assume a more active role at these occasions. No more effective way for the chamberlain to assert his dominance, they gamely insisted, than by ensuring no groom or under-steward put spoon to mouth until he gave the order. Because I knew that this was their gentle way of ordering me to say grace, I rudely stonewalled them. And then one day a ruddy-nosed noble, lately come upon the manor, barged in as Master George was clearing his voice at the head of our table.

'Hath not your chamberlain a voice?'

Master George shrugged slightly, shot me a bracing look, and sat down.

Knowing this dreadful moment might come, a couple of days before I had as a precaution commissioned our scrivener – the kindly old dear who penned the daily bill of fare in quill-etched Tudor script – to knock me out a couple of period graces. You may imagine my horror when I rose, bent to retrieve these from the belt purse I had folded them carefully into the previous morning, and found it empty but for my dice and coins.

'Prithee, I must away!' screamed a thousand inner voices. But with William licking his lips in my wobbly peripheral vision, from somewhere deep in my doublet I summoned a thousand and one more to scream them down. Before I could think better of it, I was stuttering my way through an on-the-hoof olde worlde remix of the standard text. 'For what we art to receiveth anon,' it began; mercifully I recall no more. Except that when it was done, I repaired directly through the forbidden door and there refreshed myself lavishly from Master George's vessel of squared form.

For those of us in the house, the afternoons were pleasingly low-key: most visitors, having made a beeline for the hall on arrival, did the grounds after lunch. As the shadows stretched across the Tudor Rose maze, we had little more to do than gaze into the carp-rippled moat, or mill photogenically about the court-yard. When that palled, and the coast was clear, we'd gather in the kitchen's smoky sunlight for tea and Jaffa cakes, sending out a page every few minutes to check the flag on the right-hand gatehouse. Factory-whistle cheers accompanied the news that it had been lowered: this was the sign that the last visitors had left, and we had this whole glorious place to ourselves.

Frisbees and farthingales on the front sward, mugs of Rhenish spritzer by the ice house: so schizophrenically entertaining were Kentwell's early evenings that I began to regret not experiencing them, as did the underclasses, in full kit. At least, even after hours and out of costume, I was still Master Wat; no one ever asked my real name, or used their own. Only through one rare slip did I learn that Mistress Joan's son Christian – a splendid fellow who ranked amongst Kentwell's finest archers – was in very truth a Paul. Many diehards had gone the extra mile and christened their offspring Harry, Bridget, Ned or some other Kentwell-ready name.

At around seven we all filed through the kitchen, where Patrick's Polish caterers doled out canteen nosh from big tin trays into our wooden bowls. We ate out on the front sward, watching the low sun gild the heraldic motifs that decorated the pavilions before us.

This restful prospect, and the rigours of a long, hot day, unfailingly sapped my enthusiasm for the jarring, Butlins-model entertainments arranged in the overcroft each evening. Instead, after a moderately beery deconstruction of the day's events with my fellow foremen, I would take the long way back to camp through the blue-black denouement of an early summer's day, breathing in hay and roses, and keeping an eye out for the alehouse keeper, whose nocturnal habit it was to get a little too high on his own supply, then roam the grounds with an assault rifle.

First a stroll through the delightful walled garden, a trim but fecund encapsulation of English horticulture, and then off across

the moonlit fields, glancing back at the hall's dark old brickwork
and leaden cupolas rising magnificently from the golden corn.
Out here in deepest Suffolk the prospects were helpfully timeless, a yawning agricultural flatness broken only by oaks and
church spires. It was startling to contemplate, as I did one night
after rescuing a local paper from a bin outside the time tunnel,
that somewhere out there was a world where people were racing
lawnmowers and being convicted of selling solvents to minors.
And thence, at last, to my sweatily nylon ease, waiting for barefoot sutlers in split-thigh cocktail dresses to trip over my guy
ropes on their unsteady way home from casino night.

Appropriately, I began to lose track of time. One afternoon
or other, someone's pet jackdaw got stuck in a goodwife's hair,
and in the consequent flailing she lost her wedding ring. The
morning before, or maybe after, a young gentry female split a
seam whilst cheerleading for William at some sporting event;
that afternoon, or the next, the two swapped roles and outfits
for a Shakespearian lark.

As the week wore on we started putting together what the
old hands called 'a bit of by-play for the punters'. One morning
Mistress Joan's son Christian rushed breathlessly across the
moat bridge to report that a Spaniard was abroad in the manor;
someone had plasticated a pig's heart, which we later presented
to the schoolchildren as proof of the spy's capture and execu-
tion, making two of them spontaneously retch. Three young
vagabonds were apprehended in the sunken garden with a pair
of great-hall candlesticks; a couple of hags came to beg scraps
from the kitchen, and I was summoned to expel them. ('I've
got a background in theatrical design,' whispered one, when I
passed approving comment on her soiled repulsiveness, 'so I
know how to degrade myself.')

That same mid-morning, Master George and I did take our
feudal ease about the manor, our mission to extend to the common
folk an invitation to dine upon the great-hall side-show known
as 'low table'. Even though I now expected it, the shock and awe
wreaked by our presence was still too much, or almost too much.
Forelocks were tugged until I feared they might tear loose, and

172

the standard reaction to our offer was a wordless whimper: half a dozen places were up for grabs, but in an hour we only offloaded four. No interest amongst the potters, or the mummers, or Christian and his hawser-armed comrades on the archery butts, busy ventilating a straw-stuffed Scotsman from eighty yards. And this despite the fact that they'd be dining that day, in the words of one stout bowman, 'on roadkill'.

In the end only three of our invitees were bold enough to turn up at the appointed hour, and their cowering servility was something to behold. 'Do I use a spoon or a knife to eat this?' whispered an aged seamstress, grasping desperately at my many detached hose-strips as I passed along the low table with a marchepane tart of something or other. 'And what should I say to people? Please? *Please?*'

I grimly unclamped her filthy hands from my livery and walked on by, wishing this act of haughty contempt didn't feel so good. That it did was down to my latest humiliating reverses in the War Against William, and the ego repairs thus necessitated. An hour before, as I was filling my mug from the water-butt, he'd run up, plunged his sweaty head straight in, and run off, leaving me soaked and revolted. And just a minute gone by, there he was, giving me the wink as I was once more brusquely recalled to the high table. 'Are there not two ends to the table, Master Wat? Is your head addled by the sun?'

As the week wore on I became rather deft at rationalising these petty inter-staff rivalries as an authentic part of behind-the-scenes life in a big house, but somehow that day it was all too much. Too old to buddy up with the vast bulk of my fellow servants; too thick to cut it with the toffs. *Upstairs, Downstairs,* with me marooned on the landing.

A day or three later I crossed the courtyard on the most fiery morrow yet, ducked into the darkness of the stewards' room and found it in sweaty disarray, a Vermeer reimagined by Hogarth. A flotilla of Starburst wrappers bobbed gaily about on the water-butt, the wheelchair ramp was home to many empty aluminium reminders of the previous night's cider-powered courtyard ceilidh, the two maids who now shambled in were both wearing Ray-Bans, and the first school party would be crossing the moat bridge any minute.

I was halfway into a rather impressive rant when a chorus of listless mumbles from the shadows cut me short: 'No schools . . . late opening . . . Saturday.' My furious glower melted away. Saturday; my last day. It was with some surprise that I detected a pang of regret in the emotions this information released.

Emerging from the overcroft a few minutes earlier I'd noted a spring in my flat-soled step, the spring of a man on his merry way to work, not some humiliating fancy-dress parade. A glance at my reflection in the moat confirmed the authenticating effect of a few days away from the razor: in the Kentwell vernacular, my outfit now suited me right meet. Yet again I had adapted to period life only at the death. It would be a week before I felt entirely comfortable without a hat, and purging my vocabulary of the last remnants of Tudorspeak required twice that; 'mayhap', 'most wondrous' and 'upon the yester' were the last to go.

Goodwives and gentlemen crossed my path; I graciously acknowledged or pre-empted their greetings as status dictated. A pair of sutlers ambled merrily past, and I recalled a showdown at the second open day, in which their station had been sternly warned to 'authenticate their pottage', following a raid the previous summer that netted two pots of Cajun seasoning mix. The memory failed to inspire more than a half chuckle: the fear and ridicule that once dominated my feelings for these people had progressed from understanding to admiration. Indeed I now found it impossible not to envy their detailed back stories, their mastery of ancient skills and speech, the almost heroic pedantry that made Kentwell what it was: as perfect a recreation of life at a Tudor manor as you could reasonably hope to expect. Living history was a phrase I had rather wearied of, one trotted lamely out at every 'Eye of the Tiger'-soundtracked jousting demo, but looking around at the coiffed and straw-hatted figures wandering out to their far-flung work stations, it seemed the only accurate description of my environment.

And so I'd clacked across the brickwork maze with a cocky,

almost proprietorial air, musing for the first time on my converging responsibilities in both past and present. If, as Patrick had told us, the Great Annual Recreation sustained his estate for the rest of the year, then surely in my role as the big boss man in black, I was charged with keeping this house in order both fictionally and factually. I had grown into my role, and what a very important role it was.

By gratifying coincidence an especially grand dinner had been laid on that day, with the gentry personally subsidising the centre-piece dish that some hours later I saw in the latter stages of preparation: chicken dressed as lizard, a magnificent dragon-like contrivance decorated with hundreds of overlapping cucumber 'scales', and stuffed with sausage forcemeat. No surprise to see that this spectacle had attracted a long line of pages to the kitchen, at least until Mistress Joan trotted rather breathlessly up and informed me that they were actually there to ferry a waiting array of less exotic dishes out to the frontsward picnic.

My twin tasks at this event, established by precedent and reiterated by Master George that morning, were to usher those gentry who had opted to lunch alfresco to the allotted pavilion in good time, and thence to lead the procession of dish-bearing pages from kitchen to lawn. Waylaid by sack-clothed sycophants and camera-happy visitors during my farewell perambulation about the grounds, I had only now arrived to fulfil the second of these duties, having entirely overlooked the first. For a tiny moment I wondered if this oversight might be laughed off; a glance at Mistress Joan's round-eyed, pale-faced dismay made it plain it could not. As a breach of Tudor protocol and decorum, presenting salat of portingales to an empty table was, as I now well understood, right off the Kentwell scale.

The forces of panic were massing impressively in my head, and in combination with the befuddling heat swiftly convinced me that the best course of action would be to go out in a blaze of ignominy, an in-for-a-groat sequence of outrages. I'd blow off in a minstrel's lap, jump on Patrick's back and ride him into his moat, treat that lizard to a very different sort of sausage forcemeat. Then I looked down the line of pages, saw one face radiant with amusement, and thought of something much better.

'William,' I said, resolute and stentorian, 'are those that would dine without not yet summoned?' My tormentor's glee atrophied, and from the mouth that had expressed it emerged a series of faltering protestations; I'd never previously thought of 'b-b-b-but' as something people might actually say. Graciously I offered to keep his fellow pages in a holding formation while he righted this grievous wrong, and a while later he returned, red-faced, muttering under his breath and tutting theatrically above it. I should have left it there, but my dander was up. 'Mayhap thou art weary from this burdensome undertaking?' The vocab was all wrong, but I took care to linger over the patronising form of address.

'Meaning what, Wat?' he half-spat, and for a vivid moment it seemed this whole idiotic business would end in a physical coming-together.

It was a thought that recurred to me a couple of hours later, when I looked up from a wooden bowl of leftover chicken dressed as lizard, and saw my children gawping at me from the front rank of spectators. In blending amusement, awe and concern their expressions unsettled me not – I had beheld the same mix on several thousand faces over the previous week – but the proportions would have been rather different had they discovered their long-absent father trading ruff-wristed blows with a thirteen-year-old boy.

'Come hither, childer,' I said, at the declamatory volume that was now second nature, and as one they took a small but obvious step thither.

Chapter Six

The moment I beheld Roman legionaries clanking in formation around a Las Vegas parking lot was the moment I vowed to experience transatlantic living-history at first hand. A horribly patronising sneer besmirched my face whenever I imagined the prospect, which was increasingly often now that my journey through time had nosed into the realms of non-native American history – let's not forget that Virginia was named thus in honour of the famously intact Elizabeth I.

What a deflating, sneer-wiping experience, when at last I sat down to select myself a Stateside group, to discover historical re-enactment as we know it today to be an entirely American invention. The transatlantic phenomenon that is the Renaissance Faire may have serious re-enactors choking on their pottage, but the fact remains that these beery celebrations of velvet and cleavage, which today attract five million Americans a year with their Drench-A-Wench stalls and jousting unicyclists, can trace their heritage right back to the late fifties. A young Dustin Hoffman earned his acting spurs at one, playing a dragon slain by St George.

By the mid sixties, while those pioneering neo-Vikings shuffled uncertainly up the Isle of Man beaches in their Dr Scholl's sandals, American enthusiasts were already organising incomparably more professional re-enactments as part of the Civil

War centenary festivities. The movement was soon sufficiently well entrenched for US participants to abbreviate themselves as 'nactors, and before the decade was out an American had coined what would become the globally accepted term of derision applied to any ill-equipped weekend casual: 'farb', a word of obscure etymology, perhaps most convincingly explained as a contraction of 'far be it from me to criticise that impression'. It is perhaps the greatest testimony to US living history's well-worn heritage that its participants were dissing each other for inauthenticity at a time when the Sealed Knot, the English Civil War group that kickstarted European re-enactment, was still but a pewtery twinkle in its founders' eyes.

Give or take the odd ringtone and roll-up, in terms of immersive authenticity my experiences to date had been characterised by a generally upward trajectory. If I wished to continue this trend, it would mean tracking down an unusually dedicated living historian, the 'nactor's 'nactor. And that, in splendid defiance of my lazy preconceptions, meant crossing the Atlantic.

'I have heard this fellow spoken of at re-enactors' workshops, revered as the ultimately developed character' . . . 'His persona is a truly authentic settler, like a relic from another age' . . . 'My brother said he just showed up with his animals and blew everyone away.' Clue by clue, link by link, arresting commendation by arresting commendation, I homed in on my target and began to track him down across the American scene's sprawling online territories.

The nameless cattleman in question seemed imbued with a semi-mythical status: the few who claimed a sighting told of a character apparating at historical fairs with a well-trained team of oxen, then apparating out again, leaving a profound impression but no contact details. After a couple of weeks of this I began to wonder if the whole thing was the product of febrile minds and too many nights round the campfires, like something out of a Clint Eastwood ghost Western.

I was about to move on when a name abruptly landed in my inbox. 'Hi Tim – I think you are looking for Gerry Barker, from Wisconsin.' An eager reply prompted a photographic attachment: 'Here is the gent in question at an event in Ohio. He really projects the image!'

I double clicked and found myself confronted by a senior interpretation of the *Rocky Horror Show*'s Riff Raff, casually at ease upon a recumbent, nose-ringed steer. An attendant foreground schoolboy, beaming into camera beneath a tricorn hat evidently removed from the bald pate behind him, obscured most of what went on below that craggy face and the straggly curtains of grey hair that framed it. Only the cattleman's feet were visible: utterly bare, but for a lavish slathering of bullshit.

The personal details swiftly procured an email address; the almost instant reply to my tentative approach confirmed that here was a re-enactor cut from a very much rougher cloth than any I had yet encountered. Declaring that his focus was on 'living-history experiments', not public events, Mr Barker described at length the life of a lone ox wagoner, *circa* 1775, and his zealous determination to emulate it. My eye ran through paragraphs littered with troubling phrases of intent: 'middle of nowhere . . . fifteen miles a day . . . sleeping on the ground without a tent . . . trail food – a lot of Johnny cake'. In reference to a throwaway comment I'd made regarding his bare feet, he wrote: 'I do usually walk without shoes, but I got frost-bitten this past winter and am not recovered yet, so may reconsider.'

All this meant I had to struggle very hard to accept an invitation to accompany him for a few days in the calmly gracious manner with which it was issued, and to blot out the implications of its accompanying caveat: 'I had not intended to ask any one else to take part, because it is going to be uncomfortable.' The sign-off that ended this sobering communication seemed to toll out across the screen. 'Good enough, I have to get out and beat animals. Your Obedient Serv't, Sir, Gerry Barker.'

Further contact revealed Gerry as a man of companionable charm and understated wit, but did nothing to appease my terror. Three months later, seated in the arid, air-conditioned chill of Cincinatti Airport's meeting point, I reacquainted myself with a print-out of his collated correspondence, and the improbable blend of erudite curiosity and horny-handed endurance that defined it. 'I am probably too intense for most people,' he had written early on, 'but my personal goal has been to learn from controlled living-history projects, experiments that start with a question.'

Questions Gerry had previously sought to answer included whether it was possible to turn a patch of forest into a two-storey log cabin in three months using only eighteenth-century equipment (it was); if one man could make gunpowder from scratch in a weekend (using bat crap and charcoal, he could; and how long it might take a family to clear a plot of land, raise from this a crop of flax, and process the resultant harvest into a shirt (a year, and 120 hours of labour per head). Along with a hardy crew of likeminded companions, Gerry had built roads, led pack trains through mountains and across rivers, and waged a five-month campaign against Native Americans, who from hereon in I'm going to have to call Indians, because this was 1775 and anything else just sounds silly. He had done things that were doubtless awful in ways I didn't understand, like boiling salt, retting jute and surveying 130 rods of boundary, and things that I all too clearly did: 'At the Siege of Martin's Station we wanted to see what it was like for sixty people and their animals to live enclosed in an area the size of a basketball court.'

I folded the wodge of paper back into the smutted linen haversack that had now been at my side since the first century AD, contemplating once again how richly deserved was the hallowed, almost legendary status which the 'nacting community had conferred upon the man I was soon to meet. An academic with an MA in Labour History, and an experimental archaeologist whose unquenchable thirst for calloused and malnourished adventure was expressed in the worrisome phrase that ended his final email: 'I am as careful with historical accuracy as the current law allows.' Gerry Barker: Übernactor.

'Uh, Mr Moore?'

I looked up and found a generous slice of foreground filled by a huge, panting man with a walking stick. Long grey smock, long grey hair, and an air of breathless bemusement: he looked for all the world like an acid casualty who had wandered off into the woods in the summer of 1967, and only just found his way out. 'How's flying these days?' he wheezed, having introduced himself as Butch. 'Kind of gave that up forty years back.'

Butch, I knew from our emails, was an old friend of Gerry's, and a long-term collaborator in historical endeavours: the smock, I noted with a now well-trained eye, was in truth a shin-length linen shift, and the headband which kept his hair off that moist forehead was more pioneer than pot-head. 'Gone let myself get unfit and fat,' he sighed, pausing for breath as we shuffled towards the airport multi-storey. How I regretted not expressing more forcefully a willingness to drive myself from Cincinatti to the Daniel Boone National Forest, the million-acre Kentucky wilderness Gerry had selected for his latest experiment.

Only after several further rests did Butch arrive at the extravagantly careworn pick-up truck that was to take us there. 'Someone bust into the cab last night,' he grunted, unnecessarily nodding his head at the glinting shards of quarter-light that carpeted the threadbare front seats. I brushed off the worst and climbed in, breathing in a now-familiar draught of woodsmoke and dung, and placing my feet carefully into a footwell filled with straw hats, tins of a substance mysteriously labelled 'Instant Shoe Foal Extension' and a great many balls of lead shot, which cannoned noisily into the bulkhead when Butch engaged reverse and stamped on the loud pedal.

We had about 150 miles to drive, Butch reckoned; with the odometer broken and the speedo needle hanging limply at zero, he could be no more precise. What time would we get there? Butch smiled carelessly. 'My watch fell off in 1975,' he said, 'and I never have seen a reason to put it back on.'

I gazed through the cracked windscreen as malls and motels

thinned out into primeval forest, my stubbled cheeks buffeted by waves of thick and clammy August afternoon blasting in through the broken window. Not shaving for three days beforehand was now part of my two-pronged pre-re-enactment programme, the other being to stuff my fat face like a squirrel preparing for winter. Never before had my short-term nutritional future looked bleaker – pondering the composition of 'Johnny cake' as I laid waste to my sleeping neighbour's in-flight breakfast, I imagined Gerry offering some future historical companion a runny portion of Timmy cake.

We stopped at an agricultural superstore, where Butch shuffled incongruously through clusters of check-shirted, baseball-capped good old boys in search of bovine insect repellent. Fair enough, I thought: the oxen hadn't volunteered for this trip, so it didn't seem right to punish them as part of our own perverse pursuit of period discomforts. Browsing the aisles I found my attention attracted by a display-case crammed with viciously serrated weaponry, lethal chemicals and armoured protective clothing. Presiding over this was a placard with a starkly evocative legend: 'The Stuff You Need Out Here'.

On we rumbled towards the hazy, blue-green southward horizon. Where did 'out here' start, and how would we cope in it without any of that stuff? Surveying the rolling, unpeopled immensity, and hearing of Butch's upbringing on a Wisconsin dairy farm – with his father an invalid, he'd been left in charge of the herd at the age of twelve – I realised how close so many in this great and still largely untamed land must feel to their pioneering forefathers, in a way that so few Europeans ever could. To condense Gerry's living-historical mission into a fatuous one-liner, his aim was to find out how the West was won. Out here in rural Kentucky, with a population half that of London's dispersed across an area larger than Hungary, it was easy to imagine this as an ongoing battle.

Butch's preferred mode of interaction was to intersperse long, companionable silences with arresting revelations, stridently delivered. 'Know what I do?' he'd blurt, drawing me from jetlagged slumber. 'That's right, I've got me a bee farm!'

Through this conversational process – one rendered more compelling once the sun settled towards the eastern hills and we had an already quiet road to ourselves – I learned that Butch was registered disabled with severe dropsy, that his 'nactment-phobic wife was delighted to have him 'confined to an armchair', and that a fear of 'everything going down' courtesy of a Y2K-bug government plot had compelled him to see in the millennium in the sanctuary of Gerry's house. And I learned that my chauffeur was an ordained minister. 'I hate any kind of "ism",' he yelped abruptly, 'except creationism!' With that he thrust a business card at me, and in the squinting half-light I read it: 'Dr Butch Hauri, Frontier Reform Church'. And underneath: 'Adventures with God'. 'I'm the real thing, by the way,' he added. 'Licensed to hatch, match and dispatch.'

Deep into the silence that followed, we turned down an unkempt road signposted 'Salt Lick', which inspired my chauffeur into a sermon on the effects of livestock dehydration. Fatigue and a terror of offending a licensed dispatcher had for some time restricted my contributions to the odd hum and nod, so it was something of a surprise to hear myself inform Butch that the ox was an endangered species in most European countries. 'A *what*? An ox is just an old bull, London boy!' And he laughed and laughed, like they did in the *Dukes of Hazzard*.

He was still chuckling wheezily as we drove across a huge dam, past a sign that welcomed us to the Daniel Boone National Forest, and then off into a lakeside car park, empty but for a cavernous cage-sided trailer. I climbed out, briefly entertained Butch with my flailing attempts to see off several hundred winged parasites, and climbed back in. For some time we sat and watched the daylight fail. 'Re-enactors talk about "doing it like Barker",' Butch suddenly exclaimed. 'They come up and offer to buy his old clothes, like he was a celebrity.' Another long pause. 'Do you have any idea how many thousands of people would give their eye teeth to experience what you're about to experience?'

'Is it fourteen?' I felt like saying.

Then, distantly at first, but soon with twilight-shredding intensity, a rumbling tumult of clanks and scrapes echoed forth from the dark woodland ahead of us, periodically counterpointed with the gees and hups of livestock management. Presently the cream linen bonnet of a covered wagon asserted itself through the gloaming, followed in order of luminosity by the jiggling ivory sickles of eight bull horns, two human faces, the pale blue flanks of the wagon itself and finally, huge and rusty, four lumbering, nose-ringed beasts of burden.

Gerry ambled across to us, displaying a diffident charm that had not been apparent in his online photograph, and introduced himself and his twelve-year-old wagoner's lad Jacob, a brown-eyed, white-smiled Huckleberry Finn with nothing on his feet but filth and scratches. Our greetings were pleasingly low-key, as if this was a rendezvous casually suggested that morning over a shared pot of campfire coffee. Gerry was slighter than I'd expected, the wiry side of trim; ancient, blurred tattoos embellished both leathery forearms. Since that photo had been taken he'd trimmed his shoulder-length side-straggle, thereby granting a clearer view of the cracked and crusted rivulets of dried blood that decorated much of his head, their source an awful crusted wound atop his cranium.

'One of the boys flicked a horn out at a horsefly,' he explained, in a disarmingly cultured murmur. 'Guess I wasn't paying attention.'

'Filled his whole hat with blood!' piped up Jacob, cheerfully awestruck. Gerry shrugged carelessly, showed me a poorly stocked set of front teeth, and told Butch and me of a change in plan: courtesy of some ranger-level bureaucratic stupidity, we were now required to relocate our camp to a distant corner of the forest.

Gerry tossed me a sack of well-used, self-made clothing, then with an air of quiet efficiency I would become very familiar with, set about encouraging a quartet of implacable, van-sized animals into a wheeled cage. Some years before, I had been party to a more modest variant of this challenge, involving a horsebox and a very small donkey; the task had taken three of us, all healthy adults, two profane and increasingly violent hours. In consequence, I watched in awe as with no more than a few whispered words and a prompting tweak on the nose-ring, the first ox clattered obediently up the ramp.

As he worked, I delved through Gerry's sack in the evening gloom, picking out a pair of heavily patched knee-length grey britches, a set of beige hemp chaps to cover them, white woollen socks and a wide-brimmed brown felt hat of the type a prospector might have worn, with a stubby clay pipe stuck jauntily through two holes in its high, domed crown. Teaming all this with my Kentwell shift and belt – both pre-approved by Gerry – was a process that allowed a dozen bloodsuckers to make their mark about me, and required asking a twelve-year-old boy to tighten my chaps.

Last on were the shoes, thin-soled, brown-suede moccasin-like affairs, with integral straps tied above the ankle. Of everything I'd just put on, these were the only items I'd take off in the ninety-six hours that lay ahead. And this despite my entire wardrobe being comprehensively slathered in cow crap and axle grease before the first of those hours was even fifteen minutes old.

With Gerry leading by very active example, and poor Butch a hobbled spectator, Jacob and I helped persuade the last steaming dun behemoth up a ramp now slick with fresh slurry. Then we crammed ourselves into the pick-up cab and squeaked and rattled away into the empty night, four tons of horned beef lowing behind us.

The magnitude of our primeval playground became apparent in the long drive required to traverse it in search of our re-designated camp area; I learned later that at $3,600 km^2$, the Daniel Boone National Forest is the size of one and a half Luxembourgs.

Hunched over the wheel, Gerry whiled away the journey with a health and safety lecture, one whose downbeat, deadpan tone very much belied its content, focused as this was on the many creatures whose attentions might disfigure us. First up: the brown recluse, an arachnid whose entirely innocuous appearance belied a bite that had accounted for many a

185

Kentuckian limb, as well as the odd chin and nose. When it came to venomous snakes, we'd be spoilt for choice: a month after my return one of his oxen took a copperhead bite and was lame for a fortnight. Gerry's principal tip here was to lift any rocks or logs from the far side first, giving you the opportunity to let go and crush any serpents thus revealed before they went for you.

Bears weren't generally too aggressive at this time, but they'd certainly be around; at his farm over the other side of Kentucky, he shot a couple most years. 'Remember that tub of grease you put in the trailer for me?' I could hardly fail to: much of it, obscurely, was now smeared all over my neck and ears. 'A genuine homemade animal product.' Gerry smiled at the road ahead. After a while he felt obliged to add that the reliable contemporary firearm he had brought along (a *Dirty Harry* Magnum), and the four rounds of ammunition with which it was loaded, was solely reserved for delivering a humane *coup de grâce* to any crippled oxen.

Presently the road nosed out of the forest boundaries, and passed through a sad little town, all flaky weatherboard and rust-blistered enamel, moribund and antiquated as an abandoned *Waltons* set. The volunteer fire truck was listing on two flat tyres, and the General Store had a child's trike in one mottled window and a greying wedding dress in the other. 'You know you're a redneck when there are wheels on your house but not on your car,' said Gerry, as the town gave way to a long stretch of road sporadically lined in this manner. After a few more miles of nothingness a truckstop diner glowed out of the dark, and we pulled in.

Walking into a restaurant dressed as we were, and smelling as we did, would in most other first-world countries have had us arrested, or at least taken into care. It says something about rural Kentucky that our appearance invited no comment, nor even a second glance. 'You doin' good there, boys?' asked a politely bored waitress, and in a minute there I was, eating ribs in Stinky Pete's hat and a pair of steer-soiled hemp chaps.

186

Greasily replete, we headed back into the dark rural enormity, and after a few map-squinting roadside breaks turned off tarmac and on to mud. A long hour later, following a series of treacherous manoeuvrings, Gerry reversed the huge trailer into an area of grass behind a firing range. He led his boys away into the black pasture beyond, while Jacob and I rooted blindly about in the pick-up truck for things to sleep on. Butch could only sit and talk. 'You know, he's just a big old softie,' he said, as Gerry clinked distantly about with ox-tethering picket posts. 'He's had sixteen oxen now and still don't like talking about the ones he's lost.' He chuckled gently. 'Wouldn't think he had four tours of duty in Vietnam behind him.'

Darkness, and the enormous tarpaulin I was carrying, hid my facial reaction to this news. It explained the tattoos, but sat very awkwardly with Gerry's muted erudition. Reconciling the two became yet more of a challenge as Butch sketched out his friend's military CV: twenty-one years in service, many of them as a sergeant in the 'top Special Forces unit in Vietnam'; three serious injuries, including an incident involving white phosphorus that had hospitalised Gerry for a year; a vast haul of decorations. With a deprecatory chortle Butch ended off a one-sentence account of the decade in Missouri that comprised his own Army career. Then he sighed up at the sky, and the drizzle it was starting to leak. 'Yep, Gerry and me, we've been through a lot. Both sixty-two, been re-enacting together for twenty-six years. We're closer than brothers, close as two straight men can be.'

Jacob and I had laid out everything flat we could find – two big tarps, half a dozen rough woollen blankets, a quartet of half-length mattress rolls – when Gerry ambled back. Those of us who were wearing shoes took them off, then we divvied out bedding, rustled around for a bit, and settled down as best we could. The drizzle died away, the clouds moved on and suddenly the upward view was more star than sky. The fireflies came out, the moon was full: just another perfect night out in the God-forsaken depths of *Deliverance* country.

I hoped I'd be too tired to dwell on bears and brown recluses, but soon established I was not. Rustles and creaks assailed us from all sides, some distant, some whimperingly proximate. A hundred tiny legs seemed to scuttle about my person; with sweat pooling into my ears and my limbs in rigid spasm, I restricted myself to just one swift bout of frenzied self-slapping. Would these people ever know what it was costing me to maintain this impression of a happy-go-lucky historical adventurer, feebly unconvincing as it might be? What a merciful relief, at least, to find myself sharing a tarpaulin with one of the world's very hardest bastards. At least until he rolled over, met my blinkless, who-goes-there stare and whispered, 'You know, I never really sleep.'

It was pitch black when the sounds of bovine activity awoke me, though when I removed my hat from my face it most blatantly was not. The rain had returned overnight – hence my repositioned headwear – but had now made way for a clear blue dawn, the sun falling obliquely across the great stretch of gleaming pasture before us, and the mighty wall of muscular vegetation that reared up beyond it.

The jolt of bewilderment that accompanied every re-enactment reveille had never been more highly charged: where the, how the, who the, what in the name of all that was right was I doing here, out in the million-acre back of beyond with only a trio of barefoot extremists and their enormous ginger animals for company?

I surveyed the most proximate of the latter, browsing untethered a few yards from my feet, steamy piss gushing from the tuft of hair that dangled from its pizzle. Only now did I accept the defectiveness of my nocturnal risk assessment – which had, I now recalled, obliged me to re-don my shoes in a moment of small-hours insecurity. As Gerry would later confirm, the dominant bestial threat as we slept was not a brutal or venomous bite, but the benign wanderings of his heavyweight grazers, any of whom might nonchalantly stove in our skulls with a careless hoof. After returning home I learned that death by bovine trampling has accounted for eight British ramblers in the past decade.

We'd left the wagon back at the lakeside car park, and as I laid my wet bedding out in the sun, Gerry and Jacob returned with it in the trailer. Helping to trundle this handsome and evocative vehicle down the ramp, I learned that Gerry had built it himself – all of it, right down to the last iron rivet, cast and tempered in his own forge. Two years toil, from sawing the first plank to painting his initials on the tailgate.

'I guess I'm kind of a fanatic in whatever I do,' he confessed mildly, laying to rest my post-Kentwell terror that with our scenario now established, we might be expected to converse in period tongue. Our correspondence had showcased Gerry's confident grasp of Revolutionary-era language, but in the days ahead the only archaic idiom to pass his blistered lips was the occasional 'good enough'.

I listened in wonder, and a powerful sense of inadequacy, to the whistle-stop tour of Gerry's expansive hinterland that now followed: the mountaineering, the marathon running, the multilingualism (he could make himself understood in half a dozen European tongues, including Norwegian and Polish). And – his first reference to the momentous career encapsulated to me by Butch – the military.

In Vietnam he had spent a year with a remote tribe of former headhunters, training them as scouts to track down VC supply routes; he had also, in one siege, endured 104 consecutive days in wet mud. His post-Nam military career had seen him instructing elite units across the NATO world – the SAS included – on survival techniques and the art of escaping from a POW camp. 'You could say I've built up quite a tolerance for hardship,' he said, as we manhandled the wagon through the damp tussocks. 'Maybe even got a bit of a taste for it.'

More profoundly, these experiences had also left him with a deep-seated, philosophical belief that if only man could look back over his past errors, he might avoid making them again in the future. 'I'm with that guy who said that those who do not learn from history are doomed to repeat it,' he told me, doubtless well aware who that guy was, but diplomatically allowing me to camouflage my own ignorance with a sage nod.

Breakfast was perspiring cheese and slices of limp sausagemeat, wrapped in a well-used cloth and relieved from one of the many boxes and chests that in the usual manner doubled as fireside seating. I sluiced it down with my first historically legal coffee: a handful of crushed beans brewed up in a blackened billycan hung above a neat little fire Butch had got going as I slept.

The sun climbed, the oxen browsed, Jacob gambolled barefoot through the shiny grass. Round the fire Gerry gamely launched a sadly one-sided debate on the political cartoons of Thomas Rowlandson, all the while pencilling notes and calculations in a little copybook, his handwriting a honed facsimile of the swirls and curlicues of eighteenth-century penmanship. I leaned over for a closer look: he ran a grubby finger down the columns, explaining the bushel maths detailed therein. In the days ahead, Gerry explained, he hoped to establish what was a realistic full load for an ox-drawn wagon, and how far such a vehicle might travel on lonely forest paths between dawn and dusk.

Tilting the billycan dregs into our tin mugs, Gerry laid out the historical context for his latest experiment. By the summer of 1775, Britain's grip on its American colonies had been weakening for some time; it was eighteen months since unenfranchised Bostonians had introduced their native marine life to the stimulating effects of black Bohea tea. In April, a bloody engagement between British troops and patriot militia at Lexington, near Boston, had marked the start of the Revolution's armed phase. 'The shot heard round the world,' was how Ralph Waldo Emerson described the opening salvo, but from what Gerry had to say, the bang didn't reach Kentucky. 'This was the frontier. No one out here would have known or cared about the War of Independence.' Only in 1782, with the war almost won, did Kentucky see any action.

In the latter half of the eighteenth century, the lonely lands just west of the Appalachian Mountains were known only to the boldest or most desperate pioneers, and hardly familiar even to the Shawnee Indians, the dominant regional tribe, who used the area as a hunting ground but established few permanent settlements. Most auspicious of the select colonials to stride across the Appalachians through the Cumberland Gap was Daniel Boone, a man I was only previously aware of for always getting me mixed up with Davy Crockett, on funny-hat grounds.

Boone was the hardest of the hardcore pioneers, a frontiersman whose CV came stuffed with terrifying dramas: rescuing his daughter and two others through a surprise attack on their Shawnee kidnappers; being adopted by the said tribe's chief after astounding them with his hunting and tracking skills following his own subsequent capture; surviving an ambush in which several companions were tomahawked to death as they slept.

This latter alarum enlivened a successful attempt in the spring of 1775 to hack a path into the heart of Kentucky. Boone built his fortified home at the end of what would be known as the Wilderness Road – can't imagine that went down well with the Kentucky Relocation Board – and is fondly remembered as the state's founding father. The untamed forest that engulfed us was a fitting monument to a man once described as 'a determined rejector of civilisation'. For a fitting embodiment of his legacy, I had to look no further than the barefoot figure now ambling back from a comfort break in the trees behind us.

'Good news,' said Gerry, picking idly at the huge scab on that bald and weather-beaten pate. 'Just seen an eight-foot black king snake back there, so I don't think we'll be bothered by much else.' This apparently took into account the thumb-sized ants I could see scuttling about on the nearby tarpaulin that would be my bed for the next four nights, if not the ground-hornet nest Gerry now located a few paces behind my haversack pillow. 'Watch for that if you need to visit the woods in the night,' he said, though I'd long since vowed to preclude any such excursion by the simple expedient of wetting myself. Then he squinted up at a now potent sun, assessed the hour by counting the hand-widths that separated it from the horizon, and suggested 'a little walk with the boys'.

Some years ago, while traversing Spain in the sole company of the donkey previously alluded to, my expansive ignorance of farmyard-class hoofed animals evolved into deep respect. Mutual understanding, interdependence, companionship – just some of the factors that ought to have underpinned this respect, which was in depressing reality dominated by a base fear of having my genitals pulped by an incoming Buckeroo number. As Gerry and I walked towards his browsing behemoths, one by one they raised their huge horned heads from the grass to survey our approach with curiosity, hatred, dread, affection, whatever it was that went on behind that bland, impenetrable gaze. How sad that I was already defining my relationship with these magnificent animals, each four-square and flourishing as a period livestock portrait, by their ability to injure me. Totting up the hooves and horns on display, all I saw were twenty-four new ways of meeting a ridiculous end.

Hailing George, William, Charles and James ('four of my least favourite kings') by name, Gerry brought his herd to attention and then swiftly to heel. With a series of gentle calls and grunts, and just the merest tug on a nose-ring, he somehow persuaded the rear oxen to reverse back over the various bits of tackle attached to the wagon's towing pole; another gesture and they bowed their heads, allowing Gerry to affix the pair to a mighty neck yoke burnished with age and use. In a moment more he had manoeuvred and attached the front two, then with a modest chorus of hups, a cacophony of trundling creaks and clanks and a wave to Jacob and Butch, the six of us and our wagon eased off, past the awkward intrusion of our pick-up truck, and away up the deserted earthen trail into another age.

By 1775, almost a million British colonists – religious refugees, economic migrants and convicts – had settled in North America, and it's estimated that of the four million Americans counted in the first US census in 1790, some 80 per cent were of British descent. In curious consequence, as Gerry had already reassured me, my period American accent was more authentic than his; imagining myself as a recent

arrival in the colonies, I was struck by the distorted familiar-
ities that characterised this new world. The rolling swathes of
oak and birch had provided a reassuringly English backdrop as
we'd driven by them at twenty-first-century speed, but close
up, at ox pace, there was an odd, almost psychedelic twist to
our surroundings: the blades of grass were too broad, the leaves
on the trees too green, the butterflies and dragonflies too plentiful, too colourful and far, far too large. Our rattling, rumbling
progress would send birds chirruping away through the tree-
tops; I'd look up expecting to see dun-hued anonymities making
their escape, and instead catch lurid flashes of scarlet.

I'd imagined the life of an ox wagoner as one long and
leisurely, straw-chewing stroll through the countryside, letting
the ox-train take the strain. I quickly found it was not. Our
outing, an unladen two-mile jog up the trail and back, was no
more than a brisk recce for the full-scale expeditions to come,
yet even this modest journey proved fraught with alarums.
When Gerry yelped out a warning to mind where I trod, he
wasn't alerting me to the latest wet sack of crap flopping out
on the trail, but my proximity to the cartwheels: he had once
thus bisected a dog. On even modest descents, we had to swiftly
attach a chain-brake to a rear wheel to forestall a destructive
runaway; on the uphill sections, any delay in cracking the whip
(a skill Gerry performed with forest-echoing proficiency) and
the loss of momentum would have his boys locked in strenuous combat with gravity. Though unmetalled, our trail was
certainly broader and better than whatever Daniel Boone and
his boys could have hacked out, yet even so Gerry had to
monitor every inch of our progress with a keen eye: on one
steeply pitched curve we almost dropped a wheel off the edge,
a scenario which, I was assured, would very likely have ended
in a Magnum-sponsored mercy killing or four.

'Wagoning was a hard, filthy and dangerous job,' said Gerry,
having heaved the perpetually errant Charles back on to the
straight and narrow by his nose-ring. 'Plus you'd be away from
home most of the year, so keeping a family was tricky.' Because
of this, and because ox wagons were the only supply line to

the pioneers and settlers who pushed this new nation ever further westwards, men like Gerry were richly rewarded: twelve shillings a day, his research suggested, equivalent in terms of relative average earnings to perhaps £400 now.

'Woah there, baby boys.'

Gerry brought us to a halt before a fresh dog turd on the sun-dappled path; my surge of relief at this comforting evidence of fellow humanity died away when he knelt down and ascribed it to a bear. 'Only a small guy, maybe 150lb,' he mumbled, squinting closely at the claw-tipped footprints clustered around it, but that was 150lb too much for me. Afterwards I seemed to find myself walking rather closer to Gerry's side, almost treading on his heels when he strode off into the trees to harvest sticky red sumac buds or sassafras roots, for beverage use.

Another foraging mission ended with Gerry pulling down a thick wad of broad, flat leaves that he described as the woodsman's toilet paper; I nodded distractedly, my shoulder inclined against his, my eyes darting around the treetrunks for a telltale snatch of dark fur in motion. I was still nodding when Gerry coughed gently and explained that he was rather hoping to make use of these leaves; my trudge back to the ox cart, and my vigil beside it, was long and very lonely.

A squadron of enormous, languid horseflies gathered around the boys' flanks and my face, and as I swatted away blindly with my hat, I recognised just how hard won were those twelve shillings a day. And I hadn't yet accounted for the bandit ambushes that obliged most travellers to gather in convoys – rarely an option for a wagoner, who couldn't afford to hang around waiting for company. I'd left the Age of Collective Joy and entered that of Solitary Hell.

The sky was bruising ominously when we rumbled back into the firing-range car park, now home to a huge bulldozer, and the tree it had recently felled. The three-man crew turned as one to survey our tumultuous approach with disbelief, then very vocal yee-hah-model enthusiasm. They rolled up to us, those large faces reddened by hot toil and excitement, slapping linen backs and ox flanks in a manner that betrayed a life-long familiarity with draught animals and men dressed as cowboy scarecrows.

Reluctant to confuse – and thus enrage – these substantial, uncomplicated fellows, I kept my milksop Limey twitterings to myself as their tree-necked foreman addressed us. Never has my mother tongue sounded more alien: all I took away from his speech was a worrisome pledge that tomorrow we would all have a taste of his cousin's Y-lining. As we watched them drive off in their pick-up truck, Gerry explained that in Kentucky, moonshine was known as 'white lightning'.

The supper that Butch had prepared in our absence was a parody of male-pattern culinary ineptitude: a viciously carbonised blend of rice, apple, sweet potatoes and – how? – sand, made tolerable only by the tart and invigorating sumac tea we sluiced it down with. Gerry opened a grubby chest and from it withdrew a period bottle of homebrew ale; conditioned to expect unlimited fireside alcohol as my inalienable historic right, I watched with something beyond disappointment as he poured out an espresso-sized measure into my tin mug and his own – Butch, I now learned, had long ago forsworn all liquor. (The following morning Gerry poured a carton of apple juice into an earthenware flagon; sixty hours later, having regulated the fermentation process by briefly loosening the cork once a day, we accompanied our last hours in the forest with a palatable and acceptably potent cider.)

Jacob was dispatched to wash up in the nearby river, which as a later yomp around the pasture would prove wasn't at all nearby. Taking unkind advantage of Jacob by virtue of his age and status was our sole concession to eighteenth-century inter-personal authenticity. The hierarchy was never ruthlessly imposed – tongue in cheek rather than ruler on hand – but Jacob's mother, a keen re-enactor herself, had apparently insisted that her son enjoy nothing less than an unvarnished character-building experience.

'Hey – rotten kid!'

Throughout the first day I chuckled uncertainly while Butch

chivvied the wagoner's boy with jocular period relish, as if we were doling out the workhouse gruel and he'd just asked for more. But by the last, I found myself building Jacob's character through such endeavours as fetching my canteen from the wagon, or checking my hat for spiders, or getting some proper wood, not this twiggy rubbish, and being quick about it.

It had been entirely dark for some time when Jacob blundered back to camp behind a teetering stack of crockery and utensils, just ahead of the long-threatened rain. Soon fat drops were clattering down through the oak branches above, but no one else seemed to care – not even Butch, who had come without a hat. Only when the fire began to lose its battle with the downpour did Gerry appear to notice it was raining, and by then I had already turned my shirt back to front to dry its sodden rear before the surviving red flickers. When droves of small frogs began hopping out of the storm in search of refuge, Butch reluctantly conceded the severity of the conditions: 'Like a cow pissing on a flat rock,' he drawled, his large face a delta of rivulets.

Just before our fire was reduced to a smoking hiss, Gerry swiftly brewed up eighteenth-century chocolate – hunks of sugary cocoa-cake dropped into a billycan of water. 'A nightcap for you,' he smiled, producing from another chest a lozenge-sided brown bottle whose dimensions recalled the high-end perfume industry. With the deliberation of an apothecary, he transferred perhaps half a cubic centilitre of distilled spirit from this modest vessel into my mug of ale-tainted chocolate: a gesture I did my best to accept in the companionable manner in which it was offered. A more taxing variant of this challenge followed when Gerry saw me off to bed with a sweating nugget of sausagemeat. One of the most important lessons he'd learned in Vietnam, he said, raising his voice above the thundering rain, was that a diet heavy in fatty food helped prevent trench-foot. 'Eat meat and you get greasy. Waterproofing yourself from the inside out. The Goretex diet.'

A wet while later, I hunkered under a tarpaulin awning, and though it was anything but cool pulled the heaviest nearby blanket up to my bristled, rain-repellent chin. Butch and Jacob's sleeping quarters were of identical design – a sheet of canvas pegged to the ground at one end, and propped up at the other atop two Gerry-fashioned wooden stakes – but for our leader, half a tent was worse than none: he'd laid his bedroll out under the wagon. Not that he'd spend much time on it, though. That night and every other, whenever I looked over Gerry would invariably be standing silhouetted in the frail, damp moonlight, hands on hips, just gazing at the sky, his boys, the hand-built conveyance they hauled ('I just *love* the look of a covered wagon!' he blurted one afternoon, like a wide-eyed kid at an airshow).

The awning sufficed only to cover my top half – ideal camouflage for that nocturnal toilet scheme, at least – and I had to share its shelter with equipment that coped badly with damp, which meant being prodded in the armpit or eye-socket by a musket barrel every time I moved. Raindrops shot-blasted the tarpaulin; my sodden shins steamed; something with a lot of small legs darted across my face. Could I be any more awake? The rain subsided, and a thousand quacking, honking frogs provided the answer.

The difficulties endured the previous night, I now recognised, were strongly connected to the absence of brewed depressants in my system: in ignoble reality, it was the first time I had taken to my historical bed entirely sober. In a period spanning over a millennium and a half, I had been lulled to sleep every single night by at least a lot of beer or cider, and most often far too much. What would I give now for a deep, deep draught from a redneck's Y-lining? And so began many long hours of restless fear: exhausting, but never quite exhausting enough.

The twitches and scratches and flailing slaps didn't allow for much contemplation, and what there was proved stubbornly devoted to imagining how my sorry situation might get sorrier. Yet somewhere in between choking to death on an errant amphibian and haplessly blunderbussing my face off, I exprienced an epiphany of sorts.

By attracting only willing volunteers, those eager to embrace the pains and perils of an earlier age, re-enactment was hopelessly compromised as a socio-historical tool. For every twenty-first-century Gerry, might there not have been an eighteenth-century me, someone born out of time in the other direction, who resented the damp and discomfort, who was scared of spiders and darkness, who passionately yearned for a cleaner, brighter, scuttle-free future? Or failing that, a skinful of booze to blot out the horrors of the present?

Dawn was tinging the edges of a huge green world when I finally lost consciousness, and very soon after a wet slap in the face brought me round. The awning had collapsed; I effortfully pulled it off and found myself memorably presented with the back end of a hairy orange Routemaster. A croaked yelp sent this clumping heavily away, and as I groped about in the sodden turf for the stake it had uprooted, the sights and sounds of human activity assailed me. Jacob was again dashing barefoot through the wet grass, smiling brilliantly, as if on a cover shoot for *Wagoner's Lad*. Over by the rekindled fire, and rather less winsomely, Gerry was rubbing embrocation into the folds and flaps of poor Butch's hugely distended calves and ankles. Dropsy had an authentic period ring, but it was difficult to greet its symptoms with nostalgia.

I stumbled towards them across the pasture. It was hot, it was moist, and that reheated overnight batch of ox pies was doing its olfactory worst. 'It's looking a little better,' murmured Gerry, working another gobbet of cream into those sagging, waxy bollards of flesh. Butch let out a high-pitched snort of derision, the first of his generous daily allowance. 'You said that after the Indian Wars.'

For us, breakfast was charcoal stew leftovers mixed with ground maize; for the boys, as Gerry noted just too late, it was the leather hubcaps off his wagon. 'Charles! I'm gonna cut your ugly head off and beat you to death with it!' The half-smile with which he delivered this alarming reproach was that of a soft-hearted man who had never lost it with an animal; Gerry later confessed that he'd moved on from many decades of horsemanship hoping – forlornly – that he might find it easier to bear the death of a bovine companion. As we yoked his boys up, he outlined his disgust for those who advocated a punishment-based training regime: his own self-evidently successful technique was centred on 'letting them walk towards a wall then shouting, "Woah!"' Sometimes he heard himself telling school parties to haw and hup.

Today's walk was to be conducted under authentic conditions, which meant Jacob and me filling our wagon with the period payload calculated by Gerry's research and currently stacked up under a tarp in a corner of the livestock trailer: fifteen-odd sacks of flour (or, in fact, rice chaff) with a combined weight of 1,100lb, bringing the total of wagon and load to a round ton. The boys barely seemed to notice the difference, trudging doughtily out of the car park to a cheery reception from the road crew, who had announced their recent arrival by setting fire to a truck tyre and covering it with upended vegetation.

Plainly relieved that his experiment was at last up and running, Gerry embarked on a laidback run-through of his goals as a re-enactor. 'Commonality' was the ideal: he liked to imagine walking into a local tavern in 1775, and being swiftly appraised and even more swiftly dismissed by the resident drinkers with a grunt of, 'Pah, wagoner.' You could sense he'd pictured this scene more than once, only without the bit where they peeked in his haversack and found the anthologies of Aristotle and Rousseau therein, then threw him down the well.

'The social composition at the time was ninety-one per cent agricultural and other labourers, and six per cent seamen,' he said, 'but everyone wants to be in the other three per cent.' Luring re-enactors away from the velvet end of the eighteenth-century scale was one Barker priority; another was discouraging reliance on off-the-peg outfits. 'If just one person makes his or her own clothes, not using a pattern, then I've done my job.'

Gerry's fundamentalist approach ruled out wearing, eating or doing anything 'inconsistent with the character' – taken to its appalling extreme, this had once obliged him to extract one of his own teeth, without anaesthetic. Living history, he said, required reprogramming the modern mindset. Sitting around doing nothing, for instance, was right out – park your eighteenth-century arse by the fire and you'd need some undarned socks or a dirty rifle to keep your hands busy. 'Behaviour modification' he called it, a process that had the ominous ring of electro-aversion therapy – performed Benjamin Franklin-style, with Gerry's kite flying high in a thunderstorm, and the string knotted round my testicles.

If Gerry's academic erudition compromised his bid for workaday banality, then so too did the professional perfectionism that had defined his long military career. This had become clear when Jacob watched him covering the wagon's flour sacks with a canvas sheet back in camp, and reminded Gerry that his own research suggested that wagoners hardly ever 'tarped their loads'. 'Well, they might not have,' Gerry had muttered, 'but they should have.' He set out to become a typical wagoner, but despite himself he couldn't stop striving to be the best damn wagoner you ever did see.

On we rolled, creaking up the inclines, then rattling madly down the other side, five tons of beef, wood and rice chaff on the hoof. Every so often, Gerry would tilt his head at some innocuous spoor or scratch mark and announce the recent presence of a coyote, or – stoop, sniff – that a mule had been this way three days ago. His terrifying powers of observation meant it was almost pointless trying any covert chicanery, though I did anyway. A gentle crinkling of foil, even at 100 yards, had been enough to alert Gerry to a torso-scrubbing session with an airline-issue refreshing towel round the back of the livestock trailer; no reproach on my return, just a friendly reminder that body oil was an asset to be cultivated. When he now wordlessly disappeared into the towering pines and oaks, I took the chance to inoculate myself against those relentless horseflies with an illicit blast of bovine repellent in the chest and back. At once a voice called out from deep in the woods: 'Everything OK back there?'

Gerry returned with a modest smile and yet another reward for his eerie omni-sentience. A shard of sculpted obsidian, found in a distant clearing: part of an Indian axe-head, he casually announced, that would have lain undisturbed for perhaps 500 years. I marvelled at this mystical, gleaming artefact – now resident amongst the ringhead bodkins and flint hand tools in the shelf-bound museum to my right – as Gerry revealed his probable Indian ancestry, and that he'd done a fair bit of relevant re-enacting. Six months later, in the depths of a bitter winter, he emailed me a pithy resumé of his latest historical adventure, leading an Archaic Indian hunting party in the Kentucky hills: 'It was cold, but nobody starved to death.'

Ponderous but resolute, the oxen clumped on through the silent, humid endlessness of the woods. Occasionally we stopped by a dappled glade or stream, where the boys would rest and refuel as I arduously downed a palmful of sausage or refreshed myself from the canteen Gerry had lent me – a Mateus Rosé-shaped bottle expertly encased in a bespoke leather holster. Alone Gerry would have been refilling this in streams, but with an invalid, somebody else's young son and a Limey milksop in his care, he'd thought it best to load the pick-up with several dozen gallons of supermarket spring water.

After the third such halt, Gerry consulted the map, scratched his stubble and marshalled the boys through a challenging three-point turn. Eight miles out, eight miles back: with my feet separated from gravel and rock by no more than leathery cardboard, I returned to camp at a bruised hobble. Gerry – sixty-two and shoeless – could plainly have whistled onwards through the night.

The road gang were packing up once more, another uprooted tree ablaze on their malodorous inferno. When the foreman doffed his baseball cap and sauntered up, my overworked heart leapt: here it was, that flagon of overproof hooch. But his huge, well-used hands were empty, and all he had to offer us was another stream of amiable incoherence. 'He was saying how jealous they all were,' translated Gerry as their pick-up bucked away down the trail. 'Leaving us here with everything looking so pretty and peaceful.' Very soon afterwards, a shiny new SUV crunched to a halt in the car park, and a well-groomed father walked his pre-teenage daughter towards the firing range, one hand in hers and the other clutching the handles of a weighty holdall. The first explosive report cracked out a moment later, attributed by Gerry to a .44 semi-automatic pistol. Over the following hour, this unlikely pairing employed a variety of high-calibre weapons to shred the twilight several hundred times.

After the rigours of the trail and two bowls of Gerry's rice and beans, sleep came easy: one minute I was tracking the moon across the huge heavens, the next Jacob was nudging me awake for breakfast, telling me I'd snored all night 'like Big Foot'. 'In a jungle war, a habit like that would get you killed,' Gerry called out from the fireside.

The boys had got their own back on the wagon by once again trying to eat it: Gerry had replaced the leather hubcaps, but only two remained. It was now that I learned what a 'cow magnet' was – not just an unwise way to describe yourself in a lonely-hearts ad, but a finger of metal slipped down a grazing animal's throat, which then sat in the stomach attracting bits of ingested wire and so forth, thus preventing the misery of 'Hardware Disease'.

The afternoon before, letting a horsefly have it with an in-adequately covert blast of spray, I'd wondered at the life that lay in store for an insect when coated in insect repellent: an outcast, shunned by its revolted brethren, and consumed with self-disgust. Rising from my bed, it was as if overnight I'd been slathered in human repellent. Marinaded in sausage-oil and cow crap, I had never felt more repulsively soiled; viscous with sweat and smoky grease, my hair could be shaped at will. Marching stiffly to the livestock trailer with my penultimate refreshing-towel sachet stuffed down the fetid front of my britches, I yanked a forelock tuft into a unicorn horn: it was still there, tenting out the front of my hat, when I saw myself in the pick-up truck's wing mirror an hour later.

I'd just tossed the blackened ball of tissue into the bin by the firing-range shelter when the wagons rolled. With a scrunching creak and a steady chorus of shepherding calls, the convoy lumbered into the car park; I stepped across half a Somme's worth of spent cartridge cases and other percussive detritus to join Gerry, Jacob and the boys for our final walk in the woods.

Shuffling footsore through the heavy, dank shade of those towering pines and oaks, I realised what a disappointment I had been to the grizzled, learned übernactor beside me. That morning, he'd tackled my niggling pointlessness by bestowing upon me an appropriate character history: I was an Irish emigrant, recently released from twenty-five years of indentured service, out looking for farmland and a place to build a homestead. It was a thoughtful gesture, and for a few painful minutes I'd endeavoured to get into character, calling attention to promising fields in a funny voice, and closing every pronouncement with 'to be sure'.

I couldn't hold my own in the eighteenth century, and even in the twenty-first Gerry had to hold it for me. Our early conversations suggested he'd imagined our time together as a transatlantic congress on the philosophy of re-enactment. Finding the British delegate's contribution limited to long, wondering hums, he'd moved the debate on to Anglo-American history, one downgraded to a lecture after I confidently identified Paul Revere as 'the Pony Express bloke'. Yet not once did Gerry emit even the tiniest tut of reproach, and as Jacob darted about the wagon like a restless puppy, he embarked on another genial, roving soliloquy.

Drawing parallels between the Roman invasion of Britain and the British colonisation of America, he thoughtfully connected my debut re-enactment experience with my most recent. After delivering a brief history of philosophy, Gerry's musings fast-forwarded to the near future, with the 'lazy and complacent' US and Europe eclipsed by China and South-East Asia, in a world ultimately dominated by huge EU-model regional confederations. 'Assuming we get that far without bombing ourselves back to the Stone Age,' he said, with a cheery wink.

Gerry had earlier apprised me of Mark Twain's intention to flee to Kentucky when the end of the world came, 'because there it will come twenty years later'. His words were no more than a jibe at the expense of a behind-the-times back-water, but here in these untamed, unpeopled woods it was easy – and oddly appealing – to imagine us as motley refugees crossing a post-apocalyptic wilderness, the frail veneer of fossil-fuel technology stripped away, back to basics, living off the land and on our wits. But how terrifying to picture this scene without Gerry in it: an upturned cart made from pallets and pram wheels; beside it, an emaciated man with a pipe in his hat, prostrate and giggling in a puddle of fermented apple juice and earthenware shards; a barefoot boy leading four animals away down the trail, shaking his head sadly.

At what, with a practised skyward squint, he judged to be lunchtime, Gerry parked up by a stream and untethered the boys. Then he squatted down and swiftly got a fire going with a technique I'd last seen successfully employed at Cinderbury, almost 2,000 years previously: a flint striker, a small square of scorched linen and a pinch of 'punk wood' – flaky tinder harvested from rotten, dried logs. Once again, the moment of combustion had me laughing in disbelief: it seemed more witch-craft than bushcraft.

Gerry stoked his fire with twigs, leaned a flat stone against it, and presently anointed this with a golden slurry of ground maize and water. A moment later, on the tip of a smutted knife, he passed me a floppy, lightly singed biscuit: his famous Johnny cake. Slathered in butter it was almost delicious, like giant, flattened popcorn.

An hour later, back on the road, a gleaming swish of ebony right in front of us stopped the boys in their tracks: 'Black racer,' murmured Gerry, 'one of the fastest snakes in the world.' Scanning the trailside with renewed diligence, shortly afterwards I spotted one of our leather hubcaps, evidently shed the day before and subsequently blamed on bovine canni-balism. In the heady aftermath of this, my debut act of useful participation, I embarked on a hat-swatting massacre that left twitching oxen flanks besmeared with horsefly purée.

I thwacked and splattered my way through Gerry's life history. He was the son of a wealthy, old Virginia family – 'fancy Richmond tobacco types', Butch later called them – who had first disappointed his parents by enrolling at art school, then dismayed them via the seismic life shift that still haunted him in flashbacks: he couldn't sit in the back of a car without reliving the murderous moment the VC's gunners let loose on the helicopter carrying half his platoon. He had lost one wife to cancer, and divorced three more. Children had been accrued along the way: at the age of thirteen, his daughter announced her intent to spend her leisure time as an eighteenth-century pickpocket, a role she trained for by stealing state troopers' wallets at public events; now a Maths Ph.D., her current character was that of a travelling magician. Gerry's son – a Navy Seal with thirteen years' service – pitched up at period-weapon crack-shot tournaments and was invariably triumphant.

The military veterans I'd mixed with in Denmark and Leicestershire were attracted to re-enactment by a nostalgia for hard-bitten, tough-talking camaraderie. This clearly wasn't what Gerry was looking for – apart from anything else, the worst I heard him say in five days was 'oh, shoot'. As he spoke, I understood that experiments like these – he called them 'adventures' – were a unique opportunity to meld the keen socio-historical knowledge so diligently accrued after his military days, with the low-tech survival skills he'd honed during them.

Thinking back through Butch's doomsday vigil round at Gerry's on the eve of the millennium, and Gerry's pronouncements on the first world's shiftless decadence, I recalled that the only story he'd ever told me twice was the one in which his boys hauled a crashed Jeep out of a ravine, after all mechanical rescue attempts failed. I had a sense that if not quite looking forward to a post-oil lifestyle meltdown, or something even more dramatic, they were at least relishing the challenges that such a scenario would bring, while the rest of us sat in front of blank TV screens and cried ourselves to death.

We harvested sumac, ate hot cheese, chased butterflies, turned for home. Jacob tired of our slothful progress and jogged off back to camp. At sweaty length, we led the boys up the penultimate hill; we were leading them down when I received a hot, wet nudge in the back of the head.

I turned to behold a jostling stampede at memorably close quarters: a looming logjam of minotaur heads, their expressions for once conveying more than vacant indifference. The wagon seemed much closer to the boys than it should have been; pairing this with their ragged and increasingly rapid progress I quickly saw the need to distance myself from the scene forthwith. I was fifty yards downhill and scrabbling blindly away into the trees when with a mighty whoa and a scuffling, creaking clatter of hooves and wheels, Gerry brought the runaway to a halt. By the time I crept back his incident investigation was complete: a single crooked link had detached itself, thereby loosening the rear two oxen from the wagon-pole. We found it 200 yards back up the path. 'If we'd had horses, that would have been a whole mountain of trouble,' said Gerry, though a wing-mirror check soon after showed that this apparently inconsequential alarum had drained all colour from my cheeks – and after three unwashed days in the broiled woods, and three fireside nights in a field full of crap, that meant an awful lot of draining.

Butch had fallen off the covered wagon in our absence: we found him drinking Mountain Dew and wearing bifocals. We didn't say anything. His worst leg was propped up on a wooden chest, his suffering plain to behold. He'd already boiled us up some rice, and in the chirping dusk we bulked this up with a few hunks of sausage and doled it out into our grimy bowls.

Because it wasn't raining, I'd blithely volunteered to wash up. The creek recommended for this chore lay at the outer reaches of our pasture, but, reluctant to invade the realm of the eight-foot black king, I had yet to locate it. Burdened with directions and a great stack of greasy, smutted cookware, I set off; twilight and the thrashing scuffles it brought slowed my pace and catalysed a rapid and unstoppable haemorrhage of exploratory zeal. As soon as the campfire was out of sight, I did a bad thing: I dropped the whole lot into a big puddle and thrashed it with a stick. I was blindly rinsing off bits of cholera with what was left in my canteen when a now familiar enquiry rang distantly out through the gloaming: 'Everything OK back there?'

Gerry had a tin of baccy in his lap when I got back, and, having hidden my load of shame in our camp's darkest corner, I pulled the clay pipe from my hat and requested a pinch. At this stage of my intoxicant famine, it was any port in a storm – even if that meant clearing a fluffy spider's nest out of the bowl to make room for my drugs. 'Mild, and a little on the sweet side' had been Gerry's assessment of the local tobacco – thus reassured I drew in a huge lungful through that dusty little tube, then coughed it straight back out so violently that my hat fell off into the fire. It was the right way to end my last full day in 1775.

I wondered how the Frontier Reform Church would handle Sunday, and after an entirely glorious blue-skied reveille I found out. 'We might be in the wilderness,' called Butch from the fire, 'but that's no excuse to disrespect the Sabbath.' Butch had a small and very old bible in his hand; Gerry was shaving with a mug of hot water and a deeply worrisome cut-throat razor. When he was done he handed both to me without a word. I gingerly scraped the fun-sized machete down both cheeks and across my upper lip, but baulked at the more challengingly three-dimensional sections, thus bequeathing myself an Amish-effect face-girdler.

Butch gathered us all forth to the fireside, laboriously thumbed through his bible, and in a practised mumble, began to read. The following twenty minutes included many repetitions of the phrase 'for his mercy endures forever'; at one point, Moses sacrificed an ox, and sprinkled his people with its blood. Communion followed: half a cracker and a nip of very diluted brandy.

A year before, I would have found such an intimate religious gathering unendurably awkward. But with the sun on my back and a gentle fire at my feet, Butch's unhurried psalms seemed warmly consoling – inestimably more so than Brother Balthasar's hungover medieval dronings in that frosted dungeon.

Contemplating the forest around, I felt a surge of reverence for the religious refugees who founded the nation – driven away from their homelands and out across a savage ocean, then pitching up in this dumbfounding virgin wilderness. If it seemed like God's country to them, I could understand why just a few short centuries on the Lord's word still rang out in the Farmer's Christian Academy, or the Antioch Baptist Chapel, or any of the bland, low-slung, motel-like places of worship that book-ended every town. Later, when I discreetly commended Jacob for his fidgetless placidity throughout the service, he frowned at me a little suspiciously, then described the five-hour round trip to church that dominated his Sundays at home.

Butch eased the Good Book closed, fixed his congregation with a probing stare, then launched into a sermon that amplified his reverential mumble to a bible-bashing bellow. 'We've all succumbed to a social disease!' he began, and in alarm I readied myself to shield Jacob's sensibilities by clamping my hands over his ears, or maybe – please no – his eyes. 'These days it's always gotta be somebody else's job to do things for you! Well, I'm not going to be holy for you – you've gotta go and be holy people for yourself!' And having expressed his fundamental disillusionment with the feckless modern world, Butch wound things up with a protracted emphysemic wheeze.

Packing up our makeshift travellers' camp didn't take long: pots and provisions crammed into wooden chests, flagons corked, the fire doused. Squeezing four boys and their wagon into the livestock trailer was the principal challenge, and one that left me slathered in khaki awfulness. Seeing them cooped up in a cage, my principal emotion was not compassion, but relief; a companionable way with domestic beasts was another ingrained human skill that seemed too deeply buried within me to exhume. I preferred my livestock dead.

When the others were in the pick-up and ready to go, I jogged behind a tree to decontaminate exposed flesh with the last of my wet wipes; I was finishing up when a spider – an innocuous brown spider – darted into the linen haversack at my feet. Showing a marked lack of concern for the wooden utensils contained therein, I reflexively brought my right foot down hard upon the bag from a great height, and then again, and again, and again. Many stamps later, panting and wild-eyed as I extended a tentative finger towards the carrying strap, a car door clunked open and a mild voice called out: 'Everything OK back there?'

And so we juddered off down the trail, leaving behind us a field full of ox pats, and 1,100lb of rice chaff smouldering on the embers of the road gang's fire. Watching our pasture disappear behind the oaks, I ran the historical rule over my 1775 experience. In many ways I'd gone backwards since 1578: living rough in the primeval woods, the forest floor around speckled with freshly shattered Stone Age tools and the spoor of animals long since hunted to extinction back in England. My 200-year-old shirt was still in fashion, as were the utensils in the bag at my feet, whatever remained of them. The rising sun still woke me up, and the campfire had returned as the focus of all social activity. The printed philosophy in Gerry's knapsack aside, almost nothing had changed since the Iron Age. Significantly, the principal lifestyle modification was an enhanced range of mood-altering substances: alcohol was all about unwinding, but now there were stimulants, coffee and tobacco, ingested to make men work harder and faster.

Out of the gloomy redneck woods, on to the open road and a distant, heat-hazed horizon – a disorientating, almost agoraphobic prospect after four days hemmed in by treetrunks. Shoulder to soiled shoulder with Jacob in the rear seat, I gazed out at a series of successively tidier small towns: rocking chairs on stoops, Stars and Stripes on gate posts, a sign for Knob Lick ('Everything OK back there?'). We stopped to refuel, and when the tubby forecourt attendant passed my open window I caught a quick draught of soapy, aromatic freshness. When he passed by again I sniffed more deeply: here was a fat man who stood in the sun all day pumping hydrocarbons, yet he smelt gorgeous;

it was all I could do to stop myself making that Hannibal Lecter noise. The olfactory rationale made itself plain four hours later, when our entrance divided a busy interstate McDonald's into two distantly separated camps: those who had spent five days wallowing in their own filth and that of four gingery behemoths, and those who hadn't, and suddenly weren't hungry.

Gerry had stoutly insisted on driving me to my airport hotel, and to save the rest of his party a needless three-hour round trip that meant unhitching the trailer in the McDonald's car park. It also meant taking off all of my clothes in this same location, in order to return his toxically soiled outfit. I won't pretend that pulling on a clean T-shirt and shorts felt anything other than tearfully wonderful, but as had been the case post-Kentwell I felt slightly indecent without a really stupid hat.

'You could have been an asshole,' said Butch, compressing my hand in his meaty grasp, 'but you weren't.' Good enough, I thought, exchanging farewell blank gawps with the boys and trying to ruffle Jacob's crispy hair as I climbed into the pick-up cab.

A hundred miles north, Gerry pulled up at a set of automatic glass doors. Before them reared a sign that told how far away 1775 now was, and yet how near: FREE HIGH-SPEED INTERNET ACCESS. GOD BLESS AMERICA. Beyond them a young hotel receptionist readied herself for the grisliest encounter of a short career.

'I guess I'll do this as long as my body lets me,' sighed Gerry, passing my holdall out through the passenger door, 'and then write books as long as my brain does.' And with that, this extraordinary fellow, perhaps the single most impressive human I have yet to encounter, was gone.

An hour and two baths later, I plucked a fat tick from the crook of my knee and gave it a good twenty-first-century seeing-to in the in-room microwave. Then I went downstairs, ate a large part of one of the boys' relatives, and severely impaired my ability to operate machinery.

Chapter Seven

The rain had arrived with a bang the evening before, heralded by great horizontal lightning bolts that pulsed across the sky for full seconds, illuminating the epic forests around. Neither scenery nor conditions seemed consistent with being in Texas, as I had been – alone at the wheel – since driving down the wrong side of the ramp at the car-hire depot in George Bush Intercontinental Airport, 200 jetlagged miles previously. With the road deserted and the few towns along it cast in derelict gloom, the foul and furious storm seemed aimed squarely at me. Godlike retribution for undersealing my Two-Door Economy/Compact with two coats of fresh raccoon, or for the aural company of KHPT 106.9, which for three Toto-heavy hours had besmirched its mission statement by failing to deliver the best of the eighties, and more.

The sense of being singled out for punishment hardened when I peered through drooping eyes and double-speed wipers at a succession of 'no vacancy' signs, an affront to their deserted car parks, and the other mounting evidence that I was now alone in all the world. Even when, in a state of dangerous fatigue, I came to a sudden and oblique halt before a motel with an illuminated reception area, the human behind it could only offer me the room kept in reserve for disabled guests – with the proviso that I faced summary eviction should some unfortunate wheel himself in from the storm-torn darkness in need of ensuite facilities cluttered with white scaffolding.

It was still raining when I yawned off into the trailer-trashed rural vastness the morning after, and a couple of hours later when my Economy/Compact wallowed to a standstill at the appointed muster area in Kisatchie National Forest. By then I'd stopped thinking of it as rain: the subdued monotony of water falling from the windless, off-white heavens seemed more like the product of some dependable industrial process.

Through the spindly, rain-smeared pines I could see bearded men in unusual hats milling around what must once have been a fire. Looking at them, my thoughts turned to the rival period events I might have pursued, and the indoor component that united most. Even the least appealing of these now sprang attractively to mind: a long weekend in the cells beneath Lincoln Castle, enjoying a little old-school rehabilitation with the Victorian Prison Re-Enactment Group, perhaps, or a country-house party organised by the Victorian Re-Enactment Society, driven abroad after their unnamed activities 'fell foul of British "hunt-the-perv" hysteria'.

Instead, I had signed up for five early-spring days in what the organisers' website had described as 'an isolated and historically relevant region virtually devoid of modern intrusion'. An academic spoke more evocatively of 'a sprawling, swampy tangle', and a published account of what I was here to recreate came burdened with the regrettably captivating title, *Through the Howling Wilderness*. A rival history of the event lay beside me on the passenger seat: *One Damn Blunder From Beginning to End – the Red River Campaign of 1864*.

I was here because this was where it started. No student of living history can afford to ignore the laboured rhyming maxim I'm about to make up: you just can't ignore the US Civil War. In re-enactment terms, it's the daddy. The 1961 Civil War centenary was marked with a series of pioneering large-scale battle re-enactments, often featuring a thousand or more combatants. Veterans from these events cringingly recall waddling towards the enemy in dyed scout uniforms and

wellington boots, but what they lacked in sartorial authenticity they made up for in the weaponry department: most
carried original Civil War rifles, then so plentiful and ill-
venerated they could be picked up for $50. At any rate, the
impression on spectators and combatants alike was evidently
profound: the huge popularity of these centenary re-enactments
kick-started a phenomenon, a school of re-enactment that by
most sensible estimates has attracted more pupils than all others
combined. Thirty years on, US Civil War groups were sufficiently
well established to mount full-scale re-runs of major battles: with
41,000 participants pretending to kill each other, the 1998 re-
interpretation of Gettysburg remains the largest re-enactment
ever seen.

Reading up on the Civil War, I came to understand the almost
desperate enthusiasm that has inspired an estimated half a
million Americans to participate in related recreations. Some
are expressing a fascination with the most compelling chapter
in their young nation's history. Others are paying tribute to
the conflict's 623,000 military victims – more American
soldiers died in the Civil War than in every subsequent war
combined. The Battle of Antietam in 1862 remains by some
distance the bloodiest twenty-four hours in the nation's history,
accounting for more than twice as many Americans as D-Day.

The confusing, unsettling reality for so many is that all
these Americans were killed by other Americans, and that
this happened so recently. The last Union widow died in 2003
– outlasted by her Confederate counterpart, Alberta Martin,
who at the age of twenty-one married eighty-one-year-old
veteran William Martin, bore him a son before he passed away,
married William's grandson from a former marriage two months
later, and finally pegged out in 2004 at the age of ninety-seven,
leaving the South in mourning and a very messy family tree.

Quite simply, large swathes of the nation are still struggling
to come to terms with this traumatic, divisive and horribly
bloody conflict. Naturally enough, the ones who pick away at
the scab most compulsively are those who feel cheated by the
outcome. A lot of water had passed under the bridge, but some

still saw a river tainted with the blood of martyrs. Over there through the trees, they might feasibly have found its source: thirty or forty men, and not a single blue uniform.

History is written by the winners, but re-enactment gives the losers a belated chance to scribble in the margins. In a precise inversion of the original proportions, across the US, Confederate re-enactors outnumber Unionists by two to one, and it was no surprise to see this ratio stretched to snapping point out here: the 1864 Red River Campaign was fought deep into Confederate territory, and is commonly encapsulated as one of the Union's last defeats.

One Damn Blunder From Beginning To End described a fiasco loosely orchestrated by the former newspaper editor and Massachusetts governor Nathaniel Banks, a 'political general' whose appointment by Lincoln – not a man I'd previously thought of as a ruthless schemer – was little more than a crude bribe to keep a potential rival out of the forthcoming presidential election. After a string of crushing Union victories, by the spring of 1864 the war seemed all but over, and most in the North had one eye on winning the peace. With the North's economically vital cotton mills running desperately short of raw materials, and the South a spent force, there seemed no harm in putting a military novice in charge of 40,000 troops and the bulk of the Union fleet, and sending him off to plant the Union flag in Texas, en route snaffling up 100,000 cotton bales from the riverside warehouses of Louisiana.

A two-month parade of tactical ignominy ensued: the fleet ran aground in a swamp, the Union armies got lost in the woods and ran out of water. Most deadly of the damn blunders was the failure of intelligence that encouraged a reckless assault on the Confederate lines at Mansfield, which in half a day cost 3,200 overwhelmed Union troops their lives. The Red River event came gloatingly headlined with the shambolic campaign's dismal last act: Banks's Grand Retreat.

'I'm not sure that BGR is the best event for you,' began an email response I'd received many months previously. 'It takes place over a five-day period, and will be a strenuous exercise involving a forty-mile march living with whatever you can carry on your back. There will be skirmishes, entrenchment building and so forth. Therefore a good knowledge of Civil War infantry drill, field tactics and how to live as a soldier will be essential even if you have the stamina to keep up. Thirdly and finally, the authenticity requirements for all kit will be of the very highest.'

The reply eloquently explained what had first attracted me to this biannual event, an almost mystical gathering of hard-core re-enactors in the wooded depths of Louisiana. Online comments described BGR in tones of breathless reverence: no public to show off before, no after-hours downtime, just five days of relentless and uncompromising immersion with re-enactment's seasoned elite. 'Nothing comes close,' was the simple judgement of one of the select band of veterans. 'This isn't an event, it's an adventure.' An adventure whose 2007 motto, emblazoned across the organisers' sepia-typefaced website and available on a T-shirt that I now wish I'd bought, succinctly encaspulated the defining ethos: 'No Whiners, No Shirkers, No Weaklings'.

Given the Banks-like depth of my relevant experience, it was no particular surprise to find my email enquiries to the listed admissions officer entirely ignored. Unusually, though, I found myself in no mood to give up without a fight, or at least a whine. If the US Civil War was re-enactment's well-spring, then the Red River was its purest source: the ultimate expression of living history. Kentwell's linguistic authenticity, Haut-Koenigsbourg's attention to culinary and aesthetic detail, the fear and hardships endured at all other points along the way – at BGR I'd find the lot, wrapped up in one muddy bundle. I was acclimatised; I was ready. Bring it on.

It was an Englishman who suggested a way in. Patrick Reardon was head of the Lazy Jacks, a group inspired by the thousand-odd Brits who fought for the Confederate cause, in a quest for adventure or their interpretation of social justice. He was taking a dozen men to BGR, and having swiftly dashed any hopes that I might join their ranks, tentatively proposed a suitable character:

a war reporter dispatched by a London newspaper. The more I thought through this suggestion, the more it appealed. I'd be free to roam the battlefield on my own terms, asking both sides awkward and – my prerogative as a foreigner – stupidly ill-informed questions, before retiring to a pavilion stocked with provisions and comforts befitting the golden age of Fleet Street expenses, therein to compose my dispatches, wearing a long silk paisley dressing gown and one of those little tasselled caps. These local cheroots make a damnably poor smoke, I'd think, though for sport I might just have a box sent to that old prig Johnson on the foreign desk back home.

Cursory research revealed that the first roving war correspondents as we understand them today were sent out to the Crimean War, and of the 500-odd journalists who covered the US Civil War five years later, a significant minority were doing so on behalf of foreign newspapers. William Howard Russell of *The Times*, easily the most prominent of these, saw his brief in very contemporary terms: to provide British readers with 'unvarnished and unedited first impressions of food, fashions, inns, streets, culture, fighting men, issues and politicians'.

Perhaps unfairly, to me this marked him out as the prototype for those vainglorious charlatans later parodied by Evelyn Waugh, spooling out reams of fanciful 'colour' without ever leaving their hotel rooms/cheroot-hazed pavilions. Poncifying his byline with a middle name did nothing to dilute that impression. Yet if all this should have diminished Russell in my eyes, I have to report that it did not. Already seduced by the prospect of emulating the fecklessly duplicitous lifestyle I had invented for him, I struggled to purge all trace of related frivolity in my reply to Patrick. Being brief and rather stern, his response suggested I had failed. 'Note that you would require civilian clothing of the period as well as appropriate items of baggage, etc. You would also be required to do a fair bit of research, as a good knowledge of the campaign, the personalities and the general period would be essential for first-person interpretation as, for much of the time, we hope to leave the twenty-first century and enter the nineteenth.'

Patrick finished off by explaining it was not within his power to invite me; he could promise only to 'seek the agreement of our hosts'. At this point, I went away to 1775 and forgot all about him, his kind offer, and the nineteenth century in general. By the time I very belatedly remembered, with BGR no more than a couple of months away, it was apparently too late; the website bluntly stated that admission to the event was now closed, and my emails to Patrick fell upon stony ground. At which point, with a trundling, clomping creak, a big blue wagon rolled up to the rescue.

I'm still not sure why or when Gerry Barker decided to grace the event with his appearance – Kentucky to Louisiana was an awfully long drive, even without four oxen in the boot – but the minute he offered to sponsor my own attendance, doors were flung open with dramatic haste. It was as if I'd been vainly trying to wheedle my way into some star-studded premiere, when suddenly Clint Eastwood pitches up, scoops me on to his shoulders and strides wordlessly past the awestruck bouncers, giving them one of his quizzical glares.

Gerry had promised me an outfit, and bagged me a berth at the civilian camp. This forest car park – the military's principal muster point – was our arranged rendezvous; Gerry's stock trailer and his big old pick-up dominated a puddled corner, but both were conspicuously empty. While waiting for the boys and their blue burden to rumble up out of the rain-fogged trees, I delved out the crumpled cribsheets that were my Patrick-ordained character primers.

I'd selected *The Times* – which I would soon learn to call the *London Times* – as my employer, partly due to Russell's celebrity, and partly to an editorial stance which, being solidly onside with the secessionist Confederacy, would endear me to those most likely to turn nasty. Britain was officially neutral in the Civil War, but as the mouthpiece of the landed Establishment, *The Times* aligned itself firmly with conservatives confused and alarmed by concepts such as democracy and republicanism. And who had yet to forgive their own government's stance on slavery, finally abolished only in 1833

– much to the irritation of the Bishop of Exeter, despite the
£12,700 compensation paid out for the loss of his 665 slaves.

The Times viciously despised President Lincoln, holding
him responsible for 'horrible massacres of white women and
children', and predicting he would be remembered 'among
that catalogue of monsters, the wholesale assassins and
butchers of their kind'. Yet such was the paper's global clout
that Lincoln felt obliged to welcome its fêted correspondent,
William Howard Russell, with a eulogy that must have been
delivered with that lantern jaw set in a rictus grimace: 'Mr
Russell, I am very glad to make your acquaintance, and to
see you in this country. The *London Times* is one of the
greatest powers in the world – in fact, I don't know anything
which has much more power – except perhaps the
Mississippi.' I'd just read it again, imagining Abe flicking
the Vs under the presidential desk as he spoke, when the
car shook slightly, and a familiar cry called something loud
and heavy to a slushy halt.

Just as before, Gerry greeted me with studied nonchalance.
He'd had his Riff Raff locks hacked down to a buzz-cut, which
along with his filth-slathered bare feet and careworn attire gave
him the look of a grizzled convict on the run. The boys, the
wagon and everything inside it were precisely as they had been
in 1775: as I'd discovered with my 2,000-year-old linen bag –
once more by my side – the tools and trappings of everyday
life evolved with almost glacial sloth in the pre-industrial age.

The clothes Gerry had brought along for me were in the
pick-up: I got changed, and very wet, behind the stock trailer.
From the ground up: a pair of extravagantly weathered black
leather brogans, handmade by and for Butch and two sizes too
big; thick blue trousers with a fat, smudgy pinstripe; one of
Gerry's sack-like waggoning smocks, concealed with a satin-
backed black waistcoat and a heavy black-wool *OK Corral*
frock coat; a dusty brown neckerchief, tied in a floppy bow.
Tramp-shoes aside I felt almost disappointingly normal, until
Gerry frisbeed over the pièce de résistance: a high-crowned
black felt hat with a prominently upturned brim. A Derby,

Gerry called it, but I can most usefully describe it as a bowler hat with all the silly bits made sillier.

With my feet plumped up by two pairs of fisherman's socks, I shuffled along behind Gerry as he set off towards the Confederates clustered in the nearby trees. The rain had eased slightly, and a few were ambitiously trying to restart the failed fire; a charred fist-sized hunk of wet gristle sat in a blackened pan atop it. Other than a general theme of light grey and dirty cream, there was little sartorial consistency on display: a mix-and-match jumble of caps and hats, a random assortment of canteens, pouches and knapsacks slung across all manner of jackets and tunics. Uniforms that were anything but uniform. At earlier events I'd have attributed such disparities to inadequate research or funding; how gratifying, this time, to be entirely certain that how they looked was how it was.

Confirmation that I had arrived at the outer limits of large-scale re-enactment came when their soiled and spattered faces emerged into focus. Yellowy smiles all round – they were loving this. No whiners, no shirkers, no weaklings. The abysmal conditions had cranked the authentimeter right up.

How uncommonly satisfying, then, to find these hardcore filth-wallowers reduced to a nudging, deferential hush by Gerry's arrival. 'Sharp wagon you have there, sir,' was all anyone dared say. Every 'after action report' I would read later paid lavish tribute to Gerry, sometimes by name, more often as the humbly mystical Ox Guy, trundling through the forests, trailing a dusty cloud of historical verisimilitude.

Gerry mumbled something to a pastor, a man with the look of Crocodile Dundee dressed in Lee van Cleef's *The Good, the Bad and the Ugly* wardrobe. He jogged away and returned a while later with a black rubberised sheet the size of a picnic blanket. 'Vulcanised pro-tection for you, sir,' he puffed, briskly lashing two corners of it round my neck. 'Thank you . . . father,' I said, with no appreciation of how whimperingly grateful I would come to be for this kindness, both to him and to Thomas Hancock, the English scientist who had patented the relevant process twenty-one short years previously.

The civilian camp was a few miles north, and Gerry agreed
to walk me there: his appointed wagoner's task was to deliver
water (supplied, as an unfortunate health-and-safety prerequisite, in turquoise plastic jerrycans) to both armies and the
non-combatants. As we waved the Confederate army farewell,
he theatrically cracked his big whip three times, a trio of
thwacking snaps that filled the forest around: it was the only
time I ever saw him show off.

The rain had settled into a heavy, dispiriting drizzle that
my woollen clothing eagerly blotted up; I discovered the ample,
concave brim of my black-felt head-roof made a useful gutter,
but only as long as you remembered to drain it every so often.
For a long, wet while we were on tarmac, bordered by trim
and benign pine woods that recalled my many off-fairway
adventures in Tiger Woods PGA Tour 07. Every so often a pick-
up carrying one of the BGR organisers would shoot past with
a genteel wave or a hollering Rebel yell; the only foot soldiers
we passed were a couple of sallow ganglers who identified
themselves – in nasally Midland tones – as part of the Lazy
Jack contingent. All they wanted to know from Gerry was how
bad the snakes were: 'There's a ninety-pound rule with these
things,' he said, leaning back against a steaming ox flank. 'If
you weigh over that, a snake bite won't kill you.' They nodded
uncertainly, then went on their way, bickering over the maths.

A couple of hours on the skies began to clear, and soon after
Gerry hupped and hawed us off the main road, on to a sticky,
orange-soiled track, and into a very different world. An
evidently recent forest fire had reduced the surrounding woodland to a blasted, black-stumped wasteland that hemmed us
in on both sides, grimly redolent of war and death. After a
mile of this the sound of drawled chatter filtered through the
post-apocalyptic silence, and soon we were trundling out of
the scorched-earth dead zone, into a clearing ringed by half a
dozen ramshackle marquees. Beaming pigtailed girls in
smocked dresses ran up through lines of off-white laundry, two
very old dogs stood their ground and barked, five or six white
hens clucked and scuttled amongst the churns and cauldrons

and piles of wood, and broad, homely women wearing bonnets and pebble spectacles squeezed the full skirts of their grey Florence Nightingale dresses out through the canvas tent-flaps to cheer and wave. It was the closest I will ever come to feeling part of a liberating army.

'Gentlemen, we are truly delighted to see you here,' shouted the nearest of the women, stuffing stray strands of a very complicated bun back into her headwear. 'Those Walker boys have been in the tavern, worryin' us all with their shady dealings.'

'Tavern?' I asked much too quickly, scanning the canvas awnings in urgent expectation. When my gaze returned, her dimpled face had fallen slightly; I realised that this establishment, and its associated dealings, existed only as part of the scenario.

As we unloaded the water, and a few sacks of rice, flour and salt, Gerry gave me a discreet low-down: the six civilian families here were refugees, about twenty people in all, driven out of their homes by the hated Union army. One by one the men of the camp strolled amiably up to help us, their flamboyant beards and moustaches confirming the impression I'd formed back at the Confederate muster point that the 1860s was very much an anything-goes era for facial-hair enthusiasts. All wore plain, faded shirts and trousers held aloft with braces, and all but a couple of stringy-limbed beanpoles filled their ample clothes in a manner that made ironing superfluous. It was the one weakness – along with the laminated public-information sheets staple-gunned to a US Forest Service noticeboard – in an otherwise profoundly evocative scene. I'd read on the plane that by 1864, with the war three years old, nutrition near the front lines was a hand-to-mouth affair. Soldiers pillaged what they could from the fields, and were often obliged to live on desiccated corncobs and related animal fodder; starvation was commonplace. But whatever else I might endure in this camp, going hungry clearly wouldn't be a problem.

With Gerry and his boys magnetically attracting all the attention I was free to wander unmolested through the surrounding woods, rehearsing my back story. Well, ma'am/sir, I arrived in New York – hawk, spit – aboard the *Persia*, the first iron-hulled Cunarder, which as you know eight years ago claimed the Blue Riband with a record transatlantic time of . . . oh, buttocks. Five weeks? Four days? Perhaps gloss over that. Just pad it out with stuff that rammed home *The Times*'s stoutly pro-South line, in language these simple country folk would understand. Like, I dunno, a fight I had – and won – in the first-class saloon, with a drunken liberal . . . no, a crying vegetarian . . . no, an effeminate Union colonel, wearing a pink Abe Lincoln stovepipe hat, with a Pekinese in his lap.

I didn't realise how far into the muddy pine needles I'd wandered until a distant clanking trundle stopped me in my tracks. When I scrambled back it was too late: Gerry and his lethargic pacemakers had gone. 'Mr Barker told us you might like to eat somethin', sir,' said a young boy in a Casey Jones cap, and with a feeling of deep foreboding I followed him into the largest tent.

'That was wonderful, ma'am.' I relieved the pewter dish of its last scrapings, and clinked it down on the tiny table before me; a round-faced young woman blushed slightly, curtsied, and half-ran out through the tent's open rear into the dimming forest. As the veteran of a thousand years of porridge with a hint of leek, I could now eat large quantities of almost anything, and in the previous hour had dispatched several challenging slabs of puckeringly saline pork, and two plate-denting ladles of hominy grits – a fêted rustic foodstuff that owes its existence to a moment of culinary happenchance involving congealed semolina and a sack of gravel. But there was a pickle jar, and the homemade lemonade was excellent; though once my second tin cup was drained I'd been politely steered on to water, dispensed from a barrel that still bore the Jim Beam distillery's branded imprint, and was tainted to match.

I creaked back in my chair – a tiny thing, whose design and dimensions suggested a Goldilocks-model end lay in wait for it – and looked around the tent. This astonishing construction was divided into two areas, both fully boarded-out and laid with faded Turkish rugs; I was in the bijou kitchen-diner, a caravan-sized area hung with old cookware and hand tools, and stacked on one side with tinned provisions bearing precise facsimiles of period labels: THIS CORN IS PACKED ACCORDING TO ACT OF CONGRESS IN THE YEAR 1863. Crammed in with the dolls'-house furniture was a small cast-iron, wood-fired range, permanently (and hazardously) on the go. This area opened into the much larger front parlour, a prim and trim social area ringed with dressers and side-tables, upon which rested oil lamps and candlesticks, old books and framed religious lithographs.

It was to this room, at the shy behest of another pebble-spectacled young mother, that I now repaired. Outside, amongst the chickens, a sweet little girl in an *Anne of Green Gables* pinafore dress picked up a length of rope and began skipping; I sat in a spindle-backed farmhouse chair, steam still rising off my sodden trousers, and exchanged awkward smiles with my nervously looming hostess. Presently two more children, a boy of about five and a red-faced girl I took as his slightly older sister, shuffled silently into the parlour, and sat down on a wooden chest. The woman nodded approvingly, then picked out a very, very old book with a weathered black-cloth binding and opened it at a marked page. Settling into an earnest monotone, she began to read.

'My father at last fixed upon the kettler's trade . . .'

After two paragraphs of this I could feel myself sliding into glazed stasis, yet through sagging eyelids I watched the two children seated to attention, straight-backed and fidgetless. A heavy yellow page was turned, then another, and another . . . after a while I sensed from their reactions that they weren't actually listening, just doing as they were told. At some point the skipping girl began accompanying herself with a playground chant about steamboats, but when this segued into one that namechecked the creations of Walt Disney the censorious response from the fathers gathered around a nearby fledgling campfire was immediate. 'I don't think that game's been invented yet, honey!' Looking crestfallen and confused, she shuffled away, trailing her rope behind her.

It was all but dark when a cluster of new voices approached the tent. In a moment the parlour was teeming with Custer-moustached Confederate officers with a lot of buttons and chevrons on their grubby cuffs and collars; conspicuous amongst them in his all-black outfit was the pastor. Their ongoing conversation, loud and heavy on cackling bonhomie, was centred on an absent party by the name of Old Man Johnson, who'd apparently been a hog-rustler before the war, and now – har-de-yee-har! – rounded up deserters. With ratcheting unease I waited to be noticed.

Soon the men and ladies of the camp were wedging themselves inside, obliging me to vacate my chair and inch gratefully back into a corner, between two sideboards. Candles and hurricane lamps were lit and trays of food and refreshments were brought forth from the rear kitchen: boiled potatoes, beef jerky, a pat of butter shaped into a little sack. I somehow managed to serve myself and ingest a hefty plateful, standing up, without attracting conversational attention. Then, squeezing between the haystack skirts en route to the newly arrived pickle jar, I found myself baulked by a dirty great colonel.

'How many brides have you buried, sir?'

Well, that was one I hadn't revised for. Was this some darkly comic riddle? The absence of a twinkle in those mud-rimed eyes suggested not.

'Just, um . . . just the one. Sir.'

He sneered at me over his blond, butter-speckled lip bush. 'One of our British friends?' There followed a genuine harrumph, enunciated as that precise word. 'I've married and lost his aunt, his mother and her sister.' And I followed his plump and grubby finger on its journey through the throng.

With the dining complete the womenfolk retired to wash up, leaving me alone with a pastor, three Confederate officers, four horny-handed refugee fathers and not even half a clogful of Dutch courage to face them. For a while they talked amongst themselves about mail deliveries, hog breeding and the War of 1812, whatever that was. If I failed to pick up on the enhanced level of prickliness that seemed to characterise the evening thereafter, it's because I've only just discovered – some four minutes ago – that this was fought between Britain and the United States. Even now nobody can agree if any side won, except to say that if anyone did, it wasn't the Americans.

'And what is your British guest's business here in Louisiana?'

As the fleshy, open faces of my refugee hosts puckered in doubt, I realised the extraordinary truth: these people had accepted me into their community untroubled by any understanding of who I was or what had brought me to their encampment at an ox wagoner's side. After the best part of a day spent in their company, eating their grits and muddying their rugs, I had yet to be asked a single pertinent query. For a few moments I watched the camp's menfolk exchange I-thought-you-invited-him looks. Then, with an air of deepest foreboding, I revealed that I was a war correspondent from the *London Times*.

'Sir, did you ever hear the story of David and Goliath?'

I told the pastor I had; he rested his hands on his black thighs, leaned forward in his seat, and slowly told me it again, tweaked as a parable for the current state of the war. The debate that followed began well when someone mentioned the Trent Affair, a British/Union maritime episode I'd encountered in my Wikipedia print-outs, and was therefore able to discuss, if only to confirm that an incident thus named had indeed occurred. Thereafter, however, my contribution lapsed into occasional protestations of my employer's sympathetic editorial stance. When these were ignored I settled into nods and hums, which grew ever tinier as the pastor's anti-Federal rhetoric blossomed into a passionate tirade. 'This war is about money and cotton and greed!' he half-shouted, his craggy features ominous in the hurricane lamp's flickery uplighting. 'Put that in your newspaper, sir!'

The ensuing thirty minutes, including as they did several strident repetitions of this command, were as trying as any I had yet endured in my historical wanderings. Perhaps ten had elapsed when one of the officers withdrew an opened envelope from somewhere about his considerable person and passed it to the parson. He extracted the letter within and rose to read

it aloud, jaw quivering as his eyes ranged across the neat copper-
plate hand visible through the thin paper. 'My dearest mother,'
he began, introducing a brief first-hand account of life on the
Confederate front lines.

In all honesty it sounded no worse than undernourished and
rather dull, and the final PS fell some way short as a rousingly
Churchillian call to arms: 'Please tell James to plant more
parsnips.' It was the parson's closing address, delivered through
pursed and trembling lips after he'd finished and refolded the
letter, that raised vengeance levels to an audible high.

'That young man's life,' he rasped, 'was snuffed out this
morning in a cowardly Yankee ambush.'

In the grim silence that followed, all within those canvas
walls understood that only one man was ultimately responsible for the hard life and brutal death of this fine young scion
of the South, and that he was here amongst them right now,
round-domed hat in dampened lap, eyes fixed wanly on his
oversized tramp's shoes.

'Put that in your newspaper, sir,' croaked the colonel.

'What – the parsnips thing?' I might have said; instead, I
nodded at the floor.

A terminal clatter of earthenware and pewter heralded the
end of the washing-up, and the ladies began drifting back into
the front parlour. With each new arrival it was as if another
of the many buttons entombing me in my heavy outfit had
been undone. The angry man-talk settled into bland ponder-
ings on tomorrow's weather; a refugee father flicked a moth
off his ear; somebody did the rounds with a tin ewer of coffee.
Our pastor pulled a small black bible from a small black pocket,
and read a psalm to a background of pious nods. A hymn was
sung, then a few jollier folk numbers, the voices clear and
strong. This was better: here we all were, making our own fun.

The last misgivings ebbed wearily away when one of the
female elders hauled aloft from a side-table a venerable, gold-
embossed volume the size of three encyclopaedias. Then surged
violently back, pinning me into my small, hard chair, when
she handed it to me with a gentle smile and these appalling

words: 'Sir, I wonder if you would do us the honour of reading us a little William Shakespeare?'

In impotent horror I watched as the womenfolk gathered tightly about my chair; one held out a hurricane lamp and with small, prompting motions of her bonneted head brought me to my feet. I opened the giant book somewhere in the middle and in the flickering shadows saw two pages clustered with minuscule words.

Later I would regret not riffling through in search of *Henry V*, a play with an appropriately martial theme, and which, twenty-six years since I studied it at O level, remains the only Shakespeare work I have encountered in its original text. But at the time, standing there with a rivulet of sweat tickling my spine and a dozen grubby, expectant faces clustered about mine in the candlelight, I found myself in no mood for dramatic niceties. *Cymbeline*, said the largest word at the top of the page; I lowered my nose towards the microscopic text beneath and launched blindly into a soliloquy which mentioned a horse with wings, adultery and – rather unexpectedly – Milford Haven, delivered at a speed that combined all these, and their many tiny neighbours, into a single, quiet noise.

With the speech over I moistened my lips and raised my eyes; the faces seemed frozen, as if posing for a silver-plate photograph. A slight shuffle caused me to glance swiftly behind: gathered by the kitchen entrance stood five bleary children, clad neck to ankle in grey nightgowns and evidently brought from their beds to witness this performance. There was a cough, and a protracted creak of floorboards. A drop of rain flicked the canvas overhead, then another; I drew in what breath I could and started up again, muttering out the twixts and prithees and wondering distantly if I had been pushed into some hellish crack in the Kentwell/Louisiana continuum.

After fourteen years, the hurricane lamp began to shake in its holder's failing grasp; taking this as my cue I finished the line I was on, slammed the book shut and sat down as if in the latter stages of a very competitive round of musical chairs.

'Goodnight now, children,' said a voice a short while later, 'and don't forget your prayers.'

Morning, as ever in the olden days, came early. A few short hours before, a kindly lantern-carrying wife had led me out past the officers and gentlemen, across the sodden blackness and into my sleeping quarters. Frail with the nervous exhaustion of making my own fun I was asleep almost before we got there; only now, peering weakly about in the grey dawn light, did I appreciate the efforts made on my behalf. This was the storage tent, but bar a few barrels and sacks stacked at my feet the provisions and implements I'd seen piled up in it before had been cleared away, and in their place a bed laid out, with a huge and potently aromatic buffalo skin as the mattress. On a low side-table beside me lay a winsome still-life: a tin jug of water, a linen handtowel, a candle in an earthenware holder and the means to light it (courtesy of Gustaf Erik Pasch, who had patented the safety match twenty years previously). Still the rain thrummed its staccato beat on the canvas, and I thought of the 250 soldiers Gerry had estimated were out in the woods, sleeping rough and uncovered. Twenty-four hours on, might I hear the whine of a distant shirker?

When the rain moved on I got dressed – shoes, hat, done – and ducked out through the flap. A damp mist swirled through the thin pines, the chickens were out and about, and outside a distant tent a man in a blue flannel shirt and braces was stretching a welcome to the new day. It was all very becoming; not quite a period rush, but a stirring sense that living history was so much more than unshaven men with bad breath hitting each other.

A mood of happy fulfilment saw me through contact with the anachronisms that daylight revealed to my now practised eye – the chainsaw hidden under the logpile, the CHINA stamp on the back of the iron range – and even the most harrowing breakfast I had yet endured: cold grits topped with a dollop of unidentifiable grey purée. One by one the refugee families turned up to eat, tin utensils in sooty hands; afterwards, under a clearing sky, we sat around a small campfire, drinking coffee and shooting the old-time breeze.

Jesse, one of two strapping brothers, said he'd heard that Yankees were within five miles, with horses and cannon. 'Gentlemen,' said his wife, hands clasped primly in her ample grey lap, 'I believe I would give the last of my bread to feed our fighting men.' A short plump man they called Doc reminisced about the Mexican War of '46, and how a friend had just picked himself up a real pretty Mexican bride for $100. Feeling obliged to make some sort of contribution, I announced that the first underwater telegraph cable had been laid under the Atlantic in 1857. 'You know – seven years ago.'

A morning school had been set up in the main tent's parlour, and as I washed grey matter off my plate I looked up to see a child reading aloud from a black-bound period primer, *The Eclectic First Reader*: 'Bad boys lie, and swear, and steal,' he announced, steadily. 'The old man is a beggar. We do not give him money. We may give him old shoes.' Then a vibrant young woman marched up to me with an axe, handed it brusquely over and said: 'Running short of firewood. Logs are there.' Gone now, the 'sir' stuff – this was my effective inauguration into their community, one that would be marked later with a very modest blaze assembled from misshapen splinters.

I spent the rest of the morning harvesting broom grass – grass to make brooms – from the trailside verges. A friendly chap with shaggy stubble and a hat like my 1775 number showed me the ropes, and when he glanced around and quietly told me his name was Roger I sensed we were in for a twenty-first-century chat. Having outed himself as a Bush-loathing ex-air force policeman – 'I guess this gives me a fix of that discipline and responsibility' – Roger described the extraordinary scale of the Civil War re-enactment scene; he'd been at that full-size rerun of Gettysburg, and still endured flashbacks of noise and panic.

For a serious re-enactor, the problem with such a popular period was having to share it with what Roger called 'the guys in Wal-Mart shirts' – the 'casuals', whose cringeworthy outfits and blaring historical ignorance reduced most events to fancy-dress embarrassments, and thus obliged the hardcore obsessives to organise strictly ring-fenced private events such as this. By the same token, the existence of these obsessives meant that his wife was now able to make a living by selling period shirts for $125. He fingered his own with a wink, then peered dubiously at my fistful of brown stalks. 'Uh, let me look after those for you,' he said, with a diplomatic smile.

For a couple of hours we all pottered about in twos and threes. One by one the real-life shutters went up: the associated conversations, as so often throughout my time travels, were a curious mix of the breezy and the brutal. Over a fireside coffee Doc revealed himself as another Vietnam vet – a medic – and described at length the mine explosion that had left him half-blind and obliged to treat the mutilated survivors by feel. A splendid young man whose sunny nature had earned him the name Happy told me how he'd got into 'all this' after finding his great-grandfather's axe in the garage at home – 800 miles away in Ohio. 'Got it right here with me now,' he said, smiling towards his canvas quarters. Many of his older fellow refugees, he told me, had been raised, like Butch, in homes without electricity; one or two had drawn their water from a well. If none of this seemed extreme to them, it was because they were simply re-enacting their own childhoods, not that of their distant forebears.

The sun came out through the lanky trees; I slapped at bits of wood with an axe and suppressed the gnawing realisation that I wasn't doing very much war reporting. At what felt about four o'clock the two brothers suggested a fishing trip, and soon a dozen of us were bumping down the hot trail in a big red pick-up, bamboo canes under our arms, feet dangling off the tailgate like hillbillies. After a few miles, smoke and the strains of a tin whistle wafted out of the trees: I turned just in time to see a few flashes of muddy dark blue, a chestnut flank or two and the barrel of a great big cannon. 'Union artillery,' called out Happy.

Distracted by this encounter, and the anti-bear bins and alligator warnings punctuating our way from the car park to the sandy banks of Kisatchie Bayou, I found it hard to apply myself to the fruitless rod-based entertainment that followed. For much of the time I just watched the five children who'd come along with us, marvelling at the blend of obedience and independence that underpinned their spirited but squabble-free conduct. 'No smiling!' called out a boy of nine when his father pulled out his digital camera, stuck it on sepia, and lined us all up for a group shot. If it sounded a little rehearsed when he later described re-enacting as 'way cooler than video games', his younger sister's delight in telling me how she'd won over her sniggering schoolmates was entirely genuine: 'I just wore my costume into school one day and showed everyone my layers.'

Gerry and his boys were back at our camp when we returned, sandy and fishless. Home as it was to Doc and a trio of former and current nurses, the refugee camp was the BGR M.A.S.H.; Gerry had come to request a medical visit for a Confederate infantryman who had 'bust up his knee'. One of our ladies drove away into the twilight as directed, and over fireside plates of salt pork and pickles Gerry detailed the day's rival casualties. 'Sorted the wheat from the chaff today,' he smiled ruefully, revealing that five soldiers had already been hospitalised – three with heatstroke, one with worryingly elevated blood pressure and the last, dumbfoundingly, airlifted out of the forest following a suspected heart attack. 'And all that in a five-mile march.' I listened in shocked silence, but the faces around me betrayed no more than careworn regret. 'A lot of these guys sit behind a desk all day drinking pop,' said Happy, flatly, 'and then wonder why they can't deal with this.' (Later I'd learn that the average American downs a gallon of sweetened soft drinks every week.)

An advert I'd seen on The Gentleman's Emporium, an online nineteenth-century costumier, spooled through my mind. 'How many years, beers, and nachos does a fellow need before the old tux won't button? Not to worry – we have solutions! There's Rhett, an elegant brocade vest hiding a fully boned corset, and Beau, a less duplicitous boned cummerbund.' It was certainly tempting to interpret the casualties as a parable for the state of modern America – a nation idling along in its bloated comfort zone, the lean and hungry pioneer spirit now distilled down to an overproof obsession with high-calibre self-defence. The get-up-and-go had got up and gone: if there was dirty work to do, you paid an immigrant to do it. You could turn up here with the most authentic, most expensive kit, and strap your gut in with a Gentleman's Emporium 'solution', but if anyone thought you could actually carry yourself and a reproduction muzzle-loading Springfield up and down a few hills they were whistling Dixie.

To avoid further medevac airlifts, the entire schedule had now been reworked: the forty-mile route was cut in half, and many set-piece events cancelled or rescheduled. I learned now that all the food Gerry and I had delivered the day before, and many other camp supplies, were here purely to be looted by passing armies. A refugee wife recapped for the late arrivals to the fireside: 'The Confederates are now taking our chickens tomorrow afternoon, and the morning after the Federals are coming by for the rice.'

The pastor drove up and summoned Gerry away to effect epoxy-hoof repairs on a lame horse, and for a long while after I sat in the kitchen with the brothers and their wives, stripping the veins off prawn necks in preparation for a late-evening gumbo feast. Having never encountered this dish outside the lyrics to the Carpenters' 'Jambalaya on the Bayou' this was a gastronomic encounter I was looking forward to. And still am: with the prawn-skillet already sizzling on the range, Gerry returned in almost breathless haste. 'You're missing the war,' he said, simply. 'Let's go.'

I wiped my stinking hands on my trousers, grabbed my belongings and a bedroll from the tent and said a hasty farewell at the fireside. 'Here,' said one of the kindlier of the camp's many kindly ladies, trotting up as I climbed up into Gerry's pick-up. 'You won't eat well in the army.' She handed me a bulging knapsack, smiled bracingly, and watched us barrel off into the night.

Gerry's one weakness was a fondness for enigmatic silence.

He kept his peace throughout the dark and bumpy drive, and maintained it when at length we pulled off the track. Our headlights picked out the dull glint of dirty metal; as we clunked open the doors I detected a restless equine whinnying, underpinned by a steady chorus of deeply masculine snores. Silhouetted in the glow of a dying fire a lanky, bow-legged figure shuffled down to meet us. Gerry exchanged whispered greetings with the young Dennis Weaver, conducted swift introductions which revealed that my host actually *was* named Dennis, then departed. 'Rest of the boys are asleep,' murmured Dennis, in a cowboy twang, motioning up at the fire and the tents I could now make out around it. 'Just, ah, make yourself comfortable where you can.' I watched as he crept off into the dark, then laid out my bedroll where I stood. Beside me loomed the vast spoked wheel of a gun carriage; above, framed by black pines, yawned a vast and star-peppered heaven. I shifted about, crushing most of the many boiled eggs in my knapsack, and lay there nurturing an excited thought: whatever greeted me when I awoke would come as a total surprise.

'You ugly *baaasssssstards!*'

The reveille did not disappoint. Two of the nine brown horses tied to a picket line strung out just beyond my feet were engaged in vicious hoof-to-face combat, and Dennis was separating them in kind: I watched in groggy confusion as he leapt clear of the ground and scissor-kicked the nearest participant extremely hard in the bottom. His work done, Dennis exhaled loudly, pulled a dark blue sergeant's jacket off its peg (the end of the cannon barrel), and extracted from this a packet of Marlboro. Having sparked one up with a Zippo lighter, he gave me a wink and said, 'Welcome to the Douglas Texas Battery, Confederate States Army, the only horsedrawn artillery unit west of the Mississippi.' Then, tracking my brow-furrowed gaze to his dark blue jacket and slipping into a disgruntled mumble, he added, 'Now galvanised to the damn Federals.'

I sat up, stuck my hat on and followed Dennis up to the two long, white tents. One was still home to loud snores; the four occupants of the other were trying to get some coffee going on the fire. Dennis began the introductions, but before he'd even got my name out, a portly young man let rip with a fart more compellingly repulsive than any of the several hundred that history had thus far exposed me to. A quavering anal symphony, it rose and fell and rose again, fading only at reluctant length into a drawn-out, buttock-stuttering coda. 'Oooo-eeee!' exclaimed the delighted artiste, slapping his sizeable navy-trousered backside with both hands. 'That's your beans talking, JD!'

My preconceptions of life in the Union artillery were almost entirely dismantled as the morning grew older. Most of the late risers emerged with filter-tipped cigarettes propped in stubbled mouths and partially deflated camping mattresses under their arms; our snack rations – dispensed by a man in Specsavers bifocals – comprised a sizeable Zip-Lock bag stuffed with dried fruit. 'Why ain't you got rubber soles?' called out an impatient young voice when one of our senior members slipped in the dewy grass for the second time. 'I mean, who's going to notice?'

They were nine in all: the youngest a well-fed kid of twelve, here with his well-fed pa – a Supervision Officer in the Smith County Corrections Department – and the eldest a wry and learned fellow called Russ, with something of the Walter Matthau about him, conspicuous in voice and demeanour as the solitary non-Texan. The man they called JD wasn't far behind him: a snow-haired, snow-tached old cowboy, whose enigmatic silence I would soon connect to advanced deafness. All but a couple were either below or well above call-up age; this, and the pervasive sense of spirited aimlessness, made it very hard to banish the spectre of *Dad's Army*.

We drank coffee and Coke and milled around the fire under a strengthening sun. Our cannon was a facsimile of a 2.9" Parrott rifle, one of the Civil War's most popular field pieces: cheap and easy to build, as manoeuvrable as three-quarters of a ton of iron was ever likely to be in the horsedrawn age, and capable of accurately dispatching a 10lb shell the best part of three miles.

Our flatulent maestro, name of Trey, extracted a mobile

phone from his cartridge pouch and embarked on an incom-
prehensibly drawled shit-shooting discourse with a back-home
buddy. No one seemed quite sure what was happening. The
human casualties meant a rejigged schedule, but the organisers had apparently not accounted for the loss of two of our
horses (Gerry's epoxy-hoof repair had yet to cure), or in fact
three, now that a hideous and livid crescent-shaped haematoma
was emerging from the unfortunate kickee's neck. Our captain
– a man called Wayne with a healthy Van Dyck beard – drove
away in search of instructions, and his underlings devoted the
consequent hiatus to informing, and then severally reminding
me, that none of them – with the possible exception of Russ
– was fighting for the Union by choice. The Douglas Battery's
seven years' experience of such events had been accrued in the
Confederate cause; faced with a huge shortfall in Federal volunteers, the BGR organisers had been obliged to 'galvanise' many
reluctant Southerners into donning the dark blue.

My, how this had stuck in the artillery crew's collective
craw. The Union army was loudly and repeatedly encapsulated
to me as 'rapists and pillagers', bent on destroying a proud and
honourable way of life (I was regularly told, in contradiction
of the academic consensus, that 'slavery weren't even part of
the issue'). In consequence, all that fuelled these men was stubborn pride. As the sole artillery unit present at the event, the
Douglas boys were all too aware that acquiring their weapon
was a primary opposition objective: almost every pronouncement on the Confederacy's moral superiority came appended
with the caveat that 'they still ain't getting our damn cannon'.

Presently Captain Wayne returned, a sombre and very
different man. 'Right,' he said, climbing out of his pick-up and
staring at each of us carefully. 'Is everybody rehydrated?' His
subordinates exchanged level glances. 'Anybody need a rest?'
Trey scratched an ear, then stooped to raise a wooden toolbox
at his feet. Wayne saw him and shrieked. 'Don't lift that alone!
And bend your legs, not your back!'

I'd by now deduced that Wayne's debrief had majored on
yesterday's medical alarums, and the health-and-safety measures

necessary to prevent a recurrence. Almost as an afterthought he added that the war was about to start without us, a couple of miles to the east. Having any hope of getting there before it finished meant loading everything – horses, cannon, us – into their fleet of vast and shiny pick-ups and trailers, very quickly. That this would not occur became obvious well before Wayne wound up his curiously jarring lecture. 'So if anyone's worried about a procedure, don't keep it to yourself. Speak up! Keeping quiet is a dangerous game.'

Navigational uncertainties compounded our predicament, and it was a full ninety minutes – and almost midday – before the distant sound of irregular musket fire drew us off the road. Wayne and Dennis trotted off into the heat-hazed woods towards the unseen battle; the guns fell silent soon after, and they returned downcast.

The next engagement was apparently scheduled for four o'clock, and the Union artillery abruptly worked itself up into a frenzy of determined atonement. After a lot of urgent whispering over maps, our convoy drew up at a roadside clearing: a four-strong reconnaissance party strode purposefully into the muddy, humid forest, and holding on to my hat I jogged off in pursuit.

Only after an hour did someone think to ask where we were going, and it was a great many squelching strides before the painful truth at last emerged: here was a 'but I thought *you* knew' situation, which had resulted in us playing follow-my-leader for several shoe-clogging miles. One damn blunder from beginning to end.

Our very quiet return journey was enlivened near its end by an ambush, which sent the sounds of revolver fire and human panic ricocheting through the trees. Satisfied from a very early point in the proceedings that this was all a friendly-fire nonsense, I barely bothered to take cover. Soon after, our colleagues, who had witnessed the regrettable denouement of this ill-fated mission, and long since established its farcical futility, greeted us with abusive jeers. Russ, a lone voice of muttering dissent throughout the dilatory indecision that had occupied the morning, came up to whisper what would be his catch-all verdict on most unit activities: 'Now, what you saw then was *not good*.' Then Wayne stomped up with a plastic jerrycan and almost forcibly rehydrated the pair of us.

It was gone three now; with an air of frustrated hopelessness we piled into the pick-ups, shot off in a cloud of orange dust and disembarked a couple of miles down the road. At last those seven years of experience manifested themselves. Horses were led briskly out of trailers, and four attached to the limber that bore our cannon. Equipment and supplies were hurled into the back of two wagons, one for each remaining horse, and then with a great purgative yee-hah the Union artillery was rattling off through the Kisatchie Forest. A stirring sight indeed, though for me also a rather disheartening one: by accident, or design, I was obliged to jog after them on foot.

After half an hour, the pops and cracks of nineteenth-century warfare asserted themselves above my ragged exhalations. My unit had long since vacated the undulating horizon ahead; with a lung-torching, waistcoat-ripping last effort I caught up just as they were preparing to push on to the front line. The trail had ended at a hilltop clearing ringed by hefty, venerable oaks: perhaps 200 yards away, and half as many below us, a thin line of men in blue were exchanging rifle volleys with an unseen foe. Between us lay dense pine forest, heavily sprinkled with large rocks and veined with rain-swollen streams. It was hopeless: Wayne issued a thwarted sigh, and lithely dismounted. 'We can still give supporting fire from up here,' he said, and had no sooner done so when Dennis – astride the horse that headed the four hauling our ten-pounder – yanked up his reins and with a rousing bellow thundered suicidally down the hill. Our captain launched into a complicated burst of precautionary instructions that dwindled into Dennis-centred profanity; the rest of us stared for a moment, watching the cannon limber bucking off rocks and sideswiping tree after tree, a runaway ton of very loud trouble. Then, as one, we charged off in hazardous pursuit.

237

Reliving the moment round the campfire that evening, none of us was at all sure how Dennis, four horses and our cannon – how desperately this tale called for a fond epithet, a Barbara or a Catherine, but there was none – had arrived at the front line intact. In the breathless heat of the moment, though, there was no time to appraise this tremendous feat of horsemanship and lunatic bravado. When I scrambled down to the cannon, one shoe in hand, I found Dennis already detaching his steaming horses from the limber, hard up against a dozen weary, war-soiled Union infantrymen, gunpowdered cheeks resting on rifle stocks as – crack, crack-crack – they let off another faltering volley at an uphill enemy I could hear but not see. It was still and sunny, and a fog of gunsmoke hung in the wooded valley; when it thinned, I spotted perhaps eight lines of Federal riflemen in the trees around us, loading and ramming as they prepared to return the latest Confederate fusillade.

The artillery crew were now up to full strength – in essence this comprised our unit's four most senior members, minus JD – and manoeuvring their weapon into position. Only now did I notice the violently detached vegetation lodged plentifully in its trunk-scuffed wheels. There was a lot of shouting, but all of it tightly focused: 'Number Three! Get on the right side, ready to prime!' 'Number Four, ready!' A grandly moustachioed Union commander, majestically costumed but careworn in demeanour, trudged up and distractedly approved our request to open fire. Russ, the Number Four, stretched out an arm towards the little priming lanyard – the only obvious departure from a procedure I'd last enacted nearly 400 years previously – and with a dainty little tug unleashed a thunderous, valley-shattering explosion. The world shimmered, then froze; it was long, long seconds before an enemy rifleman summoned the wherewithal to discharge his feeble and pointless weapon. Swab, ram, prime, boom, repeat . . . I watched as Douglas's Texas Battery burst gloriously to galvanised life.

It was a period rush all right, full strength and class A. And look at me go – an embedded reporter out on the front lines, wafting aside the fog of war with a steady hand, grimly prepared to sacrifice himself on the altar of unvarnished truth. I would tell my readers of peace and beauty reduced to a human hell defined by fear and furious noise, of heroism and salt pork, of unplanted turnips and $100 Mexican brides, of . . . of some old bloke asking if you fancy a go on his cannon, and you pull this little wire loop, and fuck almighty . . .

If Russ hadn't wished me to react to what followed as I did – imagine Thor scoring a decisive last-minute Superbowl touchdown – then he has only himself to blame for failing to explain that the crew had just packed in a double charge. It was one of the happiest moments of my life.

Three earth-moving cacophonies later the Union commander waved an arm to silence us; with the big red sun dipping behind a hill, it was time to call it a day. We hitched up the limber and threaded the horses carefully through the trees, crunching across a forest floor scattered with shreds of cartridge paper and – a dark glint in the leaves – Dennis's Colt revolver, thrown from its holster by the rigours of his reckless descent.

Too late now to move on: we pitched camp at the clearing. I dragged bits of dead tree in from the undergrowth and tossed them on JD's fledgling fire, then sat down in a shrinking triangle of sunlight and systematically ingested the entire contents of my emergency-ration knapsack. I'd moved on to air-sealed dried fruit when the prison officer came up, handed me a hefty old revolver and shyly insisted that I follow him.

'I just can't stop thinking about what you said this morning,' he mumbled, referring to a debate on comparative gun laws that had revealed my lifelong unfamiliarity with any weapon more powerful than an air rifle but less so than a cannon. We stopped a fair distance away from the tents. 'Just don't seem right,' he said, shaking his head, then motioning at the revolver. Despite myself, I found I was touched by this fondly paternal effort to plug a shameful hole in my manliness: I raised the gun, closed one eye and let the twilight have it, five times.

Those who had room sat round the fire and filled it with chicken tortillas and JD's famously eruptive beans; Russ proposed a visit to the infantry camp down by the front line, and I accepted. From a distance, through the forest gloaming, it looked beckoningly evocative: bearded figures, perhaps a hundred in all, clustered tightly around tiny fires, the occasional glint of pebble specs or an officer's sword. Some squatted over pots and pans, others wiped war off their rifle barrels.

As we started to thread our way through these groups a very different picture came dully into focus. Few soldiers could summon the energy to turn their heads at the sound of our approach, and those who did surveyed us with dead-eyed, blank-faced incuriosity. At the time, I'd ascribed the almost truculent indifference that greeted the artillery's arrival at the front to irritation at our earlier no-show. Now I wasn't sure. The default expression visible between astounding whiskers and flat-topped, half-squashed cap was one of grubby, vacant resignation – the look of men who knew they might well die tomorrow, and didn't even care. It was Russ who drew my attention to the silence: no singing, tin whistles, banter, not the tiniest expression of camaraderie. And certainly no Zip-Lock bags of mango slices, if the grimly charred shreds of animal being poked about most skillets were anything to go by. Was all this a brilliantly realised evocation of war's dehumanising effects, or just a load of flaccid idlers failing to cope with a few days of burger-free hard work?

A small brook was the decreed front line, and we arrived there in the middle of a prisoner exchange. Senior officers in long coats milled about on either bank, swords by their sides, looking sombre and important; one of the dark-blue lot took a suspicious dislike to me, and after a gruff interrogation by one of his subordinates ('What is your business here, *sir*?') I was ordered away. In consequence, I reported on the lantern-lit proceedings from behind a distant tree, restraining the powerful urge to loudly explain that this was only a bloody game, and how Robert E. Lee and Abe Lincoln were bum-chums.

Happily, my vantage point afforded an excellent view of the POWs' march of shame. Amongst the handful of Confederates being roughly escorted to the exchange point I spotted one of the Lazy Jacks, a whey-faced young Brummie I'd met on the first day, his grimy features etched with defeat, fear and dazed disbelief: precisely the expression I recalled seeing on the RAF pilots shot down and captured during the first Gulf War. I half expected to hear him robotically repeat a prepared statement apologising for his involvement in an unjust war against a peace-loving nation. Then the distant roar of a Rebel singalong carried down to us through the cold night air: I cocked an ear, traced it to the Union artillery and set off back to camp.

My, those boys were quite the campfire choristers. Without any alcoholic encouragement – to my substantial disappointment, their solitary nod to catering authenticity – they bellowed away for long hours, tirelessly and lustily besmirching the colours they so reluctantly wore.

Three hundred thousand Yankees laid stiff in southern dust,
We got 300,000 before they conquered us,
They died of southern fever and southern steel & shot,
I wish it were three million instead of what we got!

That was the least inflammatory number – identifying some of the others from half-remembered snatches meant visits to some very alarming websites. I wrapped my blanket around me, chewed a lint-coated strip of jerky, and rehearsed the journalistic-immunity speech I'd deliver when the outraged Union hate-mob stomped out of the blackness.

'Think of it this way,' said Wayne, detecting my fire-lit unease between verses. 'How would you feel if you were made to fight for Nazi Germany?' It seemed an ambitious parallel, even before the post-choral paeans to 'bad-assed' Nathan Forrest, a Confederate general best known for his association with the fledgling Ku Klux Klan. That was Russ's cue to turn in and mine to feign sleep: I lay there surrounded by unsavoury chortlings that effectively answered my great unasked question – What If The South Had Won?

Waking up because you're cold ranks high amongst timelessly

241

unpalatable human experiences. Through one eye and a thickening fog I saw that the fire had all but gone out; though it was still pitch black I accepted sleep was at an end. I shuddered off into the mist in search of fuel, and when I shuddered back, trailing a nine-foot branch past the unfortunate horses, restlessly stamping for warmth, my fellow firesider Trey was sitting hunched up in a blanket and wanly poking the embers. For half an hour we exchanged unhappy grunts. Then the tent flaps rustled and Wayne emerged: the Federals were scheduled to pull back at dawn, he croaked, and we had been ordered to cover their retreat. Trey pulled his mobile out to check the time: under an hour to pack up, saddle up, prepare the cannon and be off.

With a little artificial assistance – my job was to illuminate any scene of complex tackle-attachment by holding Trey's phone screen very close to it – we managed it with ten minutes to spare. I'd gathered from their anecdotes – and uncanny farmyard impersonations – that most of the artillery boys had spent at least part of their lives waking up in the dark and tending to animals; it seemed that Dennis, Trey and his younger brother were part-time cowboys. At any rate, the men of Douglas's Texas Battery rose to the challenge quite magnificently. They geed and hawed and buckled and heaved and farted and swore, and after the crippling awkwardness of The Fireside Bigotry it was a profound pleasure to watch and hear them do so.

A lone bugle called mournfully out from the valley, and presently a shredded and soiled Stars and Stripes battle standard took shape through the foggy half-light, followed by a long and silent column of dusty and dispirited infantrymen. When the two mule-drawn carts bringing up the rear were behind us we let rip with a thumping double charge, and another. So traumatically potent was the third that my brain seemed to shift in my skull: one of the cogitations thus dislodged reminded me that this day was the last. Abruptly confronted by the shamefully narrow scope of my war reporting to date, but too cold and tired to tackle this situation rationally, I snatched up my possessions and ran after the retreating

Yankees. Not a moment too soon, as I later learned: when the artillery departed shortly after, a Confederate snatch-squad ran out of the mist and grabbed JD, the unit's arthritic straggler. (Once in POW custody, he put his head between his legs until his face went purple, then made a successful run for it when his alarmed guards went off to summon medical assistance.)

I lost the Federals in the fog, then spent a long hour patrolling the forest-highway tarmac, watching the air clear. When a column did march out of the woods I could see at once they were the wrong colour: despite all that Johnny Rebel carousing, it was genuinely frightening to be confronted by men I'd come to think of as a hated enemy. Then a rusty pick-up shot past, leaking horn noise and jeering taunts, and remembering that this wasn't 1864 I trotted up and introduced myself to a young Confederate major in a filthy ten-gallon hat.

'We're driving those Yankees out of here, Mr Moore, keeping 'em out of Texas.' The major's forthright manner suggested his boys were fighting a very different war to the one I'd just experienced, and their condition confirmed it. These men had been living off nothing but corn bread and salt pork – period rations, in period quantity – yet as they marched grimly past I saw fire in their sunken eyes. Most compelling was the barefoot, pallid and painfully emaciated young soldier who strode by with a vigour entirely at odds with his appearance; take away the muddy clay pipe sticking out of his unkempt chest-length beard, and he could have recently emerged from a long spell in a medieval dungeon. Only later did I notice that the filth slathering his shoeless feet was generously blended with fresh blood.

Soon we were deep in the black-stumped forest of death that Gerry and I had walked past on day one. Everything seemed instantly more dramatic. A low boom signalled the Union artillery's distant presence: 'Here we go,' muttered a voice from behind, and when I looked back everyone was biting open paper cartridges and emptying the contents down their rifle barrels. 'I want to see a tight, *tight* skirmish line!' hissed the major, as his men fanned out across the burnt desolation. A cry, a stutter of echoing cracks and battle was joined. Everyone around set off through the smoke and shouts and charcoal spikes in a sort of crouching run, and with my heartbeat noisily filling my head I followed. We crossed a forest trail, a slash of orange through the blackness, and there at the roadside sat a group of huge-skirted ladies, surrounded by upended baskets and willow-pattern crockery. 'They took our food!' wailed one. 'They even took my bible!' I looked across at her as I scuttled past, and saw tears streaming down red cheeks.

Soon after, the skirmish settled into a stand-off; everyone took cover behind sooty tree-stumps. I found myself sharing mine with a Prussian-moustached Frenchman: one of four, he told me, who'd come all this way to fight for the South. 'For me this is nothing about politics or society,' he said, sliding easily into the declamatory philosophising that had been such a feature of my time with his Roman countrymen. 'I have a romantic sympathy for – what you say? – the hopeless cause.' His small blue eyes gleamed out of that miner's face. 'In these woods I truly feel as if I am doing something I have done before.' Then a volley of musket shots crashed out, the major barked an order and soon I was hot, tired and alone.

'What the hell is that damn newspaper man doing?'

Fearless professional curiosity had propelled me deep into no man's land, or so I'd like to claim: in truth my journey into the crossfire was entirely attributable to fatigued confusion. A Confederate sergeant-major crunched across the barbecued woodland, grabbed my arm and half-dragged me back to his front line. The major was deeply unimpressed. 'Have that man placed under arrest with the rear guard,' he muttered coldly, before striding off towards the enemy with his revolver raised.

It wasn't so bad back there. My guard was a paunchy, sallow and painstakingly lugubrious Midlander, another Lazy Jack: he'd suffered three heart attacks and was taking it easy to avoid a fourth. For a couple of hours we trudged up and down the hot and sooty dale in companionable silence, joined along the way by a handful of downcast Union POWs, who through blisters, exhaustion or disintegrating footwear had been unable to keep pace with their retreating colleagues. Then scorched earth gave way to leaves and pinecones and a familiar row of canvas peaks appeared before us. How telling of the sensory and experiential overload endured in the previous forty-ish hours that my time at the refugee camp now seemed a distant memory, and how revealing of my own feeble milksoppery that I greeted those dear civilians with almost tearful fondness.

This was their big set-piece occasion, and how they were enjoying it. Certainly more so than the demoralised Federals, who I learned had let themselves down with some very half-hearted march-by pillaging moments earlier. Still, their loss was our gain: the pebble-spectacled ladies bustled about us, proffering baskets of apples, cookies and bread. With this sort of fare on offer, and the sun now merciless, it was difficult for even the most undernourished Confederate to get too excited about the bubbling, slurried vat of hominy grits that was the pièce de résistance. One who did, though, presented the event with an iconic highlight that featured prominently in every after-action report I would read on the internet in the months ahead: 'I shall not forget the soldier hungry enough for hot food, and bereft enough of something to take it in, that he held out his hat as a bowl, and ate hominy from it with his hands.'

I missed that memorable scene, but I think we can be fairly certain that it starred our barefoot beardie: if re-enactors were awarded medals, that simple act would have bagged him one the size of the skillet dangling from his bedroll. A mention in dispatches for the soldier who scooped up one of those sweet little white hens as we tramped out of the camp, planted his boot on its head and decapitated the animal with a hearty tug. A colleague lashed the twitching corpse to his pack; I followed the trail of blood for an hour.

I gathered things were building to some sort of climax when we found the cannon crew draped across their weapon in dramatic interpretations of death. 'Hi, Tim!' hissed a couple of corpses as I trotted by with my guard. That would be the last I saw of them, and though I didn't then know it, I found myself appraising my time with the galvanised artillery. Much as I disagreed with many of their opinions – in all probability with huge swathes of everything they held dear – at the end of two long and hugely exhilarating days, these were men who had welcomed a foreign stranger into their ranks without question or hesitation, then through good old Southern hospitality let him share all they had: their food, their blankets, their high-calibre weaponry.

We pursued the Federals up a steep and messy ridge, and as must be common in war, discipline and unity steadily petered out in weary confusion. I arrived at the bald brow of the hill without my guard, and found a few Confederates slumped against a hedge, awaiting officers and orders. When a tubby young soldier staggered out of the trees and collapsed theatrically at our feet, clutching his stomach, I stifled a bored groan; many others didn't. After a minute or so of rasping death-rattles, someone wandered over and wearily bent down by his head. Then very swiftly jumped back upright, wearing a very different expression. 'OK! Guys! Cut the shit a minute – this guy's in serious trouble.'

The alacrity with which I volunteered for the mercy-dash back to the refugee camp and its resident medics was contingent on forgetting these facts: (i) the camp was now very far away, and in an uncertain direction; (ii) my shoes were two sizes too big. After three wrong turnings and a full-length, face-first sprawl on the orange gravel, I arrived there in a ragged, skating shuffle, sweat and dust congealed on my desperate face. The ladies were starting to pack things up; between rasping breaths I delivered a bullet-point summary of the situation: man, sick, follow, car.

By the time we made it back to him, struggling up the last fateful hill on foot with a trunk full of medications and many gallons of water, the semi-naked victim was sitting up between two straightfaced colleagues with a sheepish look on his big red face, and a conspicuous rubbery garment topping the pile of discarded clothing beside him. We were given a terse summary after the pastor had driven him off to hospital: man, fat, corset, heatstroke. If he'd died, I'd feel bad about hating this man as much as I still do.

Perhaps four hours later, I was lying out beneath the stars, the crackle of a very proximate campfire doing its best to drown out the in-tent snores around. I rolled over and heaved another couple of dirty planks into the blaze, floorboards from the now dismantled front parlour tent. Earlier, at a get-together with an end-of-term mufti-day feel to it, the refugees had gathered around a table there crammed with plastic vats of Mountain Dew and Pepsi, wearing jeans, T-shirts and wistful, weary smiles. Before changing they'd all taken turns to shower under a waterfall down the hill, where the following morning I'd get through two whole bars of motel soap and drown a travel alarm clock.

Something nipped my neck, then something else: I slowly levered myself half upright, and in the firelight saw a great many small brown things darting frenziedly about my vulcanised sheet. I brushed the worst of them away with a lazy hand, then flumped back down: I was going to sleep on an ants' nest, and didn't even care. It was progress.

If that was one small step for a man, mankind had dutifully come up with a giant leap. Eighteen months and 2,000 years on I had arrived at the dawn of the modern age: matches, waterproof fabric, tinned food, prescription eyewear. My role was a newspaper correspondent in the contemporary mould, reporting on the civilian backdrop to a war fought with machine-guns and long-range ordnance, a war whose last widow had died just three years before.

I'm not sure at what point I decided this would be it for me, the moment I'd take my finger off the rewind button. It might have been when I caught my reflection in a Union artillery pick-up wing-mirror and accepted that minus the hat, this was the first outfit I could have worn down Chiswick High Road without having it laughed clean off me by gales of civic derision. Perhaps it was when I saw the Stars and Stripes battle standards fluttering through the gunsmoke, and realised that having recreated the lives and times of all those long-defunct peoples and societies, I had now arrived at the genesis of the modern world's reigning superpower. Or maybe a bit of both, seasoned with the uncomfortable awareness that moving forward from this point would mean pursuing my provisional arrangement with a group of Channel Islanders who spent their weekends in wartime bunkers dressed up as Nazis.

Two summers before, on a hot hill near Wales, I'd stood outside my roundhouse and portentously speculated whether some Moore-to-be might one day call this home, whether history and civilisation might one day come full circle. Was the hi-tech, high-speed urban existence we'd been perfecting since the 1850s the ultimate expression of man's productive genius, or his destructive stupidity? Sensible opinion accepts that our current lifestyles are entirely unsustainable: the oil's running out, the ice caps are melting, the price of food is shooting upwards because there isn't enough to go round, and not much space left to grow any more. Take Ancient Egypt as your starting point, and there are more people alive today than have ever died.

Soon, perhaps sooner than we might wish to believe, we would need to lead simpler lives. Smaller scale, more self-sufficient, more physical. And what of the dehumanising effects of modern life, the insularity and mistrust? If anything united the many re-enactors I had met, it was a simple and truly heartwarming quest for gregarious community. All in all, we just weren't meant to live the way we now did: I'd spent the previous eighteen months unlearning the screen-centred, anti-social torpor and blaring practical ignorance that in two short generations had completely redrafted the blueprint of human behaviour, a blueprint which in two more might itself be dangerously redundant. In revisiting the past, I had gone back to the future.

A nearby bestial snuffle was followed by a distant, echoing howl. Above me stretched the glittering, timeless prospect that had been a constant companion throughout my travels through history. Beside me, the last glowing remnants of the past were quietly going up in smoke.